Rise of a Champion

Legend of the Cid: Book 1

By Stuart Rudge

Coming Soon

Blood Feud

Fall of Kings

Contents

Places Names and Terms

Some of the place names within the novel use the original Moorish names, mostly settlements which had been under Moorish control in the eleventh century and not yet conquered by the Christians. There is also a separate list with terms and names which use an original translation.

Arabic Name	*Modern Translation*
Al-Andalus	Moorish name for the Iberia
Al-Sahla	Alpuente
Balansiya	Valencia
Barbushtar	Barbastro
Batalyaws	Badajoz
Garnata	Granada
Ifriqiya	Africa
Isbiliya	Seville
Jebel Tariq	Gibraltar
Lleida	Larida
Qalat 'Ayuub	Calatayud
Qulumriyyah	Coimbra
Qurtuba	Cordoba
Sahlatu Bani Razin	Albarracin
Saraqusta	Zaragoza
Tulaytula	Toledo
Washqah	Huesca

Miscellaneous Terms

amir	Moorish king or ruler
alferez	high-ranking official in Christian Spain, carried the king's standard in battle. Translated from the Arabic *al-fāris*, meaning "horseman" or "cavalier", it was also translated in Latin as *armiger*, "armour-bearer". Commanded the king's personal retinue of knights.
huerta	from the Latin for "garden", it was a fertile area for the cultivation of vegetables and fruit trees for consumption and sale. The Moors mastered the art of irrigation, and many *huertas* kept the *taifas* fed.
parias	tribute paid by Moors to defer warfare.
taifa	Moorish kingdom of Iberia.

Map of Spain c.1064 AD

For my mother and father

Part One

The Betrayal

Asturias, 1063 AD

One

I was the son of a knight, yet I loathed the idea of following in my father's footsteps.

The castle yard was full of life. Seven boys similar in age to me toiled hard against their posts, wooden swords in hand; the oldest trio carried blunt steel as their training intensified. The grunts of the labour were entwined with the barks of the instructors and the clang of steel and thud of wood. The buildings on the periphery of the yard were busy as well; loud dins echoed as the smith beat his steel with a heavy hammer, the horses whinnied as they were settled in to the stables and guardsmen exchanged banter as they changed shifts in the small guardhouse by the gate. A light snow drifted from dark clouds, forming icy puddles in the yard. Patches of sloshy mud clung to boots and the hems of cloaks.

The wooden post before me was worn and dented from the plethora of blows it took daily. Around me the other boys hacked at their own with wooden and iron weapons, chips of wood coursing through the air with the intensity. My breath rose in front of my eyes as I paused and sucked winter air into my lungs. Sweat trickled down my forehead. The wooden sword in my right hand was heavy and the small shield in my left was nothing but a hindrance. It felt as though I had danced a waltz with the post for an eternity. But it was barely passed midday, and the session had only begun.

Behind me, the keep of the castle loomed overhead. Our castle was little more than a tower surrounded by a high wall with a parapet, but it was in important symbol of status and I was lucky to be raised within one. We had everything we needed, and the tower offered good views of the land, views I cherished and dreamt of what lay beyond. Surrounding the castle was a village, modest in size but with a small market and a throng of craftsmen whose sons trained with me, hoping one day to be knights of Leon-Castile.

I felt my brother's presence next to me. His hands took hold my sword arm and gently bent it into a fighting pose, and he did the same for my shield arm before straightening my back and legs. His eye caught mine and he gave a slight smile. For years I trained as Inigo did, yet I was slower, weaker and not half as brave. He liked to remind me who was the superior sibling, but he offered help when I needed it.

'Do your best, Antonio. Father is watching.'

I turned my gaze to a window in the keep as my father stared at me, the same expression of condemnation on his face like any other day. It was a vision I had grown accustomed to. My father was stern but fair, his engaging smile countered by the thunderous glower of disapproval. He always favoured Inigo because naturally he was the one who would inherit my father's lands in Asturias and continue the family name to glory on the battlefield and within the kingdom. He was strong, brave, quick and handsome, and blessed with the same sun kissed skin and jet hair.

Father had returned to Lugones only an hour before, yet he had not taken the time to greet us after such a long time away. He simply entered his chambers and spoke with our mother and the seneschal of the castle, Telo. Earlier that year he had accompanied Sancho, the prince of Leon-Castile, to do battle with the Aragonese king Ramiro in the territory of the *taifa* of Saraqusta. When we heard the news, it had come as a surprise, for he had gone to Castile to find a wife for Inigo, and it was a strange twist of fate that he found himself in an army headed for Saraqusta. While we had heard Sancho had won a battle at a place called Graus, the only news of our father was when he returned to Leon and wrote he would not be back for a while. His return before the first heavy snows of winter came was a welcome surprise. He might not approve of me, but it did not stop me loving him.

He soon strode out of the keep towards me.

I stiffened with fear. His expression was firm, and his thin lips grimaced like they did more oft than not. His green eyes glowered beneath a frown. His raven hair and beard were neatly trimmed, and his tunic and trousers were brown with a long green cloak trimmed in brown wolf fur over his broad shoulders and powerful frame; the hem and his boots were caked in thick mud. His long sword hung at his hip, fastened on to a black belt by a silver buckle.

He reached out and squeezed my arm hard. 'You still do not have any muscle on these bones,' he muttered. 'You need to work harder.'

'I try, father.'

'Trying is not good enough.'

'I am...sorry,' I said as my eyes lowered to the ground.

'You will both show me what you have learned these past few months,' he declared. I looked at my brother, a concerned expression on his face. He was a squire for a knight in the entourage of Diego, the count of Oviedo, but had been summoned back to Lugones by my father a day before he himself had returned. Inigo had considerable skill with a blade, and he knew he would humiliate me in a fight. 'Come. Show me you have been listening to your tutors. I will not believe you have been idle.'

'Father, perhaps you would like to tell us about your exploits this year,' Inigo suggested. 'I am eager to hear your tale of Graus...'

'Later. Go and get a wooden sword. I would not want you to harm your brother.'

Inigo gave me a sideward glance as he duly obeyed, replaced his blunt steel with a long wooden sword from the weapon rack. He faced me, poised for combat. His sword and reach were longer and being two years my senior he was much quicker and stronger. I already knew the outcome of the fight. It was not the first time my father had made us duel in unfair circumstances. Perhaps he wanted me to suffer.

I ignored his request. There was a tense silence as I stared at a puddle before me. Tiny snowflakes landed on the water and made delicate ripples on the surface.

'Antonio,' my father barked. 'Turn and face your brother.'

I lifted my eyes and stared at him. 'I do not want to.'

He took a step forward, close now so I could see the lines upon his furrowed face.

'I am not asking you.'

I froze. His focus was on me and I dared not move. I swallowed hard and stood my ground, hoped Inigo would join in with the small show of defiance. My father's mouth twisted in fury as his eyes bore deep into mine. Still I stood motionless, both in fear and attempted defiance. I had no intention of being publicly humiliated.

Then he struck me.

It came out of nowhere, a fierce backhand that hit me full in the mouth. My head snapped to the side and I fell to the ground. The wooden sword and buckler flew from my grip, and my hands and knees were covered in thick mud from an icy puddle. I held myself and tried to regain my composure as the pain throbbed in my mouth. A crimson patch appeared on my glove as blood dripped, the sweet metallic taste of it filling my mouth. A tear welled in my eye, such was the pain and shame, but I forced myself to be strong. I hauled myself up and faced my father.

Those in the yard had stopped to stare at my degradation. It was deathly quiet as the snow continued to drift gently, and the wind caressed my cheek. I sniffed as a dribble of snot ran from my nose and looked my father in the eye. There was no shame on his face, only the determination to do it again. I could not stop the tear trickle down my cheek.

'Why can you not be more like your brother?' he snapped. 'He listens. He is strong and brave and acts like a man. For four years he has served well as a squire. You? You're nothing but a coward.'

'Father,' Inigo called. 'Perhaps that is enough for one day.'

My father glared at Inigo; his mouth twisted in fury at my brother's intervention. But after a few moments he nodded and beckoned him forward.

'After your lesson with Father Santiago I want a word with you both. We will have a drink together, as men.' He cast his eyes over me with a hint of scorn. 'I will share my experiences with you, for it has been a good year for our family. Perhaps you might understand why you need to grow up.'

He marched back into the tower as the yard came back to life. I looked at Inigo and gave a slight smile, relieved and embarrassed his intervention saved any more humiliation.

'Thank you.'

His face was unflinching, stern, as if his assistance was reluctant. 'Thank me by putting a smile on father's face.' He turned and retrieved a blunt steel sword from the rack before resuming his own gruelling regime.

Dishevelled, I retrieved my own sword and buckler, looked at the post and hacked at it with all my strength, eager for the ordeal to end.

*   *   *

My father was waiting for us in the hall of the keep.

The early evening sun descended fast and the purple sky outside deepened like a bruise. The winter winds whistled around the hall and turned the air bitterly cold. I had wrapped a fur cloak around my slender frame, but it did not deter the chill. The scent of burning pine filled my nostrils as wisps of smoke rose from the dancing flames of the braziers.

My mouth still ached, and father's strike would leave a mark, but I put on a brave face regardless.

The hall was empty save for my father. He sat on the low dais where our family ate our meals, overlooked the other benches. When we approached, he beckoned for us to sit at a long table on the ground level, where upon were two jugs and three goblets, all crafted from fine silver. We sat as he poured blood red wine in to two of the goblets then placed them in front of himself and Inigo. He filled the third with cider from the second jug, pouring from height to add a foam and fizz to the drink before he placed it before me. He was content to let me have cider, but he considered wine a man's drink, reserved for guests and those in his household who had his approval. I clearly was not among them.

'This has been a good year for our family,' he declared, taking a sip of his wine. 'Our prestige rises in the court of King Fernando.'

I sipped my cider, savouring the tart taste as he recounted the tale me and Inigo were eager to hear of.

Earlier in the year he had been in Burgos, searching for a suitable wife for Inigo, when Ahmad al-Muqtadir, the amir of Saraqusta, had called for aid from King Fernando. Saraqusta was a Muslim kingdom surrounded by Christian realms: Leon-Castile was to the west, Navarre and Aragon to the north, and east were the Catalan Counties. All looked on the city in the valley of the Ebro with envy and so al-Muqtadir was content to pay tribute to Fernando for protection against his enemies, be it Christian or Muslim. King Ramiro of Aragon had encroached in his territory and seized the town of Graus. Fernando had incentive to fight because Ramiro was his only remaining brother, and so honoured the terms of the agreement. Their father, Sancho III, had divided the Kingdom of Pamplona between his three sons, with Fernando being granted the county of Castile. Fernando had already killed his brother Garcia of Navarre at Atapuerca almost a decade previous, so the chance to defeat his last dynastic rival was all too tempting.

My father had offered his sword to the fight and had been part of a force of knights that marched to Saraqusta with Sancho, the eldest son of Fernando. They had met with al-Muqtadir's men at Saraqusta and marched to Graus which was under Ramiro's control.

'It was there we met the enemy,' my father said. 'Ramiro was arrogant and marched from the city when he heard his own nephew opposed him. Between the high hills to the west and the river to the east the battlefield was narrow, so we were two densely packed forces opposing each other. The skirmishers exchanged their volleys and we formed our lines on the fields outside the town as the sun beat upon us. Then we charged.

'We kept our shape and held our line as our horses galloped hard, and Ramiro's knights charged to meet us. I still remember the thunderous crash as we collided with the Aragonese, the screams of dying men and horses, the deafening clang as steel swords clashed, the crunch and crack of broken limbs and the battle cries in the Christian and Moorish tongues.' Excitement gripped him as he relived the battle in his head. But his demeanour turned grim as he stared into his goblet.

'There was so much blood. The world descended into a red cloud. The paint of my shield was hacked off, replaced by bits of clot and jellied flesh splattered on the front. My mail hauberk too was slick with blood and the smell was rancid, imbedded in my gloves. I tried scrubbing the death from them but gave up and burnt them. Nothing would relieve the stench.

'But the horrors I witnessed that day were worth the glory. God heard my prayers and blessed me, for it was I who delivered the killing blow to King Ramiro and won the battle for Leon-Castile.'

My eyes widened at the news. To survive and win a battle was one thing, but to kill a king in combat was a heroic deed worthy of a song.

'How did you achieve such a feat?' Inigo asked, astonished.

My father filled his and Inigo's goblet with wine before continuing. The flickering flames highlighted the proud smile on his face. 'A stray javelin caught the king's horse in the neck and they both tumbled to the dirt. The horse was dead, but Ramiro was alive, and he fought on valiantly, hacked at the legs of our horses and bested any man who faced him. I showed no fear as I charge towards him, and our swords sang the song of battle. I was relentless as I pressed with my attack, drove him back but unable to pierce his guard. But he slipped on a patch of blood and gave me the opening I needed. I hacked at his neck and his body went limp. His army lost the will to fight and a great cry of triumph in Christian and Moorish tongues rang out as his body was dragged back to Graus along with the rest of his defeated men. There was no doubting my achievement. Prince Sancho witnessed it and he praised me after the battle in the eyes of men and God.

'I have been in Burgos and Leon since we returned from the battle. The king embraced me and gave me gifts for my actions, such as the silver you drink from now. And he has also granted us new land to the south and east of Lugones, and soon I will receive new estates in Castile so our income and prestige will grow with time. I have other things for you both, mainly a few trinkets and some silk from Isbiliya to make fashion new tunics. But I come with something even more valuable. Opportunities.

'The king knows our family now, and he will expect great things from the house of Pedro Valdez de Lugones. Can I count on you both to raise our family name and continue our legacy?'

'You know I will not let you down father,' Inigo beamed.

They both looked to me. I wanted to tell them I would do what I could to raise our prestige and make him proud, but I could not. I did not want to. I opened my mouth, but no words came forth. All I managed was a slight nod. Father was not amused.

'Inigo, leave me with your brother.'

He gave a nod, drained his wine then he exited the hall.

My father's cold stare numbed me more than the winter air.

'It is about time you squired. You need to get the feel of what it takes to become a knight and have some discipline drilled into you. Lucky for you I have found someone willing to take you on.'

8

I lowered the cup, stunned by the unexpected statement. 'Who is he?'

'His name is Sebastian Alvarez. His own squire died at Graus and so in return he has agreed to take you on. He considered it an honour to train my son. He holds land near Palencia. You will leave to reside with him in the spring.'

My mouth hung slack, unable to speak. 'You're sending me away?' I squeaked after regaining my composure.

Father frowned. 'Well you cannot squire for him here. He is a knight of the realm with land of his own.'

'But I thought you would send me to Oviedo, like Inigo. I am happy here!'

'You spend all day with your head in a book instead of trying to be a man. You do not become great by reading about the lives of others; you make others write about the deeds you achieve, like I have this past summer.'

'Father Santiago is a good teacher.'

'And Sebastian Alvarez is a good knight and will be a better teacher than Santiago. You will learn everything about being a knight from him.'

'But I do not *want* to be a knight. I cannot do it.'

'No son of mine will be a damned priest!' His fist slammed on the table, knocking Inigo's empty goblet on its side. A silence ensued as my father seethed. I did not move, did not breath lest I incur his wrath again. I clasped my hands together to stop them trembling, hoping my fear would subside. He closed his eyes, breathed in deep and softened his tone. 'This is a good opportunity for you, Antonio. Your brother will be jealous, for Palencia is close to the frontier with the Moors. You will likely see some action. Here in Asturias Inigo will not. You do not deserve a chance like this, but I believe this is right for you. I cannot help you here. So, you will go and squire for Sebastian. You will leave a boy and return a man.'

There was no arguing. His mind was already made up. He was willing to send me to Leon until I was sworn as a knight.

And that process would take years.

'For the rest of the winter you will stop your lessons with Father Santiago and practise in the yard twice as much.'

That was something I could not adhere to. Santiago's lessons kept me happy, devouring knowledge and letting my mind wander with inspiration from the crisp vellum pages of the manuscripts. I wanted to become a man of the cloth, spread the word of God and compose histories whilst Inigo conquered the *taifas* for Leon-Castile. My mind was my weapon.

'Please, father, I beg you...'

'There will be no discussion,' he cut me off sharply. 'You are my son and you will do as I say.' He rose from the table and marched towards the door, pulling it open with a creak. He stopped and turned to me, his face still hard and stern.

'Stop being a disappointment. Make me proud.'

The door slammed as it closed, leaving the hall quiet and still. The wind no longer whistled, but slight gusts filtered through cracks in the walls and the cold nipped at my cheeks. The fire cracked and sent tiny flecks of ash gliding through the air. I watched one soar high and slowly descend, its path manipulated by the gusts, spiralling one way and the next before coming to rest on the table, nothing more than a grey smear. Like the speck of ash, I knew my fate was out of my hands; it would be decided by my father.

And he wanted to abandon the embarrassment he called a son.

*   *   *

The heavy winter snows settled. The rolling green hills of Asturias were pale and desolate, and the peaks of the Cantabrian Mountains were shrouded in thick mist and seemed to stretch to Heaven itself. Our boots crunched off fresh snow and cracked through frozen puddles. I did not mind the cold weather if sat by a fire or brazier with Father Santiago. But my mood dipped now I was outside in the bitter air, toiling away and trying to invent different ways to strike a wooden post. Every day was more demanding than the previous.

Inigo returned to Oviedo whilst my father played host to new faces, usually petty lords from elsewhere in Asturias and some even from Leon, eager to make his acquaintance. My father surprisingly took the time to introduce me to his new guests, explaining I would be moving to Palencia to become a squire to Sebastian Alvarez. The name was received favourably, which more than likely meant he was a good knight and I would be trained well. Despite the praise I still abhorred the notion of going.

It was soon our turn to be the guests. We were invited to attend a feast with Diego Fernández, the count of Oviedo, in the weeks leading to Christ Mass.

Oviedo was once the seat of the kings of Asturias and they ruled from there until the court was moved to the city of Leon to the south, but it still retained its status as an important city. It was only a few miles to the city and a little further to the palace itself on the southern side of Monte Naranco, but the journey was slow as the wind whipped at our cloaks and the cold rain lashed our faces. We pressed on, grim and cold with hoods around our heads and scarves around our faces, wandering in a white abyss. But we soon reached the palace close to nightfall where we were met by the seneschal and immediately ushered inside, offered fresh cloaks and placed by a roaring fire to dry ourselves.

I had been to the palace only twice before, but I still marvelled at the complex every time I visited. The Asturian king Ramiro I had built the palace a few hundred years ago and the kings had used it as a residence until royal affairs were moved south to Leon, where it had become the residence of the count of Oviedo. It was a truly wonderful building built entirely of sandstone and marble, something rare in the north realms. Most buildings of our people had timber cages to hold the ceilings, yet the ceilings of the palace were perfectly smooth arches of sandstone and the golden exterior and the red tiles along the roof served as a beacon to those travelling the hills. The complex incorporated a main hall, a church dedicated to Santa Maria, the royal apartments and guest chambers, stables, kitchens, a smithy, a library and archives, guardhouses and several underground vaults, whilst galleries connected all the buildings together. Diego Fernández may not have been a king, but it did not stop him living as one.

When our clothes were dry, we were escorted to the main hall. The pale winter sun had already set so the chamber was well lit with torches, and braziers burned around the exterior to provide heat to the guests. Fresh rushes had been laid on the floor and the scent of lavender filled the air. Long tables had been set out, already crammed with guests feasting and drinking. At the end of the tables was a small raised dais where Diego sat with his wife and two sons. Along the walls hung the alternating banners of Leon-Castile; a purple lion on white, and a golden castle on red, and beneath each banner was a medallion carved in to the walls with the image of some animal, bird or mythical beast, surrounded by a circular knot pattern.

As a squire Inigo was charged with serving the dishes to the lords and guests, cutting meat and filling goblets with wine. There was roast boar with crisp skin, wild fowl and game, fresh bread and fine cheese, all washed down with flagons of deep red wine from Rioja and Washqah and sharp apple cider. Figs, cherries and apple tarts were provided for the sweet. My father was adamant I did not touch the wine, but when he was talking to the count on the dais my mother passed me a small goblet of full-bodied red wine and winked to show her approval. I drained it eagerly and the potency hit me in an instant.

For me the feast was a quiet affair. My father was uninterested in introducing me to any of the men he talked to, Inigo was busy serving, my mother was engaged in small talk with the guests beside her and I did not have any intention of talking with my two sisters who sat and gossiped. It was as if I was non-existent, so I quietly sipped my cider and eavesdropped on gossip and snippets of news.

'The king will march on Saraqusta in the spring,' grunted a squat man to my right.

'Do not be stupid,' a taller man with a long beard and a left eye that drooped protested. 'He has just fought a war on their behalf. The *parias* gives him a steady stream of gold.'

'Which he should use to regain more land in Portugal,' added a third. 'Qulumriyyah would be the logical choice, and a war in Portugal might give us men of Asturias a chance to wet our blades with Moorish blood. The Galicians cannot have all of the glory.'

'Bollocks!' barked the squat man. 'Portugal is a feral land, and Qulumriyyah will not fall without a fierce fight. Our king is not so stupid as to throw away the lives of good men for a piss poor land. Besides, Saraqusta is the big prize.'

'I hear it is not the king who will fight the Moors, but men from outside this land.' Another man with a huge scar on the left side of his face was eavesdropping too and decided to add his opinion to the debate. The other three men turned to him.

'What have you heard?' asked the taller man.

The newcomer sipped from his wooden cup. 'Apparently the Pope is not happy our king aided al-Muqtadir against Ramiro. He thinks it unacceptable for a Christian to aid a Moor in fighting other Christians, and so he's appealed to men to take up arms against the Muslims. And, perhaps, those who fought *with* the Moors.'

The other men were silent for a moment, absorbing the news.

'And who will he ask to fight?'

'The Normans of southern Italy, for they have fought the Moors before. But he has also appealed to the Franks, Burgundians, and Aquitanians. He is even looking for support from Aragon and Barcelona.'

'And you think they will march on Leon-Castile?' asked the third man.

The scarred man shrugged. 'Stranger things have happened.'

'The Pope will not fight Fernando,' the squat man barked. 'He needs him to spread the word of God and reconquer the *taifas* from the Moors.'

The talk was similar throughout the hall, mainly of Fernando's intention to march to war come springtime. I do not know how long I had been listening in for, but I felt a presence next to me. Inigo loomed over me with a jug of wine and motioned to the dais.

My father and five other men were with the count by the dais. In the low light of the hall they looked jubilant as if good news greeted them. Diego climbed from the dais and took my father's arm and embraced him, like one would embrace a brother.

'What is happening?' I asked.

'Count Diego honours our family. Father has been chosen to collect the *parias* from Saraqusta this spring.'

The *parias* was proof the Christian kingdoms in the north were feared by the Muslim *taifas* of the south. Every year the amirs sent yearly tributes to Leon-Castile in return for the promise of not being attacked, and even assistance when needed. They feared the power of our knights on the battlefield and found offering gold for peace was the best option. Being surrounded by enemies, Ahmad al-Muqtadir of Saraqusta always offered the most lucrative *parias,* but the tribute had paid dividends when Fernando had defeated Ramiro and won a war for him.

And in the spring my father would go to Saraqusta and retrieve the tribute.

I realised Inigo was staring at me, his mouth curled into a grin.

'Why are you so happy? Are you going too?'

'Other things are happening in the spring, little brother. Father has promised me his new lands in Castile when I receive my knight's belt. And now I am betrothed. When I become a man, I am to be married to the count's daughter.'

14

I gasped and turned back towards the dais where a girl only a year younger than me now stood facing my father and the count. 'Jimena?'

Inigo nodded and his grin enlarged. 'Yes brother. She will be mine.'

My hand gripped my cup tighter, to the point I could have crushed it. Inigo was not grinning because he was to marry the daughter of a count, increase his prestige and one day become a famed knight of Leon-Castile.

He was grinning because he was to marry the girl I loved.

*　　*　　*

When I was young Jimena was the only true friend I had.

We met when I was twelve and she was eleven, when her father had hosted a great hunt in the hills and forests around Oviedo. Being in Diego's service my father had attended the hunt and brought the family along for the occasion. This was prior to his feats at Graus, so during the hunt he was on the peripheries of the group where he would mingle with the lesser known lords as they galloped through the forests of Asturias, skewered boars and felled game with well-placed arrows.

I first noticed her hair, black as pitch, yet it shimmered in the light of the sun and billowed past her shoulders in great curls. Her emerald gown was fine silk, and her sun kissed skin glowed. She turned my way and she smiled, which sent my heart in to flutters. We were only young, and I did not know anything of love, but I stood there and stared at her for a long time. A frown appeared on her face and she stared back at me, puzzled. I averted my gaze as my heart thumped against my chest, hoped she had looked at something else.

'Why were you staring at me?' I turned to see her before me. She was even prettier than I thought, despite the frown on her face. I blushed and no words came out. 'Are you a mute?' she pressed after a pause.

'No. I...I like your dress, that's all.' It was the best I could think of, but the comment was well met, and she smiled.

'Oh, thank you. It's lovely, is it not?' Her eyes were the same vibrant colour as her dress and sparkled in the sunlight. She spun on the spot so her dressed whooshed and provided a gust most welcome in the summer heat. 'The silk is from some Moorish city in the south. I forget the name. My father had it made.'

'Who is your father?'

'The count.'

A pang of panic gripped me. 'You are Jimena Díaz?'

'Yes. Who are you?'

'Antonio Perez,' I managed after a pause. 'I come from Lugones.' She was the youngest daughter of the most powerful man in the region, and I the son of a petty lord, but she was unfazed by it.

'That's not far from here, is it?' I shook my head. 'I have seen it from a distance when I walk on the hills of Naranco, but I have not been before. Is it nice?'

'It's small, but its home.'

'Who is your father?'

'Pedro Valdez,' I motioned to where my father stood with Inigo, who gently stroked the feathers of the falcon on his wrist. 'And that is my brother.'

'He is handsome,' she said with a smile. The comment left me dejected. It appeared Inigo would be better than me at everything; even taking the affections of girls.

'There is my father,' Jimena pointed as a group of young men crowded round the count. They admired the huge falcon perched on his wrist as it pecked at the guts of a rabbit. 'Those are my own brothers, Rodri and Fernando. Rodri is older and is strong and likes to talk to girls. Fernando is the better swordsman and is protective of me, but most of the time he is an idiot. Why are you not with the other boys?'

'I do not fit in with any of them.'

'Why not?'

16

'These boys want to be squires and one day knights. I do not have the same desire, or the ability. I am weak.'

'All boys your age are weak. You have not got any muscles yet. But should not let them boss you round. Stand up for yourself, Antonio. You will not get anywhere in life if you shut yourself away.'

'It's not as if I do not try,' I said, harsher than I would have liked.

'Well try harder,' she frowned. A voice called to her and she turned and waved in recognition. 'I have to go now. It was nice to meet you, Antonio Perez.' She turned and started back towards her mother.

'Wait!' I called. She turned and looked back. 'I'd like to walk around Naranco as well. Can we be friends?'

She frowned again. 'Will you not be spending your time training?'

'I'd rather spend time with you.'

Her frown lifted as she chewed her lip. 'You really are not like the other boys, are you?' I shook my head as she cocked hers slightly. 'Meet me at the hill fort in two days' time. Come at noon.'

For the next three years the hill fort became our refuge from the world. The fort was on the eastern side of Monte Naranco, but most of it was hidden from view. The ancient stonework was buried beneath a thick blanket of grass and mud, as if the earth had claimed the ruins for itself. In one of Father Santiago's lessons I had asked him about the ruins, and he said it was a castle built by a people called the Celts hundreds of years ago, even before the Romans came, and there were many dotted all across the north of Hispania. They were built on hillsides or along rivers and the coast to protect the land, each one with a series of ditches and walls to deter attackers. The one on Naranco might have been huge, but only a few of the houses and the larger outline of a hall were still visible. I used to look at those ruins from our own castle and wonder if it was an important settlement for the people who dwelt there; what they did, how they lived, what gods they worshipped. I found no answers in the overgrown ruins, the secrets forever buried with the inhabitants.

We sat in the remains of the hall and talked for hours. She spent most of her time with her mother and a few of the daughters of nobles who lived in Oviedo, but sometimes she escaped to walk the hills with her brothers. Her father felt his lands were safe enough for his children to explore unhindered, but he drew the line at letting Jimena out alone. She never listened. When she returned her father would scold her for her stupidity and disrespect, but it did not deter her.

'He cannot keep me on a leash,' she said. 'One day I will be married to the son of a famed knight I will have no hand in choosing. That is when I will be shackled and bound to serve him for life; bear his children and raise them, uphold the family honour, run the estates when he marches to war. So why is it wrong to be a free bird for a few years before I am given a life sentence?'

Jimena was level-headed and mature for her age and, like me, she enjoyed her education. When she was not learning to sing or dance, sew or embroider, she was with her own tutor, a young priest named Osmundo. Osmundo's good nature certainly rubbed off on Jimena and she was a clever, witty girl, articulate and wise. She had her moments of immaturity, like how she loved to hide in the hill fort before I arrived and jump out and tackle me to the ground, but I did not mind. It was nice to have a friend.

Our friendship blossomed and over the years we met as much as we could. I would bring books from Father Santiago's small library and read the pages to her, and she would listen intently. And she would bring her flute and make sweet songs as I sat there with my eyes closed, took in those precious, tranquil moments with relish. In the spring we would wander the forests and look at the new life blooming, and in the height of summer we would clamber to the top of Monte Naranco. Everywhere we looked there was rolling green hills and small settlements, and to the south and east the snow-capped peaks of the Cantabrian Mountains towered far in the distance. In the same summer my father fought at Graus I looked at her and adored the way her curly locks fluttered in the breeze. She returned my gaze and smiled; a gesture that melted my heart. I knew I loved her, and I prayed to God one day she would be mine.

The blissful memories disintegrated until I was back in the hall. Inigo still loomed over me with his irritable grin.

I looked at Jimena engaged in conversation with our fathers. She glanced my way, a forlorn smile on her face. She had reluctantly accepted her fate as a pawn in a game of politics, married off with a handsome dowry to the son of a knight who would soon become a lord rather than for the promise of love. I had no doubt she would be content with Inigo and he would treat her well, but she would not feel the same love and affection if she were to marry me. Inigo would inherit my father's land in Castile, and Jimena would spend the rest of her days there whilst I was elsewhere, unable to see or speak with her. Anger and shame and woe boiled within me. Would my father find me a girl of similar stock, or would he feel a bride of a noble family would be wasted on his inferior son?

It should have been me marrying Jimena.

I grabbed the jug from Inigo's grasp and filled my goblet despite his protests. I did not care what I was meant to do, what was acceptable and expected of me. I was being forced from my family home by my own father. It was a cruel exile. I was fifteen years old and felt as though my life could not get much worse.

But it did.

In the spring my life fell apart.

Two

'I am leaving for Saraqusta, and when I return you will go to Palencia,' my father said in his stern voice. He stood by the door to the hall dressed in his riding gear, covered by a long grey cloak and fastened by a gold and garnet brooch shaped like an eagle in flight. A shaft of pale light from the first of the spring sun filtered into the room and cast a dark shadow across his face. 'It has been decided your cousin Emiliano will be joining you, so you will not be alone in your venture.'

Emiliano was two years my senior and I enjoyed his company. His father Velasco was my paternal uncle and had a small castle near the northern coast at Santurio. 'I will be back in a few weeks. Prepare yourself.'

My father left for Saraqusta, and for a time I was happy.

I spent most of the time in the company of Father Santiago. He was an ancient man, with a tuft of white hair sitting on his pocked head, tiny eyes and a bulbous nose. His plump lips always carried a gentle smile. He was a good teacher and came from the monastery at Tol along the coast to the west. He took residence in Lugones after my father requested he tutor me and Inigo. He even had his own chapel in our castle and a small room with shelves for his books and scrolls. He looked ancient and moved gingerly, but while old age took away the mobility in his legs it gave him vast knowledge, and his eyesight was still as good as mine. He seemed to know everything.

No question was beyond him and I was fascinated with the stories blossomed from the smallest of prompts; I learned of the great wars between the Romans and a people from a city in Ifriqiya named Carthago, the history of the Visigoths who settled in Roman Hispania and laid the foundations for the northern Christian kingdoms today, and the tales of the saints of the land who incited pilgrimage and attracted men from north and east of the Pyrenees. I took to reading several of Santiago's tomes under his guidance. The more I asked the more I wanted to learn. I learned to read and write before Inigo did, despite him being three years my senior. He grew stronger in body as I grew enhanced my mind.

When Santiago was copying out a manuscript, he would make me read the passages to enrich my reading. It took a lifetime for him to copy out even a few pages, his quill delicately scraping along the velum in a small neat script. The daylight dictated his writing time and I watched in awe as the bluely black ink dried on the vellum.

The book he was copying that spring was a history of twelve of the Roman emperors, named Caesars in the Latin tongue, by a man named Suetonius. He was making me read a passage about the emperor Vespasian, but I did not feel like reading.

'What troubles you, child?' he said in a croaky voice.

'I do not want to go to Palencia.' I muttered.

'It will be good for you.'

'Why would you say that? I thought you enjoyed tutoring me!'

'I do, dear Antonio. But to be a squire for a lord of Leon is a great opportunity. You will receive training from brave knights who have fought the Moors before. You may go on to be a famous knight yourself.' He offered a smile.

'You could come with me. You could still be my teacher.'

21

'I am old, and my uses run thin,' he grimaced. 'When you go, I believe it will be the last time we see each other. If I am lucky, I will spend some time in a monastery with others of my order. If not, I will take my place next to the Lord. Either way, I fear our lessons will soon end. Enjoy these moments with me.'

I adhered to his wishes and spent a blissful few weeks in my favourite surroundings with familiar company.

But the bliss did not last.

A procession of men came along the road from the south one morning, my father at the helm. I went to the yard with my mother and sisters, Maria and Eva, and waited for him. The gates swung open and the horsemen cantered into the courtyard. The horses' heavy hooves churned the muddy ground softened by rain. My father swung from the saddle and strode towards us along with my uncle Velasco and cousin, Emiliano. Velasco was taller than my father and clean shaven with the same stern green eyes. The brothers were dressed in new silk tunics, blood red in colour with white trim above loose white trousers. If they had worn headdresses, they would have looked more like Moors than men from Leon-Castile.

My father embraced my mother and kissed her passionately before greeting my sisters. He turned his gaze to me. I expected some comment laced with scorn, but he embraced me with as much enthusiasm.

'Welcome back husband,' my mother beamed. 'How was the journey?'

'Long and hard, but it was a success. Al-Muqtadir delivered his tribute promptly, given the king's assistance at Graus. And when we made our acquaintance with each other once more he was quick to lavish us with gifts.' He motioned to a laden cart behind him, which I now saw had rolls of silk, some silver trinkets and a sack or two of spices. One of his men carefully removed a fine Moorish sword and helm and took them in to the interior of the keep.

'He is a man who looks after his friends,' my uncle added.

'You look like a conquering hero returning from a successful campaign,' Eva said.

'I believe I was not sufficiently rewarded for killing Ramiro, and al-Muqtadir agreed. The spoils of war were a little late in the coming, but I received them nonetheless.' He gave my uncle a sideways glance and they both smirked as if pleased with themselves. He looked at me, not with contempt but as a father would look at a son he had missed. 'Are you well rested, Antonio?'

'I am.'

'And have you been practising since I have been gone?'

'I have.'

He gave a grunt of satisfaction. 'Good. Your uncle and cousin will stay and refresh for a few days, then we depart for Palencia.'

Emiliano seemed in good spirits at the prospect, but I was not. Nothing had changed in my mind. I knew I was being sent into exile.

They feasted well that night, but my mood was still glum, and I seldom spoke. My father described the journey to Saraqusta, yet I had no interest in his words. I ate little and kept a steady flow of cider down my gullet, and when the sun had set, and my father and uncle called for more wine I took my leave. I doubt they noticed, or indeed missed my presence.

I lay in my bed and tossed and turned as sleep would not come to me. Deep in my mind I had hoped the trip to Saraqusta would have changed father's mind about sending me away, but it only served to fuel his desire to see me gone. But before I was banished, I had unfinished business.

If I was to leave my home, I would confess my love to Jimena.

*   *   *

Around the back of the keep was a hole at the base of the castle wall big enough for me to wriggle through. The wall of the keep was not built flush to curtain wall and so there was a gap wide enough for me to walk. I had dug out the ground over the years, but the squeeze was tighter as my frame filled out. It had been my escape route when I wanted to leave and avoid detection from the guards patrolling the parapet. I wished I could pass through one last time and run away and not have to go to Leon. But my fate was already sealed.

I left at dawn and crept out of the castle. The guards were oblivious to my presence. I slithered out of the hole, pulled my hood over my head and stalked between the wooden houses of the village of Lugones, stuck to the shadows. The only movement came from a pair of dogs who stirred and glared at me before lowering their heads and resuming their slumber. Father beat me once when the guards discovered me trying to sneak out of the postern gate to meet Jimena at the hill fort, saying I should be training or studying. The next time I tried, Father Santiago covered for me and told my father I was with him, and I used the hole in the wall to make sure I was not discovered again. It became all too easy. Though now I was going to Palencia I was sure he did not care where I went before I left my home. He would drag me there if he had to.

I reached the periphery of the village and made my way to the river. Behind me the pale orange glow of dawn rose over the Cantabrian Mountains and illuminated the rolling green hills ahead, banishing the gloom of Monte Naranco's shadow. The river Nora wound delicately to the south and east past Lugones, the gentle waters lapping around stones and shimmering in the low light. There was no wind and it was eerily silent, but I savoured the solitude and tranquillity.

Over the small bridge I took a turn to the right and made for a line of oak trees at the base of Naranco. It was safer in the shade of the wood. The new light of day poked through the canopy as the trees stood like silent sentinels, forever in a state of watch. New leaves sprouted from the gnarled branches, fresh and green, and flowers bloomed as the spring took hold of the world. Hares scampered ahead and the birds banded together in a morning chorus. It was a paradise; no one to order me around, no one to make me do what I wished not to. I was determined to cherish one final walk of freedom.

I continued for a while then stopped to break my fast on stale bread, an apple and a few scraps of cold boar. The sun had crept well over the mountains to the east, but a chill hung in the air, as winter's grip was still not fully broken by the spring sun. The rumble of hooves cut through the tranquillity. I peered out of the undergrowth to see a large troupe of horsemen galloping on the road towards Lugones. Helms, mail and spear tops glinted in the rising sunlight. I found it odd for a party of armed men to be riding hard in the early morning. Perhaps they were going to visit my father, come to congratulate him on his role in the victory at Graus. They were too large a group to be my escort to Palencia, or to discuss a marriage proposal for me. The thought made me shudder, or perhaps it was the early morning chill. I wrapped my cloak tighter to my body as I continued along the hillside.

It was another hour before the tower of the cathedral of San Salvador loomed over the houses and walls. The city shone golden in the bright sunlight and acted as a beacon for the serfs from outlying fields and villages to conduct their business of the day. I re-joined the road and made my way to the northern gate, sparsely populated with travellers headed in the same direction. There was a buzz in the air and lots of excited chatter, but I was too far out of earshot to hear any of it.

The walls of the city were the height of three men with a parapet for guards to walk along. I knew none of them would recognise me but kept my hood up, tried to remain incognito. The city gates had only just opened by the time I arrived, and a steady procession of traders, serfs, carts and mules shifted through under the watchful eye of the guards. Here and there people were stopped for questioning, but I escaped their gaze and slipped into the city unhindered.

I followed the crowd on the main road through the city. The close press of the houses kept the avenues well shaded from the sun, but a warm wind wound through the tunnel like streets, filtering stuffy air in to my lungs. The heat baked the piles of shit laid by horses and mules and masked the subtle fragrance of cooking fires and morning meals. The bells of the cathedral rang loud over the grunts of pack animals and general chatter of the serfs and traders going about their business. Oviedo was a hub of trade, the principal city of old Asturias and attracted wealthy clientele to its markets. And the market was my destination.

The street opened in to a wide square. On one side was the cathedral of San Salvador, its gleaming limestone façade bright in the morning glare. Two other churches flanked the square whilst on the opposite side to the cathedral stood a large building enclosed by a high wall which was the residence of the count of Oviedo, also Jimena's home. It would be folly to even attempt to gain access to the enclosure, but I knew I did not have to.

In the centre of the square was the market, already a hive of activity. The merchants engaged in their daily bartering war, duelling with discounts and waving their wares towards potential customers as they buzzed and weaved their way between the stalls. A thin Castilian trader shoved an ivory statue of the Virgin Mary in my face, tried to force a sale, but I dodged out the way and scanned the stands. Every morning Jimena walked the markets and perused the wares, particularly the Moorish wares; glass beads and goblets from Balansiya, silk from Qurtuba in every colour under the sun, and statues and ornaments fashioned from ivory from a desert far to the south across the sea.

Jimena was not difficult to find. Her dress was a vibrant blue and her hair was covered with a white headdress, made her stand out from the crowd. I pulled my hood back and strode forward, not wanting to wait another second. I had not noticed her brother Fernando a few feet behind her. It was he who saw me first, with a startled look on his face.

'Antonio,' he frowned. 'What are you doing here?'

Jimena looked alarmed at first, and then smiled. At least she was pleased to see me.

'I have come to say goodbye,' I said to Jimena, ignoring Fernando. He looked at Jimena, who gave a sideward smile of approval at my presence. He stepped out of earshot and returned to the market stalls. Jimena embraced me and squeezed tight. The scent of jasmine in her hair filled my nostrils.

'I have missed you, Antonio. You must be excited to be going to Palencia.'

'I do not want to go. It's why I have come.'

'What do you mean?'

'I want to stay here. I do not want to be a damned knight.'

Jimena frowned. 'But most boys your age desire to be a knight.'

'Not I. My best talents are reading and writing. I will not be able to do any of that in Palencia. There will just be a new set of people to laugh at how weak I am. I belong in Asturias with my family and my friends. And the girl I love.'

Her mouth hung open in surprise and a frown formed on her brow. 'You mean…me?'

'If you tell me you love me too, we can go.'

She looked nervous, took half a step back. 'What are you talking about?'

'We will leave Oviedo.'

'You're not making sense.'

'We will run away and be together and start a new life somewhere new.'

'You cannot be serious!'

'I have never been so serious in my life, Jimena. I am ready to defy my father and do what *I* want, not be a pawn in his game. But I need you to come with me.'

'Stop it. Now,' she said sternly, pointing a finger at me. 'Your words are folly. If we leave, we will be hunted down and punished. I will be reprimanded by my father and you will be thrown into the prison for kidnapping me. If you are lucky, you will go back to your father who will send you to Palencia; otherwise you will be hanged. You do not get to decide my fate. My father has seen to that and nothing will change his mind. Not even what I want.'

Jimena's reaction was more intense than I had anticipated. Tears glistened in her eyes. I remember her saying she resented the notion of being shackled to a man she did not love and there was nothing she could do about it. Her fate was sealed. And she made it perfectly clear she hated what she would become.

'You do not want to marry Inigo, do you?'

A tear trickled down her cheek. 'I am betrothed to the wrong brother.'

It was all I ever wanted to hear. I had loved Jimena from afar for what seemed like forever and it pained me I could not have her. But now her words were bliss.

Yet any hope of a future together was short lived.

'Jimena, are you all right?' Fernando rushed to his sister, the tears now streaming down her cheeks. He put a comforting arm around her and glared at me. 'What have you said to her?'

'I am fine,' she replied, wiping her face. 'I am just sad to see Antonio go.'

'You should leave,' he said through gritted teeth.

'I have not finished saying goodbye.'

Fernando squared up to me. He was approaching twenty years old and his larger frame towered over me. I stood my ground and tried to remain defiant.

'Leave her alone,' he growled.

'No.'

He pushed me hard and I fell to the floor, grazing my hands on the dirt. Those around us stopped and stared at the commotion, looks of concern or intrigue on their faces. I got to my feet and stood firm.

'I am warning you. Leave her alone.'

'No!' I cried.

He lunged, grabbed my cloak and drew his arm back, his hand tightened into a fist. Gasps of shock came from the crowd as Jimena started forward and screamed for her brother to stop. I braced myself for the blow to come.

But it never did.

'Antonio!'

A familiar voice called from behind. Fernando lowered his fist as a horseman emerged from the crowd, reined his mount in hard and came to a stop next to us. It was Jorge, an older boy from the village of Lugones who trained in the yard. His father was the blacksmith and he had the same broad shoulders and solid face.

'You have to come. Men are at the castle. They have arrested your father and uncle!'

I tore myself from Fernando's grip. 'What do you mean? What has happened?'

'Royal knights from Leon have seized your father. There are claims he and uncle are guilty of theft, treason and conspiracy against the crown. They are taking them to the king!'

The news shocked me to my core. Only a few months ago my father had been celebrated as a famed knight who had delivered the killing blow to Ramiro. Now he had been arrested for being a traitor.

The crowd stared at me. Murmurs of shock and whispers of gossip rippled through the congregation. They knew who I was now, and one man shouted to fetch the guards and arrest me for being the son of a traitor.

'Go,' Jimena stepped forward. 'Go to your family before it is too late.' I blinked and hesitated. 'Go!'

I looked at Fernando behind her, his seething nature now cooled. He nodded his agreement. I wanted to stay with Jimena and run away and plan our future together, but with the arrival of Jorge and the ill news he brought I knew that path was firmly closed forever. And so, I took Jorge's hand, vaulted myself on to his horse and held on tight to his waist as he spurred the beast in to action.

I took one last look at Jimena with a grim expression upon her face, not knowing what the future held, before Jorge's horse sped through the streets of Oviedo.

*   *   *

The ride to Lugones was agonizingly long.

My mind played out the different scenarios of what would happen to my father. According to our laws the best outcome my father could ask for is a pardon from the king, but he would be blinded first so he could not look upon the people again and they would look upon him in shame. But the worst outcome would affect all my family. He would be sentenced to death and his property would be seized and we would be left with nothing, and the king would grant our land to anyone he deemed worthy of it. None of the outcomes were favourable, but I prayed King Fernando would show mercy. Surely the man who killed Ramiro of Aragon, the king's brother and last dynastic rival, would be shown clemency?

I knew I was being naïve.

It was close to midday by the time Jorge's horse cantered over the bridge near the castle. We took cover in a small copse at the side of the road. I dismounted and stalked into the undergrowth, looked towards my home. Plumes of smoke drifted from the courtyard, and the gates to the castle were wide open and men with shields bearing a rampant black bull stood at the entrance, held back a crowd of curious villagers.

'You will never make it through without being spotted,' Jorge said.

'Do not worry. I have been sneaking in and out for the past few years. They will not spot me.' I smiled. 'Thank you for warning me. It's nice to know some people are willing to help me out.' Jorge was one of the boys who would not humiliate me during our training, knowing I was much weaker than he was. The bruises did not hurt so much from a reluctant blow.

He nodded his gratitude. 'Thank Inigo. He was the one who sent me.'

The statement drew a frown from me. I believed Inigo would have been at Oviedo where he squired, so I could not understand as to how he had gained entry to Lugones after the soldiers had arrived.

30

'Do you know where my brother is now?'

Jorge's expression turned grim. 'He was in the yard with me, but I could not tell you where he is now. With any luck he will have evaded capture. Good luck.'

I retraced my steps from the morning, skirting the periphery of the village and stalking between the stone and timber houses. There were no guards in this part of the village and only a handful of serfs mulled around and exchanged their gossip, so it was easy to find my escape route under the wall. After squeezing through I dusted myself off and crouched low, kept close to the wall and edged around the corner to survey the carnage in the yard.

The bodies of my father's men were everywhere. Twisted and bent, forever in death's embrace, visages of agony and horror embedded on their faces. Blood leaked from wounds on their torsos and necks and stained their garbs and armour. Even the stonework of the walls and stairs dripped red, marking death around the whole courtyard. Enemy soldiers now patrolled the ramparts and busied themselves around the castle, ransacked the outlaying buildings and gathered any man they had not yet killed. Several wagons waited in the centre of the courtyard, surrounded by a small troupe of mounted knights.

And there, in the middle of the enemy, was my father and uncle.

They knelt with their hands bound behind their backs. Their fine garbs were slick with mud as if they had been thrown around the yard like animals. Velasco's expression was grim, yet my father was defiant. He looked at his captors with scorn, even when he was at their mercy. I had no doubt he would show the same level of bravery until death came for him.

A loud click sounded from behind and I spun to find the source of the noise. There was a small storeroom at my back, but the door was closed, and no one was there. I held my breath and my gaze lingered in case one of the men had spotted me but, content I remained hidden, I turned back to the yard and tried to form a plan.

I was alone in a pit of snakes, and one wrong move would result in my capture, but my options were limited. If I stayed concealed until they left, I would be isolated. My mother and sisters would be confined to a convent for the rest of their lives and the castle would pass to a new lord, rendering me homeless and helpless. Presenting myself to the attackers would see me imprisoned with my father or condemned to slavery. It was too dangerous to go back to Oviedo and seek help from Jimena, for her father was loyal to the crown and harbouring the son of a traitor would harm his reputation.

I did not hear the storeroom door swing open, nor see the shadow emerge.

A hand covered my mouth, an arm wrapped around my midriff and yanked hard. My cries were muffled as I was hauled into the storeroom. I thrashed and tried to break free from the grip, but my assailant was too strong. The door creaked shut and a lock clicked, the sun disappeared, and I was plunged in to darkness, shrouded in shadow. My assailant heaved me up a flight of stairs and threw me to the ground. I lay there a moment, caught my breath and regained my wits. Footsteps scraped off the wooden floorboards as two figures circled me.

The familiar face of Inigo manifested from the darkness.

'Where have you been?' he demanded.

'I went to Oviedo.'

'Why?'

I hesitated. 'To see Jimena one last time, before I went to Palencia.'

'You need to understand neither of you are going to Palencia anymore.'

I turned to see Emiliano behind me. He gave a sad smile and my spirits lifted. At least I was not left alone with Inigo.I knelt and frowned at him. 'Tell me what is happening. You are supposed to be in Oviedo. Why are you here? I do not understand any of this.'

Inigo walked over to a window. The shutters were closed but shafts of sunlight filtered through and cast stripes along my brother's face. He peered through one of the shafts.

'I rose at dawn to start my duties. A large group of armed men were already in the central square. I do not know how many there are – forty, fifty perhaps? – and their leader spoke with the count. I could not hear what they were saying, save for a few discernible words.' He turned and stared at me with intense eyes. 'Pedro Valdez…traitor.

'I followed them back to Lugones. Even as I approached, they were through the gates and smoke rose from the interior. The main gate was guarded, but one of our men had unlocked the postern gate and must have fled for his life. I slipped in that way and only the grace of God allowed me to find Emiliano unharmed. Together we hid in here. The men were killed, and the boys taken captive. We have been lying in wait, looking for an opportunity to kill that knight.'

'What knight?'

Inigo motioned outside and I peered through the shutter.

In the centre of the courtyard was a man on a huge bay horse. A long black cloak hung around his shoulders, fastened by a gold chain that glinted in the sunlight. Gold too adorned his belt buckle, and his mail coat and the helm cradled under his arm were polished to a gleam. I had no doubt the long sword with the jewelled pommel at his hip would be the same.

'He is Bernardo Garces, but most know him as Azarola. He is the lord of Dueñas and is a powerful figure in the south of Leon. They say he saved the king's life at Atapuerca a decade ago and his stock has risen ever since.'

The knight surveyed the castle with squinty eyes. His hair was raven black, short and cropped and his weather-beaten face was clean shaven. His squashed nose resembled the snout of a pig and a sinister smile was embedded upon his bulbous lips. It was a face I would remember for years to come, a visage to haunt my dreams every night.

A group of soldiers exited the keep with bundles of possessions, loading them on to the wagons as my father and uncle looked on helpless. They were the same items my father had brought upon his return to Saraqusta.

'Who is that?' whispered Emiliano.

Amongst Azarola's knights was a tall man dressed in a long, pale yellow gown trimmed in green and a headdress in the same fashion, yet his skin was darker than the other men. He was not Leonese or Castilian, but a Moor. He stood next to Azarola and studied the bundles in the arms of the soldiers as they were brought out. His beard was cropped and neatly trimmed, and his frame muscular. A savage scar ran over his left cheek, glinting silver against his olive skin, whilst the eye was deathly pale.

The Moor barked something and a soldier stopped. He snatched the bundle and looked it over carefully before he marched over to my father and shouted something I could not make out. My father must have said something he did not like for the Moor kicked him in the face. Blood poured from my father's nose as he lay in the muddy yard amongst a chorus of jeers from the gathered soldiers. When the Moor turned, he held the elaborately decorated Moorish sword and helm. Clearly it had some immense value to him.

'I do not know who he is,' replied Inigo, 'but I will kill that bastard as well.'

'And how do you propose to kill him?' I said.

'I do not know, but we have to do something.'

'We cannot fight fifty men on our own.'

'We have to do something!' my brother hissed.

A tense silence hung in the air and we watched as the last of the items were loaded on to the wagons. Azarola shouted something and my father and uncle too were thrown on to the back of a wagon, hands still bound behind their backs. They resembled disgraced serfs more than knights of the realm. The driver whipped the reins and the horses lumbered into motion, starting a steady procession of wagons out of the gate.

A commotion sounded from inside the keep and my mother and sisters burst forth, making for my father. The guards restrained them as they screeched and my father shouted back to them in reassurance, but his words only added fuel to the fire. My mother tore herself away, tried to scramble on the wagon to comfort my father. She did not see the Moor as he stepped out and struck her.

He caught her mouth with the back of his hand. She cried as she fell and lay on the floor, sobbing. The Moor shouted something in his native tongue and spat in her face, before he mounted his horse and rode behind the wagons. Her wails were like torture to my ears as the grief of losing a lover took hold. The guards released my sisters, who ran to her side and comforted her. I clenched my fists as anger boiled within me. I wanted to run out and help my family, but all I could only watch their abuse from afar.

'We wait until the cover of darkness,' Inigo said.

I and Emiliano exchanged puzzled glances. 'And do what?'

'We will go to the militia's armoury and arm ourselves. It does not look as though Azarola's men have ransacked it, so we might be able to grab some weapons. Emiliano, you're good with a bow, are you not? We could use a good shot.'

'You cannot be serious.'

Inigo rose, determination embedded upon his face.

'We're going to Leon. We go, free our fathers – and kill the man they call Azarola.'

*   *   *

We waited until darkness before we made our move.

Inigo inched open the door. The cool evening breeze caressed my cheek but carried the stench of death and smoke in the air. Torches had been lit to illuminate the courtyard in a vibrant glow. The bodies of my father's men had been looted of weapons and possessions then taken outside the castle. The blood-stained ground and walls served as a reminder of the massacre.

Azarola's soldiers remained but their presence had diminished. A handful patrolled the walls and manned the gate, and some had entered

35

the keep, no doubt to enjoy the comforts we once took for granted. My mother and sisters had been taken back in to the keep too, but we had heard nothing of them since. I feared for their safety, yet we were devoid of ideas on how we could free them. There cannot have been any more than twenty men left in the castle. Twenty was still too great a number for three young men to challenge.

We crouched low and scurried along the periphery of the yard, sticking to the shadows. My mouth was dry and my palms slick with sweat. The armoury was on the same side as we were, but there was plenty of ground to cover and there was always the chance of being spotted by a vigilant guard. But those on duty must have thought no threat would come from inside or out and instead chatted casually to their comrades and drank pillaged wine from the stores. Inigo slowly opened the door to the armoury, and we slipped inside.

The militia's armoury had been untouched. The scant torchlight of the flickering flames revealed a pair of racks for weapons lining the walls: one for swords and knives, and another for spears and javelins. Plain round shields were hung upon the wall, and a couple of bows and crossbows were stored next to barrels of arrows and quarrels. Five mannequins stood in a row down the centre of the room with boiled leather jerkins, padded tunics and cheap steel bowl helms upon them.

Inigo walked over to the rack of swords and weighed them, felt the edge of the blades and tested the tips. Emiliano twanged the string of a composite bow. Satisfied at the draw he slung a quiver of arrows to his belt before moving over to the swords.

Inigo pulled two knives from a rack and held the handles towards me.

'Get some sheaths that fit, grab a whetstone and go stand guard.'

'But I have never used one before. You know how dreadful I am in a fight!'

I must have sounded pathetic. My father had been captured and Inigo had taken the lead, devised a plan to try and free him, yet I moaned I could not use a knife and did not have the stomach for a fight.

I regretted my words and thought he was going to strike me. Instead, he held up the larger of the knives; straight and sharp, made of good steel.

'What we are doing is mad, but it is the only way we can free our father. We need to take matters into our own hands. And what I need you to do is sharpen this knife every night and pretend it is going to be the knife to end Azarola's life. Can you do that?'

I did not have a choice. There was no alternative but to stick with Inigo and Emiliano and embark on a mission of folly. I took the knife from Inigo's grasp and nodded reluctantly. There was no reassuring smile from him, just a grunt of acknowledgement.

I duly followed his instructions, found sheaths for both weapons. The larger knife was the length my forearm and could have been passed off as a short sword. In the right hands it could do some damage. The smaller blade was nothing more than a knife a man might cut his meat with, but it could be easily concealed from view. I hid it at the back of my belt underneath my cloak and hung the longer knife by my side. I placed a small whetstone in a satchel which I slung over my shoulder and pulled on a pair of worn leather gloves.

'So, what is our plan when we get to Leon?' Emiliano enquired. My brother was silent as he ran a finger along the length of a long sword with a worn leather tang. 'You do have a plan, do you not?'

'It's a long way to Leon,' Inigo replied. 'There is plenty of time to conjure one.'

I and Emiliano exchanged nervous glances.

'So, how do we get out of the castle?' my cousin pressed.

'I have not thought that far ahead yet.' Inigo was growing increasingly agitated. It was obvious he did not know what to do.

'Are you expecting us to fight our way out?'

'I do not know.'

'Well…should we wait until dawn, or try and get out now?'

'I do not know!' Inigo slammed the sword into its sheath.

A tense silence hung in the air. It was clear Inigo's plan was farfetched and fabricated out of desperation. He was the dominant brother, his father's son, and he had a responsibility to take the initiative and be the hero. But at that moment it was beyond anything he was capable of.

'I know a way out,' I broke the silence.

Inigo's gaze snapped towards me.

'Then let us hear it. I am sure it's a wonderful plan.' He could not mask his sarcasm.

'I have been sneaking in and out of this castle for years. The postern gate will be locked and watch by men, but around the back of the keep is a hole, at the base of the curtain wall on the western side. It might be a tight squeeze for you but it's better than walking to the gate and kindly asking to be let out.' Inigo sighed and shook his head. 'You may not think much of me, but I have my uses. Have you got a better idea, *brother*?'

Inigo did not like my tone. He was dominant and enjoyed holding sway over me. If there was an idea to be had it had to be his, otherwise it was insignificant.

'Fine. Lead the way.'

'I have one condition, though. I have to see Father Santiago before I go.'

Inigo's laugh was laced with scorn. 'Do not waste your time with that old oaf. Chances are he's dead. With any luck one of the guards will have gutted him like a boar.'

Anger made me draw the knife and raise it Inigo's way. I did not think I had it in me to threaten my brother with violence, but Father Santiago was a dear friend and I would not have him ridiculed.

The glow of the torches cast a dark shadow across Inigo's face. He looked even more menacing when he gritted his teeth and stepped forwards, placed his neck on the point of the knife. I was stunned and my arm started trembling at his bold action.

'Have you got it in you, *brother*?' he taunted me. 'Show me you can be a man. Do it.'

Of course, I did not have it in me. I was a fifteen-year-old boy who abhorred violence yet was subjected to it daily in the practise yard. I did not have it in me to kill anyone. And so, I backed away and lowered the knife. Inigo said no more on the matter. My refusal to act was enough to prove his moral victory over me.

'Lead the way.'

*   *   *

The guards let out an almighty roar of laughter as we scurried back through the darkness.

Black clouds masked the moon and the torches did not illuminate the full yard, which gave us ample cover to conceal ourselves. We were armed for war; I with my knives, my companions both with good swords and Emiliano with his bow, all of us with long grey cloaks to hide our weapons. We would have appeared like spectres moving in the shadows. Inigo and Emiliano wore leather jerkins under their cloaks, knowing mail or helms would slow them or attract unwanted attention. I decided against wearing one; no matter what happened I had no intention of getting involved in hand to hand combat.

We kept low as we passed the storehouse and turned the corner to the back of the keep. There was no light here and we could not risk a torch lest we be discovered, so I crouched and let my hand brush along the rough stone of the outer wall. Our boots scraped along the ground until I found the gap around a third of the way behind the keep.

'We are here,' I whispered. 'You squeeze through and wait for me on the other side.'

I continued to the other end of the keep as Inigo and Emiliano grunted and cursed, trying to squeeze through the gap.

Father Santiago's chapel was on the northern side of the courtyard next to the burned out stable. Its limestone façade and red tiles glowed in the faint torchlight. I peered out to make sure the guards were still engaged in their banter and hurried to the chapel door. It was slightly ajar, and a faint glow emitted from the interior. I pressed my back against the heavy oak frame and pushed it open a touch, enough to slip my slender frame inside.

The air was warm and close from the many candles burning throughout the confined space. Before me was a stone altar beneath an arch, flanked by two more archways, and on the altar was an embroidered cover with a depiction of the crucifixion. The pungent scent of incense filled my nostrils, and I noticed a censer on its side on the floor, wisps of smoke still curling into the air. Other items came into view; a chalice, a jewelled crucifix and a candle stand, all scattered on the floor between the overturned benches. I feared the worst and dashed through a second door which led to Father Santiago's private chambers.

The room was a mess. Two candles burned low, the pale wax dripping over the iron stands. The bookcase had been toppled, manuscripts and scrolls now strewn throughout, precious knowledge damaged without a hint of regard for their worth. And in the middle of the floor, still as a statue, lay Father Santiago. Blood stained his vestments, and crimson trickled from a large gash in his midriff and another across his forehead, congealed in dark pools on the floor. I crouched, removed a glove and placed my hand on his, his flesh deathly cold and pale. There was no life left in his vacant eyes. I was too late.

It took me a moment to realise he was gone. My hand passed over his eyes and closed his lids, and he was finally at peace. I did not hold back my tears. In the subtle candlelight in the chapel of Lugones I wept for my mentor and friend, for the man who had taught me so much. I wept for the man who was more of a father to me than my own, then muttered a prayer to God to guide his servant to Heaven and made a silent vow to safeguard the values he taught.

The glint of something shiny caught my eye amongst the detritus. It was the final manuscript Father Santiago was working on; smaller than most books, it was bound in leather with an ivory plaque of the crucifixion in the centre and a gleaming sapphire in each corner, with smaller pieces of blue glass surrounding each jewel. I wrapped it in a rag I found on the floor and carefully placed it in my satchel, before returning my gaze to Santiago's lifeless eyes.

'I promise to take care of it,' I whispered, 'and give it to someone worthy of its beauty.'

I spent some time by his side before I gathered my wits and left. My eyes were still glossed with tears as the cooler air outside greeted me. I was numb and empty, drained from the brutality of the day. Only this morning I was to go to Palencia to begin a new life, yet now the future was bleak and uncertain. I wiped my eyes with the back of my sleeve and prepared to make my escape.

'Who are you?'

I froze at the unfamiliar voice. A guard had exited the keep and now squinted at me, flaming brand in hand. In the torchlight I must have looked like a shadow as I exited the chapel, but the glint of steel betrayed the dagger at my hip. The guard's eyes widened.

I darted to my right, made for the rear of the keep. My heart thumped against my chest and adrenaline coursed through my veins at the fear of being captured. The alley behind the keep slowly illuminated as the guard followed me. I skidded along the dirt and held my hands out to stop myself slamming into the wall, then scurried down the narrow passage between the keep and castle wall.

'Show yourself, cretin!'

I paid him no heed. The light of the torch crept behind me again and I risked a glance to see the guard turning the corner. But my haste proved to be my folly. The ground was precarious, littered with broken stones and small holes, and my foot kicked a large stone and I was sent flying through the air. I landed with a thud and the wind was knocked from me as pain engulfed my ribs. I scrambled to my feet and staggered forward as the torchlight grew brighter and the footsteps louder.

'Get here you little bastard!' the guard shouted.

'Antonio, get down!'

The faint outline of Emiliano appeared ahead, bow in hand, arrow notched and ready to release. I dropped to my knees as the shaft flew from his grip. It was black as pitch, but the torch in the hand of the guard made him an easy target. A loud thwack was followed by a sickening gurgle, and I turned to see the arrow embedded in the guard's neck. He dropped the torch and collapsed as he clutched at his throat, a crimson tide pouring forth. His body twitched uncontrollably for a few moments as he gasped for air. Then he was still, his eyes lifeless, glinting in the torchlight.

My knees crumbled. It was only a few moments before I had seen Father Santiago pass away, and now the sight of the guard writhing in pain was too much to handle. A cold sweat came over me and a great surge swelled in my stomach. The vomit came relentless, burning my throat and causing me to double over, retch and cough.

As strands of spittle and bile dangled from my nose and mouth Inigo hauled me further into the darkness.

'Shut up or you will get us bloody killed!' he hissed as he dragged me to the hole in the wall. I said nothing, tried to regain my wits. Any chance of respite was short lived as Inigo pushed me through the hole and into the village beyond. Frantic shouts came from within the walls. The commotion must have attracted the attention of the guards. Inigo cursed as he squeezed through the snug gap, followed by Emiliano, and soon the three of us were trudging through the village. We moved swift through the shadows, stayed away from the main street. I shut my mouth and let my wobbly legs carry me in the same direction of Inigo and Emiliano, hoped the rest of our escape would be uneventful.

We passed along the bridge over the river Nora as the bells of the guardhouse rang loud in the twilight and more shouts erupted from inside the castle, more torches lit in the blackness of evening. We had escaped, but there would be men searching for the murderers of their comrade in the morning.

We left enemies at our backs and pressed on in to the unknown.

Three

'You are a fucking idiot.'

I yelped as a sharp blow struck the side of my head. 'You try anything like that again, and I swear I will gut you myself.'

I looked at Inigo but held my tongue. We had stopped in the woods around Naranco to regain our wits. The sky was a grey smudge where the first hints of dawn crowned the Cantabrian Mountains to the east. The air was cool, calm and refreshing. We had trudged for an hour, around the river Nora, and climbed the slopes of Naranco. I could not comprehend how much my life had change in a day.

'I could not leave without saying goodbye,' I muttered.

'You should have stayed with the rest of our family in the keep and saved us the trouble of having a nuisance in our ranks.'

'Lay off him,' said Emiliano. 'We would not have got out if it were not for Antonio.'

Inigo knew the notion was true but could not bring himself to admit one of my ideas proved fruitful. Instead he unslung his satchel and rummaged around before he pulled out a small loaf of bread.

'Where did you get that?' I asked.

'We took it upon ourselves to look for supplies. We had to steal from our own people. I am not proud of it, but at least we can eat.' He took a bite of the bread and tossed it to Emiliano before drawing a smaller loaf and throwing it my way. The sight of food brought a surge of hunger and I tore great chunks from the bread and snatched a water skin from Inigo's grasp when offered.

'So how do we get to Leon?' Emiliano enquired.

'If we walk it will take at least ten days to cross the mountains, maybe longer, and that would be following the old Roman road. Finding an isolated pass to keep us out of sight would be preferable. But we need horses; otherwise we will not make it in time.'

'And where do we get horses from?'

Inigo chewed his lip. 'We will have to steal them.'

A low rumbling sounded in the distance. We crouched and were well concealed with a commanding view of the road to Oviedo. Five horsemen galloped along the road and made for the city. Even in the low light we could knew they were Azarola's men with their bull adorned shields and mail coats, riding horses we desperately needed. If they had sent out more than one search party the numbers inside the castle would have been diminished and we might find what we needed there. But going back would be folly. After finding one of their own dead, the guards would be vigilant. The fear of death from the shadows makes a man sharpen his wits and stiffen his back.

'They're watching the road,' I said.

'They do not have the manpower to watch it,' Inigo replied. 'They will ride a little further, realise there's no hope of finding us and ride back to Lugones. We will not have to worry about them anymore.'

We climbed a little further up the slope of Monte Naranco to gain a better view of the surrounding land. The sun rose and brightened the world, illuminated lush fields and sparkling silver rivers, pockets of woodland and the rolling green hills that rose to the Cantabrian Mountains to the south. And beyond them was Leon.

The journey would be hard. A Roman road ran through the easiest of the passes, but for all we knew Azarola would have men patrolling the road and so we had to find an alternate route. The mountain passes were cold, and snowfall was frequent, whilst wolves were known to stalk travellers and pounce on them when most vulnerable. And if the passes were free of snow and the wolves looked elsewhere for their meals it would take days to find our way to the other side without an experienced guide. It was a journey I did not relish.

The five horsemen cantered back to Lugones like Inigo had predicted. We started our descent, stuck to the undergrowth and pockets of woodland and, when the horsemen had cleared the road, we headed south.

We travelled the road to Oviedo and headed south a mile from the city into the countryside. Three young men with long grey cloaks travelling the road would have aroused suspicion among travellers and we needed to remain vigilant. We passed flowering orchards, herds of goats and sheep grazing in the pastures, and a group of serfs felling strong oak from a nearby wood. Two small villages passed us by, but they were nothing more than a cluster of homes and we kept our distance lest we arouse suspicion.

But we did not remain anonymous for long.

They must have been following us for a while, and they only caught us because I tripped over a rock and hobbled along at a slower pace because of my throbbing ankle. The first we heard was a high-pitched shout and we turned to see two horsemen in the distance. One of them was calling my name. My eyes widened when I saw her.

'It's Jimena. Her brother Fernando is with her.'

'Shit,' Inigo muttered.

'They can help us.'

'You really think they will help the sons of a man who was arrested for treason? Do not be fooled. Their father is a staunch supporter of King Fernando. They will have branded us traitors.'

I insisted we meet with them. Jimena was relieved to see us alive and leapt into my arms when she dismounted. Fernando glowered at us but held his tongue, kept a watchful eye over his sister.

'I was so worried,' she said, drawing away. 'Is it true? They have been arrested?' I nodded. 'What are you doing out here?'

'The castle has been taken. We could not stay there. They killed my father's men and imprisoned my mother and sisters. They killed Father Santiago, too.' Jimena covered her mouth with a trembling hand whilst Fernando looked at the ground. They had both known the priest and were fond of them, and no doubt his death shocked them as much as it had me.

'It looks like we are no longer to be wed, my lady,' Inigo said in a bitter tone before he looked at Fernando, 'and I will no longer serve your father.'

'That is a shame. You showed a lot of promise. My father thought so highly of you he intended to bring you in to our family.'

'And would that high regard stretch to him granting us a favour, by helping to release my father from captivity?'

Fernando narrowed his eyes. 'My father is a count, and the order came directly from the king. His hands are tied. Besides, if the king brands your father as a traitor there must be some truth to it.'

Inigo strode forward and squared up to Fernando, fury embedded in his face. 'The king is a liar! My father is an honourable knight and the king was lavishing praise on him but a few months ago. The charges are fabricated lies, and I would gladly cut the throat of any man who would suggest otherwise.'

Fernando was about to argue back, but something made him look at Inigo's belt. He took a step back as a look of concern descended over his face.

'Why are you armed?'

The pommel of Inigo's sword poked out from his cloak, and now he placed a hand on the hilt and brought it in to plain view.

'We are taking matters into our own hands. My father is innocent. We are going to Leon to set him free and kill the bastards who sullied his name.'

'What you are talking of is madness. You will get yourself killed!'

'I would rather die with honour than live with shame.'

Fernando shook his head. 'I cannot allow you to go to Leon. I must inform my father of your intentions.' He turned towards his horse but stopped when he heard Emiliano notch an arrow and aim his way.

'We cannot let you do that, lord.'

Fernando glared at Emiliano.

'Are you mad? You dare threaten the son of a count?'

Emiliano maintained his focus and kept the arrow fixed on Fernando.

'It does not matter who you are, lord. My father has been taken too. If you get in the way of me finding a way to free him then I will kill you.'

There was a look of genuine fear on Fernando's face. He must have seen the desperation of our plight and the lengths we would go to if we were to succeed.

'Antonio, do something!' Jimena hissed. I looked at her but said nothing. It was futile to attempt to intervene; Inigo was calling the shots and Emiliano had shown where his loyalties laid. Jimena turned her attention to Inigo. 'Stop this now! If Fernando will not help you and if my father cannot...I will.'

Inigo turned and walked over to her. She stiffened and averted her gaze when he came close, intimidated by the way he looked at her, the way his breath caressed her cheek and neck. He towered over her, thumbs hooked through his sword belt, sizing every inch of her. He was staring at her like she was his possession and only God knew what dark thoughts passed through his mind. Anger brewed inside me and I clenched my fists to suppress it.

When he spoke, his tone was cold and calculated, almost a whisper.

'You could prove useful yet.' His sadistic smile was unsettling. After a pause he continued. 'This is what is going to happen. Emiliano and Antonio are going to stay here with your brother. You and I are going to take these horses and get enough supplies to see us to Leon. If I am not back by nightfall, I will be presumed captured, and your brother will die. If men are sent to rescue Fernando he will die, and my own brother and cousin will flee. If you want your brother to live, you'd better do as I say.'

'And what if I do not comply?'

'Any outcome other than the one I want will result in your brother having his throat cut. And I cannot guarantee you will not be free of pain.'

Jimena let out a slight gasp and her eyes widened.

'You would not dare.'

'Oh, I would dare, my lady.'

'Enough, Inigo,' I called. 'Please, Jimena, do what he wants. All we need is horses and supplies. Once we have them, we will leave you alone.'

She was scared, reluctant, but she did not want to show it. She was smart and strong willed for her age, but she was just a girl and when violence was threatened against her or her family her vulnerabilities became apparent. A great grey cloud drifted over the sun and sent a gloom over the land and a chill down my spine.

After a moment of deliberation Jimena looked to her brother.

'I will be back soon.'

'No, Jimena! Do not go with him.'

'I will be fine,' she stressed. 'Come, I will make sure you get what you need.'

Jimena mounted her horse, as Inigo took Fernando's.

'If he tries to run kill him,' he said, motioning to Fernando. 'I will be as long as need to be.' An uneasy feeling settled within me as Inigo slotted in beside her, yet the most important thing was to get to Leon

48

and devise a way to free our fathers, and so I let them go on their way with a heavy heart.

'Sit,' Emiliano said to Fernando as he sheathed his arrow. 'We might be here a while.'

They were gone longer than anticipated, but after midday the low rumbling of hooves signalled their return as the silhouettes of three horses and two riders came into view. The horses were jennets; there was a black one which Inigo rode, who also led a bay, and a grey ridden by Jimena. They were smaller than warhorses and provided a smoother journey, and though they looked in a healthy condition I had my reservations to whether they could cope with the rough terrain and harsher conditions of the mountains. But a horse was better than walking and so I counted myself lucky.

'Greetings,' Inigo beamed as he reined the steeds. 'I hope we did not keep you too long?'

'Judging by how fruitful your journey was we do not begrudge how long you took,' Emiliano replied. The horses had saddles and were laden with supplies, more than enough to see us through the mountains. 'Did you have much trouble getting them?'

'No. Jimena did well and made sure we got everything we wanted,' he nodded at her.

'Just take your things and go,' she spat. She dismounted and glowered at Inigo.

'But I was beginning to enjoy your company. You were quite the travelling companion.' He dismounted, sauntered over to her and towered over her slender frame. 'Perhaps you can come with me, my lady.'

'I would rather burn forever in the fires of Hell.'

'Oh, do not be like that,' he spoke softly. 'After all, we were meant to be together.' He removed his gloves and ran a hand through her raven hair, cupping her ear. 'Come with us. I will be the husband you have always dreamed of.'

Fury fuelled Jimena's hand as she slapped Inigo hard across the face.

The thunderous sound shocked us to silence. Even Inigo was stunned and glared at Jimena. 'Do not touch me again, cur,' she spat, her face as hard as stone.

Inigo's face twisted in fury as he drew his hand back and struck her across the face. She was knocked to the ground with a cry. Dust coated her dress and a small drop of blood dripped on to the earth.

'Inigo!' I called. 'Leave her alone.'

My brother drew his blade in one swift movement and pointed the tip at my heart. 'Shut your mouth. Another word or you will receive the same treatment.'

Fernando ran to his sister and cupped her face with both his hands, studying the blemish that now marked her perfect features. They spoke to one another in hushed tones and then Jimena looked at me with raw eyes. Inigo's strike had cut her lip and a long streak of blood dribbled over her chin. A tear trickled over her cheek as those emerald eyes flashed to Inigo, her gaze now full of malice. Fernando followed suit with a cold stare, then rose and made for Inigo, his complexion crimson, but before he made any headway my brother raised his sword and the cold steel tip was at Fernando's throat.

'Do not even think about it. We are done here. Take the bitch and go.'

'My father will hear of this,' Fernando seethed.

'I am sure he will, but we will be long gone. And if your father does come for us, believe me when I say he will die. Then I will come for you.'

It took a moment for Fernando to comply before he led Jimena away. But instead of going with him she tore from his grip and ran to me, threw her arms around my neck and embraced me. I held her tight, closed my eyes and savoured the moment, knowing I may not experience it again. She trembled and breathed heavy but did not let go of her emotions.

'Inigo is evil,' she whispered. 'He will lead you to death. If you ever have the chance to stick a knife in his back, do it. Do it for me.' She released her grip and looked me in the eye. 'You really are not like the other boys, and that is good. I do not think we will see each other again. But do not ever change who you are, Antonio. I have always loved you,' she whispered and wiped away a tear. 'Goodbye.'

Jimena kissed my cheek, turned and walked away. She did not look back. Fernando gave us one final stare of contempt before he put a comforting arm around his sister and began the long trek back to Oviedo.

'Saddle up lads. We have a long journey ahead,' my brother called.

I looked at Emiliano, and by the expression on his face he had not approved of Inigo's conduct as much as I. He knew we had no choice but to follow my brother, and so he mounted the grey horse whilst I made my way to the bay jennet.

We moved swift on the road to the mountains, knowing time was against us. Our plan was folly. I no longer had the desire to follow my brother in a heroic attempt to rescue our father. We were outlaws, and now I was a traitor to Jimena and knew my actions played a part in the injustice against her. We were reliant upon Inigo, but it did not stop my resentment for him. He had crossed the line by striking the girl I loved.

It was something I would never forgive my brother for.

*   *   *

The journey through the mountains was harder than any of us anticipated.

We pressed on towards the great mountain range before us. The snow-capped peaks were shrouded in mist, made it impossible to judge their size. The straight, cobbled Roman road dissected lush valleys dotted with small villages where serfs tended their fields and livestock, but we stopped only for brief respite and to fill our water skins. There would have been talk of an incident at Lugones and three hooded

51

figures travelling south, so we made with hast, remained anonymous as best we could. A goat path turned off the Roman road and led to a step pass, but it was isolated, and our anxiety lowered once we were out of sight of suspicious eyes.

By the end of the second day the temperature had dropped from the higher altitude, and we camped beneath an overhang of rock under a star-studded sky. We ate a small meal beside our fire and Inigo and Emiliano chatted about plans and ideas, but I ignored them and found a patch of damp earth to make my bed. I had my back to them and pretended to asleep, but tears trickled down my cheek and I did my best to mask my sobs. If they heard me, they had the good grace to leave me. I was a reluctant companion in their quest and struggled to comprehend the events of the last few days. I held no hope for finding a way to free our fathers.

The weather was favourable as we entered the northern side of the range, and there was beauty in the way the early morning sun bathed the snow-capped peaks in orange and pink rays. But by midday thick grey clouds loomed overhead, brought a light drizzle which intensified into a savage downpour as our horses traversed the rocky paths, making the steep tracks slow going. Even worse were the snows that clung to the peaks and conjured a bitter cold in the air. The chill nipped at my nose as we climbed higher into the pass, the walls of rock around us slowly extending further into the heavens and now sheer. Caves were a welcome sight when we came to rest. Fire was a rare fixture with flammable material sodden and soaked from the torrents. I had a mind to stay in one of those caves and live like a hermit, distancing myself from the world, but fear of being alone forced me to haul the wet cloak back across my shoulders, mount my horse and follow Inigo's lead, back in to the drab world.

I let my mind wander as my horse followed my companions further into the rain-soaked passes. Jimena flashed in my mind, and I could not shake the image of her beaten face. My mother and sisters could have been subjected to the same torture, or worse, a notion which made me shudder. I prayed to God they would be shown clemency by being locked in a convent for the rest of their lives instead of becoming the playthings of the new lord of Lugones, whoever it might be. And I prayed God would show mercy to my father.

He was a hard man to break and he would be defiant against any punishment directed against him. The charges would be denied, and his mouth would be twisted in to a snarl, or a scornful laugh. Years of training and battle had toughened him. I would not be so brave. I would crumble and sob like a child. Perhaps if I had listened and showed enthusiasm in the training yard I might be prepared for the undertaking at hand. Inigo and Emiliano were confident fighters despite their tender age and could hold their own in an even fight, but I was nothing more than a liability. I hoped my father would be proud I was here, doing my best to be brave.

We were huddled in a sheltered copse in the mountains as mist swirled between the rock faces and hovered over the treeline, shrouded the world and left us wandering aimlessly through the passes. We had no idea where we were going, and every day we climbed higher. Only a handful of other brave souls had passed us by, and they seldom offered a word to us, weary of the blades at our hips. Our faces were glum as we shivered in our damp cloaks, longing for the smallest of flames to warm us.

'We could find where they are held, and try to overcome the guards if they are moved through the city?' Emiliano suggested.

Inigo shook his head. 'Once they are in the prison, they will not be coming out for anything but trial. They will be too heavily guarded.'

'We could pose as guards and infiltrate the prison?'

'We are too young. We'd be discovered.'

Emiliano sighed in frustration.

'Well…let's hire a bloody army and lay siege to the city and demand they hand us back our fathers!'

Inigo did not react, brooding for a few silent moments.

'The best hope we have of freeing them is to release them on their way to trial, or when they are out of prison. It will be tricky, but I believe we can do it if we get a feel for the layout, know where the guards patrol.'

'What if they have already been placed on trial and their sentence passed?'

Inigo paused. 'Then this journey is one of folly.'

Four days of climbing passed before our route descended. As we gazed south the land looked different to Asturias, for a high plateau stretched far to the south and covered much of the interior of Hispania. Where Asturias was wet and green the plateau was dry, dusty and rocky, but it was full of new towns and sturdy castles as the Christians pushed the Moors further south. I had expected to travel this mountain pass bound for Palencia to prepare for a new life as a squire. Now I travelled unsure of my future, obscured by uncertainty.

The rain lightened, the mist lifted, and it was not long until we found the source of a small river. We followed it as it trickled south through deep valleys and thick forest alive with the song of birds and scurry of animals. It wound west then east and south again, and as the water lapped over rocks and tumbled over small falls it quickened, and so too did our pace.

After six days of hard travelling we finally saw our destination.

The city was much bigger than Oviedo. A long, low palisade encompassed a large urban area packed with homes and workshops, market stalls and churches, smudged here and there by plumes of wispy smoke. In the centre of the city was a grander stone wall, rectangular in shape with strong towers and stronger gates. It was built by the Romans and marked the boundaries a fortress which once stood to protect an army stationed there, and it was within the shell of the fortress the old city stood. That wall marked the heart of the city, and I knew it was where my father would be.

We descended the hills with haste and followed the river until we reached the outskirts of the city. It was midday and a trickle of travellers wandered to and from the northern gate, mainly merchants and farmers preparing for their daily business. We tethered our horses in a concealed copse by the side of the road and planned our next move.

'We might be able to get in the first gate,' Inigo said, looking towards the palisade, 'but father and uncle will most likely be in held within those Roman walls. No doubt it will be heavily guarded.'

'Which means we will not be getting in with weapons,' Emiliano sighed.

'All the gates will be like this, and by the look of these walls there will not be any small holes we can squeeze through at the base. There's no hope of sneaking in.'

'Perhaps there is.'

I was watching the passers-by on the road when I noticed two men; one old with a crooked back and the other not much older than Inigo, stood next to a cart pulled by a pair of mules. The cart had veered into a ditch and no matter how hard they tried they could not budge it. No one seemed interested enough to offer a helping hand. I snatched the opportunity, wandered over to them and caught their attention.

'Excuse me.' The older man frowned and backed off a little as the younger man looked startled. 'I was wondering if you could help me.'

They were pilgrims, with the distinct wooden scallop shells of Santiago hanging around their neck. Leon was a stopping point for those who wandered the Camino de Santiago, the pilgrim route to Santiago de Compostela. Others passed on the road in a similar fashion, but they were so caught up in their undertaking they hardly gave us a second glance.

'What can I do for you, boy?' the old man enquired.

'I and my companions need to get into the old city.'

'So why not walk in?'

'The guards will not let us pass.' I drew back my cloak and revealed the knife hanging on my belt.

The old man's eyes widened, his tone tense now. 'I do not have anything to gain by smuggling vagabonds into the city. We are humble men travelling to Compostela. Tell me why I should not alert the guards right now?'

'We have gold.' Inigo had managed to secure a pouch of coins when he retrieved the horses with Jimena, and the mention of riches piqued the man's interest. He raised an eyebrow. 'We would be willing to get your wagon out of the ditch, as well. All we want is to ride in your wagon with our belongings and get into the heart of the city. No illusions, no trouble.'

He considered my offer, twisting his mouth as he looked at his companion. The younger man shrugged.

'Show me the gold.'

I turned to my comrades and motioned for them to come over.

'Give him some of the gold.' Inigo glared back at me. 'He said he will smuggle us in for some gold and assistance with the wagon. He will let us bring all of our gear.' I stressed the last part, as if getting our weapons passed the guards was the pivotal point.

Inigo cursed as he pulled out a handful of Moorish dinars, counted them and passed them to the old man. Dinars were worth much more than the silver pennies traders and workers usually dealt in, and the old man knew he was being paid well. A few gold coins would go a long way on his journey to the western coast of Hispania. He studied the coins and, satisfied they were real, shoved them in his pouch and took a step back.

'I do not know why you are armed, and I do not want to know. But now you are pilgrims, like me and my boy here. Take off those cloaks, wrap the weapons within them and throw them in the wagon. You will need some shells.' He nodded to his son, who went to the back of the cart and rummaged around before pulling three wooden scallop shells on cords. 'Get to work.'

We duly followed his instruction, stowed our bundles underneath their belongings and pushed. Sweat dripped into my eyes and my muscles burned, but with a great creak the wagon lurched in to life and wobbled out of the ditch. Satisfied with our assistance the old man gathered us together, each one of us now with shells around our necks.

'You are to pretend you my boys, and you will keep your mouths shut. If you are questioned say you wish to kneel at the side of Santiago and be forgiven for your sins, nothing more.'

We mounted the wagon and our pretend father drove the beasts towards the gate. Being the youngest I sat beside him in the wagon whilst Inigo and Emiliano walked at the side with the younger pilgrim, who did not look pleased having to walk the rest of the way. We would have appeared as the driver had intended; a father and his four sons stopping off in Leon during a long pilgrimage. The traffic at the first gate moved passed the guards and, though they kept a watchful eye on us, they let us through unhindered. I hoped our disguise would be good enough to fool the rest of the guards within.

Wide dirt roads wound between the buildings, and the towers of the churches reached high into the sky. Small squares opened here and there, ringed with market stalls and workshops ranging from blacksmiths and potters, tailors and weavers, stonemasons and carpenters. Taverns and hostels provided the pilgrims with accommodation on their long journeys, and dotted around them were beggars knelt or sat with arms stretched out, pleading for charity monks from the hostels did their best to hand out chunks of bread and small sips of water from wooden bowls, bestowing blessings as they went. The air was full of chatter and shouting and moans from beasts of burden, and a foul stench lingered from the tanning pits as we passed lavish town houses with smooth columns.

The city was sacked by the Moors less than a hundred years ago and a significant portion of the people who came to repopulate it were Mozarabs from the south. Their influence was everywhere, from their distinct headdresses and costume to their architecture and art from their time living under the Moors, blending Christian and Islamic influences to create something seldom seen back in Asturias. It was strange to see people who were essentially Moorish in appearance yet spoke our tongue well, but with a heavy accent. Despite their divergent culture there was no conflict with the Christians of the north who too called Leon their home. They were united in their quest to serve God and see the Christians restored as the masters of Hispania.

The sites of the city had gripped me so much I did not see we had reached the gate to the inner city. The Roman gateway was surrounded by a high wall and looked to be some sort of barracks, so an archway to the side now served as the main portal. My stomach formed in a knot when I saw the row of guards by the gate.

There was half a dozen of them, armoured in leather with helms and spear points glinting in the sun, ready for a fight if it came to it. They watched over the crowds with vigilance as they passed in and out the gate. And they were interrogating every one of them.

I was convinced we would be discovered. The guards would become suspicious of us, they would find our weapons hidden in the wagon, a scuffle would ensue, and we would be cut down or else captured and thrown in to the prisons with our fathers. At least we would be with him at the end when we were brought before the king and our fates decided.

'What are you looking at?'

I had been unintentionally staring at one of the soldiers and I froze at the unwanted attention. When I did not answer he marched over and stopped a few feet from me. His face was scarred, and his breath was rife with garlic. 'Got something to say?'

'Do not mind him. He's a mute,' the driver said with a wave of the hand. 'Mother dropped him on his head when he was a babe and has not spoken a word in his life. Dumb bitch, she is.'

The guard studied me, looked for a reaction. I held my tongue.

'What's your business?' another guard enquired.

'We are pilgrims on the way to Compostela. We seek refuge for the night, but first I wish to kneel before the bones of his most holy San Isidoro in the basilica. May we pass?'

The guards looked at each other. One gave a grunt and nodded in my direction.

'Do yourself a favour and pray for this one to stop being a gormless bastard.' The other guard chuckled before stepping aside and waving us through. I sighed in relief and offered a half smile of thanks to the driver, who nodded in receipt.

And we finally entered our destination.

Within the walls the roads were wider and cobbled, though here and there missing stones posed a hazard to horses and mules, even clumsy humans. Some of the more affluent citizens lived within the safety of these walls and silks in a variety of vibrant colours were on display, complete with trinkets crafted from precious jewels set in gold or silver. There were not any beggars here, nor were any of the buildings in a dilapidated condition. Some of the buildings were constructed from the shells of old Roman barracks or storehouses filled in with fresh stone lighter in colour to create a patchwork effect along the exteriors. There was even a church constructed from an old Roman granary, the doorway freshly hewn and carved in a traditional Mozarabic archway shaped like a horseshoe.

The old man parked in an alley and allowed us to retrieve our gear before departing with not another word. He had his gold and wanted nothing more to do with us. We spent a few moments strapping our weapons back on and pulling our dark grey cloaks to conceal ourselves.

The bells rang loud overhead.

The great *dong* echoed throughout the city. We stopped and listened and watched as a buzz overcame the people in the streets, and many headed off in the same direction. I shot a nervous glance towards Inigo and Emiliano, who had the same expression. I leaned out of the alley and eavesdropped on the passers-by.

'I hope they flap around for a long time.'

'Me too. There has not been a good hanging since the Flaínez. Traitors always get the worst treatment!'

'Death is too good for them. Burning in Hell with the Devil will teach them for conspiring against our king!'

Those word cut through me. Fate had not been kind to us after all.

'What is it?' Inigo snapped.

'We're too late,' I murmured.

'Come on,' Inigo cried, and he set off after the crowds.

I and Emiliano followed him, weaved our way through the mobs. We slowed our pace and blended in as guards appeared at the side of the road. We still carried our weapons and did our best to conceal them; Emiliano had slung his bow over his shoulder beneath his cloak, whilst his quiver was concealed by the length of it. All the way I shook with apprehension and fear. I had been reluctant to come in the first instance; I was even more so now I knew those bells signalled the death of my father.

The street opened into a wide square in the heart of the city. Here was the palace of the king, which had been constructed within the ruins of the headquarters of the Roman garrison and further enlarged by Fernando with more elaborate decoration. The crowds were excited as they spread out to fill the square. Inigo was still with me, but when I looked to the side Emiliano was gone, lost in the surge of people. I had to push and shove hard to make sure I stayed by Inigo's side. I could not bear to lose him as well.

The crowds came to an abrupt halt and I collided with the man in front of me, who turned and grunted at me. A hanging frame had been set up in the middle of the square, the worn ropes swaying in the breeze. Guards stood vigil along the edge of the square, protecting the site from the crowds baying for blood. A great roar erupted as two guards hauled a pair of men on to the platform. Their hands were bound behind their backs and they wore nothing but a long knee length tunic, splattered with dirt and spotted with blood.

It was my father and uncle.

Their faces were battered and bruised; their skin was blotched with blue and deep purple, and the occasion slash of crimson. My uncle's

60

front teeth had been knocked out, and my father's left eye was swollen shut. They could hardly stand as ropes were looped around their heads and tightened, but slack enough not choke them yet.

Beside them stood Azarola, dressed in black tunic and trousers with a sword at his hip, his horrid visage on show to the world. His bulbous lips curled into a smirk as he raised his hand to calm the crowd.

'Good people of Leon,' he shouted, his voice echoing across the square. 'Today you see the justice of your king enacted. These two men have been found guilty of treason against our king and theft from one of our own allies. Pedro Valdez de Lugones and Velasco Valdez de Santurio were charged by our great king Fernando to deliver this year's *parias* from Saraqusta. That they did, but not before they filled their own coffers with gold from the *parias*, wealth intended for the realm. Furthermore, they stole items from the amir of Saraqusta himself, including the sword that was handed from his ancestors for generations. They accepted his hospitality and abused it to become thieves in the night! And not content to end the betrayal there, they conspired to use the money they stole to arm the enemies of our king in Aragon, still loyal to his late brother, to bring fresh war upon the kingdom. But by the grace of God the conspiracy was discovered, and now the king has sentenced these two brigands to death, to answer their crimes before God himself!'

Throughout the speech the crowd shouted abuse at the condemned, but I stared in disbelief. Treason? Theft? They had returned from Saraqusta with a cart each laden with riches, but my father claimed they were given by the amir of Saraqusta in thanks. It did not make sense. My father had killed Ramiro in single combat and become a famed knight of the realm. He was an honest man, proud of his heritage and status as a knight. It made no sense he would steal from the king, join with the enemy and jeopardise all he had achieved.

I saw him staring straight at me.

When he had ascended the platform, he had appeared beaten but not broken, his face etched with defiance at the baying crowds. Now he stared back through his one open eye, mouth hung open. We would have been the last thing he expected to see, his two sons stood in the crowd at his own execution, hooded in cloaks to conceal their identity. A tear glistened in his eye and he gave a sad smile, relieved to see us yet forlorn we were to watch him die.

'What do we do?' I asked. Inigo could do nothing but stare back at our father. Seeing him tied up and moments from death had knocked the fight from him. I hit him on the arm and tried to goad a reaction.

He turned and looked at me with defeated eyes. 'What can we do?'

On the platform Azarola had turned to his prisoners.

'Do you have any last words, traitors?'

The square was deathly silent as the spectators anticipated the prisoners' final moments. My uncle held his tongue, trying to be brave but the fear was evident. His final prayers were nothing but an inaudible babble. My father held his head high and stared at the crowd.

'I am innocent of any and all charges,' he shouted, his voice stern and defiant. 'I am the victim of jealously, a conspiracy to punish those loyal to the king. I am Pedro Valdez de Lugones, the slayer of King Ramiro I of Aragon, and for this I am condemned to die! Where is the justice in that?' His voice softened and he looked me dead in the eye as another tear trickled down his cheek. 'Restore our family honour. Avenge me, my sons.'

The guards kicked, and they were thrown from the platform.

A great roar erupted from the baying crowd. The ropes creaked as they swung and strained. The prisoners thrashed as the rope ground into their necks, burning into their flesh and constricting their throats. My uncle flapped around, trying to squirm his way free, but my father only tried to gasp for air. He had accepted his fate.

Tears welled in my eyes. We were desperate, helpless and angry we could do nothing. The sway of the ropes diminished, the thrashing and struggling eased and the crimson complexion upon their faces deepened.

An arrow whooshed through the air, thwacked into the hanging frame.

Everyone stopped and turned to the source of the arrow. Emiliano was in the middle of the crowd, empty bow in hand. A look of horror had descended over his face. An eerie quiet gripped on the crowd. My muscles seized as I waited the inevitable.

'Shit,' I heard my brother whisper.

The chaos commenced.

Azarola shouted and pointed towards my cousin. Guards from all over the square sprung forward and shoved spectators out of the way, made for Emiliano. He was long gone before they reached him, and soon I found myself heading in the same direction, pushing through the sea of people, curses and jeers thrown my way. Inigo shoved a woman to the ground and her head smashed against the cobbles, knocked her out and left a crimson stain on the stone. Some in the crowd backed away and gave us enough space to squeeze through, lest they meet the same fate. The human wall dispersed before us and offered us a path to freedom.

And we ran for our lives.

The road through the northern gate was now lightly defended and only two guards stood there, waving citizens through. They saw us sprinting towards them. I slowed my pace and called for Inigo and Emiliano to stop, but Emiliano had dropped his bow, and both had drawn their swords. The guards had no time to bring their spears round into a battle stance as my companions crashed in to them; Inigo hacked at the neck of one as Emiliano plunged his blade through the midriff of the other. Both guards fell to the floor, blood pouring from their wounds as Inigo turned and screamed at me to follow. I had no time to look on at the horror before me. Despite the dizziness in my head I duly followed Inigo.

We darted through the city pursued by soldiers. Citizens stopped and stared at us, curious as to our haste and shouted encouragement to us or our hunters. Some of the guards had mounted horses and I could hear the clomping hooves drawing closer and closer. Inigo, sword still in hand, kicked at the wooden framework of a potter's stall by the side of the road. The flimsy frame snapped under the force of the blow, caused it to crumple into a heap and block part of the road. We ducked into a side street and hoped the broken stall would slow them, but it only put a few extra feet between us before the gap closed again. It mattered not if they were hampered; they were a pack of wolves pursuing their prey, driving themselves hard in the hunt, allowing nothing to hinder their pursuit.

'We have to split up,' Inigo shouted. 'Make for the river.'

He darted into an alley to the right as fast as his legs would carry him as Emiliano scarpered down one straight ahead of us.

'Which way is the river?' I screamed after them, but they were too far gone to hear. Isolated and petrified, I looked left then right. The guards closed in. I chose an alley and darted forward.

My lungs and muscles burned, and I wanted nothing more than to stop and rest, but to do so would risk the same fate as my father. As I twisted and turned through more alleys the sound of hooves faded away, but the faint shouting of men still reached my ears. I slumped behind a barrel and tried to catch my breath. I could not hold back the tears. I was lost, terrified and confused, and so I wept for my father, the man who had scorned me throughout my life, but I had loved regardless, and the uncle I had lost too. I was a fifteen year old boy whose family had been imprisoned, who had been forced to cross mountains in a vain attempt to rescue his captive father, and now I was being hunted in a city I did not know, nor did I have any hope of finding allies. I was broken.

But I knew I had to grow up.

I composed myself, wiped my raw eyes and took several deep breaths. The image of my father swinging like a fresh kill from the hunt was embedded in my mind. His final words were what haunted me most. *Restore our family honour. Avenge me, my sons.* He had not only appealed to Inigo; he was placing the responsibility upon my shoulders as well.

I looked towards the sky, tried to figure out where the sun was. I knew the river was to the west, but the narrow walls of the alley blocked out everything but vibrant blue. My only option was to stick to the back streets and hope one of them would lead me to the river.

As I stood a strong hand grasped my cloak and yanked me back.

'Where do you think you're going, little bastard?'

I twisted as I stumbled back and came face to face with a guard. A pale scar ran across the right side of his weather-beaten face and his greasy raven hair and beard were wild and unkempt. He bore a savage grin at the ease of my captivity.

'It's to the dungeons for you, boy.'

His grip was too strong to escape. In desperation I flashed my left arm and hit him on the cheek, but the strike was feeble, and he laughed as he returned the favour and smashed my eye with a hammer blow of his own. I fell to the floor and cried in agony as my vision blurred. He loomed over me, ready to haul me away.

I instinctively slipped my hand behind my back and pulled the small dagger free from its sheath as the guard grabbed me again. I thrashed out at him and forced him back, and before he recovered, I screamed and lunged at his face. Desperate eyes widened in shock as the dagger plunged in to one of them, and I gritted my teeth as I pushed harder until the full blade disappeared into his socket. The eye burst and thick jellied mess poured forth, followed by a gush of crimson. A horrific gasp escaped his throat and he stood there a moment looking gormless, staring, before he collapsed in a heap. His limbs twitched before his body was still. No breath rose from his chest, no life shone in his eyes, just a vacant expression, motionless, tranquil.

I do not know how long I stood and stared. I intended to scare him off, but my limbs had moved on their own as if they had been possessed, seized the knife and stabbed with intent to kill. A surge of vomit rose from my innards and I throw up the contents. I wiped my

65

mouth with the back of my hand and tried to compose myself, but a terrible thought would not leave my head. I had committed murder, and I knew I would burn in Hell for it.

More shouts filled the air and I panicked and ran in the opposite direction, back through the alleys. I soon arrived at a wider street full of life, pulled my hood over my head and walked along with the traffic, tried to blend in. There were no guards and I prayed to God it would stay that way. An old woman sat on a stool by the side of the street, watching people as they passed by. I stopped next to her and bowed my head in respect.

'Excuse me, my lady,' I asked in a quivering voice. 'Do you know the way to the river?' She narrowed her sunken eyes before she pointed over my shoulder, presumably west. I nodded my thanks and walked with haste, sticking as close to the edge of the street as I could. My heart thumped as my eyes darted from side to side, looking out for those who still hunted me. Citizens went about their daily business with not a care for a young lad wandering the streets.

It was not long before I reached the wide street leading to the river, and in the distance, beyond the edge of the city, was the bridge that led to Compostela, flanked by steep drops into the river below. I breathed a sigh of relief to have found my quarry and prayed Inigo and Emiliano would be waiting.

I should have known it was not that simple.

Pounding hooves sounded from behind and I spun to see Inigo sprinting hard with two guards at his back, gaining ground. I started towards the river, so close now, my legs burning as I drove them hard. Guards stood by the entrance to the bridge and turned when they heard the commotion. That way was closed. There was only one alternative.

I stopped myself at the edge of the drop and looked at the river below. The water moved swift and appeared deep. There could have been hidden rocks below which could shatter bones or knock me out.

But as I turned to Inigo, guards upon him, I knew I had one choice.

'Jump!' he cried.

I turned around, took a deep breath and plunged into the torrent below.

Part Two

Outlaw

Leon, 1064 AD

Four

A week before I had been the son of a famed knight.

Now he was dead, and I was an outlaw.

How cruel it was God could take everything away in the blink of an eye. I was a boy who was taught to be courteous, display good manners and be a respectable person. Every day I knelt in the chapel and said my prayers and harboured ambitions of being a man of the cloth like Father Santiago had been. I was a loyal servant of God. So why was he punishing me, sending his divine retribution to bring the good name and fortune of my family crashing down? Was it my reluctance to follow my father's orders and become a squire in Palencia? Perhaps it was in response to what Inigo had done to Jimena, because I allowed it to happen. Or was he punishing my father?

The swift passing of my father's sentence and the overwhelming evidence against him pointed to one outcome; he had indeed been guilty of treason against the king. But it was a notion inconceivable to me. He was honourable, a devout servant of the realm and had risen to be revered throughout Leon-Castile for his feats at Graus. If he had been guilty of treason, he would have begged the king's forgiveness and suffered any punishment save death. It was not his nature to lie.

I had to uncover the truth and clear my family's name.

*   *   *

First, I had to clear my own name, redeem myself in the eyes of men and God.

I had committed murder, plunged a dagger through the eye of my hunter to evade capture. His body would have been discovered, and for all I knew Azarola had figured out who we were. The three hooded figures, the sons of the accused, who tried to stop the execution of traitor. We would be branded with the same iron as our fathers. Men would be looking for us. Nowhere would be safe.

My limbs ached and trembled as I knelt on my hands and knees. My lungs and throat burned as I coughed up river water. The pain subsided and I turned on to my back, opened my eyes as the sky purpled with the approaching dusk. A cool breeze caressed my skin and ears picked up the delicate sound of water lapping around the rocks. I lay there and let the pain ebb away, tried to gather my thoughts. The ache throughout my body was overshadowed by a stabbing sting in my head. I placed a hand on my forehead to find blood dribbling from a great gash. My vision blurred and my mind span. I was alone, bleeding, confused, weak.

The last thing I remembered was jumping into the river, hitting the water with enough force to send searing pain through my shins. The water was strong, and I fought against the current as I was swept downstream, clattered off hidden rocks and fought the urge to breath. Everything had faded to darkness.

I was on a ford in the river surrounded by trees. To my right the river flowed steadily on, and I knew Leon was somewhere to the north on my left, yet it was impossible to know how far I had drifted down river. I could have been a few miles or so from the city. Inigo and Emiliano were nowhere to be seen.

Hauling myself to my feet I staggered into the cover of the trees. The sun had not yet set but the interior of the woods was already masked in darkness, making it seem like a shadow realm conjured from a nightmare. It was eerily quiet, save for the shuffling of my feet in the undergrowth and the occasional howl of some nocturnal creature. A chill hung in the air, yet I could not tell if it was the cold or my fear compelling my limbs to shiver. My hand was in front of me, feeling out for hidden dangers as I wandered in the darkness.

A twig snapped to my left and I froze.

The low light created menacing silhouettes around me. Shadows stalked me, ever present, waiting for the right time to strike. The tree branches moved towards me, groaned as they tried to grab me, and I stumbled through the undergrowth, tried to outrun them all, but they closed in, reached for me, the snapping twigs closer and closer now. My legs were thrown from under me as a branch swiped and knocked me over. They came ever closer. I closed my eyes and tried to scream, but only a tired croak came forth.

A strong pair of hands grabbed my cloak and hauled me to my feet.

'Antonio!'

I gasped when I heard Emiliano's familiar voice.

'Thank God you are alive!' he embraced me. He reeked of sweat and damp, but I did not care. 'I cannot believe we made it out alive.'

'Not all of us made it out alive,' I said, reminding him of our fathers who had succumbed to the hangman's noose.

'We have time enough to grieve later,' he said, controlling his emotions. 'We need to regroup and figure out what we are going to do. If we thought we were damned before we got to Leon, we really are in trouble now. Are you hurt?'

'I took a knock to the head and its bleeding.'

'Can you walk?'

I did not have a choice. We could not stay in the woods all night, and we had to find Inigo. North, we trudged, through the woods with sodden clothes and cloaks. Emiliano told me he had jumped into the river after Inigo and had seen him wash up on the shore further north, but Emiliano could not reach him and was swept downstream. When he managed to scramble ashore, he waited a while, in case one of us followed him as far south, but as the light of day waned, he set off to find us. We were out of range of any guards from Leon, but we knew we were going back into the jaws of the beast.

Night fell and great clouds obscured the light of the moon. The chill intensified and the silence was terrifying. My teeth chattered as I shivered and prayed for a warm fire and cosy bed to rest in, but there would be no such comforts. The bleed on my head had stopped but the pain still lingered, intensified with every movement. I wanted nothing more than for the nightmare to end. I knew it was only the beginning.

A light appeared ahead, followed by the thud of heavy hooves in the undergrowth. Emiliano pushed me behind a great fallen log, and we crouched and pulled the hoods of our cloaks over our heads. Two guards mounted on powerful coursers came into view. The light of their torches illuminated all around them.

We would not stay hidden for long.

We knew we would have to fight.

Emiliano carefully drew his sword from his scabbard. The sound carried in the silence and the guards' heads snapped our way. It was the turn of the guards to draw their swords, and they guided their horses at a canter towards us. Emiliano cursed as panic set in. I froze at the sudden prospect of having to fight and drew my large knife. My father always said it was better to die with a blade in hand.

But the guards never got as far as us.

One of the guards yelled in agony and dropped his sword and torch as a spear pierced his torso. The horse panicked and threw the rider to the ground, bolted off into the night. The second guard turned in confusion before a shadow charged at him, screamed a war cry as it came with steel glinting in the torchlight. A duel ensued as swords clashed in the darkness, the shadow moving swift to try and flank the rider as he reined his horse and desperately deflected the blows that came for him. But the shadow was too quick, and a swift cut caught the guard in the throat. The crimson blood appeared black in the night, and the guard fell to the floor in a heap to join his comrade in death.

Before the second horse could jolt the shadow grabbed it and pulled hard to stop it from thrashing, stroked its flank to calm the beast, offering soothing words. But the horse was panicked from the bloodshed and knocked the shadow to the ground before it galloped off like its brethren. The shadow cursed, but I was filled with elation.

'Inigo!' I hissed.

'Antonio?' he called back. We leapt from our hiding spot as Inigo rose and retrieved one of the flaming brands. Bruises littered his face and a gash adorned his chin. He looked as though he'd been through far worse than I, but he still offered a relieved smile. 'It's good to see you both.'

He handed the torch to me as he wiped blood from his sword before he sheathed it and searched the bodies.

'What happened to you?' I asked.

He took a deep breath before motioning to the dead men.

'These are not the only men I have killed this night. More will come. Azarola will not give in until we are found, so we have to move.' He found a water skin and a small coin purse of silver on one of the guards, which he fastened to his belt. He unstrapped one of the sword belts from the guards, sheathed the dead man's sword and held it towards me. 'You're an outlaw now, brother. You will need this, and you will be expected to use it when the time comes.'

I could not say no. Given Inigo's ordeal already there was more fighting to come. We were in this mess together. I took the sword without argument. It was heavy and cumbersome, a cheap steel blade, but I strapped it on and prayed to God to grant me the courage to fight when the time came.

'Ditch the cloaks,' Inigo ordered.

'But we will freeze!' I exclaimed. We were still damp, and the night brought a chill that would make a fever fester inside us if we did not get warm.

'If we are discovered by the guards, they will know who we are. Do you still have your shells?' Inigo pulled out the scallop shell given to him by the old pilgrim who smuggled us into Leon.

'Yes, but there will be no point in putting it on,' Emiliano said.

'Why?'

'I am pretty sure pilgrims do not travel to Compostela with swords by their sides.'

'Actually, they do,' I put in. 'Father Santiago once said knights from lands further afield carry their blades when on pilgrimage. Even if your intentions are peaceful it is always better to be prepared for a fight.'

We dragged the corpses of the guards into the undergrowth and covered them with our cloaks before setting off to the north. Moving quickly was the only way to keep warm against the nipping cold. My limbs ached as we trudged through the woods and hurried across open fields, stopping for brief moments when the torchlights of our hunters came into view. We needed to reach our horses which we had left north of Leon, for they held our supplies and gave us a means to flee far from the city. It was the last place any of us wanted to stay.

Conversation was sparse, each one of us focused on reaching our goal. My legs gave way and my companions were forced to carry me between them lest I was left behind. The thud of hooves and shouts of men pierced the silence of the night and we moved in constant fear of being discovered, but the darkness and ample cover throughout the terrain allowed us to stay hidden. Long hours we travelled throughout the night, the lack of moonlight causing us to stray from our path and wander aimlessly for longer than we would have liked, but we crossed the river well north of the city and, with the first light of dawn piercing the gloom, we managed to find our way to the thicket.

But we were mistaken if we believed we would find respite.

'Where are the horses?'

Our beasts we no longer tethered to the trees. All that remained was mine and Emiliano's packs on the floor, our supplies strewn across the undergrowth. Inigo's pack was nowhere to be seen.

'Where are the horses?' Inigo seethed. He turned and glared at me and Emiliano, pure anger crossing his face. 'Who tethered them?'

Emiliano looked at me and I remembered it had been my responsibility to secure the horses until we returned. My attempt proved to be insufficient because the horses were gone and our means of travel with it. Our hope was ebbing away, too.

'Yet again you fuck everything up,' Inigo yelled at me. 'You really are nothing more than a stupid idiot incapable of doing *anything.*'

Emiliano took half a step forward. 'Inigo, he made a mistake…'

'The only mistake made was by my mother and father, when they brought this whelp into the world!' He drew his sword and I thought he would turn it on me, but he turned to the nearest tree and hacked at the gnarled bark. Chunks of bark and wood flew, sweat dripped down his face as he shouted and cursed. I flinched as the steel struck the tree, imagined the blade hacking at my head instead, and I knew Inigo was right. I was useless. So much was expected of me, yet I could not deliver on any front. I was a disappointment to my father and now to my brother.

Inigo panted as he ceased his assault, his sword notched along both edges, before he turned and glared at me.

'All our lives you have been a failure,' he took small steps towards me. I backed away. 'Father only ever wanted you to become a squire and one day follow in his footsteps in becoming a knight.'

'I never wanted to learn to fight. He could not make me.'

'It was expected of you. You were the son of Pedro Valdez de Lugones, the slayer of King Ramiro of Aragon. No son of his was destined to spend his days with his head in a book. Steel was the path you should have chosen. It has been that way ever since our people settled this land. Instead, you chose to be idle and spend your time with that old oaf Santiago. Why try and reason with men with words when you end an argument with the tip of your blade?'

'But I have killed a man!'

'Bullshit.'

'He was a guard who chased me through the alleys. I stuck my knife in his eye and left him to die. I had no choice.'

'Did he die with steel in his hand?'

'No. He just…grabbed me, tried to take me away.'

'A coward's kill,' he snorted. 'Five men I killed last night, all of them seasoned soldiers who had seen war before, all coming for me with blades in hand. Father would have been proud.'

'I have not been useless. I have helped.'

Inigo scoffed. 'What have you done since this whole mess started?'

'I got us out the castle, and I got us in to the city.'

'All hail Antonio, the saviour of the moment!' he cried. 'You did not save father from death, did you?'

'You could not save him either,' I spat back at him. 'You are just as useless!'

The pommel of his sword smashed into my cheek. I yelled and crashed to the floor. Tears streamed from my eyes as the pain in my head intensified. The strain and stress of everything was unleashed and I lay there and wept like a child, wept for my father and uncle, for Father Santiago, for Jimena and the rest of my family. I was broken and would have stayed there for the rest of my days and wept, curled in the undergrowth, safe from all the bad things life could throw at me.

I do not know how long I lay there, but when I lifted my head everything seemed calm. Emiliano gathered the discarded supplies. Inigo was now sat at the base of a tree, arms resting on his knees, his head towards the ground. It was rare to see the vulnerable side of Inigo, to see him reduced to nothing. I wandered over to where he sat. His raw eyes refused to look my way.

'I know you have always hated me…'

'I do not *hate* you,' he butted in, 'you just frustrate me.'

'Because you are so perfect, and you can do everything?'

Inigo chuckled and looked at me with sore eyes.

'I am not as perfect as you think,' Inigo frowned. 'Being the eldest placed a lot of weight on my shoulders. Have you ever served meat and wine to your masters, exhausted after a full day of training, and kept your composure even when every little mistake, every missed detail is chastised? Count Diego and his family tried to instil discipline in inventive ways. They once rode me to the coast, threw me from my horse and expected me to walk back to Oviedo, without any food or water and with nothing but the shirt on my back. The tales omit the gruelling details of knighthood. Being a squire is tough, but I grew up and got on with it, put a smile on my face even when I was low and did what was expected.'

'But it worked. You can fight as well as any man I have seen.'

He gave a half smile at the compliment. 'I am not that good, but I was taught by the best. The count had good instructors.'

'Teach me to fight like you do.'

'What's the point?'

'You say I am useless, so why not help me become what I was expected to be? You were ready to become a knight. Let me be your squire.'

Inigo rose and looked at me, grimaced when he noticed the mess he had made of my cheek. 'You're all the family I have left, Antonio. Father is dead and only God knows what has become of mother and our sisters. We need to stick together. All of us.' Emiliano wandered over to join us. 'Whatever has happened will not break us; only strengthen our bonds. From this moment we stick together. So yes, I will teach you to fight. Who knows, we may make a warrior of you yet.

'I remember our father saying you were meant to squire for another man. Is that why you were going to Palencia, before you fell ill?' I nodded. 'Can you remember the name of this knight?'

'Sebastian Alvarez.'

Inigo paced where he was. 'I know his name. Father mentioned him once or twice. He fought at Graus. He claimed he is young and full of promise.'

'He lives in an old Roman villa,' Emiliano added. 'My father said I was going to squire for an old knight near Valladolid, but Antonio was the privileged one because some of the lords still lived amongst the ruins of villas around Palencia, or else constructed their castles around them. Sebastian was one of these men.'

'You know who else has lands near Palencia?' Inigo stopped pacing and stared at us wide eyed. 'Azarola.' I could picture his snout of a nose and smug smile, and wished I had the opportunity to stick a dagger between his eyes. My fist tightened and anger gripped me at the mention of his name. 'He is the lord of Dueñas, a town just south of Palencia.'

'I wish my arrow had hit its target,' Emiliano said. I had thought he aimed for one of the ropes, but it seemed Azarola was his intended target. Emiliano was a terrible shot. He had left his bow back in Leon when we fled the city square, but perhaps it was not a bad thing.

'We have unfinished business with him,' Inigo said. I narrowed my eyes at my brother. 'Once we leave this place, we should not arouse too much suspicion. He will not know who we are, and neither will his men.'

'Are you suggesting we track Azarola down?'

'No. I say we burn his castle to the ground.'

There was a stunned silence as Emiliano and I stared at Inigo. The idea was utter madness. We wanted revenge for the death of our father, but what Inigo proposed was suicide.

'Just the three of us?' I said.

'Perhaps Sebastian will take pity on our plight?' Emiliano suggested. I frowned at him, stunned he was backing Inigo up.

'Or he may hand us over to Azarola,' Inigo grimaced.

'If we are lucky Sebastian will hate him as much as we do.'

'This is madness,' I whispered.

'We have not got anything to lose,' Emiliano shrugged.

'That's true.' Inigo folded one arm and placed the other under his chin. 'If we can get close to Azarola's castle we might be able to sneak in. We have an expert in smuggling us in and out of impossible situations.' He gave me a sideward glance, a smile upon his face. 'But first we need horses, food and new clothes. We will not survive long in these rags.'

Our fine tunics and trousers were torn and soiled from our travels and tumble in the river, and a fever was festering inside me. I knew we would need to find shelter and a warm fire for the night.

'Are we seriously doing this? You're both crazy!' I exclaimed.

Inigo and Emiliano looked at each other before nodding their agreement. I wanted to protest, but knew I had no choice but to give in. The alternative was to face a future on my own.

'We will follow the Camino de Santiago east, but stay off the road so as not to arouse suspicion. We regroup, and then figure out how to bring Azarola's world down.'

*   *   *

'There's an old monastery up there.'

I caught Inigo and Emiliano's attention as I re-joined them, disturbing their rest. The early evening sun gently warmed the plains of Leon, but the air was stifling from the strong wind, hot gusts and grains of grit swirling around us. We had endured a tough and tiring trek through open country parallel to the pilgrim road, east and south from Leon for a day and a half. But soldiers were seen riding along the road, questioning pilgrims as they went, forcing us to turn slightly north to a range of hills. Inigo had sent me to a nearby village with the last of our silver to buy food, simple garbs and cloaks and a mule to carry it all. The beast was slow but responsive and did its job well. My companions were pleased enough with my efforts but frowned at my sudden statement.

'Where?

'At the top of that ridge,' I pointed east towards one of the hills about a mile away. 'You cannot see it from here, but it's there. And more importantly it looks abandoned. It might be a good place to hole up for the night.'

'Why would it be abandoned?' Emiliano enquired.

'The Moors sacked Leon and the surrounding area less than a hundred years. Perhaps everywhere was not repopulated?'

Emiliano frowned. 'How do you know that?'

'I read it in one of Father Santiago's books.' It was common knowledge the Moors, under a man named Almanzor, caused widespread devastation and sacked many settlements in northern Hispania, including Santiago de Compostela to the west and Barcelona far to the east. A series of wars which spanned over two decades forced the Christian kingdoms in the north to join together to end his threat, and upon Almanzor's death the Caliphate of Qurtuba was plunged in to a devastating civil war which left the once powerful state nothing more than a collection of *taifa* kingdoms. The ravaged regions were slowly rebuilt and repopulated, but the scars still blighted the countryside.

'I guess I never read that one,' Emiliano muttered.

'What do you say, shall we go and look?'

Inigo shrugged. 'It's better than sleeping under the stars again.'

It was passed dusk by the time we climbed the steep approach to the monastery. From our vantage point the view was clear; mist swirled above the mountains to the north, whilst to the west Leon was no longer within our sight. The land stretched far to the south, hilly, barren and baked by the sun in most places. It was a foreign sight to me, for I was used to the lush fields and green hills of Asturias. I thought of my old home, the forests and streams and great Monte Naranco where I had spent much of my childhood and wondered if I would ever find a home like that again. A part of me doubted I would ever find a new home at all.

We approached the monastery from the west as the air cooled, the wind whistled, and clouds drifted over head. The building was smaller than anticipated, squatter yet far longer than the chapel back at Lugones. A tower held three bronze bells that rang sporadically in the breeze. The small plateau was sparse save for a few scraggy bushes and large boulders. It was isolated, commanded a good view of the surrounding land and appeared undisturbed by human hands for a long time. It was the perfect place to recoup our strength before the long march to Palencia.

But it was not as deserted as we first thought.

As we passed a large boulder to our left a horrific noise sounded from nowhere, and I jumped back and reached for my sword. A goat bleated our way. Two of his fellows followed suit, and a handful other goats had stopped what they were doing and stared back at us with demonic eyes. They were holed in a large pen with wattle fencing, some chewing on clumps of fodder, others resting, but one by one the beasts stood and watched us. We returned the gesture in a perplexed manner.

'You said it was abandoned,' Emiliano frowned.

'Someone's home,' Inigo said as he drew his sword. He nodded to one of the high windows of the monastery, where the light of a torch glowed from within. Emiliano unsheathed his own weapon, and I was compelled to follow his lead. Our boots scraped along the dirt as we crept closer, weary of who might be within the building. Was it a community of monks? Bandits perhaps? My mouth dried as apprehension gripped me.

Before we reached the door, I guided the mule to the wattle fence and went to tie it, only to have Inigo grab the reigns.

'I will do it,' he said with a wry smile. 'Would not want a repeat of last time, would we?'

I let him take over without protest and took a deep breath. Satisfied our beast was secure Inigo led us to the door. The wood was old and gnarled, chipped and weather stained with a great iron handle. Inigo nodded at us to indicate he was ready and turned the handle. There was a slight click as the lock lifted from the latch on the other side, followed by a low groan as the door creaked open.

The nave was gloomy, and darkness clung to the recesses where the orange glow of the candles failed to pierce. Small horseshoe arches were carved into the walls, and above were high windows which let through small shafts of pale dusk light. The odour of damp and decay lingered, and few candles burned on iron stands along the dusty stone floor. Debris was strewn throughout the building; broken bits of wooden furniture, smashed roof tiles and a pair of tattered tapestries, their vibrant colours now faded with time and the elements. Part of the roof had fallen in, big enough for water to pour through when rain came and for the wind to send a biting draft during the winter. At the far end stood an altar with a concentration of candles and objects I could not quite make out, and behind was a semi-circular room, the sanctuary, shrouded in darkness. An eerie atmosphere hung in the monastery.

Our boots echoed along the nave, scraped on the gritty floor, cut through the unnerving silence. My eyes darted back and forth, chasing the ever-changing shadows, vigilant against the darkness. My boot crunched on something and I stopped. A bone had snapped under my weight.

The bone of a human leg.

Not far away was a human arm, and another leg bone, and across the whole floor skeletal remains were dispersed amongst the wreckage. Fragments of clothing still clung to the decayed bones. I swallowed hard as a skull glared back at me in the darkness, mouth hung open as if screaming in agony for all eternity. I tightened the grip on my sword. It was heavier than usual as fear sapped my strength. The monastery had been inhabited and the aura of death lingered within, but who dwelt here or for how long remained a mystery.

A low chanting sounded from the sanctuary; a dreary drone which intensified my anxiety. Easing ourselves forward, tip toeing over the debris, we passed the altar and peered into the sanctuary. Few candles burned here, concentrated near a long wooden table in the centre of the room. Two bookshelves stood on either side, empty for the most part but the faint outlines of tomes and scrolls stood out of the darkness, illuminated by the dull glow of the flames. More literature dotted the thick layer of soiled rushes covering the floor, and a blanket strewn on the floor appeared to be a makeshift bed.

And we saw the hunched figure at the table.

He moved like a shadow, ethereal against the glow of candlelight. I could pick out words from the low drone, as if the figure chanted a prayer as he scribbled on a manuscript. The vellum pages cracked, and the goose feather quill scraped as he worked. His hand flashed to a horn of black ink, paid no heed to the droplets which splashed over the table and book.

Inigo took another step forward and raised his sword in both hands, ready to strike. I held out a hand and motioned for him to move back. He responded with an intense glare, but a more vigorous wave of my hand had him lower his sword and retreat a few steps. I did not want to spook our host; we needed his assistance.

'Hello?'

The figure let out an almighty shriek and leapt to the side, pressed its back hard against the wall, glared wide eyed. A scraggy white beard hung loose below a gaunt and wrinkled face, bright eyes like white abysses. His bald head was smooth and shiny in the flicking candlelight whilst his mouth hung wide, revealing yellow teeth rotted with time, a sordid maw from which a frantic wheezing sprung forth.

'Stay away! Stay away!' The quill in his hand dropped to the floor. 'What are you doing in my home? Leave this place at once!'

I held out my hand and took a step back to give him some room.

'It's all right. We're not here to hurt you.'

'You expect me to believe you when you carry steel in the house of the Lord?' His eyes further widened at the swords in our hands, shining bright in the candlelight.

'We mean no harm.' I sheathed my sword, hoped it would stop quell his anxiety. After a moment's hesitation Emiliano did the same, followed by a reluctant Inigo. The old man relaxed a little, but the look of fear still masked his face.

'What makes you think you can enter the house of the Lord armed as such?' he spat.

'Because the Lord welcomes all of his children into his house,' I said calmly, 'especially those who need respite. And he even accepts those who are armed, as long if their motives are peaceful.'

The old man leaned forward. His wrinkled face screwed with a look of cautious curiosity. 'Why did you not simply knock on the door and ask for it, instead of scaring an old man halfway to death?'

'This place looked abandoned. We meant to look around before we set down for the night. All we ask for is a roof over our head.'

'This is no hostel. You do not use the Lord's house for sleep.'

'I was under the impression the Lord looked after his servants. A man of worth once told me God welcomes all into his house, whether they come for worship or sanctuary. We seek the latter.'

'It looks as though you have made yourself pretty comfortable here,' Inigo called from behind me. The old man flinched at his abrupt tone. 'Does God approve of you using his house as your own?'

'I carry out the Lord's work,' our host stammered. 'He told me to come here.'

'What work?'

'I will say no more until I know your names.'

Inigo placed a hand on his chest. 'I am Inigo. This is my brother Antonio and my cousin Emiliano. And you are?'

'Father Juande.'

'And where are you from, Father?' I asked.

'I do not remember,' Juande's eyes shifted from side to side. 'I have journeyed far and wide. Home is forgotten to me.'

'And are you responsible for these remains?' Inigo crunched the nearest bone underfoot. The old man winced.

'Inigo, enough of the interrogation,' I snapped. I was trying to gain Juande's trust, but Inigo was hell bent on intimidating him. 'Let us sit and talk. Are you hungry, Father?'

Juande bit his lip with crooked teeth. 'I could eat. What do you have?'

'We have fresh trout and some hard bread. Would you like to join us?'

His eyes lit up and a smile appeared on his face. 'The same feast Christ served to the five thousand. I would be delighted to share a most holy meal.'

We lit a fire under the hole in the roof and set about cooking the fish we had caught earlier that day, plucked from a shallow river which flowed from the mountains. Juande lingered in the sanctuary for a while, making sure we were cooking our meal before he stalked over and squatted by the fire.

He was old and frail, and the squatting must have been painful, but he seemed more comfortable than I was on a stool. Long nails sprouted from his fingers and toes, as discoloured as his teeth, and his skinny limbs were covered in sores and scratches. His right eye was milky white and sagged, and when it was not staring ominously it twitched. A long strand of drool dangled from a permanent gurn. He may have been petrified of us, but his appearance and demeanour did not fill me with joy either.

I motioned to Inigo to give Juande some of the fish, and the old man flinched when Inigo rose and passed him a share of our catch, but accepted it when he knew there was no danger. He broke it up in his dirty hands and scooped it into his mouth, sucked at any loose flakes which tried to escape.

'It's good!' he exclaimed in a childlike manner.

Inigo divided the rest and we sat for a few moments in silence, savoured our meal. The scant light revealed columns decorated with leaves and flowers and the capitals carved as wolves' heads, a sign the monastery was built by the Visigoths and had stood for a few hundred years. With the remains of so many bodies it felt more like a mausoleum than a monastery.

Inigo finished his meal first and stared at Juande, who rocked back and forth where he squatted, looking into the fire.

'Why is this place full of the bones of dead men?' he asked.

'They serve as a reminder of what the Moors did,' the old man replied.

'These are bones of monks, here for almost a hundred years?'

'Yes.

'You could have shown them dignity by giving them a proper burial.'

Juande frowned. 'My holy brothers are at peace in the house of God. What more dignity do they need?'

Inigo picked up a skull from the floor, discoloured by years of filth with half its teeth missing. 'Does this look dignified to you?'

Juande did not reply, only stared at Inigo, the twitch in his eye more intense. It was clear he felt threatened by my older brother.

'Why are you here?' my brother pressed.

'To carry out the will of God.'

'How, exactly?'

'I heal people with the touch of San Cyrinus.' I exchanged a perplexed look with Inigo. 'Would you like to see it?' Juande exclaimed. Before we could answer he had scurried back to the sanctuary.

'I think we have stumbled upon a mad hermit,' Emiliano whispered.

'He's more of a child than Antonio,' Inigo replied.

Juande scampered back with a long wooden box in his hands. Only when he held it up to the light did I see it was in the shape of a human arm, with its fingers clawed, as if it grasped something. The wood was old and gnarled, stained by the weather and worn by ware, suggested it was many years old.

'This holds the bones of the arm of San Cyrinus,' Juande said, astonished at the item he now held towards us. Rusted iron hinges squeaked as he lifted a panel on the side of the arm. Inside, nestled within a tattered red cloth which lined the interior, were the skeletal remains of an arm. The cartilage and tendons that held the joints together were still intact, and it looked as though it had been freshly exhumed. The stench made me scrunch my nose. The wooden hand opened too, and within were fragments of finger bones. 'This has the power to heal afflictions and diseases. Through this relic the power of the almighty Lord runs rife!'

We sat in stunned silence, which was not the reaction Juande expected given the look of dejection on his face.

Inigo picked up a bone from the floor and waved it towards Juande.

'This must be the thigh bone of Santiago; a most revered relic said to cure leprosy and burn all heathens who look upon it.' Inigo threw the bone at the wall, which clattered on the stone. 'You are lying, bastard.'

'I speak nothing but the truth,' Juande spat back as he rose. 'I brought this relic back from Roma where the holy saint was buried. The Lord instructed me to go on pilgrimage to Jerusalem to find my purpose in life, and as I knelt on the hill where Christ was crucified God give me a mission; to heal the pilgrims travelling to Santiago de Compostela through the touch of a saint.

'I received a vision, in which the blessed San Cyrinus came to me and said his touch would heal ailments and afflictions, disease and deformities. And so, I set out to find his tomb, travelling far and wide before I was directed to Roma. There I found his resting place and uttered a blessing as I carried away his arm and took up residence in this place so I could set about the task God assigned to me. Pilgrims pass along the Camino de Santiago, and I am there to offer a healing hand to those who need it.'

'Do people really fall for this?' Emiliano frowned.

'It sounds like bullshit,' Inigo added. 'I have never heard of a San Cyrinus.'

Neither had I, and I had good knowledge of saints.

'This is no trick! The touch of San Cyrinus heals those who believe!'

'Do people pay for the privilege?' I asked.

The comment caught Juande off guard. 'A suitable contribution is always appreciated. But it is worth parting with some silver because the touch of Cyrinus can heal pox, sores, and afflictions to the skin…'

'You're nothing but a thief,' Inigo growled, rising to stare Juande down. His voice echoed as anger fuelled his words. 'You claim to do God's work, yet you cheat innocent pilgrims from their coin for your own gain? I would stake a claim you have a hoard of silver and gold right here, do you not?'

Juande shook his head. 'The money is used to preserve this house of God, and some of it goes to the hospices on the road to Santiago de Compostela. I keep none for myself!'

'Liar!'

Inigo leapt forward and grabbed Juande by the scruff of his neck. The wooden arm clattered on the floor as he screeched and clawed at Inigo's arm, but he had no strength in his feeble limbs and the squirming alone served to feed the fire within Inigo. I wanted to help the hermit but hesitated. Something about Juande did not seem right.Holy men claimed to have relics of saints to heal and bless those who were willing to pay for the privilege, but most turned out to be hoaxes. I had no doubt Juande's was the same, and his scheme of cheating pilgrims for money seemed immoral and was a sin in the eyes of God. Perhaps the punishment Inigo intended would not be such a bad idea.

'Tell me why I should not kill you now. God would thank me for smiting one of the great sinners in this world.'

'Please, I beg you!'

'Begging is not good enough.' Inigo threw Juande to the ground and drew his sword. He raised it with both hands as Juande yelped and covered his head with his hands, expecting the killing blow to come.

90

But it did not come.

Inigo lowered his sword and let the tip rest on the stone floor. The subtle clang pierced the silence. Juande peered from behind his arms, wary as to why he was not dead, and rose to his knees. His blind eye stared vacantly, the other intently.

'Perhaps I will spare you,' my brother whispered with scorn. 'But I expect you to comply with our wishes.'

Juande cowered. 'What would you ask of me?'

'We need coin.'

'I do not have any. I swear it on our Lord I gave it all away!' Juande's hands clasped together in supplication.

'That may be so, but if what you say is true you can get coin. You have proved you can extort the wealth of pilgrims for your own gain, so you will continue to sell your story of miracles. But you will take from the pilgrims and give it to us.'

Juande's eyes widened, his voice full of uncertainty.

'Why…why would I do that?'

'Because if you do not, we will make a martyr of you,' Emiliano hissed, standing at Inigo's shoulder.

'I could sell a story to the pilgrims, too,' Inigo continued. 'I would weep as I lamented for San Juande, the hermit who was butchered by bandits because he refused to reveal his great hoard set aside for the poor pilgrims travelling to kneel before Santiago. I could turn this place in to your shrine and have your skull on display. But whilst your name may be remembered, the manner of your death will stick most in the minds of men. And we both know you would not be raised to live in the Kingdom of Heaven but burn forever in the fires of Hell for your sins. So, what do you say, old man? Disgraced in life, or disgraced in death?'

Juande did not have a choice. Three strangers threatened him with death, and so he reluctantly nodded.

'Excellent!' Inigo exclaimed as he slapped Juande on the shoulder. The old man winced and rubbed his aching limb. 'We will discuss it more in the morning and we can go through exactly how you extort all this money.'

Without saying another word Juande retrieved the reliquary and sank back in to the shadows of the sanctuary, muttered something as he went. Night had descended and the only light came from the candles around the monastery, flickered in the breeze that filtered through the hole in the roof. Inigo beamed as he sheathed his sword and rubbed his hands together.

'And there we have it; we have a means to get to Palencia and equip ourselves for war. We will get as much wealth out of this old bastard as we can, slit his throat and be on our way to avenge our fathers. Good idea, is it not? I will take the first watch. I do not trust this creep.'

As I lay on the cold, dirty floor I caught glimpse of the sadistic grin on Inigo's face, the shadows adding to the menacing visage. He was enjoying this. He had power and he loved every moment wielding it, bending Juande to his will. Inigo thought it would be so simple, but I had my reservations.

Soon my doubts would be justified.

Five

It was a gruelling trek.

The monastery was only a mile or so from the pilgrim way as the crow flies, but Juande had led us south and east from the monastery, descending from the high ground through open fields, into thick woodland and across the ford of a swift river. It was more than a few miles walk, which was not easy going through precarious terrain, and for an old man like Juande it would have been even harder for his frail frame, but he knew every detail of the paths we trod; where to step on a steep descent and which rocks to tip toe on through the river. He seemed fresh enough when we arrived at our destination. Sweat coated my brow and my calves ached. I was beginning to think there was something unnatural about the old hermit.

We stood by the edge of a worn cobble and dirt path wide enough for two carts to travel abreast. The Camino ran along the remains of the Roman road from Catalonia to Portugal by way of Leon, but only part of the cobbles remained and proved more of a hindrance to travellers. A small wooden signpost with a scallop shell nailed to it pointed to the west for the benefit of pilgrims. It was the main artery for pilgrims coming from the east, used mainly by those from the Catalan counties, the south of France and the Italian peninsula. There was another route along the coastal mountains passed Oviedo, and I sometimes watched the pilgrims from the walls of Lugones; some in great groups and others traveling in solitude, all seeking the blessing of Santiago.

'I speak many different tongues,' Juande said. 'I know enough to make any pilgrim part with their coin for San Cyrinus's blessing. Let me do the talking.'

'I will not know what you are saying. I never learned another tongue.'

'That's good. Pretend you are a mute.'

'It's not the first time I have been asked to play that part.'

The road was deserted. Juande's plan was simply enough; I would wait with Juande by the side of the road, ready to greet any travellers, and was to hold the reliquary as he worked his magic and spun his story of miracles. Inigo and Emiliano kept vigil from a small thicket behind us up the slope in case things turned sour. Juande assured us there would be no violence; though sometimes armed, pilgrims wanted to travel in peace.

To complete the look of Juande's assistant I wore black robes Juande had found tucked away in a chest in the sanctum of the monastery, fastened around my waist with a length of robe. It was too big for me, and in the midday sun the heat inside was stifling and intensified the musty stench it emitted, but any complaints fell on deaf ears. Around my neck was a simple wooden cross, stained by the weather and gnawed by time, but I felt like a man of the cloth. It was strange at first, yet the longer I sported the attire it the more I liked it.

San Cyrinus's reliquary rested on a cushion I held steady, beneath a discoloured white cloth. The bones within were a sickly beige hue covered in grime and dirt, and the rotten muscle released a foul stench. If Juande was to be believed the relic was over nine hundred years old, but for all I knew it could have been the arm of some poor soul who was buried in a local graveyard just several months ago. The reliquary itself was plain and simple, did not look holy or special. But perhaps I would believe in its power when Juande demonstrated its abilities.

'How often does this ploy work?' I asked.

He turned and looked at me, the twitch in his eye intense.

'Not often,' he shrugged.

My eyes widened. 'Why did you not mention this before?'

'You did not ask! And besides, your brother would have hurt me. It was easier to comply with his wishes.'

Inigo was counting on the money we earned to get us to Palencia. If things were as bad as Juande claimed Azarola would die of old age before we reached him. His reaction would be violent.

'Look, they come!'

To the east a procession rounded a bend in the road obscured by a wood. As they drew closer, I could pick out at least ten of them, men and women, some on foot and others on horses. There was even a young girl on a pony guided by a man, and a woman in a wagon who cradled a new-born baby. They wore fine tunics of brightly coloured wool, and above them were the trademark wooden scallop shells hanging around their necks. Once a pilgrim arrived in Santiago de Compostela, they would trade their wooden shell for a real once, picked from the western coast of Hispania, as proof of a successful pilgrimage. They looked affluent and the unease lifted when they noticed us and slowed their pace.

'Greetings, friends of Santiago!' Juande called in his shrill voice, his arms spread in welcome.

'Greetings traveller,' one of the men replied. His accent was strange, but he spoke our tongue. A royal blue cloak adorned his shoulders, fastened by a glinting silver crucifix clasp, worn over fine white silken garments and strong leather boots. 'My name is Miquel. I and my companions are travelling from Barcelona to Santiago de Compostela. Are you from one of the hostels along the route?'

'I am Juande, and this is my assistant, Antonio. But we are not travellers, nor do we hail from any hostel. We are men of the Lord, come to spread his word and show the world the wonders of his power!'

The pilgrims exchanged curious looks.

'What wonders?' Miquel asked.

'The wonders we speak of are channelled through a most holy relic revered by God himself. Behold the reliquary of San Cyrinus, healer of ailments and disease!'

In one swift movement I pulled the sheet and revealed the reliquary. The pilgrims stared at the wooden arm with curious eyes.

'One touch from this saint,' Juande continued, 'will aid a traveller upon any road they trek. He has been known to heal pox, afflictions to the feet and legs and give travellers renewed strength in their journeys. His blessing will see you safely to Santiago de Compostela, to kneel at the side of the holy saint.'

Juande picked up the reliquary and opened the box to reveal the bones within. Some of the pilgrims were now mesmerised and chatted enthusiastically between themselves, including Miquel. I found it incredible the pilgrims listened to what Juande claimed; it was clearly rehearsed, and the delivery was desperate. But I have learned in this life a man fears the wrath of God and equally marvels at the miracles of his power.

The solitary child within the group was ushered forward and stood next to Miquel. It was a little girl, no more than five years old with dress of green wool trimmed in gold. But when I looked closer at her I gasped.

'This is my Agnes, and she is sick,' Miquel said with a grim expression on his face. Agnes's sun kissed face was blighted by pox; dozens of big, white mounds covered her skin, and most looked ready to erupt at any moment. Agnes looked at the ground and tried to turn away, embarrassed by her affliction, but Miquel forced his daughter round so Juande could study her. She was so young yet hideous. 'Can you help her?' Miquel pleaded.

'The hallowed San Cyrinus would be glad to!' Juande slammed the reliquary shut and held it towards her. 'Come here and let the power of God heal you.' Agnes whimpered and clung to her father's leg.

'There is no need to be shy.' Juande coaxed Agnes forward as he grinned with his crooked maw. She clung tighter and even Miquel put a reassuring arm around his daughter, unnerved by Juande's behaviour. Age had not been kind to Juande and when he smiled, he looked terrifying; discoloured, crooked teeth, a furrowed face and a pale, twitching eye. He looked more like a demon of Hell than a servant of God.

I placed the cushion on the floor and walked to Agnes, then knelt before her. Her eyes widened; no doubt unnerved by my presence.

'There is no need to be scared,' I said softly. 'I do not know why God punishes the innocent ones. I too have been punished, yet I committed no crime against our Lord. Do you feel as though you have been punished?' Agnes nodded her head and released her grip on her father's leg. 'And do you still believe in Him, despite the punishment?' She nodded again. 'That is good. I still believe in Him too; despite all the bad things he has allowed to happen to me. But I kept my faith and he rewarded me.'

'How?'

'The touch of San Cyrinus healed me.'

The little girl gasped, as did her father.

'How?' Miquel enquired.

'When I came to Juande I was weak. I had not eaten for days and there was no strength left in me to carry on. But Juande uttered a prayer to God and San Cyrinus and touched me with this precious relic. By the grace of our Lord I was filled with renewed vigour and vitality I had never experienced before, and from that day on I vowed to serve Cyrinus, so others might be healed as I once was.'

Just like that, they were convinced the power in a dead man's arm in a wooden box could change their lives and heal Agnes's affliction. I was amazed the lies that came from my mouth had such power. I almost felt guilty.

'Do you believe in God, my child?'

'Yes.'

'And do you believe in miracles?' Agnes nodded. I smiled. 'I confess I cannot help you, for I am simply a man of God. But if you believe then God will heal you. Believe now, sweet one, and God will set you free from this curse.'

Agnes relaxed but looked to her father for guidance. After a stern look at me and Juande he nodded his approval and ushered Agnes towards to Juande. She still looked unnerved but there was a newfound determination there too, fuelled by my words.

'Do not worry. He will be gentle,' I reassured her. Juande's eye twitched as he gave a delicate nod, before he placed the claw like wooden fingers over Agnes's face. She stiffened as they rested on her cheeks and forehead.

Juande closed his eyes, tipped his head back and breathed deep.

'Blessed Saint Cyrinus,' his voice shrieked, 'heal this child of her affliction. Let the pox that blight her face wither before your power. Let the poison within her ebb away and be replaced with purity!'

Without warning Juande pushed forward with the arm. Agnes cried as she was shoved backwards and landed on her behind. Gasps came from the gathered pilgrims as Miquel rushed to her side before he glared at Juande.

'What did you do to her?'

'It is not what *I* have done, but what San Cyrinus has done. He has blessed your child. She will be healed.'

'Did the saint demand you assault her?' A streak of crimson trickled from Agnes's nose.

'Just be glad she was not older. I struck Antonio thrice in the face before I was satisfied San Cyrinus's power was alive. Such was the level of sin within him it took a more intense blessing to beat the evil out of him.'

'But Agnes is without sin,' I added, 'and so this will be sufficient for her to be healed.'

Miquel calmed his temper. He was desperate to see his daughter healed. 'How long will it take to work?'

'I cannot say for certain,' Juande said. 'But you must do exactly as I say. There is a hostel a few miles along the way, not far from Leon. Take her there and ask the monks to bathe her skin in fresh water infused with rosemary and juniper berries. Juniper berries are sacred to Cyrinus and will help fight the pox. Prick her finger and allow a leech to suck the poison from her and burn it when it becomes fat with evil. You must pray every hour from dusk through to dawn until the affliction subsides. Only then will your child be set free from her curse.'

Miquel drank in every word. Renewed optimism masked his face as he held his daughter's hand. 'You hear that, my little dove? You're going to get better.'

A small smile curled on her lips. She looked at me, her bright emerald eyes twinkling in the sunlight, showing a small glimmer of beauty underneath the hideous warts. Pox could be fatal, especially in children, and what we had given Agnes and her father was better than any poultice or remedy conjured by the hands of men: hope.

'How can we ever repay you for this kindness?'

I looked at Juande who gave a shrewd smile. He may have winked, too, or it could have been the twitch in his eye.

'Whilst we do not represent the hostels of the Camino de Santiago, we do still offer them support when we can. Financial support.'

Without hesitation Miquel reached for the purse hanging on his belt, tipped a few coins on to the palm of his hand and offered them to Juande. A golden dinar sparkled in the sunlight amongst the silver pennies. For a moment a twinkle appeared in Juande's wide eyes as his mouth curled now with a gluttonous grin, but he composed himself and gave a slight bow.

'The Lord welcomes your donations,' he said, then plucked the coins with his bony fingers. 'May God bless you on your venture to Compostela.'

'Thank you both,' Miquel replied, 'and may God bless you too.'

Agnes gave me a wave and a parting smile full of warmth as she was ushered back to her pony. The party continued west on the dusty track towards Santiago de Compostela, full of hope her affliction would be healed in no time.

I wondered how long it would be until Agnes was dead.

A face afflicted by pox was something I had not seen until then, but even I could guess Agnes had a severe case. Death would not be far off. The pox would burst, a fever would develop, and no amount of water infused with rosemary and juniper berries would help. Her father would cry with anguish and question why God had taken his precious daughter, even when San Cyrinus blessed her, and a suitable donation had been made for the welfare of other pilgrims. Grief would be replaced with anger. Miquel would look for us.

'You never told me you were a priest,' Juande croaked.

'I am not.'

'Well you could have fooled me! That was a good showing. You should take this up as a living.'

'It is a wonder you make a living out of this at all,' I snapped. Juande looked taken aback by my outburst. 'Rosemary and juniper berries? Even I know enough to know rosemary and juniper berries will only make her smell a little nicer in death. And waving a wooden box in their faces to convince them it will heal them? How do people fall for this nonsense?'

Juande frowned. 'Well…it works…sometimes.'

'Thrusting a dead man's arm into their face will unnerve them. You have to make them *believe* it will heal them.'

'This is not just any arm. It is the arm of San Cyrinus!' he cried, the bones shaking in the box in his grasp.

A voice cried from the west and a single figure ran towards us.

It was one of the pilgrims. He was a burly man with shaggy, sandy coloured hair and a dark green cloak hanging from his shoulders. He puffed his cheeks as he caught his breath after his jog back to us.

'I too wish to be healed by San Cyrinus,' he said, composing himself.

Juande straightened. 'Of course. You have pox too?'

'Not pox. It's more…personal. Embarrassing, almost.' His complexion deepened to crimson. 'My wife and I are desperate for a child. We have tried for many years but…nothing.'

'Ahhhh, of course,' Juande sighed. 'Your manhood is broken.'

The man stared at the ground in shame. 'All I want is a son. Does Cyrinus…heal that sort of thing?'

'That is something Cyrinus reveals in curing!' Juande exclaimed. He prepared San Cyrinus's arm. 'Come here, and the saint will see you have a son!'

'Remember, Father,' I interjected. 'These are delicate matters. Be gentle.' Juande grimaced at my cautious tone, but none the less approached the man with fervour. His counterpart stiffened. The hermit placed the curled fingers around the man's crotch. I winced at how uncomfortable the man looked.

Juande drew his head back, closed his eyes and shouted to the sky. 'Oh, holy San Cyrinus, bless this man's manhood so he may bear children! Let his seed be fruitful and his family name passed on for generations! Banish the evil within that prevents his wife from carrying his child. Let thy will be done!'

Without warning Juande thrust the arm into man's crotch, which was met with a mighty yelp as he fell to the floor. He cupped his hands around his throbbing crotch and winced. Juande could not resist a smirk at the man's discomfort.

The man got to his feet, still in pain. 'This will work?'

'Yes, you will bear children. Wait until the next full moon and apply honey to your manhood before you fornicate with your wife. Then pray to the Lord at dusk every night until your wife's bloods

101

cease, and her belly begins to swell. Then the sound of a babe will fill your ears in due course.'

The promise of a child filled the man's face with hope, and he reached into his purse. He pulled out two silver pennies and held them towards Juande, but the old man shook his head.

'Matters concerning the genitals are trickier than all else. The rewards are more…generous.' Juande raised his eyebrows and the man knew what was meant. He fumbled around in his purse again and this time produced a shining gold dinar. He placed it in to Juande's open palm with the silver pennies. The coins clinked as Juande slid them into his satchel.

'Thank you,' the man said with a nod, 'and God bless you.'

'May God and Saint Cyrinus bless you, too,' Juande replied with a shrewd smile as the man hurried to re-join his companions. He looked at me and grinned as he shook his satchel, the clink of the coins inside like a sweet harmony to his ears. 'The Lord has been good to us this day.'

'Rubbing honey on a man's manhood will not help,' I said in disgust.

'A man will believe anything you want him to believe when it comes to the Lord and afflictions,' Juande shrugged. 'I could have told him to rub nettles on his manhood and drink his own urine, and he still would have done it.'

'This is wrong.' I was angry at cheating innocent people out of money and promising them salvation in exchange. Agnes would always bear the scars of her pox, if she lived, and the man who pleaded for a child would most likely remain childless for the rest of his days. I had helped convince the pilgrims San Cyrinus would heal them and I hated it. 'You are using the faith of innocent people to extract wealth for something that does not work.'

'Cyrinus heals!'

'What you are doing is immoral.'

'So is robbing a man of his earnings at knifepoint, which is exactly what you and your companions are doing! Robbing me of my coin! We all sin in this life; God choses to grant salvation to those who sin for the right reasons.'

'Then tell me who is the greater sinner; the man who extorts money from the innocent, or the man who would relieve the thief of it?'

'Looks like we are cut from the same cloth. Just like your bully brother,' he motioned behind me.

'How much did we get?' called Inigo. He and Emiliano had wandered from their vantage point and now approached our position. Juande put his hand in his satchel and pulled out our earnings, grinned like an eager child hoping to impress a peer. With one fell swoop Inigo snatched the money from Juande's palm and counted, despite the old man's protest.

'Not bad,' is all he said. Emiliano's eyes beamed at the coin.

'Inigo, wait,' I called as they turned and made his way back up the hill. He turned and frowned. 'This is wrong.'

Inigo frowned. 'We do not have time for idle chatter. There's another group coming from the east. Prepare yourselves.'

As he wandered back to the thicket Juande placed the reliquary of San Cyrinus back on the cushion then folded the dirty cloth over the relic.

'The more money we make, the less time you will have to do all this. It is best to block out the hate and just do it, like he said.' He took his place by the side of the road and waited for the new group of pilgrims to arrive.

I took a deep breath, picked up the cushion and took my place beside Juande. Agnes's visage would not leave my mind and I started to worry about her fate and the affect her death would have our own fortunes. I shivered at the thought of the fires of Hell waiting for me when I met my end.

I just hoped we would kill Azarola before it happened.

103

*　　*　　*

Our ploy proved fruitful yet left a bitter taste in my mouth.

Within two weeks we had managed to fleece a small hoard from gullible pilgrims. Even Juande was surprised by our success rate; he was used to a few pieces silver here and there, but with my influence people believed in the healing powers of San Cyrinus and queued to be healed by his touch.

And every coin added more weight to the sins I committed.

Inigo decided we needed a fortune before we moved on Palencia. We required horses, food, clothing, weapons and armour, all of which would not come cheap. But we at least had an isolated base to hole in until the time was right. Juande explained he had an agreement with a village on the other side of the hills where he would leave coin within a small copse by the side of the road, and the villagers would leave supplies and the occasional goat. But now Emiliano went to the nearby villages with our mule and bought essentials to keep us going. One day he came back with a hunting bow and a big grin on his face, something that did not go down well with Inigo.

'You waste our coin again and I will cut your throat,' he seethed.

Emiliano defended his decision. 'I needed a new bow. Now we can hunt around the hills and catch game.'

'You need to learn how to use one. You're an awful shot,' my brother had retorted.

'One day you will see how much of a good shot I am.'

We had cleared most of the debris from the nave of the monastery and moved into the dormitories at the eastern side of the nave. They were big enough for around ten monks, maybe more, with a library and kitchen attached, but they were hollow shells now. Empty bookcases gathered dust and the ovens were stone cold, having not been used in years. It was better than living in squalor and it felt like a new home, despite the musky smell. Juande kept to himself in the sanctuary, and at night I heard him as he scribbled at his desk, ranted about something inaudible. We locked the door every eve in case the old hermit suddenly felt threatened by our presence and tried to be rid of us in the dead of the night.

But things were unusually quiet one night; the subtle crack of our fire was blocked out by Inigo's snoring, but Juande was silent. He only slept a few hours before dawn, yet tonight no frantic rants came from the sanctuary. I was restless and decided to investigate to ease my curious mind. I pulled on my boots, strapped on my long knife to be safe and crept to the door. I turned the key and made sure it opened with a delicate click before creaking it open and tip toeing into the nave.

The light of a full moon beamed through the hole in the roof and covered the nave in a lunar glow. Delicate wisps of smoke from the candles drifted out into the warm evening air. Such was the tranquil atmosphere in the monastery the thud of my boots cut through the silence. The sweet scent of incense filled my nostrils. Juande's shadowy figure moved in the darkness of the sanctuary, hunched over his desk one minute then drifted around the next, black against the faint candlelight. The silence made me suspicious.

We had been with our host only a few weeks, yet we knew nothing about him apart from him being a blabbering idiot and a thief. I was determined to uncover who he was.

Juande did not react as I entered the sanctuary.

'Who are you?' I asked.

'Juande,' he replied flatly, not taking his eyes off his manuscript.

'No. I mean…where did you come from? How did you end up here?'

'I told you when we first met.'

'I mean before God told you to seek out Cyrinus?'

'Do not want to tell you.'

'Why not?'

'None of your business.'

'If you tell me who you are, I will tell you who we are.'

'Do not want to know.'

'But…'

'I do not care!' he snarled; his eyes narrowed with scorn.

'What are you writing about?' I pressed.

'You would not know. You would not understand.'

'Try me.'

He sighed as he set his quill down.

'I am copying a manuscript, a laborious task best conducted without distraction.' He stressed the last few words paired with a glare.

'What manuscript?'

'*The Historia de regibus Gothorum, Vandalorum et Suevorum*, a great…'

'History of the Goths, Vandals and Suebi,' I interjected, 'the people who settled in Hispania after the Romans left. Composed by Isidoro de Isbiliya. It is considered one of his best works.'

Juande's crooked jaw hung slack. He had mistaken us for brigands, uneducated, used to nought but violence. He did not expect a young man who knew how to read, write and was versed in history. I walked over to the manuscript and read the most recent passage. It told of the Vandal king Geseric, who led his people over the straits from Jebel Tariq to Ifriqiya and formed a kingdom in the old city of Carthago. Ifriqiya was where the Moors originated from, and I wonder if Geseric's invasion of their homeland prompted hatred for the people who inhabited Hispania, which in turned caused the Moors to invade our homeland. Or perhaps living in the desert was too much for some and they desired our fertile land.

'Your script is neat for your age,' I commented.

'Thank you,' he said, bemused. 'You never said you were educated.'

'You did not want to know.'

'Well…where did you learn to read?'

'None of your business,' I said with a smirk.

'Fine. You have made your point. Tell me who you are, and I will tell you all you want to know about me.'

I found a stool and sat. 'My name is Antonio Perez de Lugones. Do you know where Lugones is?' Juande shook his head. 'It is a few miles from Oviedo.'

'I know where that is.'

'My father was a great knight,' I continued. 'He fought in the battle of Graus, where he won great renown when he slew the Aragonese king Ramiro.'

'He killed a king!' Juande exclaimed.

'He did,' I said with a smile on my face. It slowly disappeared. 'He was executed.'

'For killing an enemy king?'

'He was accused of treason. A knight named Bernardo Garces de Dueñas arrested him and hung him in public.'

'Sounds like he was guilty.'

I glared at Juande. 'He was innocent.'

'Then why would they execute him? They do not arrest innocent men for no reason, so there must have been a good cause to have him killed.'

Anger boiled inside of me. What did Juande know? He was a hermit who believed a skeleton's arm healed men of their afflictions and charged a fee for the spectacle. He was touched by madness and knew nothing of how the world worked. He did not know my father, the fierce, honest, hardy hero of Graus. And yet what he said made sense.

My belief was my father had been set up by Azarola, or someone else who wanted to see him fall. A man with my father's growing reputation would be in line for a bright future, and an even brighter future for his sons. But I remember the way he looked when he returned with the *parias*; the way he claimed he had finally received suitable payment from al-Muqtadir of Saraqusta for slaying Ramiro. Perhaps he was not as honest as he made out and was blinded by greed. Did he really steal from the *parias*, and take possessions belonging to the amir of Saraqusta? I was determined to extract the truth from Azarola, by any means necessary.

'Your father paid for your education?' Juande asked.

'He did. I had a private tutor. He used to teach me about these things,' I motioned to manuscript on the table.

'Then you a lucky boy. Many are not so privileged!'

'That opportunity has disappeared. I wanted nothing more than to move to a place like this and read the histories, study the bible, live my life in peace and solitude.'

'It's not a very pleasant life. A man gets lonely when he has nothing but goats to bleat at him. What is stopping you from finding peace?'

'Inigo.'

'Ah, the bastard bully.'

'He is full of anger because of what has happened to our father. We have lost our family, our home. All we have is the clothes on our backs and the weapons at our sides.'

'So why are you here?'

Juande seemed genuinely harmless, but I did not trust him enough to tell him of our plans. I did not know how he would react if I told him the only reason we were gathering money was so we could go to Palencia and kill Azarola.

'I was due to squire for a knight before my father died. He resides near Palencia, so we need supplies and horses to see us there. With any luck he will take pity on us and allow us to become squires, or at least serve in his household.'

'You could always stay here!'

'Why would we stay here?' I frowned.

'To help spread the word of Cyrinus! You are very good at getting people to give money. We could restore this place, fill it with books and build a shrine to Cyrinus, like the one at Santiago de Compostela. You would not have to go to Palencia. You could be a man of God – right here.'

It was a tempting offer. I had cherished my education during my early years, and the opportunity to restore a monastery and create a shrine for pilgrims from all over Hispania to visit was something I considered for a time that night. But what would Inigo say? His focus was to reach Palencia; to suggest an alternate plan would be to receive some retort or even a backhand around the face. Perhaps I could do both. If we survived the encounter with Azarola I could run away from Inigo and return to the monastery, restore it to its former glory and become Father Antonio.

But they were farfetched dreams. The future I saw was nothing but steel and blood.

'It's not an option. Inigo would not allow me to.' Juande looked disappointed. 'Anyway, it's your turn.'

'I was a monk.'

'I guessed as much. Where?'

Juande stared at the nearest candle stand, narrowed his eyes and hesitated as if trying to remember some distant memory. His gravelly voice was softer than usual. 'I am Galician by birth. I forget the name of my birthplace. Age has caught up to me. I was a young man when we celebrated a thousand years since the birth of Christ. I might have been your age,' he said, casting his glance my way. 'My mother and father abandoned me when I was young. Too poor to feed me. I came into the care of monks. They raised me with a bible in one hand and a quill in the other. And when I was deemed worthy my life was nothing more than preparing parchment, mixing ink and producing these.' He ran a hand over the cracked vellum pages, the script of black ink neatly finished in delicate flicks and dots. 'But I would not have had it any other way.

'The written word is a thing of beauty. The Germanic and Celtic tribes used to pass their history on orally, but the Romans brought writing to their world and soon great histories like these were composed for us to marvel over. And the word of the Lord has been transcribed for centuries, allowing His message to be preserved for future generations. Long hours spent copying every word, every detail, every single day. But they are needed. Books like these can be weapons as much swords.'

'Weapons for what?' I asked.

'The fight to take Hispania back from the Moors.' His tone became more intense as he spoke. 'They came to our lands with fire and steel, burned our towns and monasteries, killed our people and settled in the lands of the south. They tear down our churches and replace them with their mosques, enslave our people and force us to bow to Islam. The Christian kingdoms need to put aside their differences and unite under the banner of Christ, drive the infidel from our shores and restore Hispania to the glory days when the Visigoths ruled and prospered! Leon, Castile, Navarre, Aragon and Catalonia; weak divided, but unstoppable united!'

What Juande said was true to an extent. The Moors did come and conquer vast swathes of Hispania, but they were not the barbarians he was making them out to be. Those Christians who dwelt in the Moorish cities were not forced to convert to Islam; in fact, they happily embraced the customs of their new masters and became Mozarabs. They lived side by side in harmony with the Muslims, for the most part, and though they were subordinate they still enjoyed a better quality of life in southern Hispania than they would in the Christian north. Or so Father Santiago had told me. His father had been a Mozarab from Isbiliya who moved north and became a stone mason in Leon, in a period when the Christians were striking back against the Moors and the Mozarabs were encouraged to settle in the new conquered territory. He came north so he could put his skills to good use and build new churches, else he would have stayed in the south.

'How will you aid the fight for Hispania, Antonio?' Juande continued. 'With the sword, or with the word of God?'

'Perhaps both.' It would be with the sword if I lived long enough, but perchance there would be an opportunity for me to become a man of the Lord, reside in a church or monastery and spread His word when we had avenged father's death. I ran a finger over the words on the manuscript, black on the beige pages. 'It has always been a dream of mine to produce something like this.'

110

'I plan on composing a life of San Cyrinus soon. The world will know his power, and more pilgrims will come flocking to be healed by his touch.'

'My tutor was composing a manuscript before he died. I brought with me...for safe keeping, I guess.'

Juande's eyes lit up. 'Do you still have it?'

'Yes. Would you like to see?' Juande nodded like a child.

'Antonio.'

We spun to see Inigo stood at the entrance to the sanctuary.

'I will take the next watch. Go and get some rest.'

I duly obeyed and bid Juande farewell as I left the sanctuary. He slinked back into the shadows and resumed work on his manuscript. Inigo fell in beside me as our footsteps echoed through the nave.

'I do not want you talking to him,' he whispered.

'Why not? He's harmless.'

'I do not trust him. How has he stayed alive so long on his own?'

'His faith has kept him strong.'

'Faith counts for nothing in the presence of steel.'

'I would not be so sure. His faith is his armour. For some people faith is worth more than all the swords in the world.'

'Did Father Santiago's faith keep him alive when Azarola's men gutted him like a pig?' The comment touched a nerve, but I held my tongue. 'He's dangerous. For all we know he is only gaining our trust so he can stab us in the back in the middle of the night. I am not taking chances. So, from now on you only discuss ways to extract more coin from pilgrims. Understood?' I nodded. 'Now, you mentioned you have a manuscript?

The question caught me off guard and I froze. I had kept it hidden ever since we left Lugones. If he knew the value of the precious stones set with the binding, he would berate me for keeping it from him, and he would pluck the treasure and add it to our hoard.

'It's nothing, just a tattered old bible,' I replied. 'I only keep it as a reminder of his memory.'

Inigo narrowed his eyes then nodded. 'Go and get some rest. I want you to get some more practice before we set off in the morning.'

Ever since we left Leon Inigo had been true to his word and was committed to honing my sword craft. He was a patient teacher, because he knew I would need to be ready to fight once we reached Palencia. Lashing out and criticising me would achieve nothing.

I started towards the door to the dormitories, but Inigo was still.

'Are you coming?'

Inigo looked to the sanctuary, watched Juande's shadow. 'No. He's quiet, so I might sit in here a while. It's peaceful.' He turned and gave a smile. 'Go, get some rest.'

I left Inigo and settled down in my blanket as Emiliano's snoring rang loud, disturbed the peace. I wondered how the building would have been in its zenith, before it was abandoned or sacked by the Moors. I could imagine the chants and songs in the morning prayers and the scrape of quill on vellum, the way the early morning light filtered through the high windows and the candles made shadows dance on the decorated walls. Peace and tranquillity, a life safe from distractions and danger. It was a life I secretly desired, but now nothing more than a dream shattered by God.

We had grown comfortable taking money from gullible pilgrims travelling to Santiago de Compostela, and if things carried on the way they had been we would have the wealth we desired to see us to Palencia.

But, given the tragedy of everything that had happened in such a small space of time, I learnt good things would not last forever.

I knew the fall would come, but I could not anticipate the scale of it.

Six

I had an uneasy feeling from the moment I woke.

The scent of incense lingered in the air as the sun shone bright through the high windows of nave, illuminated flecks of dust as they danced through the air. Our footsteps echoed around the walls as I wrapped my cloak around my slender frame to fend off the chill. It was always cold in churches and monasteries, no matter how many braziers burned or how much the sun's rays tried to heat the air within the hollow structures. Perhaps it was the cold that heightened my anxious mood, or my stomach did not agree with the goat we had feasted on the night before, but I could not shake the sense of dread.

Emiliano packed his bow and arrows and Juande carefully folded the cloth over the wooden reliquary on the cushion. Inigo watched the old man with a look of disdain, as if Juande had insulted him, and his knuckles turned white as he gripped the bag he was holding.

Without warning Inigo strode over to Juande. The older man stiffened, and I heard them whispering but could not make out the words. Inigo grabbed Juande's arm and squared up to him, his whispers more intense. Juande whimpered and stared back wide eyed, fearful of my brother. Inigo shoved Juande back and stormed out into the warm summer air. He gave me the same look of distain before he left.

Emiliano and I exchanged puzzled looks.

'What was that all about?' he asked.

'I do not know.'

Juande had a look of dread embedded on his face as he carried the cushion towards the door, and he followed Inigo outside.

'Keep an eye on Inigo,' I said to my cousin as we followed Juande.

'Why?'

'Just keep an eye on him. Something is not right.'

No one spoke on the walk to our usual greeting point. A tense atmosphere hung in the air, but it was difficult to figure out why. Inigo had become threatened by Juande's presence, yet I saw no change in the old man. The only difference was he was unusually quiet, and he was not keen on sharing why. I thought it best to keep my questions to myself.

We took our positions beside the side of the road and waited. It was mid-morning and the summer sun was warm. Sweat trickled down my brow and back.

'Why were you burning incense last night?' I asked Juande, trying to break the silence. 'Was it the feast day of a saint yesterday?'

'No. I have just always liked the smell of incense.'

'Oh. I see.' Silence ensued once more, and it was then I realised Juande was shaking. 'What's the matter with you? You do not seem right.'

'And exactly what is "right?"' he bit back. 'You do not know anything about me, so do not tell me I do not seem *right*.'

I held my tongue, taken aback by his reaction. He saw my hesitation and the stern look on his face melted away.

'After you left me last night, I had a vision. From God.' My eyes widened in surprise. 'It frightened me.'

'What did He say?'

'Nothing good,' he swallowed. 'He showed me our end.'

'*Our* end?' I exclaimed.

'Forget about it,' he hissed as a pair of pilgrims wandered up the track.

The day proved to be fruitless. Juande did not engage with the pilgrims with the same gusto as he used to, and not a single pilgrim was interested in our words. It continued in such a manner under early evening. Clearly displeased with our effort, Inigo called to us from the thicket with a sour glare.

'There's a big group coming from the east,' Inigo called. 'About twenty. Easy pickings. Do not fuck this one up, otherwise there will be consequences.'

We had never encountered twenty pilgrims in a single company before. The most we had addressed were Miquel's group of around ten and the rest were only handfuls of pilgrims. A larger group might be harder to handle, or else walk on by, but Inigo expected us to fleece every one of them for as much as we could.

The pilgrims rounded the wood and advanced up the dirt road towards us. Seven of them rode horses and three were finely dressed; another four guided two wagons with creaky wheels laden with goods pulled by a pony each, and I counted ten on foot clad in unremarkable garbs, some with hats upon their heads, leaning on staffs and walking before the horsemen. Those on foot seemed engrossed in conversation and one of them waved his arms around emphatically as he spoke, which drew laughter from his comrades.

As they drew closer, I could pick out discernible features of some of them; three of the horsemen were members of the clergy, one of which was a priest with a gleaming golden crucifix hung around his neck and a frown permanently embedded upon his brow. Another two of the riders were knights with fine tunics and cloaks fastened with silver chains, and the remaining two were their squires. All had swords at their hips. Although they wore wooden scallop shells around their necks, the sight of steel brought a touch of unease.

Juande shuffled nervously beside me. His silence increased my anxiety. Is this what he meant when he claimed he had seen our end, that these men would somehow harm us? I swallowed hard and tried to breathe deep to calm my shaking limbs, but the sight of weapons now filled me with dread. I remembered the way my father's men had been slaughtered within the walls of Lugones and prayed to God we would not suffer the same fate. But Juande's words had me disconcerted. I took small comfort in knowing my long knife hung by my side, hidden by my robes.

The troupe stopped before us as Juande extended his arms in welcome.

'Greetings, travellers!' he said with enthusiasm. No one replied. Juande's bravado ebbed away. 'The servants of the Lord welcome you this day.'

The priest looked at one of the knights, before looking back to us. He said something in another language, his voice as stern as the frown on his face. Juande hesitated then replied in the same language. They conversed for a few moments, and one of the men on foot barked something which made Juande flinch.

'What is he saying?' I whispered.

'These pilgrims hail from…Pisa, on the Italian peninsula. I cannot deduce where the priest or knights are from. Take the sheet off.'

I did as I was told and removed the sheet, expecting a chorus of gasps from the pilgrims as Juande revealed the secrets and powers of the reliquary. Some of the pilgrims on foot came forward for a closer look, but they did not seem impressed. There was silence save for a few murmurs and whispers, until the whole group seemed to turn their gaze towards the priest. He in turn glared then barked at us. Juande stammered and his counterpart repeatedly cut him off. There was none of the usual enthusiasm and bravado Juande normally displayed. Something had him startled.

'What's wrong?' I whispered.

'The priest, the knights…are from Roma.'

'What's wrong with that?'

'They know who Cyrinus is,' Juande hissed. 'He has knelt at the saint's tomb before. He says this cannot be his arm, and he is incredulous about us claiming it is. He says we are blasphemers!'

The priest shouted something and motioned to me. Juande smiled awkwardly and picked up the reliquary, moved cautiously towards the priest and tried a charm offensive. But the priest would not believe any word that came out of Juande's crooked maw. He nodded to the knight, who in turn called to the pilgrims on foot. Two of them moved towards Juande, swatted the reliquary from his grasp then seized Juande's own bony arms. A third struck him in the midriff with his staff. The old hermit yelped as he was forced to the floor. The priest continued to berate him, and the other pilgrims hissed and jeered. He looked at me, desperate eyes brimming with pain.

'Let him go,' I growled. Instinct made me drop the cushion and pull the knife from beneath my robes. All eyes turned at me, shocked by my action. I even surprized myself with my bravado. But I had already seen one man of God die at the hands of brutes. I was not prepared to see another hurt right in front of my eyes.

In an instant I regretted my bravery.

The knights drew their swords, and the pilgrims raised they sticks in a hostile manner. Those who had not apprehended Juande marched forward, ready to seize and beat me. Fear gripped my limbs as I backed away, devoid of ideas.

A pilgrim cried and fell to the floor, an arrow embedded in his back.

The men of Pisa spun to see Inigo skirting down the slope as Emiliano drew back his bow again, loosed another shaft that caught one of the knights in the neck. His body slumped from the saddle and twitched in the dirt. My brother shouted our father's name in a war cry as he raised his sword and clashed with the nearest pilgrim, swatted the staff away and plunged the blade in to his midriff. The tip exited the man's lower back, drenched in crimson, and when Inigo ripped the blade free the pilgrim slumped to the floor in a heap. He paid his victim no heed as he sought his next foe.

The ambush had caught the pilgrims by surprise and there was hesitation in their actions now, checked by Inigo's furious assault and Emiliano's arrows. They were not men trained in a fight. Fear flashed on their faces. The priest barked and waved his arms at the remaining knight to intervene. Juande desperately called for the conflict to stop. But it had gone too far. Inigo had the taste for battle, and I could not leave him to fight on his own.

The pilgrims had their backs to me, distracted by my brother. I shuffled forward and thrust at the lower back at the nearest one. The thrust was feeble, but the tip pierced his tunic and bit into his flesh. He growled as he turned and tried to bring his staff around, but I had already drawn my arm back and lunged with all my strength. This time the blade punctured his belly. The pilgrim gasped and I stabbed again and again, frantic and wild, felt his warm blood gush over my hand. The staff clattered on the floor as he fell to his knees and I cried my father's name as I turned the blade in my hand and stabbed into his neck. A horrid gurgle came from his throat as blood poured forth, and he toppled into a heap. There was no finesse in the kill, only desperation and brutality, a style more suited to tavern brawls than the battlefield. I did not care. I intended to stay alive no matter what.

I squared off against the next pilgrim. He glared back, wide eyed, staff held in a defensive pose. I took a cautious step forward, which was met by a bark in his native language as he swung his stick to dissuade me. I hopped back, tried to figure out how to get close to him. The pilgrim glanced to his side as one of his fellows fell with an arrow in his calf and screamed in agony, and that distraction gave me enough time to slash at his hand. The blade scraped over his knuckles. He yelled as he dropped his staff, but before I could strike again, he lashed out with a fist and caught me in my mouth. The blow knocked me off balance and I stumbled to the ground. My vision blurred and a throbbing pain engulfed my head for a moment. My knife had skirted along the ground from my grasp. I stretched and tried to grasp the hilt. The muscles in my arm ached as my bloody fingertips slipped on the bare pommel.

The pilgrim reached it first and flicked it away with his boot. His shadow loomed over me and I flipped on to my back as he reached for me. His heavy hands wrapped around my throat and squeezed hard. My whole body tensed as I gasped for air, clawed at the man's arms and his face. I remembered Juande's words, how he had seen our end and wondered if this was what he meant, killed on the side of the Camino de Santiago, unmasked as frauds and punished by God for our actions. It was what we deserved for our sins, but I saw my father's face, the way he looked at me and the words he spoke to us before he was executed, and I knew I could not fail in my quest to avenge his death.

Using the last ounce of strength within me I brought my knee up to my assailant's groin. A howl escaped his lips and the pressure on my throat alleviated as his hands cupped his bruised balls, and I stopped only to suck in deep breaths before I rose to my feet. Fury guided my boot into the side of the head. I cursed him as he slumped to the ground, and I retrieved his fallen staff. The will to survive guided my limbs as I staggered over to where he lay, lifted it and smashed it upon his head. The force of the blow knocked him unconscious, but I did not stop. A bestial rage had consumed me. The staff rose and fell numerous times. Only when his skull had caved in and a jellied mess seeped forth did I relent. The staff clattered on the earth.

Emiliano's arrows had killed a squire, unhorsed the other and injured a handful more pilgrims. All around Inigo were dead or dying pilgrims. He panted like a wild animal, and upon his face was a savage visage which sickened me; I never knew a man could appear so bestial. His sword was slick with thick crimson, his hands and face and tunic splashed with more. He resembled a butcher slaughtering livestock for the winter. This was not Inigo my brother. Before me was Inigo the warrior, possessed by the battle joy a man experiences when he steps into the fight. But there was no glory here. Only survival.

The surviving pilgrims had backed away, dismayed at the horror before them. Inigo pointed his blade at the remaining knight and bellowed a challenge. Unfazed by the carnage the knight snarled, sword already in his grasp and spurred his horse forward. As the two came together I expected to hear a great clash as the steel blades kissed, but instead Inigo dropped to one knee at the last moment and swung with all his strength. The blade bit into the horse's knee with a sickening crunch and the beast screeched as it tumbled to the dirt.

The knight was thrown forward and took a tumble himself, rolled across the ground before he came to a halt in a heap. He lifted his head, his face now bloodied, but Inigo was on him and plunged his blade through the knight's mouth, pinned his head to the ground. Blood trickled down the edges of the blade, seeped into the earth below as the knight's eyes glazed over, lifeless and unmoving. The knight, far from his homeland, was now a corpse slaughtered under the Hispanic sun, bereft of the dignified death his rank should have allowed him.

Everything was eerily quiet. The remaining pilgrims who had escaped the carnage had fled the way they came along with the wagon drivers. Their wares remained. A handful of pilgrims were either dead or else moments from death, along with both knights and one of the squires. Their blood was a blight upon the pilgrim way to Santiago de Compostela. Only the priest remained alive, trapped underneath his horse's carcass, felled by an arrow to the neck. He squirmed and whimpered like a wounded animal unable to escape. I ignored him as Inigo wandered over to me, wiped the blood from his sword.

'I am glad you were not a coward,' he said. His hair was slick with sweat and his face splattered with the blood of his foe.

'If I were a coward, I knew you would have come after me. I'd rather face this lot than face you in a rage.'

'What happened to make them become aggressive?'

'They knew who San Cyrinus was and accused us of being frauds. Juande did try and persuade them but…'

I stopped because I had looked at Juande. My eyes widened and panic gripped me. Emiliano skirted his way down the slope towards the old hermit, a look of concern on his face. Inigo too turned and looked.

'Shit,' he muttered, before we both hurried over to Juande.

The old man was slumped over his now dead assailant. An arrow was embedded in his chest. His whole body twitched in a spasm as blood seeped from his wound and mixed with that of the pilgrim. He moved his head and stared at us; his mouth twisted in agony and a streak of crimson trickled over his pale skin and snowy beard. He tried to speak but no words came forth. His neck slumped and one final gasp escaped his lips, then he was still. Only his deformed eye continued to twitch after his death, glaring at us accusingly.

No one spoke. The wind picked up and dark clouds approached from the north, threatening rain. I was numb with shock. Juande's death was what I had tried to prevent, yet God had chosen this time for him to go to the Kingdom of Heaven; or perhaps for the devil to drag him to Hell for his sins.

'You idiot!' Inigo screamed at Emiliano. His shrill cry carried along the hillside as Emiliano winced. 'Did I not say you were a shit shot? Did I not?' Emiliano held his tongue, not wishing to add fuel to the inferno that raged within Inigo. 'You killed Juande! Now what are we supposed to do? We have nowhere near enough money to get to Palencia, and now you just killed our main source of wealth.'

Without warning Inigo marched over to the priest, still trapped beneath his horse. He tensed, and there was fear on his face when he saw the long sword in Inigo's hand. An inaudible babble escaped his lips and he desperately tried to wriggle his way from beneath the horse carcass. It was to no avail.

'You are the reason Juande is dead,' Inigo snarled. 'You could not have just left us be, could you?' Inigo knelt and leaned in close to the priest. There was raw anger in his malevolent eyes as he whispered. 'Perhaps you thought you would deliver God's retribution for the sins we have committed. Let me show you the true meaning of retribution.'

The priest's eyes widened as Inigo stood, lifted his blade in both hands, then cried out as the edge fell with frightening speed. His head was severed clean from his neck. It rolled down a steady decline, left crimson smears where the stump brushed the dirt, then came to a halt. Eyes full of fear glared back at me; his face was forever contorted in a visage of agony. Thick crimson trickled from his neck and congealed in a pool amongst the dirt.

I looked away, disgusted. We were not meant to be murderers. We were meant to enact revenge for the death of our father. How had it come to this, spilling blood on the Camino de Santiago, taking the lives of pilgrims who wished to kneel beside Santiago? I was confused, repulsed at our actions and slipped into a trance where I could no longer comprehend what had happened. The only thought that stuck in my mind was we were sinners, and we were destined for Hell.

'Check the wagons,' my brother called as he wiped his blade clean. He knelt beside the older knight and stripped him of his valuables. 'These chaps looked wealthy enough, so perhaps they have something of worth.'

The drivers had fled with the remaining pilgrims, but the ponies and wagons remained. I did my best not to look at the bodies that littered the ground. My boot slipped on a patch of blood, but I closed my eyes, took a deep breath and managed to keep myself from falling. Emiliano made for the first wagon whilst I headed to the rear of the second wagon, hauled myself up and drew back the cover.

My eyes lit up.

The wagon was laden with churchly treasures; two reliquaries of wood and ivory, a handful of fine leather backed bibles, several exquisite bolts of silk and wool and a silver incense burner. The priest liked to travel in style and parade his wealth. On his dead corpse were a trio of gold rings, two with sapphires and one with a ruby, and a silver crucifix hung next to his scallop shell on a leather thong around his neck. I rummaged through the belongings, but a long streak of crimson sullied the incense burner and I realised my hands still had blood on them. It was a stark reminder of the carnage around me and I felt the colour drain from my face.

'This is wrong,' I called out. 'We should leave this place now.'

'Keep your mouth shut and do as you are told,' Inigo barked.

'No,' I said defiantly.

'Do as you are told,' he seethed as he marched over.

'I cannot,' I gasped with tears in my eyes. I jumped down from the wagon and felt my legs wobble. But if I believed I would be given any form of respite I was gravely mistaken.

My nose exploded in a fountain of blood as Inigo drew his fist back and thumped me. I cried as I fell back, felt the sharp pain shoot through my face and the taste of blood as it trickled into my mouth. Blood poured on to my cupped hands. The sight of it made my limbs tremble even more profusely.

'You are in no position to tell me what to do,' Inigo barked at me. I got to my feet, pinched my nose to try and stop the bleed, and winced at each touch. 'If it was not for me you would be dead, so show some bloody gratitude. I cannot stand the sight of you now, so this is what you are going to do. You will walk that way,' he pointed to the east, where the pilgrims had come from, 'and you will walk for a few miles, and then stop. If another group of pilgrims come along you will claim you have been robbed and ask them to take you east to the nearest hostel. If not, wait somewhere comfy. Only when it is dark can you go back to the monastery.'

'You expect me to find my way back in the middle of the night?'

'That is *exactly* what I expect you to do.'

'What will you be doing?' I asked reluctantly.

'Cleaning up this damned mess.' He turned and called to Emiliano. 'Clear the road of these corpses. Get everything out of that wagon and load it on to that one. We will have to load the bodies on to the empty cart. We cannot risk being discovered like this, else there will be a bounty on our heads. We will take them back to the monastery and decide what to do with them there. Leave the horses. There's no way we can shift them.'

'What about all this blood?'

Inigo looked to the sky. Dark clouds continued to drift in from the north. 'The rain will wash it away. But we will not be here by the time someone discovers it. We are going to lay low for a while.' He turned back to me with a scowl. 'You, get walking and do not come back until nightfall.'

As I turned and began my journey east, I heard Jimena's final words to me echo in my mind. *You are not like the other boys. Do not change who you are.* And I recalled her final request, one I never dreamed of following through with, but at that moment felt so appealing.

If you ever have the chance to stick a knife in his back, do it.

Dark thoughts crept into my mind. Innocent men had died because of our actions, and initially fear engulfed me. Now anger coursed through my veins. If Inigo and Emiliano would not repent for the blood that had spilt on the Camino de Santiago, I would make them repent for their sins.

I would redeem myself in the eyes of God and kill them.

*   *   *

I had waited long enough.

The dark clouds manifested into a savage storm, lashed the land with rain guided by a strong wind. Lightning lit up the sky as thunder rumbled like a thousand horses galloping overhead. I trudged on, soaked and miserable, but I was glad to feel the drops of rain as they dripped off the end of my nose and trickled down my cheeks. I looked to the heavens and let the elements cleanse me of the grime that caked my body, rubbed my hands until my pale skin showed. My hands may have been clean, but my conscience was not.

The cold numbed the pain in my face, yet the ache lingered. But I did not care. I felt blessed to be alive given the swath of deaths. Many of the pilgrims we encountered would never return home, and that weighed heavy on my mind. Two men of God had perished because of our actions, brave knights and a host of innocent pilgrims too. Those who fled would return home and spread news of the disaster, and the people of Pisa and Roma would see the Camino de Santiago as a hostile place to those who wished to kneel at Santiago's tomb at Compostela.

Dusk had arrived and I pressed on with haste along the Camino de Santiago to the comfort of our sanctuary. The return journey was made longer as darkness crept over the land, but I came to the spot where the blood had been shed earlier that day.

The last hints of the waning light revealed a bare site. The dead horses remained but else it was deserted. No corpses, no wagons, no Inigo or Emiliano. Even the blood had been washed away for the most part, nothing more than dark patches on the rain-soaked ground. The low howl of wolves in the distance persuaded me had I lingered too long, and so I trudged up the hillside.

The darkness and the ache in my limbs made progress slow. Guided by scant moonlight I lost count of how often I tripped on a rock or fell in a hidden ditch or stream. Soon I shouted curses, unleashed my anger in tirades aimed at no one in particular. Juande would have known the way back unhindered and I wished he was there to guide me, picking his way around the hidden dangers. Long hours of wandering in the dark passed until I reached the monastery.

The two empty wagons greeted me. Dried blood covered the back and the wheels of one of them, presumably the one used to transport the corpses. The bleating of the goats in their pen broke my gaze, joined now by the two ponies Inigo had brought back who quietly snorted in the darkness. I left the goats and entered the monastery.

A great glow emitted from the centre of the nave. Shadows danced along the walls as the flames devoured a mass of objects at the heart of the blaze, and the smoke drifted through the hole in the roof. I tried to make out what was burning but most of it was nothing more than charred remains of blackened wood. A gut-wrenching stench akin to roasting flesh made me gag and I covered my nose with my sleeve to block it out. Steam rose from my sodden robes as the heat hit me. The crackling of the fire drowned out the thud of my boots as I walked towards the sanctuary.

Inigo was stood like a sentinel, studied an object in his hands as Emiliano stamped on something, broke it with a great crack before he threw it on to the blaze. It was part of one of the bookcases that held Juande's manuscripts. The sanctuary had been stripped of all furniture.

'You cleared the road, then,' I called to them.

I received no reply. Neither of them acknowledged me.

'What is that stench?' I tried again. Still nothing. Something was amiss, but exactly what was beyond me. Was Inigo still angry about Juande's death?

'Ivory is expensive,' Inigo said, not taking his eyes from the object in his hands. 'It fetches a very good price in the markets in the Hispania. I'd imagine this ivory came from Ifriqiya, from an elephant. Do you know what an elephant is, Antonio?' he looked at me with a calm expression. 'They are reportedly magnificent beasts with a great nose and tusks that can skewer a man, so big they can trample anything underfoot. A great general from Ifriqiya named Hannibal marched them through this land and into the heart of the Roman Empire. But you already knew that from reading one of your damned books, did you not?'

'What are you talking about?'

'Ivory is expensive,' he stressed. 'And so are sapphires.'

He showed me the object in his hand, and fear gripped me.

It was Father Santiago's final manuscript. The cover had been stripped of the ivory plaque and gleaming sapphires. Inigo reached into his satchel and produced the loot which gleamed in the fire light.

'When were you going to tell me you had these?' he spat. I found no words to answer. 'Oh, but you were going to tell me about them, were you not?'

I swallowed hard. Emiliano had stopped throwing material on to the blaze and glared at me.

'It was Father Santiago's...'

'We could have been at Dueñas by now!' Inigo barked, made me flinch. 'Do you have any idea when you have done? If you had given us this, we could have avoided all this pointless bloodshed. All these deaths are on *your* conscience.'

He marched over to the fire and tossed the manuscript on to the glowing embers. A tiny flame licked the corner of one of the pages. A blackened ring appeared where it had charred, before the flames spread and engulfed the rest of the precious book. Beneath it was the scorched remains of a human arm. Juande's body was on the pyre. His flesh was charred or blistered pink, his scraggly white beard singed to reveal his crooked maw twisted in a silent scream forever in death. Beneath him, amongst the broken furniture, were the bodies of the pilgrims, similarly twisted and scorched by the flames. The sight made me recoil in horror.

'Why did you throw them in the fire?' I cried.

'They're all dead. What does it matter?' Inigo retorted.

'You had no right.'

'After the way you have acted ever since father died, I have every right!'

'I wanted to bury Juande, give him the proper rites.'

'Then go ahead,' Inigo waved to the fire. 'Drag his body out and bury as you will. Bury them all if you must. With any luck you will join them in the ashes.'

'You're a bastard,' I shouted. 'You're nothing but a bully and a bastard. All my life you have treated me like shit. Even when we only have each other left you still put me down. You beat the girl I love, and I had to watch whilst you did it. You killed innocent men today, all to

127

satisfy your bloodlust and greed. Well I may not be brave or have the strength you do, but I have morals.'

'Morals?' he scoffed. 'Murderers have no morals. Need I remind you that pilgrims died by your blade this day? You're as much a cold-blooded killer as I am.'

'And I will love every minute of killing you!'

I drew my knife and screamed, rushed forward and thrust, aimed to pierce my brother's heart. The attack caught him off guard and he stumbled back. I continued my assault and tried to land a blow, and in his attempt to dodge his heel clipped an upturned floor tile. He barely managed to keep his footing, and I seized on his misfortune to throw my body at him. He toppled and I leapt on top of him, raised my hand to plunge my knife in to his heart, only to find it had slipped from my grasp too.

I screamed in a mad rage as I pounded his face over and over. Inigo was bigger and stronger, and he managed to block a few of the blows, but anger fuelled the strength in my limbs and soon his face was a bloody mess. A dazed expression glazed his eyes and I reached for my knife, wrapped my fingers around the hilt before raising it above my head, and screamed at the top of my lungs.

Only Emiliano's intervention saved my brother from death.

Strong arms wrapped around my neck and gripped my hand, rendered me immobile. I was hoisted off Inigo and flung against a column like a doll. My head clashed with the cold stone and my vision darkened. I lay slumped against the wall, dazed. Pain engulfed one side of my body. Blood trickled from a fresh cut, warm against my skin. The flames of the fire reflected off Emiliano's blade, pointed in my direction, a steely expression upon his face.

Inigo coughed and spat blood as he got to his knees. He took his time as he retrieved his sword and came to me. I expected Inigo to beat me bloody or even stick a knife in my gut. But he did not. There was no anger on his face. Instead, he drew his head back and barked with laughter. Even Emiliano was puzzled by his strange behaviour and cast a confused glaze his way.

'Good, Antonio. Very good. I have taught you well,' my brother chuckled as he wiped his dripping nose with the back of his hand. 'We might make a killer of you after all.'

'I do not want to be a killer,' I said meekly.

'We're all killers now, brother, whether you like it or not. What did you think would happen when we reached Dueñas? We would slip some poison in Azarola's wine and be on our way? It is best to get the feelings of guilt and shame of killing over and done with now. There's more blood to be shed.'

'Say you are with us,' Emiliano put in.

I looked deep into their eyes. There was no emotion there, no remorse for their actions. Would I ever feel like that? Would I take the life of a man and feel no guilt or shame? It was a life I abhorred, but it was the life I would now lead. I had no choice.

'I am with you. Until the end.'

My words were said without conviction, but it was enough to make Inigo smile and nod. He ruffled my hair.

'Good. It is the right choice.' He began to walk towards the fire in the nave but stopped and turned back to me. 'Another thing, Antonio.' His tone turned sour. 'Do anything like that again, and I will burn you alive.'

As Emiliano joined my brother, I laid my head against the wall and quietly wept. It had been a day of blood and I hated my part in it. The blood of Juande, the priest and all the others who died that day would remain on my hands forever.

I was no longer the innocent boy who wanted to be a scholar.

I was a killer, and my future was paved in blood.

*   *   *

We holed ourselves in the monastery and avoided the outside world as much as we could. We no longer woke early and travelled to the Camino de Santiago to extort wealth from the pilgrims. Instead we rose at our leisure, ate our breakfast and set about training on top of the cliff where the monastery stood. The weather was glorious for a time and the only other company we had was the pen of bleating goats and horses. The pyre inside the monastery was left as it was, provided a grim reminder of the dark days gone by.

There was still a tension in the air, but time healed the rift. Four days passed before Inigo threw a sword my way and told me to pick it up. I hesitated at first, but when I retrieved it and stood opposing him, he gave me instructions on how to fight like he had before. The animosity faded with each strike of our swords, every bruise and embrace. He made a point of sharing our food equally between us all, taking equal watches and dividing the labour fairly. I felt like their companion again.

The wagons we had captured were laden with fine possessions and food, including a few jars of wine from the Italian peninsula. A goat was butchered each night and devoured, washed down with the potent wine that got me drunk far too quickly. We even adorned ourselves in the exceptional wool and silk garments, paraded around the monastery as if we were nobles attending a feast in their finery. Our laughter echoed around the cold stone walls and for a time we were happy. We lived like kings.

But the wine ran dry, only two goats remained and boredom crept in. Our primary goal came to the fore of our minds and the preparations had to be made. It was time to go to Palencia.

'Me and Emiliano will be gone for a while,' my brother said as he prepared the horses. 'We will go separately and get the rest of the supplies we need. Try to stay out of trouble whilst we are gone.'

It's not as if I could do much, or go anywhere, or get in to trouble. I was isolated from the world in a small piece of paradise in the hills south and east of Leon. And I loved every minute of it.

It was peaceful in the monastery. There was a book within the priest's possessions which had not been thrown on the fire, so I spent time pouring over every word and savouring the tranquillity. It was a tome on the lives of saints and was hard to read because the script was messy, but the illustrations were vivid and vibrant. When I became bored of the book, I took to practising the techniques Inigo had showed me, slow and precise, rehearsing them time and again until they were almost second nature to me. I even found myself sat on the fence of the goat pen, talking to animals as they stared at me. They were good listeners. My father, Inigo, Jimena, Azarola; I told them all about my thoughts and troubles and plans, and occasionally they bleated in reply. I imagine this was what Juande was like most days. No wonder he went mad.

A week had passed before I heard the whinnying of horses and rushed outside to see my brother and cousin dismounting. Inigo led a third pony for me, and all three of them were laden with supplies. He untied a large leather bag from his horse and threw it to me.

'What's this?' I asked.

'Armour.' I opened the bag and pulled out a leather shirt with hundreds of iron scales sewn on to it to resemble the scales of a fish.

'Scale armour?'

'Yes. It suits a skinny, nimble fighter.' He himself had claimed the coat of mail from the knight he had killed, as well as his exquisite sword. 'It will deflect a glancing blow but will not stop a piercing strike, or an arrow.'

'That's reassuring. Why could I not have had chainmail too? I'd rather stay alive than move around quicker.'

'The price I got for those sapphires only went so far and I did not get as much for the incense burner as I would have liked. I had to sell everything of worth I had with me to get your armour, and you're lucky to have a horse. Thankfully Emiliano bought all the food.'

'You should have sold the whole book,' Emiliano said. He had looted a leather jerkin from one of the squires and had replenished his supply of arrows. 'It might have fetched a better price.'

'If you tried to sell the whole book you would have ended up giving it away for free,' I replied.

'Would a priest not pay for it?'

I shook my head. 'He'd expect it to be donated. They are rare and precious things, not suitable for a pyre.'

Inigo grimaced. 'Well that does not matter now. I got a price and you got scale armour for it, so be happy.'

'And if I am not happy?' I received no reply, just a look of reproach.

The horses were tethered, and we traded the warmth of the sun for the cool of the monastery. I slid the scale shirt on and secured it with a belt, felt the snug fit against my waist, before I strapped on my sword and dagger. Inigo, in his fine clothes, mail and looted sword, looked as much a knight as the one he had killed. There was a look of my father about him; tall and dark, strong and confident, imposing and impressive. I wondered what father would make of me now, dressed in my scale shirt, weapons strapped to my side. Perhaps he would have cracked a faint smile of pride.

When we were ready, we all stood in the sanctuary. Light streamed through the windows on to our faces, and I basked in the warm glow and tranquillity of the holy place. We took a moment for private reflection, readied ourselves for the road ahead.

'The time has come, brothers,' Inigo said. 'We ride for Dueñas, and there we will kill Azarola for the shame he has brought upon our fathers. Vengeance we be ours.' We looked at each other and nodded our commitment to the cause. There was a mutual understanding it was a death or glory situation, but we were prepared for it. 'Leave everything we do not need behind.'

Within the hour we had loaded the horses and were on our way back to the Camino de Santiago, this time as travellers.

I was sad to be leaving the monastery. For all the misery it had brought us it was a tranquil place, isolated from the world and a perfect place for a man to devote his life to God. I vowed to return one day and restore it to its former glory. But for now, the path I rode led to war.

We wound west through the hills, back towards Leon, then joined the Camino de Santiago and travelled east under glorious sunshine. Our plan was to follow the Roman road to Carrión de los Condes then turn south to Palencia and on to Dueñas. We kept our swords by our side but wore scallop shells above our armour. Though mercenaries and other armed men travelled throughout the land we did not want to seem as if we were ready for a fight. There would be fighting aplenty when we arrived at Dueñas.

Pilgrim parties were common on our journey. They were unnerved by our weapons but were relieved enough once we passed with a curt nod, and they saw the scallop shells around their necks.

'News of what happened must have spread far by now,' Inigo muttered as a band of monks rode by.

'Do you think men will be after us?' I asked anxiously.

'Only God knows.'

It was not long until we came to the site of the massacre of the pilgrims.

The area was tranquil. The rain had washed the worst of the bloodstains away. The dead horses had been dragged on to the edge of the road and became carrion for wolves who roamed the land. Little more than the skeleton remained, covered here and there in patches of rotten flesh, the innards nothing more than a hollow space inhabited by a few buzzing flies. Though the scene was now barren, the ghosts of the conflict haunted me as I passed through.

My mind played through the skirmish and it all seemed so familiar. The screams of the dying, the stench of blood and death, the blood that sprayed through the air to coat anything it touched with a crimson smear, and the ache in my limbs from the fight, the burn in my throat and the sweat that dripped from my brow. I had almost died, but God had spared me for a reason. And that reason was to enact revenge for my father's death.

'Let's stop for a while,' Inigo ordered. 'I need to piss.'

'Here?' I asked, perplexed. 'We should move on as soon as we can.'

'Relax. Tie up the horses and get some bread out.'

Any protest was bound to be overruled and so I cursed as I tied the horses in a thicket away from the road, before we prepared a small meal of hard bread and cold goat. But as we sat there and ate Emiliano crouched and peered out of the undergrowth.

'There are two horsemen coming from the east.' he said. He had the eyes of a hawk and saw further than any man I knew. We joined him and looked to where Emiliano stared as the two riders came our way. 'One more spot of banditry before we go south?' he said with a grin.

'Need I remind you what happened the last time?' I exclaimed.

'We do not have to kill them,' he retorted. 'Just something to get the blood pumping again. It's been a while since our last bit of action.'

We looked at Inigo who had remained silent.

'Can you see who they are?' he asked.

Emiliano squinted. 'Looks like a trader or a lord, with a servant.'

'The extra coin will not hurt us.' He turned to Emiliano. 'Just one more.'

Emiliano grinned, yet a horrible feeling formed in my stomach.

Something was not right. Pilgrims sometimes travelled in isolation, but the perils of wandering the roads in small numbers could cost a reckless man his life. And a savvy trader would have a cart laden with goods with a guard of some sort, whilst a lord would travel with more than just a squire or servant, usually with an entourage of knights. It did not make any sense.

The lord wore a fine silk tunic of blue and white stripes and rode a magnificent black stallion, whilst the squire rode a chestnut mount and wore dark blue garbs. Both had swords strapped to their sides, but no armour. The only finery the lord wore was an amulet set with garnets which hung from his neck. He did not look wealthy but offered easy pickings for a group of bandits.

My cousin led the way and sauntered down the slope to meet the horsemen with his bow in hand. I and Inigo cautiously followed. My brother's hand rested on the hilt of his sword, in view of the travellers. He did not want a fight but needed to intimidate them in order to get what we wanted.

'Greetings!' Emiliano shouted. The horsemen stopped and waited until we were no more than a few meters from them. 'Lovely day, is it not?'

'That it is. God blesses us with fine weather,' the lord replied. He was middle aged, well built with a crop of mahogany hair and piercing brown eyes.

'Did he bless you with that fine amulet as well?' The horsemen looked at each other before the lord shrugged.

'We are humble pilgrims travelling to Santiago de Compostela. Our wares are none of your concern. Please, step aside and allow us on our way.'

'They are our concern now. You will give them to us.'

'Why would we want to do that?' the squire asked. It struck me that he looked too old and well built to hold the rank.

Inigo drew his sword and stepped to the side of Emiliano to block the road, as my cousin plucked an arrow from his quiver and laid it over the bow but did not draw it.

'We do not want any trouble. Do as we ask, and nobody has to get hurt.'

'You boys do not scare us,' the lord smirked. 'We will not bow down to the demands of cretins. Move aside and be on your way.'

'Just give us your gold and we will let you be.'

'Give us the road, or you will die this day,' the squire retorted. His voice was gruff, laced with authority. The comment silenced my cousin.

Something did not seem right. These two men were bold. It was as if they had expected our hostility. News of the death of the Roman priest would have spread, so pilgrims would wary of bandits and be vigilant. Yet their behaviour was highly unorthodox.

Then it struck me.

'They're not pilgrims,' I muttered.

The squire smirked. 'No, we are not.'

'How do you know?' Inigo frowned.

'They're not wearing scallop shells!' I cried. 'And how many lords travel on pilgrimage with only a squire? This is not right!'

Inigo flashed his gaze towards them both, and a look of realisation descended upon his face. He raised his sword and took a step back from the horsemen. I could hear the string of Emiliano's bow tighten and I knew trouble was coming. More death was coming to the Camino de Santiago.

But it would not be the blood of the horsemen that was spilt.

The lord whistled, and I thought the ensuing whinny of horses were our own from the thicket, but then a troupe of horsemen emerged from the woods to our right. They shouted war cries as they charged towards us. The ground shook with the rumble of hooves. The steel of spears and javelins and swords glinted in their hands, and iron and leather adorned their bodies.

We had no time to react before they were upon us. I was frozen in fear, but my comrades had other ideas. Emiliano loosed an arrow which flew past its target, then drew and notched another. But the second arrow never left Emiliano's hold. Two of the riders mounted on swift horses drew back their arms and launched a pair of javelins. I ducked to avoid the missiles and was relieved when they sailed over my head, but I heard a cry and spun as one of the javelins embedded in Emiliano's chest. His body was thrown backwards and slammed on to the ground. His limbs twitched profusely, before he was still.

The horsemen cantered around us in a circle, cut off any route of escape. I tried to count their number, but their swift movement made it impossible. Another band came up the road from the east. There was nothing but a wall of horseflesh, steel and leather.

The ground stopped shaking as the riders reined their horses in and stood motionless, all eyes glaring at us with contempt. Most were lightly armoured with leather or quilted cuirasses, round shields and carried javelins or spears, but there were a handful with mail coats and coifs or iron helms, kite shields and long spears or fine swords. Knights of the realm they were, who served landed lords and stood with the king in times of war. It was a position my father once desired for me, now no more than a distant dream.

I looked to my brother, who stared at the knights with a look of scorn. His sword was still in his hand and his grip tightened on the tang. He took a step forward and his voice was stern when he spoke.

'Who commands here?' No one spoke, no one moved, eyes still on us. 'Who commands here?' he said with more intensity.

One of the knights passed his spear to a comrade before he dismounted and stepped forward. He looked impressive with a fine iron helm with a nose guard trimmed in gold, and a polished mail coat that gleamed in the sunlight. He looked young to be a knight in charge of a troupe of horsemen, with his youthful face and bright hazel eyes.

'Who are you?' my brother demanded.

'I am Rodrigo Díaz. And you are murderers. I am here to make you pay for your crimes.' He drew his sword.

'You are bold,' Inigo sniggered. 'I shall enjoy killing a fancy piece of goat shit like you.' Inigo lunged forward and swung his blade.

But the outcome of the fight was set in stone right from the start.

Inigo was skilled but his opponent made him look a novice. Each one of my brother's attacks was swatted away with ease. The swords kissed with loud dins. Inigo's brow dripped with sweat as he laboured and toiled to find an opening, yet his assailant was calm and composed, simply matched each strike and defended himself. Inigo lunged too far and missed Rodrigo, and the young knight sidestepped and slashed at Inigo's calf in a single fluid movement. My brother screamed in agony as he was forced on to his knees and swung in wild arcs to try and catch his opponent. But Rodrigo was out of range as he circled him like a wolf taunting its prey, licking his lips for the blood to come. Inigo tired and stopped the futile attacks. He knew he was beaten.

Inigo looked at me with eyes full of pain and offered a sad smile.

'Forgive me, brother. Forgive me for everything.' He closed his eyes and tilted his head back, before he whispered to the sky. 'Forgive me, father.'

Rodrigo's blade sliced across Inigo's throat and sent a shower of blood spurting on to the ground. My brother choked for a moment before his body went limp and fell to the floor, lifeless.

And I was alone.

Rodrigo snapped his gaze to me and marched my way. I was numb with fear and could not move or speak.

'Where are the rest of your men?' he shouted at me. I could not respond. 'Tell me!'

'This is it,' I finally managed. 'Just the three of us.'

'You lie,' he snarled through gritted teeth before turning to the knights behind him. 'The pilgrims from Pisa said there were more than a dozen. They said they swarmed them like wolves to a slaughter!'

'There were only ever three of us, I swear.'

Rodrigo studied every inch of me. He seemed disappointed there was only me before him. I was a young man barely out of adolescence, yet he expected armed bandits who would offer a fight.

'Draw your sword,' he growled as he took a few paces back and levelled his own at me. He was in the mood for a fight, to slay me like he had killed my brother. But where Inigo was brave and would face such a man, I was nothing but a coward.

Against a single man I could perhaps muster enough courage to fight, but against the troupe before me, my resistance crumbled as I drew my sword and laid it on the ground in surrender. Rodrigo's posture relaxed at my behaviour. I unsheathed my knife and threw it down and ripped the scale coat from my body to show there was no fight in me. Rodrigo seemed offended by my actions, but he eventually wiped the blood from his sword and sheathed it.

'Who will have the pleasure of killing this one, Rodrigo?' an older knight with a weather-beaten face and strange accent called.

'No one, Mancio. We will take this one back to Sancho. He will want to question him. And who knows? He may repent for his sins.' The older knight looked displeased but held his tongue. Rodrigo strode to me, close enough so I could see the intensity in his hazel eyes. 'Enough blood has been shed upon this road. You are now a prisoner of the Kingdom of Leon-Castile. Tie him up.' He turned and mounted his horse.

'What about them?' a man shouted. He motioned to Inigo and Emiliano.

'Strip them and leave them for the wolves. They do not deserve burial.'

As I was bound by hand and foot and slung over the back of a horse, I realised how lucky I was to be alive. My companions, the family I had suffered through so much with, were now nothing but corpses. Their deaths represented not just the last resistance of our shattered family but the near failure of our mission to avenge our fathers and kill Azarola. I alone remained to fulfil the quest we had set out to achieve. But for now, I was a prisoner of a young knight of Leon-Castile.

And that is how I came to meet Rodrigo Díaz de Vivar.

The man I would serve all my life.

Part Three

Slave

Seven

I was going back to Leon, but this time in chains.

All eyes were on me as we travelled the road to the eastern gate of Leon. Pilgrim and trader, serf and noble all looked at me with intrigue; a young brigand, garbs soiled and torn, bound and paraded as a captive of the crown. Cheers rang out when the knights rode by, and jeers were aimed my way. I caught the occasional rotten vegetable or stale heal of bread in the face which throbbed with pain by the time we reached the city. All I could do was wince and stare back with contempt.

The Roman walls loomed overhead as I was escorted through the massive gate. On my first trip to Leon I had not appreciated their grandeur. It was hard to believe they were built by men. Father Santiago once told me the Romans were master builders because they used a material called cement to bind their masonry together. It was made from ash and lime to create a bond that dried as hard as steel and even dried in water, allowing the Romans to construct bridges with cement in their foundations. No one has been able to replicate the cement, or even match the Romans for their strength in building.

I tried to imagine what my father would have felt when he passed through the great Roman gateway, bound in chains, clad in nothing but tattered garbs such as I was. He was the slayer of King Ramiro of Aragon, the Fernando's own brother and last dynastic rival, and he should have been raised to glory by the king himself. But it had not worked out that way. Azarola had arrested him for a crime I was certain he did not commit. As he sat there, helpless and bereft of hope, I imagined he would have been defiant, spitting scorn in the face of his accusers. But deep down I knew there was fear. There would be no scorn coming from my lips, just pleas of mercy.

The wide streets opened to the main square of the city. When my father was executed it had been crammed with people eager to catch a glimpse of the killing. There was none of those crowds now; only citizens of Leon finishing their daily business, perusing the market and bartering for last minute wares, scurrying around the heart of the city. Dusk approached, and as the sky developed a purple haze the bells of the churches called for evening mass.

We did not enter the palace as I thought we would, but instead I was escorted towards the northern gatehouse. A high, oval shaped wall had been constructed around the main Roman gatehouse and was used as a barracks and a prison. We entered a long, narrow courtyard as men practised with wooden spears, sharpened steel and fixed armour. Some of them stopped to stare at me with ominous grins curled upon their faces.

'Fresh meat, lads!' one of them called, greeted by a chorus of whoops and whistles. 'We will have fun with this one!' shouted another.

'He's not to be harmed,' Rodrigo barked in reply. For a young knight his voice commanded authority, and the excitement died as he guided his horse to an older guard, presumably a senior figure in the barracks. 'See he is placed in a cell. My lord Sancho will call for him when he arrives.'

'Sancho is coming to Leon?' the guard said with surprise.

'He does not conduct all of his business from Burgos. He will be here soon enough. I will personally collect this one when the time comes.'

The guard nodded, and Rodrigo turned and spurred his horse out of the gate followed by his entourage, left me to the mercy of the guards.

A tall soldier grinned as he hauled me by the scuff of the neck and dragged me in to the guard house. The bonds on my feet were cut so I could walk, but my hands were still tied behind my back. I lost my footing several times and stumbled through the corridors, but my captor simply kicked me when I was down, or else dragged me along the hard-stone floor. The waning light of day was replaced with dim torchlight as I was led down a staircase into the bowls of the gatehouse, where the air became stuffy and carried a foul stench. My bearings were lost in the relative darkness as I passed a row of gnarled wooden doors with small windows covered in iron bars. A great cry came from one of the cells which scared me witless, and when I looked at the door a scarred face twisted with anger and crooked teeth snarled at me.

A loud click sounded behind me and I was thrown into a black abyss.

I slammed into a wall and fell to the ground. Pain shot through my side, and something wet and putrid splashed on my face. I opened my eyes as the guard marched towards me, a knife in his grasp, and slashed the bonds that bound my hands. He gave me a swift boot to the midriff for good measure before he slammed the door and locked it behind him.

I winced with the pain as I sat and surveyed the cell. The rank smell of damp filled my nostrils, entwined with the gagging stench of shit. Mould lined the walls of the cramped space with barely enough room to lie down, so I huddled in the corner and simply stared at the bare walls. The faint glow of dusk illuminated a portion of the cell through a small window with rusted iron bars. I knew I would be plunged into complete darkness. Being cold and alone in a dank cell only enhanced my fear.

The vibrant sounds of the city faded. Silence settled as dusk blanketed the world. The darkness came, and the first of my tears along with it. Everything I once knew was gone and I was reduced to nothing. I buried my head in my knees and sobbed like the child I was, tried to comprehend the nightmare.

Life had not been perfect, but I did not hate it. Being forced to train as a warrior in my father's castle was a small price to pay for being allowed to learn with Father Santiago and live in comfort. Inigo and I had not been close throughout our childhood, but he had been there for me when our father had been taken and executed, and despite the fresh anger caused by grief he had tried his best to guide me as we tried to avenge our father's death.

Jimena's face flashed in my mind, with her radiant smile which lit up my heart, and I wondered whether she missed me or hated me for allowing Inigo to hurt her, and my failure to defend her honour. I prayed I would see her again, but given my heinous sins I doubted God would listen

The first night was the hardest. Sleep did not come, and I lay there and sobbed and stared at the wall with raw eyes, where the pale moonlight moved through the night. All I could hear was the rumble in my stomach, the only smell the putrid stench from the past inhabitants of my prison and the only touch the cold stone of my cell that chilled my bones. I was beginning to think this was what Hell was really like.

In the morning a guard brought me a bowl of thin gruel which resembled vomit, accompanied by a heel of stale bread. I forced myself to eat it, gagged after every mouthful but grateful I had something inside me. And then I waited. There were sounds outside my window and I imagined what was going on out there, put faces to the various voices and wondered who they were, what business they had in the heart of the city. When I was bored of that menial task I stood and paced the tiny cell to stretch my legs, felt the ache alleviate.

And that was when I saw it.

Graffiti was etched on to the walls, mainly the names of prisoners who had inhabited the cell, or else random expletives or prayers. I had glanced over the names in the waning light of the previous night, not interested in who they were, but there was one I had not seen before which now stood out clearly.

Pedro Valdez de Lugones was here, an innocent man doomed to die.

Emotion numbed me as I read the words. I ran my finger over the grooves of his name and a tear trickle down my cheek. It was the closest I had felt to him for years. He had always preferred Inigo to me because Inigo was content to be what my father desired, yet I showed reluctance, which he deemed a sign of weakness. He rarely smiled or told me he loved me. My only hope was he had seen me be brave when it mattered and stood up for myself when faced with death.

A second night in isolation came, and a third and a fourth before the door finally swung open and Rodrigo Díaz stepped in.

'Come with me.' He wore a scarlet tunic and his blade hung by his side. A stern look was embedded on his fresh, youthful face. His dark hair was tied in a leather thong behind his back, and his beard was neatly trimmed. His piercing eyes unnerved me.

'Where are we going?'

'Come.'

I stood and limped after him as my legs struggled to cope with the sudden freedom. Climbing the stairs was painful, but by the time we reached the top some of the feeling had returned and I could at least keep pace with Rodrigo. Outside the air was warm, and the waft of freshly baked bread and roasting meat made my stomach grumble. A quartet of guards fell in behind us as we exited the courtyard of the barracks and into the city.

The palace was in the centre of the old Roman fortress and was converted from the headquarters of the garrison commander. Some of the plaster façade had worn away to reveal crude brickwork underneath, but the kings of Leon had added to it over the years, so it was now a sprawling palace complex. We passed through a forecourt with colonnades around the periphery and entered the great hall in the centre. Cool air greeted me as my eyes adjusted to the relative gloom. It was a large open space with the capacity for several hundred people when full, centred around the two thrones sat upon a raised dais. The roof was held by long columns with capitals adorned with leaves or flowers, and along the walls hung alternating banners of the lion of Leon and the castle of Castile. Today the hall was empty save for a few guards standing vigil, and our footsteps echoed as we exited through a door on the right.

Galleries branched off to other parts of the complex. The roof was vaulted and freshly painted with biblical frescos. A trio of priests carrying parchments marched straight for us as they rowed over something I could not hear, oblivious to our presence, and Rodrigo eased me out of the way as he himself stepped to the side to make way for them. They never thanked Rodrigo; their business was seemingly too important for manners.

We turned at a smaller gallery with several doors along the sides, each one with a guard stood outside. Stopping at a door around halfway down, the guard took one look at Rodrigo and stepped to the side, allowed us access. My escort knocked thrice on the freshly hewn wood and, once a voice called from inside, opened the door.

The room was large and well furnished with an ornately carved bed, shelves and a desk, upon which a large golden crucifix stood, studded with precious gems. Fresh summer air scented with lavender circulated the chamber through the open window shutters, and the white linen curtains swayed gently in unison. Shimmering crimson silks adorned the bed, and tapestries were hung on the walls, depicted famous passages from the bible; one showed David and Goliath in battle, and the blood from Goliath's head so vivid it reminded me of the horrors I had seen in recent weeks. A mannequin stood in the corner, on which hung a gleaming coat of mail, a conical helm with a gold nose guard and gilded with golden patterns, and a sword with a large, crescent shaped cross guard and pommel of gold.

Behind the desk, staring out of the window, stood a tall, well-built man in his late twenties. His bronzed skin was smooth, and his mousey brown hair and beard carried a tinge of blonde and were well groomed. A silken shirt of green and white stripes adorned his massive frame, fastened by a leather belt with a silver buckle. He turned to face me, and the first things I noticed were his piercing green eyes, strong jaw and stern expression. He radiated power and authority, and his mere presence intimidated.

'Rodrigo,' he said with a smile. 'This is the criminal?'

'Yes, lord.'

The smile disappeared as he sniffed.

'Did you not think to throw some water on him? He smells like a cesspit.'

'The smell did not bother me, lord.'

The man grimaced before turning his gaze back to me. 'What is your name?'

I hesitated because I did not think it wise to reveal who I was. For all I knew I was a wanted man; the son of a convicted traitor would not be welcomed, and I myself would stand trial for my part in the crimes I had committed. And so, in the confines of my cell, I had created a fake name and rehearsed a fictional upbringing. I prayed it would be believed.

'Santiago,' I said meekly, after hesitation.

'Santiago, *lord*. My father is the Emperor of Hispania. A street urchin like you will show me the proper respect.'

This was Sancho, prince of Leon-Castile and eldest son to King Fernando and Queen Sancha. He had been in command of the army at Graus and would have known who my father was, were I to mention his name.

'Santiago who? Where are you from?' he pressed.

'Santiago Iniguez de Gijon, lord.'

'You are a long way from home.'

'Yes, lord.'

'What made you leave? How did you end up here?'

I took a deep breath. 'I am an orphan, raised by my uncle. But he was a poor man, only a carpenter by trade, and he could not afford to feed me as well as the rest of his family any longer, so I ran away. I wandered from village to village, lived off scraps and tried to find a purpose in life. From Gijon I travelled to Oviedo, and it was there my companions found me. Bandits, they were. They offered me a chance to join them or face a painful death. What was I to do?'

'Where are the rest of your comrades?' he continued his interrogation. I hesitated as I remembered my brother and cousin, slaughtered by Rodrigo and his men. 'Speak, boy, and things might go a little easier for you.'

Rodrigo's gloved hand smacked the back of my head. I winced and rubbed my head as he looked at me with a steely gaze.

'Do not make my lord ask you again,' he growled.

'My comrades are dead,' I replied. 'There were only three of us.'

'The men from Pisa and Roma said there were at least a dozen of you,' Sancho frowned. 'How did three of you overpower a pair of knights and a host of pilgrims?'

'We set an ambush and had an archer with us. He was graced with a good aim and strong arm.'

'And it was this archer who caught the javelin in the chest, you say?' The question was directed at Rodrigo who replied with a simple, 'Yes, lord.' Sancho grunted before continuing. 'And who was your leader?'

'He only called himself Domingo. He never told me his full name.'

'They said there was a priest with you, as well,' Rodrigo put in.

'A hermit. I wanted to leave him alone, but my companions decided to keep him as a plaything, something to keep them occupied when they were bored. He died in the fight.'

'Along with a priest from Roma and a host of men on a peaceful mission of pilgrimage.' Sancho shook his head in disgust. 'Bandits raiding the Camino de Santiago so close to Leon; it's a fucking travesty.' He planted his hands on the desk in front of him and sighed. 'So where are the bodies of the men you killed?'

'We burned them, far from the road. It was easier than burying them.'

'And the Roman priest, him too?'

'The priest too, lord.'

'The Pope will hear of this and he will not be best pleased. The Camino de Santiago is used by hundreds of pilgrims a year who wish to kneel at the side of the tomb of Santiago. This attack may put many of them off. A holy man should be able to walk on pilgrimage unhindered and, more importantly, in safety!' Sancho slammed a fist on the table, making me flinch. 'If he is guilty of these heinous crimes why did you spare him?' he berated Rodrigo.

'May I speak freely?' Rodrigo was unfazed by Sancho's abrupt nature.

'You know I value your judgment, Rodrigo. Speak.'

'Look at him, lord. He is barely a man. I do not believe him capable of being part of the killings.' I risked a surprised look at him, and even Sancho frowned, but he allowed Rodrigo to continue. 'When we confronted the perpetrators, it was his companions who fought us; this one stood and watched, made no attempt to intervene. He threw his weapons down without hesitation. There was something different about him, no warrior's build, no bravery. And so, I thought it would be prudent to bring him for questioning before we passed judgement, rather than killing him and learning nothing of their motives.'

Sancho nodded. He placed his arms behind his back and stepped from behind the desk to stand in front of me. I tried to avert my eyes from his gaze as he towered over me.

'Have you taken a life before?'

I swallowed hard. 'I have, lord.'

151

'Willingly?'

'I had no choice.'

'Did you kill on the Camino de Santiago?'

'No, lord.'

'I have a hard time believing you, boy,' he snarled.

'Rodrigo told you my companions were brave. I am a coward and only fell in with them for safety, because I had nowhere else to go. It was best to receive food from bandits than not eat at all.'

'It is better to cast aside those who would sin and walk your path alone, so your soul would remain pure. Were you not taught that God punishes sinners?'

'Yes, lord. My soul is condemned for the choices I have made.'

'Indeed, it is. I do not doubt your soul will burn for all eternity for your part in these murders. You have brought a great shame to my father's kingdom. He wept when he heard the news and will be required to send a letter of reassurance to the Pope. I should have you hanged for conspiring with bandits,' he sneered. I swallowed hard at the thought of sharing the same fate as my father. 'But…I am merciful. You are young and as such I believe a weak-willed boy would be easily swayed when faced with adversity and difficult choices. So, I will give you the chance of redemption.'

'You are most generous, lord,' I replied meekly. 'What would you have me do?'

'God was deeply offended when one of his agents, a most holy priest from Roma, was slaughtered whilst on pilgrimage. You may not have delivered the killing blow, but you are accessory to the crime. Therefore, you will grovel for His forgiveness. You will do public penance for your crimes by walking through the city to the Basilica of San Isidoro, where you will kneel at the feet of my father and the bishop of Leon. I will gather every lord, every knight and man of the cloth and let them hear you beg for God's forgiveness, such is the shame of this crime.'

Most men would throw themselves at the feet of Sancho and thank him for such a punishment. But as I considered the implications, I became fearful. I could not risk being recognised. My father had played host to a number of lords and knights after his return from Graus, and though it was unlikely all the leading men of the kingdom would attend the event as Sancho had claimed, it would only take one of them to confirm my true identity. I would be branded the son of a traitor, fellow conspirer against the king, murderer of men of the cloth. Death would not come quick enough.

'No,' I squeaked.

Sancho folded his arms. 'You are in no position to reject this proposal.'

'You cannot force an innocent person to repent for something he had no part in.'

'As far as I am concerned you are as guilty as your comrades. The punishment I offer you if very generous.'

'I tried to stop the killing. I wanted to save the priest.'

'Prove it.'

All I had was my word, and Sancho did not believe the lies I had spun. He had been generous with the fate he had chosen for me, and I did not care about being publicly humiliated, but all I could think of was being discovered and seeing Azarola's smug face in the crowd, revelling in my anguish. The next time I saw Azarola I wanted to stick a knife through his throat. My hate for him and desire to avenge my father had not diminished.

'My lord, I have another suggestion.' Both I and Sancho turned to Rodrigo, surprised the young knight had interrupted us.

'Go on,' Sancho said curiously.

'He does not have to die, nor does he have to grovel, but I believe he will be duly and rightly punished. I will take him with me to Vivar.'

Sancho frowned. 'For what purpose?'

'I always have room for a slave. Whatever strength keeps Santiago going will be shattered once Arias is done with him. When his body and mind are broken, I believe he will beg for you offer of penance.'

Sancho crossed his arms and tapped a finger on his chin. A servant entered the chamber with a golden goblet and jug of blood red wine and set it on the table, then filled the goblet for Sancho. I wondered if I would be doing the same for Rodrigo in due course.

'You do not usually keep slaves, Rodrigo, and Arias will more than likely kill him before he is broken,' Sancho said. He picked up the goblet, took a sip and smacked his lips, savoured the taste. havery well. Santiago Iniguez is your new slave. He is to suffer in every task he is given. But make sure he does not die. Death would be too good for this one just yet.'

I swallowed hard and regretted my decision. I was now a slave, reduced to nothing, a subordinate in a strange land.

I wish I had accepted the offer of penance.

*   *   *

We left the lush fields of Leon behind and entered the barren steppe of Castile. It is a desolate landscape where not much more than small clusters of trees grow and water is scarce, the land more suited for grazing flocks of sheep and goats on the dry grass than attempting to cultivate crops. The wind howls from the mountains, fierce and arid during the day and bitterly cold by night. It was late summer, and the nights grew longer. I was glad to be taking shelter in a castle when the harsh winds of winter descended upon the land, even if I was a slave.

It was a four day ride to reach Rodrigo's castle, located only a few miles north of Burgos. My bonds were cut, and I could ride my own horse. I was also dunked in a barrel of cold water and made to scrub with soap fragranced with jasmine, so I no longer stank like a cesspit, and provided with fresh garbs, plain but practical. I was still a prisoner, escorted to Castile by a troupe of hardened knights led by Rodrigo himself. I seldom spoke on the journey, but one night an old warrior named Osorio, who looked too ancient to wield a blade, was on guard duty and chatted to me. He was pleasant enough and talked about his life most of the night, particularly the battles he had fought in. But there was a reason for his kindness.

'You will find no pity or compassion if Arias has anything to do with you,' he croaked.

'Why not? Who is he?'

'He is the castellan of Vivar in Rodrigo's absence, and is charged with recruiting and training men to garrison the castle and fight when called upon. Everything pisses him off. Even looking at him in the wrong way will send him in to a rage. You must have done something bad to end up in his company,' he chuckled.

'I have met worse.' Arias sounded like my own father.

Osorio smirked. 'I beg to differ, lad. Even Rodrigo is wary of him some days. He does command respect, but most do as they are told out of fear of his temper. They say he once struck a boy so hard it killed him, all because he did not clean the blood from a coat of mail properly.'

I stared wide eyed. 'You surely jest?'

Osorio grimaced. 'Wish I was.'

'Do you have any advice on how I can stay alive?'

'Sure. If you piss him off, make sure he has not got a sharp blade on him.'

The castle of Vivar stood in a low valley surrounded by rolling fields, no more than an hour ride north of Burgos. It was modest in size, with a keep that stood only slightly taller and wider than the one I grew up in. Around the stout stone wall was a village with throng of workshops and a small market. The spears and helms of a handful of militia patrolling the walls glinted as we approached. The stout wooden gates were already open, and before them stood a lithe man with a royal blue tunic, and white trousers. He had a thick crop of dark hair in contrast to his pale skin, and his small, piercing blue eyes narrowed often as he stared at us. He was flanked by a pair of servants, one with a tray with goblets of wine, and the other with a bowl of fresh water and a linen cloth draped over his arm. He gave a slight bow of greeting.

'Welcome home, lord. Did you have a successful hunt?'

'We did, Martin,' Rodrigo replied as he dismounted. 'Bandits will no longer plague the pilgrim way. Where is Arias? I have brought something for him.'

'He is away hunting boars, lord,' the man replied through thin lips, polite yet cautious.

'That man likes to slink away whenever I am not here,' Rodrigo growled, removing his helm and gloves. He splashed cool water on his face, patted it down with the cloth and took a goblet of wine. He motioned to me. 'This cretin is to be given to Arias.'

'Who is he, lord?'

'One of the bandits we hunted down. It would have been too easy to kill them all, so I brought one back to give to our friend as punishment. He is our slave now.'

Martin raised his brow in apparent surprise as he kept his gaze fixed on me. 'Oh, is that so? You must have been very naughty. I hope you do not mind lots of shouting with the occasion clip around the ear.'

I swallowed hard but said nothing.

'Do not spoil the surprise, Martin,' Rodrigo smirked. 'Take him to Arias's chambers and have him wait there.' Without another word Rodrigo moved into the castle with his men in tow, and servants came forth to guide the horses to the stables.

Martin turned back to me and gave a wry smile. 'I am lord Rodrigo's seneschal. I look after the estate whilst my lord is away. And you are?'

'Santiago Iniguez.'

'Well, Santiago, I am sure we will be seeing a lot more of each other. Come, I will escort you to Arias's chambers.'

Between the gate at the south and the keep at the north, which was three stories high and made of sturdy stone, was a central courtyard, large enough to fit fifty men at any time, though it looked as though Rodrigo did not command even half that number. Along the eastern edge of the courtyard were the sleeping quarters and stables for his knights, whilst the western side housed the smith, the storerooms and armoury, and the chapel with quarters set aside for a priest were situated at the south west.

'Rodrigo seems young to be a lord,' I said as we made our way across the courtyard.

Martin frowned at me, perhaps annoyed a slave would dare talk to him. 'Yes, he is. He inherited this estate from his father when he died some years back, but he was too young to take up residence here. Sancho took him to Burgos as his squire. He was knighted only a few years ago, and I believe he is the youngest man to be knighted in recent memory. Despite his tender age he is a good lord.'

'So is Arias really as bad as people say?' I asked as we entered the hall. Tables and benches were laid out, and servants prepared for a feast and set out decorations.

Martin sighed at my persistent questions. 'It depends in what context. He can be a little heavy handed if one's actions cause him offense.'

'Like the boy he killed?'

Martin frowned. 'Who told you that?'

'One of my escort.'

'Arias is not a murderer, if that is what you are implying.'

'Then what happened to the squire?'

Martin grimaced with disapproval. 'Ask my lord about it when he returns. I am sure he would be delighted to tell you.'

We climbed the stairs to the second floor and arrived at Arias's chambers. It was not a large room but commanded a breath-taking view of the sun-baked fields and hills to the north through a great window. There was no affluence here; Arias seemed to live an austere lifestyle, with no fancy silks on his bed or tapestries adorning the walls. Everything was plain and understated. The only glint of gold came from a wooden crucifix hung upon the wall, which was engraved with golden patterns and the crown of thorns upon Christ's carved body shone like a halo.

Martin motioned to a desk near the window. 'Sit.' He turned and left me in silence.

On the desk were several parchments with lists of names and items scrawled upon them, next to a small ink pot and quill. A long, sharp knife had the tip of its blade embedded in the wood amongst a collage of small nicks in the wood. Opposite the window was a bed covered in black and brown wolf furs, and two heavy chests sat at the foot of the wooden frame. A brazier stood in the corner, and the coals had been allowed to cool whilst the warmth of the day still lingered outside. Underneath the crucifix was a small folded piece of cloth big enough to kneel on.

Where his furnishings were simple, his tools of war were not. Hung on the wall was a white kite shaped shield with a red boar's head painted on it, which was unusual because such a shield was said to be used by a people called the Normans, whose knights rode huge warhorses and carried long spears with their kite shields. I had once heard my father talk of such men, for the Norman art of war had spread south through Francia and into the Catalan counties, which in turn had started to creep in to the other Christian kingdoms of Hispania. On a mannequin was a fine coat of mail, and a conical helm with a long nose guard and mail hood to protect the neck. Beside it on a weapons rack was a long sword in a red leather sheath trimmed in silver, the cross guard and pommel polished silver as well.

A servant entered the room with a tray of food. It was nothing more than a heel of bread and a handful of olives, but I devoured it regardless. As I ate two more servants entered with a tall stand with a wash basin. They came back not long after with the water. Steam rose gently from the rippling surface. Neither of them paid me any attention before they left me in silence again.

As the sun began to set, voices rose in the hallway. A tall, lean man strode in, followed by Martin. His dark hair was bound in a knot which hung past his shoulders, and his sun kissed skin was blighted by dust and specs of blood, just like the dark green hunting clothes he wore. A long hunting spear was grasped in his hand, the tip coated crimson, which he leant against the wall and crossed over to the water basin.

'Rodrigo can protest all he likes. He's knows I love hunting boar, and if I want to let off a little steam in the absence of war then damn it, I will.' He stopped when he saw me, glared at me with penetrating dark eyes. 'Who is this little cretin?'

'Lord Arias, he is the reason I require an urgent word with you. He arrived earlier in the day. He is our new slave.'

'Slave?' Arias frowned. 'On whose authority?'

'Sancho's, lord. He is one of the bandits who plagued the pilgrim way. Rodrigo insisted on keeping him alive and letting you give him orders and duties. I think it may have something to do with your reputation for being a rather stern man. Our lord expects you to give him some…special treatment.'

Arias barked in laughter. 'Stand up, boy.' I did as I was told, and he strode over to study me. A heavy hand clasped around my arm and squeezed hard, made me wince, which seemed to amuse him because he grinned at my discomfort. 'You need some meat on your bones for what I have got planned for you. Far too skinny.'

I did not have much of a physique. The few weeks of intense training with Inigo at the monastery had made me stronger and fitter, but there was still a long way to go before I would be considered to have a man's frame.

Arias crossed his arms. 'So, you're a murderer?'

'I am not.'

'Martin says you are. Are you a liar, Martin?'

'No lord.'

'Are Sancho and Rodrigo liars?'

'No lord.'

'I am not a murderer,' I reiterated, 'but I was in the company of killers.'

'Let me guess. You were the runt of the pack, the coward that survived?' My silence was enough to answer the question. 'Then it is a cruel world, is it not, that the innocent ones are punished for what the guilty have done? And if punishment is what Sancho and Rodrigo desire for you, they have chosen the correct place.'

Arias pulled his tunic over his head to reveal a ripped body marred by scars. A particularly nasty one stretched from his shoulder to the other side of his lower back.

'He does not mean that,' Martin reassured me. 'You might learn a thing about discipline and honour here, but I hardly doubt our lord will hurt you.'

'We will see about that,' Arias growled. He threw water over his body and scrubbed himself with olive oil, washed the grim of the day away. 'Have you ever served food at a feast before?'

'No, lord.'

Arias turned to Martin as he wiped dripping water from his body. 'Take him to the squires for now and instruct them to talk him through how things are done. He can be Rodrigo's cup bearer for the night. If the other boys want to beat him a little, then do not stop them. He will get worse treatment soon. Tomorrow, the real fun begins.'

Rodrigo, Martin explained, selected boys from local families in the village to squire for the knights in his employ; they were then chosen for their skill, courage and courtesy by Arias. I was placed in a room with two of the boys and they frowned as I entered. One of them scrubbed coats of mail and helms with sand whilst the other sharpened a spear point with a whetstone. The work ceased as they stared at me with gormless expressions.

'Santiago, this is Esidero and Gotinus,' he nodded at the pair.

'Lord Rodrigo got *another* squire, has he?' Esidero said. He was tall and thin, a year or two older than me with a face pocked with spots and dark, shaggy hair. 'He does not look so special.'

160

'He's nothing but a skinny little runt,' grunted Gotinus. He was broader in the shoulders with a block of a head and shaven hair. 'He does not look like he belongs here, Master Martin.'

'And there are only two beds in here, and I sure as hell am not giving him mine!'

'Oh, do not worry yourselves. Santiago is Rodrigo's new slave. And suitable accommodation has been set aside.'

'Where?'

'The goat pens. By order of Prince Sancho.' Esidero and Gotinus exchanged a puzzled look. 'Best not to ask about the particulars. Instead my lord has asked you to show Santiago how to prepare for tonight's banquet. He will be carrying out the same duties as you for now, as well as what is expected of a slave, and Arias has requested he be the sole cupbearer for the lords' table for the evening.'

Esidero sniggered but Gotinus glared at me, as if my new role caused him offense.

Martin turned back to me. 'I shall leave you in the care of your new comrades. Be gentle with him,' he said to the squires, offering a pleasant smile before leaving.

A tense silence hung in the air as both boys stopped their work and stared at me. I swallowed hard and shuffled on the spot, unnerved by their glares. They put their tools down before standing and taking a step towards me. I instinctively took a step back.

'Where you from, runt?' snarled Gotinus.

'Gijon.'

'A bloody Asturian. You're a long way from home.'

'I do not like Asturians,' added Esidero.

'What have Asturians ever done to you?'

'It does not matter what you did to me. It's what I am going to do to you that you have to be worried about.'

Gotinus lunged at me, took me by surprise. He moved around me and looped his strong arms through my own so I could not move, no matter how much I flailed, as Esidero drew a small knife from the back

161

of his belt. My eyes widened as the blade was waved in front of my face, slow and taunting, an ominous grin on his face.

'If you tread on our toes do not think we will hesitate to cut you…'

'Leave him alone.'

A young woman appeared in the doorway. As she stepped into the gloom of the room her features became more discernible; bright green eyes, flowing chestnut hair and full lips pursed in to a pout. She had high cheekbones, and her face welcoming and strikingly beautiful. She was a few years older than me and carried herself well, dressed in a simple gown of crimson trimmed in gold. Esidero and Gotinus tensed whilst I stared, taken by her beauty.

'Is that mail clean?' she snapped, made my new companions jump. 'You know Rodrigo does not like the men to fight in rust.'

'It will be, my lady.'

'Good. Now you're both to go and muck out the goats and place fresh straw for our new guest. We do not want him to be rolling around in dung as he sleeps, do we?'

'No, my lady. We will be on to it straight away.'

The two squires scurried out, left me with the woman. She stood and stared with a curious pout on her lips. A knot formed in my stomach; not because I was intimated, but because I had instantly fallen for her beauty. She had subtle curves, full breasts and an enchanting aura. A soft smile appeared at the side of her luscious lips.

'Welcome, Santiago Iniguez.'

'You know my name?'

'Nothing escapes me in this castle. I like to know everyone's business.'

'Who are you, if I may ask?' I asked cautiously.

'I am Constanza, Arias's daughter. But you will refer to me as "my lady", else my father will hear of it. And if I know my father that would be a punishable offense.' The pleasantry disappeared from her face, replaced by the same stern look as her father.

162

I dropped to my knees and bowed my head in her presence, realised now why the squires were so nervous when she appeared.

'Forgive me, my lady. I did not know.'

She could not stop herself from giggling.

'Get up you fool. I am jesting with you.' She held out a hand and I took it as I rose, felt the smoothness of her skin, delicately kissed by the sun. 'In private you may call me whatever you please, but in front of anyone else be sure to show respect, especially my father. If you have any trouble with the other squires do tell me, and I will see to them. That goes with anyone in this castle. Men do not seem to stand up to highborn girls, especially if their father would not hesitate to cut off their manhood. You may be a slave, but I will not stand for anyone to be mistreated in any way.'

It seemed impossible for a man like Arias to produce a beauty as Constanza. She was kind, graceful and had a sense of humour, something I had rarely seen in a woman.

'You'd best prepare for the feast tonight. We are hosting some nobles from Burgos, so Rodrigo will demand perfection. I will see you around, Santiago Iniguez.' She winked as she left, left me to stew over the new feelings of lust I felt.

I had known her only a matter of minutes, but I was in love.

*   *   *

There was no honour in being a cupbearer, but if it was classed as punishment, I relished the responsibility.

I was stood behind Rodrigo and his guests at the main table with my jug of blood red wine, ready to step forward whenever a cup was raised. The lord of Vivar sat with an official from Burgos, and though their conversation seemed intense I was out of earshot of their hushed tones. On his other side was his mother, Teresa, a woman in her mid-forties with a sour face and an appetite only for wine. I filled her cup many a time, but the wine did not seem to affect her. She was quiet most of the evening and only gave a half smile when more jugs of wine were brought in to the hall. Arias had a place on the lord's table with his wife Dometza, who was tall and graceful but with a squashed face and a slender nose, with dark eyes that darted around the room. Constanza was there too, and shamelessly flirted with the handsome young men who vied for her affections. She always had a smile or wink for me whenever she caught me staring. I averted my gaze often, in case her father caught me looking.

Garlands of herbs were hung from the walls to give the air a fresh scent which was broken by the aromas of the food on offer; cuts of the boar Arias had skewered earlier that day roasted in spices, with freshly baked bread, eggs and olives. After the main feast was done and the night dragged on the women retired, left the men to continue their discussions, drinking games and boasting. The benches were crammed with Rodrigo's own household knights, of which I counted twelve, along with knights from the lord from Burgos. They were deep in conversation, with one event of the last few months dominating proceedings.

An army of Christians had marched over the Pyrenees and laid siege to the Moorish city of Barbushtar, which was under the control of the *taifa* of Saraqusta, on a holy war issued by the Pope himself. Pope Alexander had preached the importance of driving the Moors from Hispania to the many states of Europe, asserting the threat they posed to the Christian world. A few hundred years ago the Moors almost conquered Francia but were stopped by a Frank named Charles Martel, and the Pope made a point it could happen again.

Men from Francia and Burgundy, the Papal States and Normans from the southern tip of the Italian peninsula answered his call and marched on the city, where they were joined by local forces drawn from Aragon and the Catalan counties. The Christians agreed to spare the inhabitants of the city if they surrendered, but when the Christians were given entry, they massacred the Muslims. One man shuddered as he reported the streets were meant to have flowed with the blood of the dead like a river. The men who conquered Barbushtar were still in the city and were fortifying their position against the Moorish counter attack to come.

'Our great king should take encouragement from the Pope's involvement in our affairs,' a young, clean shaven man said, 'and strike at the other *taifas*. They are fearful of the power of God!'

'Fernando grows fat on the *parias* he extolls,' argued another. 'There is no need for unnecessary war.'

'The men of Christ wage a war of conquest for our land and we are to do nothing? I will not accept such a travesty!'

'These actions will bode ill for us,' added a brute of a man from Burgos. 'The Moors will unite against this hostility and march north to confront us, as they did under Almanzor not a hundred years ago.'

'The *taifas* are forever divided! Each of them has their own agenda and will not band together. They are weak whilst we grow strong. They pay us to leave them alone because they know we will defeat them.'

'Why do we not join the war, lord?' All eyes turned to Rodrigo, who had sat quiet and listened to the debate rage on. He took a swig from his goblet then held it out. I stepped over and let a stream of blood red wine fill the cup to the brim.

'Let me hear your thoughts, Santiago,' Rodrigo said as I took a step back. All eyes were now on me.

'Lord?'

'Would you join the Franks and march on Barbushtar?'

'I do not know, lord.'

'Answer this then. Would you do nothing and grow fat on the profits that pour in through the fear you instil, or would you lead the charge against the Muslim *taifas*, bringing the word of God back to the regions that have lost their way? Peace, or war?'

'I would take up arms to fight for our land, lord.'

'Of course you would,' Arias snarled. 'You are a cold-blooded killer. Violence runs through your veins, does it not?' I circled the table, tended to the others who required a refill.

165

'This is my new slave,' Rodrigo called to his guests. 'He is a murderer sent here for redemption.'

'Him? A killer?'

'He used to be a bandit, though I have serious doubts he could played the part. There is nothing intimidating about him.'

'There's more meat on these ribs!' a portly man called, waving around a half-eaten boar rib which was met by a chorus of laughter. But Rodrigo's face was stern, saw no amusement in the jape.

'There is not much difference between him and many of the boys who look to become knights of the realm. Am I expected to believe that boys like this represent the next generation of warrior, to join the battle to take back Hispania? I find it a mockery of the great men who have fought and died for that ideology. Some of the boys will make fine knights, I have no doubt, but when I look at some of the cretins who are sent to me I lament when I think they will be given their belts, wed highborn women and whelp even more weak bastards in to the world. Castile has but a small population in a vast land, and each man trained to fight needs to be perfect. We need *men*! Strong men who can stand in the battle line and rout our enemies. But I fear that is naught but a dream, and when our king dies, we will become as fragmented as the Muslims.'

It had already been decided upon Fernando's death his kingdom would be divided between his sons; Sancho would inherit Castile, Alfonso would be given Leon and the youngest Garcia would get Galicia. The strongest Christian kingdom in Hispania would be weakened, and most likely descend in to war like the *taifas*.

Rodrigo continued. 'The king has been a beacon who has united the kingdoms of the north and pushed south against the Moors. But he is old and will not live for many more years. We need another strong leader who can keep us united and drive the Moors out once and for all. It is achievable, but perhaps it will not happen in our lifetime.'

'That man could be you, lord,' one of his knights said with a wink.

'Me?' Rodrigo grimaced. 'If I had a thousand men, I would have taken Barbushtar and held it for our king. But I am nothing more than a petty lord with a handful of loyal knights and a throng of boys that need training. That is why I have Arias. A bit of rough treatment from a bastard like him puts meat on a boy's bones and courage in to his heart.'

His men laughed at the comments. Arias smirked and locked his eyes on to me. He drained his cup before holding it out for me to refill. 'Turning boys in to men is what I do,' he growled. 'They mature or they break. You will know about that soon enough.'

Come dawn I was woken by a bleating goat as Arias kicked it out of his way, his shadow stark against the early red rays of the rising sun.

'Saddle up, boy. We ride.' He threw a long green cloak at me.

'Where are we going, lord?' I rose, fastened the cloak around my neck.

'It is not your place to ask where we go. Just get ready.'

Within an hour a small troupe of us filtered out of the gate and galloped east. The fields basked in the morning glow as we passed small villages that dotted the landscape. The heat brought a coating of sweat upon my brow, and I wished to throw the green cloak from my shoulders but thought better of it in case I incurred Arias's wrath.

Rodrigo rode at the helm with Arias, and his twelve knights accompanied us, carried spears but with no armour. We were not armed for war and no squires rode with us. I believed we were on a hunt which Arias seemed to enjoy so much. Boars and deer were abundant in the forest, but we did not enter any of the wooded areas and instead stuck to the rough tracks that led north and east to a low valley. After a brief stop, we continued through the valley as grey clouds rolled in from the west, threatened a deluge. Miles of open field passed us by, gave nothing away to the purpose of our journey.

Our pace slowed when we ascended a range of hills. Rocky outcrops sprung from the hillside and pockets of woodland grew along the rough track as we climbed higher and higher. The wind picked up, the clouds darkened, and I thought they would burst at any moment, but thankfully they held off. Then we descended the high ground and skirted the periphery of a dense wood. The land opened, but in the distance more hills surrounded us to the north, east and south. It was here, early evening, when Rodrigo called a halt.

Arias led his horse a few spear lengths before the rest of us and surveyed the beauty of the land. He turned and beckoned me over. We stood in silence for a few moments. The valley was silent save for the snorting of horses and the rustle of trees that swayed delicately in the breeze. The world seemed so peaceful.

'Do you like my daughter, boy?' Arias broke the silence.

'She is a very comely woman, lord,' I replied, unnerved by his choice of conversation.

'I'd wager you want to suck on her tits.'

'I...no lord!'

'I hate liars,' he growled and glared at me.

'I am not a liar. I have not looked at her in that way!'

'Every man who comes through the gate of Vivar looks at her in that way and wants to plough her. I have lost count of how many lords have been disappointed when I rejected their marriage proposals. There were a few knights I could have come to an agreement with, but most are dead or else are fathers to worthless cretins, and now I must wait to find another worthy of calling my daughter his wife. They are a rare breed in these lands.'

'The man to wed your daughter would be a very lucky man, lord.'

'Are you lucky, Santiago?' Rodrigo put in.

I looked at him, then each of his men. All eyes were on me. Something did not seem right.

'Sometimes, lord. I consider myself lucky to be alive.'

'Right now, you need all the luck you can get.'

The world span as I was thrown from my horse, landed on the earth with a painful thud. I gasped as the wind was knocked from me. My horse was led away as Rodrigo continued to glare at me. He drew a knife and tossed it my way, then guided his dazzling white horse forward and scowled at me.

'There is something curious about you, Santiago Iniguez. I have a hard time believing you could survive a journey from Gijon to Oviedo, then to the Camino de Santiago, regardless of whether you were with bandits or not. So, here is a test for you. A test of survival. Show me how lucky you are.'

Rodrigo turned his horse and started back the way we have come. Panic gripped me as I scrambled to my feet and stumbled after them.

'Lord, you cannot leave me here!' I yelled. 'How will I know how to get back?'

'Head west,' he called as the horses galloped in to the setting sun.

I stood motionless, stunned at what they had done to me. I watched them crest the hill and hoped for a moment it was all a cruel jape, but when they disappeared over the ridge, I knew it was no ploy. The first winds of autumn blew a chill which made my spine tingle and my limbs shake. I picked up the knife and sheathed it on my belt, pulled the cloak tighter to my body and searched the land for somewhere to take shelter for the night.

I was alone in the wild.

Eight

God had abandoned me.

Luck had nothing to do with my fate; it was God's will and His will alone. Father Santiago taught me God has a plan for us all, a plan for us to follow and earn our place in the Kingdom of Heaven when our time in this world is over. But there are things to coax us off the path, temptations set out by the Devil and his demons, enticing us to commit sin and so earn a place in Hell for all eternity instead. I was sixteen years old, but I felt as though my sins were irreconcilable, and God had sent Rodrigo to be my punishment, to chastise me for all I had done wrong.

He had left me alone and afraid in a land foreign to me.

I stood and willed my lord to return over the hill. They could berate and beat me as much as they wanted so long as they returned and took me back to Vivar. Enduring the taunts of the men was something I could deal with, for I had lived with Inigo's comments long enough. I would have given anything to be back in the goat pen. It took a while for reality to sink in before I turned and surveyed the area.

To the north, south and east the country was barren and desolate, stretched to hills far beyond. It was a place devoid of life where a man could become easily disoriented if he lost his bearings. Birds chirped in the lush woodland that swayed with the breeze. It was a tranquil spot, one I would enjoy given the opportunity, but the sun was descending to the west, dusk not far away, so I set about finding shelter for the night.

I pulled the cloak closer to my body and stuck to the edge of the forest, headed back the same way we had come. The interior was already gloomy and the silence within unnerving. A sense of dread hung over me as I peered in to the darkness, wondered if something, or someone, lurked in the darkness. I did not see the rock jutting out from the ground. My toes clipped it with force, sent searing pain shooting through my leg and forced me to the ground. My cry of agony reverberated throughout the valley and echoed through the forest.

Curses rolled off my tongue as I slipped my boot off to see throbbing toes already starting to bruise. Blood seeped from the big toe nail, half hanging off. I touched it and winced as the pain intensified. I cut a piece of cloth from the cloak, wrapped the toes as tightly as I dared then carefully slid the boot back on, breathed deep to try and block out the pain that flared with the deftest of touches.

I had spent so much time focusing on my injury I had not realised darkness had descended. And I was not alone.

A snort to my right was followed by a low rumble. Initially I felt a surge of hope, thought a horse and rider had stumbled upon me. Then a mass of fur and meat lumbered from behind a small copse. It was a great bear; its fur was a deep brown that shimmered gold when it moved. Its monstrous paws padded softly on the dirt as it sniffed the ground. It did not pay me any attention at first, but when I gasped at the sheer size it turned its head my way. Two bright amber eyes stared back.

I risked a look around to assess my options. I could not run along the track with my injured foot, but at the edge of the forest were a few large trees whose gnarled branches hung to the ground and were climbable. I knew it was my only option for escape.

I looked back at the bear as paws thudded my way.

Using slow, steady movements and gritting my teeth to fight the pain, I rose and backed away towards the treeline. My breaths were short, laboured yet muffled, clutched by fear. And the bear wandered closer still. My heel clipped a large rock and I stumbled back yet managed to keep my balance. But the sudden movement was something I had tried to avoid.

A great bellow reverberated around the hills, and without hesitation I scrambled towards the tree. I could hear the panting and heavy thuds as the bear charged, but I did not look behind, instead kept the nearest tree in my sight, scurried as fast as my injured foot would allow me, gritted my teeth against the searing pain. The distance seemed to take an age to close, but as I reached the base of the tree, I clambered up the gnarled bark, gripped my fingers on anything I could. Higher and higher I climbed, and for I moment I believed I had escaped the monster that stalked me.

I screamed as the bear's claws ripped in to my calf.

Crying in agony, I hauled myself on to a high branch and straddled it as the bear reared on to its hind legs and took another swipe. This time it found nothing but air, and even when it tried to bite with its vicious maw did it fall short again. I winced and panted, and tears streamed down my cheeks as blood dripped from a gash on my calf, sent the bear in to frenzy. The world shook as another thunderous bellow sent birds in to flight.

'Leave me be!' I screamed back.

The bear did not leave. It paced back and forth, waited for me to fall, and anticipated a fresh kill. Only when the last light of day disappeared over the hills did it abandon its pursuit, but I did not come down from the tree. Cold, injured and disheartened as I was, I felt safe above ground. The bleed on my leg only stopped when I cut another piece fabric from my cloak and wrapped it around the wound, cursed as the pain flared again. I settled back against the trunk and rested.

That was one of the longest nights of my life. I did not sleep lest I fall off my perch, and so I filled the time with memories of my old life, the people who I had lost. Tears came and went as the nocturnal birds called out their midnight melodies, and as much as my eyes ached from exhaustion, I stayed vigilant.

I climbed from my perch when the gloom of dawn arrived. I travelled in to the unknown and did not know what lay ahead, what dangers I would face. But I was determined to reach Rodrigo and prove to him I was not weak. Too much had happened to me for me to stop now. I picked up a fallen branch to lean on, took a deep breath and hobbled west.

The early morning glow warmed my back as I made my way up the hill where Rodrigo had departed. The air was muggy, and though rain clouds greeted me overhead the showers held off for the day. The woodland thinned and steep hills with rocky outcrops appeared on both sides, and from there the land descended with a rough track that snaked down the hill side. My injured leg made progress slow and painful, and I spent my second night amongst a copse, warm but hungry, unable to salvage anything but a few sour berries. I pressed on when the dawn poked through the trees, and by midday the valley opened to wide plains with hills to the north and south. It took the best part of the day to stumble through the valley, but I was lucky enough to find a small village at the base of a hill. It was nothing more than a cluster of huts for the shepherds who grazed their flocks on the hills, but the hours of walking had taken their toll and they were kind enough to offer me a few scraps of lamb and water and patch my leg up with fresh cloth. They said Vivar was to the south and west.

As I pressed on the heavens opened, drenched the world in a deluge of warm rain. My boots squelched on the fresh mud and the air became humid so I ducked under the nearest set of trees and waited for the worst of it to pass, but the downpour continued well in to the night and so I was forced to seek refuge under those trees, shivering and damp as the cool evening air greeted me.

It was approaching dusk the next day before Vivar's keep came in to view. Relief overcame me and my limbs were injected with fresh optimism as I staggered forth once more. Burn as my legs might, the promise of the stack of hay next to the goats spurred me on. The sun was beginning to set as I stumbled through the village. Man, woman and child all looked at me with intrigue; some even followed me as I wound my way to the gates of the castle. To my surprise, the gates creaked open as I approached. My pace slowed to a painful limp as I passed through the stone gateway and entered the courtyard, to a sight I certainly did not expect.

Arias stood in the centre of the courtyard, flanked by some of the squires with smirks on their ugly faces. Moments later a host of bystanders exited the keep; Martin was there, along with a priest and several servants. Arias held his blade in his hand with the point rested upon the dirt, and some of the squires too had steel in their grasp. The way they stared unnerved me.

'You are tougher than you look, Santiago Iniguez de Gijon,' Arias called. His tone and demeanour reminded me of my father.

'I do not feel like it, lord,' I replied weakly. My limbs trembled and the wound on my leg throbbed. I planted the stick in the ground and leant on it to stop myself from falling. 'It was a long way back.'

'We are impressed. Part of me believed we would never see you again.'

'Prince Sancho said I was not to die. Given I have offended him already I thought it best not to leave him disappointed a second time.'

Arias smirked and looked up at the keep. Rodrigo gazed down at us from his room on the highest floor, his hands planted firmly on the stone ledge. His piercing stare was fixed on me for a while, before he looked at Arias and gave a nod.

'Give him a sword,' Arias called.

Esidero threw his long sword, which skidded along the floor and came to a stop before me. 'You will fight him,' Arias nodded to Gotinus. The block headed squire marched forward and stopped a few meters before me. He licked his lips and loosened his limbs for the contest to come.

I stared in disbelief. 'I am no warrior, lord. I am too exhausted to fight.'

'You will do as I say, cretin,' Arias snapped. 'You are no warrior, but you have shed blood. Now you are a slave of my lord, here under royal orders. You will do as you are commanded.'

'I never wanted to take part in the bloodshed. I…'

'Pick up the damned sword and fight him.'

There was no escape from the fight. I had to obey or else face even more consequences. I wanted to scream in his face, show defiance like my father would have, but I hobbled over to the sword and picked it up. The practise sword was much heavier than a battle blade, with blunted edges and a worn black leather tang. It took an enormous amount of effort just to lift it. Gotinus was confident and smirked as he circled me. I winced as I lifted the sword and took a fighting stance, however pathetic it might have looked. I swallowed hard and my heart thumped against my chest as I waited with apprehension.

'Begin!'

Gotinus was much quicker than I had anticipated, and before I knew it, he was on me. Our blades kissed and such was the force of Gotinus strike I stumbled back and fell to my knees. Pain shot through my arms and I wanted nothing more than to yield, but Rodrigo watched me like a hawk from his perch, took in my every movement. I would not allow him to see me weak, and so I planted the sword in the ground and hauled myself up, stared at Gotinus defiantly.

My opponent's smile simply grew, and he came at me time and time again, drove me back or to the ground. He toyed with me, his blows intended to keep me down and take advantage of my weak state, but as the contest went on Gotinus gritted his teeth as his attacks became more forceful. I went down again, and before I could stand Gotinus drove a boot in to my stomach, made me curl over and cry in agony. I turned over on to my back and his heavy boot rose to stamp on my face, and I narrowly avoided it as the boot thumped in to the dirt next to my ear. I pushed myself on to my hands and knees, felt the dirt between my fingers as sweat dripped from my brow. Gotinus loomed over me and grumbled with laughter as he prepared to finish the contest.

But I would not be beaten.

I gritted my teeth as I hefted the sword and caught Gotinus's strike mid-air. The force of the clash jarred my arms and the burning sensation intensified, but I fought through the pain to get to my feet. It was my turn to attack now and I aimed strikes at all parts of Gotinus's body, kept him guessing, used the techniques Inigo had taught me to drive him back. The look on his face was priceless; the confident smirk had been replaced with disbelief, fear almost. The tirade took him unaware and he had no answer for it. I shifted to my right and swung at his midriff, and as he spun to block me, he slipped and fell to the floor. His sword skidded from his grasp and he lunged after it, but I got their first and kicked it out of reach. He knelt there on one knee, motionless, waited for my next move. I could have let him yield and called an end to the contest, but would he have done the same? Rodrigo watched and I needed to show strength.

I screamed as I swung in an arc. The flat of the blade smacked Gotinus in the cheek with a sickening crunch. Blood spurted through the air as he fell to the floor in a heap. With renewed vigour I lifted the sword in the air with both hands, cried aloud as my whole body ached, ready to smash Gotinus's head. Men surged forward as they saw the danger. But my arms would not allow me to attack. I had beaten him, cast him to the dirt with blood on his face, and when I heard him groan and struggle to rise the strength in my body vanished. I let the sword drop. My vision darkened and I crashed to the floor. Distorted voices shouted as I lay there, grateful for a moment of respite.

Two blurry faces appeared over me, and their voices were barely recognisable.

'He is in a bad way, lord,' Martin said grimly.

'Days in the wilderness will do that to a man,' Arias growled.

A delicate hand pressed against my forehead. 'He is burning up. I believe he may have a fever, lord,' said a man dressed in the garbs of a priest. 'He needs urgent attention.' A silence ensued, which left the priest concerned. 'My lord, he could *die*.'

I opened my eyes enough to pick out Arias's face glaring at me. At first, I swore it was my father frowning at me like he used to, disapproval scrawled all over his face. But then his stern expression seemed to relax and there was a flicker of pity in his eyes.

'Get him patched up, feed him, do whatever you have to. And put him in a bed for a few days. He's earned that much.'

He turned and stormed in to the hall as I was hoisted up and taken to the chapel. The world darkened once more as I felt consciousness slip away, but I afforded myself a slight smile for my victory and the rewards that came with it.

For the first time in my life I felt as though I had proved myself.

*   *   *

Cool air caressed my cheeks as I opened my eyes.

The pain in my limbs had subsided for the most part, but an ache lingered when I moved. It was comforting to feel the soft bed stuffed with goose feathers beneath me, and the fresh scent of jasmine filled the air. I pushed myself up to find I was in a small infirmary attached to the chapel. A gnarled wooden crucifix hung above the bed so God would bless those who were sick. Elsewhere the room was furnished with tables lining the walls with fresh linens, various tools and instruments and a shelf packed with glass bottles and an assortment of ingredients to make medicines and poultices.

A priest stood at one of the tables and happily hummed a tune.

'Good morning,' I said with a croaky voice.

I caught him by surprise, and he jumped but offered a smile when he turned. 'Ah, Santiago! It is good to see you awake. But morning has now passed. It is much closer to afternoon.' He crossed over to me with a small cup of water, which I drained eagerly. I handed him back the cup, happy to see a pleasant face. He was young for a priest with short, sandy coloured hair, a long, pointed nose and bright blue eyes. He was my height but plump where I was lithe. A jowl hung beneath his chin, his cheeks were full, and a paunch clung to his long white robe. 'I am Father Auderico, Rodrigo's priest. And you made quite a mess of young Gotinus's face!'

'I am glad it was him rather than me,' I winced as I sat up. 'How long have I been asleep?'

'This is the third day. You must have been quite tired.'

'Exhausted.' I was suitably refreshed, but my stomach growled.

'You must be hungry too!' Auderico guffawed.

I nodded. He hurried to one of the tables where he retrieved a little loaf of bread with a pot of honey, which he offered to me. I devoured the small meal, tore chunks from the bread and did not care that honey dribbled over my chin and the bed linen. Auderico looked on in amazement. Once I finished, I let out a great belch.

'Is there any more?'

'Unfortunately, that was the remnants of my breakfast and you have scoffed it all! Come, let us visit the kitchens.'

'Will Rodrigo allow that?' I asked warily. 'It seems like a luxury for a slave.'

'He and Arias are in Burgos and will not know. Besides, he is not as bad as he seems. And, quite frankly, I am surprised you are here.'

'Why?'

'I will explain over something hot.'

The young priest helped me out of bed and let me dictate the pace. My legs were stiff, and my body still ached so I took my time, despite the hunger that ravaged my stomach. He took me through the chapel as

178

we made our way outside, where the sun shone through the intricate stained-glass windows and cast coloured murals on the walls. We exited through the open doors in to the warm autumnal air. Several men practised in the yard or patrolled the walls; villagers sought an audience with Martin in Rodrigo's absence with qualms or matters of business, a smithy toiled away at his forge and servants hurried here and there to carry out urgent tasks.

Esidero and Gotinus practised in the yard. My heart thumped as they both stopped and glared at me. Gotinus's face was a bruised mess from the sword strike across his face. I expected some sort of abuse or unfavourable greeting, but instead they both offered a curt nod and continued their duel.

'You certainly taught him a lesson,' Auderico said quietly. 'He was getting too big for his boots. I am glad you put him on his behind. It should put him in his place for a while. He might even grow up a little.'

We made our way to the kitchen where we were met with mouth-watering aromas of warm bread and fresh boar roasted in pepper and cumin. The cooks made up two bowls of hot broth with a small loaf of bread each, and a small plate of boar for the priest. We sat in the kitchen and eagerly ate.

'Lord Rodrigo seldom hunts, but Arias loves the thrill of it. If you are lucky, he might take you on one.' Auderico attacked a piece of boar and let the juices dribble down his chin. 'He hunts, and I enjoy the fruits of his labour.'

We spent several moments in silence as we each savoured our meal.

'So why is it a surprise I am here?' I asked.

Father Auderico swallowed the boar and tilted his head. 'How many slaves have you seen in Vivar, Santiago?'

I frowned then thought for a moment. 'Well, none, I suppose.'

'That is because Rodrigo does not keep slaves.'

'All lords keep at least a couple of slaves.' Most lords would keep domestic slaves to work in the household and do the tasks that servants and maids did not, and some kept groups of men to work the fields. My father had had two, one man and a woman. They were treated fairly but were subordinate to all others in his lands and were the recipients of beatings for laziness or shoddy work.

'Not Rodrigo,' Auderico said. 'He does not believe in it. Which begs the question; why are you different? What is your purpose here?'

'Has Rodrigo not told you of my crimes?'

'Only that you were a slave. He did not divulge in the particulars.'

I had not known Auderico long, but I liked him, and he was a priest, so I trusted him. I told him the same tale I had told Sancho, where I had no part in the killing of the pilgrims and only fell in with the bandits for safety. There was a look of shock on his face when I described how the priest had died.

'May I ask you something, in confidence?'

Auderico frowned. 'Of course.'

'Will I go to Hell, for what I have done?'

He leaned forward. 'Have you committed murder?'

'I did not kill the priest, nor did I shed blood on the Camino de Santiago. But yes, I have murdered.'

'Then you are going to Hell. But half the soldiers in the kingdom will be going to Hell once war breaks out, so you will not be alone.'

'War with whom? The Moors?'

'Oh no, God smiles on our efforts to expel the heathens from Hispania. I mean the war between the sons of Fernando. Each son of the king has already been assigned his own county which will become a kingdom once their father dies. Do you think they will all stay allied, uniting to expel the Muslims? Of course not. They will fight to control all the Christian territory north of the Duero, and many men will die, and the land will be plunged in to civil war. But God willing Fernando will not die for years. Peace may endure for a while.'

'I hope I am not dragged in to conflict. I'd prefer to live.'

Auderico grimaced. 'Rodrigo is your new lord and he is bound to Sancho. Wherever the prince goes, Rodrigo will follow. I'd say there is a very good chance you will be going to war. As a slave I expect he will make you do all the menial tasks required on a campaign. Mainly mucking his horses and keeping them fed. He may even send you forth to fight.'

'Is there a way I could gain God's forgiveness?'

'There are ways; you can kill Moors in battle, do public penance, or you can even devote your life to God and become a member of the clergy. Do you feel like joining me in becoming a man of the Lord? We get to eat well.'

'Not yet. I have business to attend to first.'

'What business?' He narrowed his eyes.

'Never mind.' I quickly changed the subject. 'What is it like living here? Rodrigo seems very young to be a lord.'

'He is, but he is one of the better lords around. He inherited this castle around four years ago when his father was executed.'

'Executed?'

'His father was Diego Flaínez.' The vacant expression I gave was enough to indicate I did not know the name. Auderico raised an eyebrow. 'The man who rose against King Fernando?' I shook my head. 'You must have been living under a rock, Santiago! Diego Flaínez was a Leonese lord who held lands in both Leon and Castile. He was given this castle by the king after he helped liberate it from the Navarrese. But with a handful of rebellious lords he conspired to overthrow the king and seize power, before inviting the king's brother Ramiro of Aragon to take the crown of Leon-Castile. The attempt was thwarted, the conspirators executed, and all their lands were seized. Well, except this castle.'

'Why was Vivar not seized?'

'It was Sancho who persuaded his father not to punish Teresa and Rodrigo. The prince had grown fond of Rodrigo when he took him as his squire, saw his potential as a loyal knight, and he respected Teresa too much to simply expel her from her home. And so, Sancho arranged for Arias to take up residence here to act as a mentor to Rodrigo and be the castellan of the castle. Arias once held the castle of Frias to the north east, on the border with Navarre, but he made the mistake of offering refuge to Diego when the fugitive sought sanctuary. Fernando stripped him of his lands for the insult.'

I had heard of the attempted coup from overhearing my father whisper to nearby lords when they came to Lugones, but I did not know the particulars of the situation. By giving Ramiro of Aragon the crown of Leon-Castile, most of the Christian kingdoms in northern Hispania would be united. But it seemed folly to attempt to dispose Fernando, for he was a popular and powerful king who was generous to his loyal subjects, and Diego Flaínez seemed to have had good land throughout the kingdom. Why would he throw it away for the king of Aragon whom he owed nothing to?

'Is that why Arias is always angry,' I asked, 'because he lost his lands?'

Auderico chewed loud as he thought. 'To an extent, yes. There are other reasons I shall not delve in to. But anger is what makes Arias who he is. Men become warriors under his watch because of his quest for perfection and his constant niggling when his instructions are not followed. But in Rodrigo's absence he maintains the castle and the garrison and can be a generous lord. And I get to stare at Constanza every day. That is worth almost anything else in this world.' He gave a sheepish grin as his cheeks blushed.

'She is very pretty.'

'Pretty?' he exclaimed. 'She is a thing of beauty, proof God is good to us mortals, that he may send such a sweet angel to live amongst us!'

'A lot of people seem…wary of her.'

'And rightly so, given that Arias is her father. I'd be careful with her if I were you.'

'Why?'

'I have seen the way she looks at you.'

I stopped eating and stared at Auderico. 'Is that a good or bad thing?'

havery good,' he giggled. 'She is a flirty one, and she likes to toy with men because of her father. I think it gives her satisfaction to see them squirm under his glaring eye. She is still virgin and that makes men more eager. The look she gives them is meant to entice then disappoint. But with you...she looks at you with curiosity and intrigue. I'd watch out if I was you.'

'But I am a slave. Slaves do not wed highborn ladies. If I even looked at her Arias would cut my manhood off.'

'He'd do worse than that. But God works in mysterious ways, and if it is indeed His will then perhaps you will have a future with her. Even a grievous sinner like you might find some luck.'

Life within the walls of Vivar was not as bad as I had anticipated. After my exploits against Gotinus, Rodrigo had me moved to a small room of my own with nothing but a heap of straw and a blanket, yet it was more than I deserved. He claimed it was because winter approached and the winds howled from the mountains to send a chill that froze the ground and brought blankets of snow, so it was unsuitable for me to stay in the goat pen. I had hoped proving myself against Gotinus would change his opinion of me, but he would still frown and make sarcastic retorts.

Despite being a slave, I surprisingly struck up a friendship with Father Auderico which flourished, and I visited him in his chambers whenever I could. There was a lot of Father Santiago in him; he was kind, he always had time for me, despite me being a slave, and he sat and talked to me about tales from the Bible or events from history that fascinated me. I marvelled at the books on the shelves, desperate to take one, but it would go against the lies I had spun to conceal my identity. As far as Rodrigo was concerned, I was a peasant and an orphan who had not had the luxury of an education. I had to play the part lest my identity was revealed, and I still feared the same fate as my father. Instead I let Auderico read passages to me and he promised he would teach me to read, if Rodrigo permitted it. My new lord declined time and time again.

I never forget who I really was. I reminisced about my family at all times, but as the days went by my father's face slowly distorted so I could not remember it as clearly as I once did. Even Inigo's smug expression faded away. I had loved my brother but could not truly forgive him for the atrocities he had committed. But it did not stop me missing him and my father. It had been over six months since he died, long months of hardship and heart ache and grief that had slowly began to heal. I knew part of the grief would stay with me forever, but that would only serve to fuel my desire to seek vengeance on Azarola.

I had not forgotten his arrogant mug, with his pig nose and smirk. Every night his visage haunted my dreams and I renewed my vow to avenge the death of my father. I wanted to make him scream in agony as I twisted a sword in to his belly, to watch the blood flow from the wound and smile as the life ebbed from his flailing body. Only then would I find some sort of peace, and perhaps I could start on a path of redemption to cleanse my soul for the sins I had committed and start a new life somewhere. I wanted a wife, I wanted sons and daughters and a home to call my own where I could live in tranquillity, away from the horrors of the world and to die in peace. But such a world was only possible after I had my revenge, and it had to start with Azarola's death.

Months of hard labour took its toll on me, but I grew stronger and fitter from the hours of mucking out the horses, cleaning armour, emptying the privies, hauling firewood, serving and cleaning dishes in the hall, and the hundred other tasks given to me. The first snows of winter settled on the ground and our breaths fogged before our eyes. The low sun brought darker days, and a blanket of mist shrouded the plains of Hispania and masked the tips of the mountains. It was a time when I welcomed the hard work, just to stay warm.

It was late one afternoon, and I shovelled frozen piles of horse shit from the stables when Arias came to me. I stopped my work and stiffened at his presence.

'We are going on a hunt tomorrow. Lord Rodrigo has grown bored this winter and desires to shed some blood.'

'We?'

'You will be coming as well. You will carry our spears.'

'I look forward to it, lord.' Of course, I did not. If anything, a hunt in the freezing cold, potentially gored by a boar was not something that filled me with enthusiasm.

'Good! I will try not to throw you off your horse and leave you out there this time. The cold might kill you before you returned. And I was ordered not to kill you, after all.'

'That is generous of you, lord,' I said calmly.

Arias frowned and took a step forward. 'Are you mocking me?'

'No lord,' I replied, held his gaze. He looked for an excuse to start a rant. It was a trait I had noticed more often since I had arrived. According to Martin such a reaction was common in the autumn and winter months, when the armies of Hispania disbanded to gather the harvests and hibernate from the cold. Fighting in the harsh winds and biting frost was folly. Arias was a hot-blooded warrior who loved battle, and idleness irked him to the core. Hunting was one of the ways he could satiate his lust for blood.

Arias, satisfied I had not mocked him, gave a nod.

'Good. Go to Gonzalo and collect the spears, then make sure the horses are well fed tonight. Get a good night's sleep. We leave at dawn.'

'Yes lord.'

Arias returned to his chambers as I finished with the horses and trudged across the courtyard towards the blacksmith hut. A voice called to me from the chapel.

'Santiago.'

Constanza stood by the door, wrapped in a long white cloak hemmed with grey wolf fur. Her chestnut hair was pinned high and covered with a white headdress, and her vibrant green eyes stood out in the bleak wintery conditions.

185

'Good afternoon, lady,' I said with a slight smile and a bow of the head.

'You are looking well. I can see a bit of meat on your bones now,' she said with a soft smile. 'My father's rigorous ways are doing better than harm, it would seem.'

'I have learnt not to shy away from hard work. I will admit it's nice not to feel like a skinny runt anymore.' She giggled. 'Your father has asked me to collect his spears and prepare for the hunt tomorrow. I am to accompany him.'

'How exciting!' she beamed. 'My father is yet to allow me on a hunt, but I'd love to go along one time. There's something satisfying in seeing men bringing home a big pig in triumph or felling a graceful deer. Women are not allowed to hunt, but I'd love to try my hand at it one time. Did you know I am rather good at handling a spear?'

'Really?'

'Oh yes. I like to run my hands down the shaft and squeeze it tight, feel the power within.' She narrowed her eyes and enacted a provocative hand movement. 'And I love the way they are thrust repeatedly, strong and firm and relentless. It brings me such pleasure. I'd be happy to show you my techniques, if you're lucky.'

I opened my mouth to reply but no words came. She pouted and raised her eyebrows, expected some sort of flirty comment, I imagine, but I just stood there, gormless.

'What...do you mean?'

'Oh, come on, Santiago,' she giggled. 'You must have been with a woman?' I shook my head, much to Constanza's astonishment. 'Well, we will have to change that. Come to my chambers tonight and I will show my spear craft.'

She gave me a wink. I felt my face flush a deep shade of crimson, so I turned and hurried out of sight. Constanza called after me but I did not pay attention, only stopped when I was safely inside the blacksmith's workshop, ducked behind a rack of weapons which scattered across the floor when I bumped in to it. I cursed and picked them up.

'Clumsy idiot.'

Gonzalo the smith stopped his work and stared at me. He was tall, broad and strong as an ox with a black goatee and a shaved head that glistened with sweat from the hours he toiled at his forge. He looked like a giant and was not one to mess with in a quarrel, but his heart was gentle and his smile genuine.

'I am sorry,' I said, trying to figure out which weapon went where on the rack. Gonzalo grimaced, put his tools down and helped me stack them.

'Something spooked you?'

'It's nothing, honestly,' I insisted. I picked up a long sword and studied it as I figured out where it went. The steel was polished to a gleam, the blade light and well forged.

'I would wager you'd like a sword like that. Most men do.'

'I am a slave. I am not afforded the luxury of a weapon.'

Gonzalo grunted. 'I see. If you ever are then pay me a visit. My steel is the best in the kingdom.'

Judging by the quality of the arms on display it may well have been true.

'Lord Arias wants spears for a hunt tomorrow.'

Gonzalo grunted, wiped his grubby hands against his apron and crossed to a bundle of weapons propped against the wall.

I hefted the spears on to my shoulder and winced under their unexpected weight. There were five of them, shorter but heavier than a normal spear, with two small bars jutting out below the blade to prevent the quarry, once skewered, from working its way down the shaft to attack the hunter. Boars were fierce and would fight on even when severely wounded, so any advantage to pin the beast in place before a killing blow could be dealt was welcome.

We departed in the dawn when the frost clung to the ground and patches of mist hung in the air. Pink rays of sunlight crowned the streaking cloud overhead. There were around fifty of us, our numbers swelled by a pair of lesser lords from neighbouring castles named Enrique and Belliti, who brought their own squires, servants and trackers to add to our own. We headed north from the castle and arced to the east, to the slopes of the densely wooded hills where game was reportedly plentiful. The land was peaceful as the low sun peaked over the mountains far to the east, with no movement on the plains or in the forests. Snow covered trees lined the hills and reminded me of Monte Naranco as it loomed over Lugones and Oviedo, and I wondered if I would ever return to my home.

Rodrigo had sent a small baggage train ahead the previous day, and plumes of smoke rose from the cooking fires between the clusters of tents that had already been erected. The lords feasted on a fresh rabbit stew and warm flat bread to warm their innards before we prepared to head in to the forest. The trackers were already far ahead, scouting game.

'Who is that?' Enrique said to Rodrigo in between mouthfuls of food. He was tall and broad with short black hair, and squinty eyes that darted around and took everything in. I unloaded gear and prepared the horses as Rodrigo turned and scowled at me and made sure I could hear every word.

'This is Santiago Iniguez, a gift from Sancho. He is my slave.'

'I heard rumours about this one,' Enrique said as he brushed crumbs from his beard, before he pointed at me. 'News of his atrocities came to Burgos at the end of the summer. Allegedly, he gutted some pilgrims on the Camino de Santiago. And if that was not enough, he stripped them, threw them in a grave and pissed on their corpses before they were cold.'

'To my knowledge the bodies have never been found,' Rodrigo frowned. 'Besides, do you believe he is capable of something like that?' The last comment surprised me. I was convinced Rodrigo believed I was guilty. 'He was a runt when he came to Vivar, but with a bit of discipline and hard work, and Arias barking in his ear, he is getting some meat of his bones. He managed to knock Gotinus on his arse after being out in the wild for a few days when he first came to me, which is no easy feat. He may look like a miserable little shit, but he's got some fight in him, that's for sure.'

'Let us test him against a boar and see how he fares,' Belliti sniggered.

Within the hour we traversed the forest, guided our horses around fallen logs between the pockets of trees. The air was bitter, and frost clung to the bark of the oaks and sycamores, but I wore a long green cloak lined with wolf fur to keep the worst of the chill away. In my hand I carried one of the hunting spears with another two strapped to my back. The only sounds were the thud of hooves on the undergrowth, their heavy snorting of horses and the gentle chatter of men as they jested and traded news and stories.

We had marched a mile or so when two trackers returned through the trees, and the knights gathered around them.

'There's a nest of boars not far ahead, home to a big beauty and a couple of its offspring,' one of the trackers said. 'A narrow track leads to a clearing where she has made her nest.'

Arias turned to Rodrigo. 'Do I have your permission to have this one, lord?'

'Even if I said no you would not listen.'

Arias grinned. 'There will be others around, lord. I will even serve you the first cut of the meat myself tonight.'

The other knights nodded their agreement and settled their men, left us to stalk ahead. We wound through the trees, steady and silent like wolves. The forest was eerily quiet save for the crunch of fresh snow under our horses' hooves, and the bitter air nipped at our cheeks.

The tracker crouched low and waved at us to dismount.

'Just through there, lord.'

Arias passed me the reins of his horse, which I tied to a tree as he joined the tracker in in the undergrowth. Arias whistled.

'She is a beauty,' he grinned. My view was concealed by trees and undergrowth, but I could hear the rustle and grunts of the beast. He snapped his gaze to me and held out a hand. 'Spear.'

I held out the weapon and he snatched it before he stalked forward and waited at the edge of the undergrowth.

'Nobody delivers the killing blow but me,' he hissed. 'Pen the beast in and make sure it does not get away, but do not harm it. Know that there are consequences for coming between me and my prize.'

Without warning Arias darted through the undergrowth and out to in the clearing. The other knights and their squires leapt after him, as did the tracker, but when I tried to follow, I tripped on a fallen log concealed by snow. The wind was knocked from me, pain shot through my chest and the snow numbed my face. I lay there for a moment, let the pain subside and allowed my breath to return before got to my feet, only to realise I was alone.

Frantic footsteps, the shouts of men and the shrieks of the boar sounded from all around me. I scanned the trees for any sign of movement but there was nothing, only noises that softened and intensified with every passing second. The source moved off to my left, so I grabbed one of Arias's spare spears on my back, threw the other down and headed off, kept low but moved swift, tried to keep pace with the chase. I ducked under branches and hopped over logs, but my quarry was always out of sight. I stopped and paused as I regained bearings and caught my breath, but everything was quiet, still. I gripped the spear tighter in my hands. The silence was unnerving.

A monstrous black shadow emerged from my right and I had barely enough time to spin before it crashed in to me. The force of the blow knocked me off my feet and I landed in a heap. A snap in my right leg had me screaming in agony. I lifted my head to see the behemoth before me, larger than any boar I had ever seen, covered in thick black hair and with long tusks protruding from its maw. A trail of blood seeped from a wound in the boar's side which served only to fuel the beast's rage, and it turned and stared and snorted at me. I could taste my own blood in my mouth, sickly and sweet, and more trickled from a gash in my tunic where a tusk pierced my side. The beast must have been frenzied by its wound and seemed intent on killing anything in its path. Including me.

The ground shook as it thundered forward. I fought through the pain and brought the spear round, pointed it at the incoming boar as it shrieked, and I screamed. The beast slammed in to the metal blade and jolted my arms as it vaulted in to the air, impaled on the spear through its mid riff. A light snow began to fall, and I heard the cries of men in the distance. My heart stopped as the boar hung on the end of the spear. It squealed and flailed. My arms lost their strength. I let go of the spear shaft and the boar crashed on top of me.

I felt nothing but pain, and everything faded to black.

*   *   *

My body burned in a distorted realm. Muffled voices, blurred figures and spectres manifested in a shadow world. Demons haunted my mind, and when I tried to run from them my limbs froze, and the pain was like a thousand daggers stabbing in unison. My screams only served to intensify the glee of the demons as they rejoiced at my suffering. This was Hell. The face of the Devil himself appeared before my eyes, only it was the smirking visage of Azarola with horns protruding from his head and razor-sharp teeth, and he laughed as I burned and fell forever in to a fire. God had forsaken me, and I prayed for death.

But God truly does work in mysterious ways. Justice dictated I would die for my sins and be sent to Hell. The boar was monstrous in size and should have killed me but, strangely, God decided to spare my life. For what purpose I was not sure of, yet I was determined to take hold of my new lease of life and repent for my sins. My first task was to get away from Rodrigo, Arias and Vivar, and forge my own destiny.

The pain slowly subsided and a light appeared. My eyes opened to see a wooden roof, the planks old, gnarled and familiar. Candlelight filled the room and I stared at the corner where the shadows danced. I

191

expected to see a demon glaring at me but there was nothing there, just a pale orange glow flickering here and there. A faint scraping pricked my ears and I turned my head to see Father Auderico sat at a desk next to a window with the shutters closed. He squinted as he dipped a quill in a small pot of ink and wrote on a piece of vellum with concentration embedded on his face.

The sound of my groans caught his attention and his beaming smile greeted me.

'Welcome back, Santiago!' He placed his quill on the desk and crossed over to the bed. 'It is a blessing to see you awake again. These charters are murder to my eyes in this candlelight, so it is a welcome relief to take my focus from them. I am beginning to think you will be a permanent fixture in my infirmary.'

'It is not my desire to be in here.' I tried to sit but screamed as pain flared in my torso and the right side of my body.

'Do not move! You are very ill and will harm yourself even more if you try to get up.'

'What happened to me?' I winced.

'You faced a boar and won, though it did not go down without a fight. Several of your ribs are shattered, and your right knee and lower leg are broken as well, so we have had to secure them.' I looked to see two wooden boards secured by strong, thin ropes, which kept my shattered leg stiff. 'You developed a fever too, but the worst of it has died down. There's been a bit less screaming on a night. You're lucky to be alive and well.'

I did not feel lucky. All I felt was excruciating pain.

'I...killed the boar?'

'That you did. And may I say thank you, because it tasted delicious.' Auderico smacked his lips and grinned. 'Although between you and me, Arias was not best pleased. He wanted the glory for himself.'

'No. He is not best pleased.'

Auderico stiffened and turned to see Arias stood in the doorway.

192

His footsteps echoed through the chamber as he loomed over the priest's shoulder and stared at me. His eyes moved along my body, taking in the extent of my wounds.

'Most men would have died being bowled over by a boar of that size. But you just refuse to die.' His tone was cold, and he sounded disappointed.

'I am not ready to go to Hell yet, lord.'

Arias seemed amused. 'As long as you serve Rodrigo you will be put through hell every day. I will make you sweat and bleed and your muscles burn. Make sure he gets back on his feet as soon as he is able,' he said to Auderico. 'I want him back to his duties as soon as he is healed.'

'Yes lord.'

Arias's intense glare unnerved me.

'You took my prize away from me. I do not forget such injustices.'

As Arias left Auderico breathed a sigh of relief.

'Could you give me something to slow down the healing process?' I asked. 'Break a few more of bones if you have to.'

Auderico let out a nervous laugh. 'With all due respect, Santiago, if I did that, I think I'd be in your position by the time Arias was done with me.'

The healing process was long and arduous. There were only so many hours of the day Auderico could sit and write his charters next to me and keep me company or read passages from books to pass the time. I craved to be given one to read myself but knew it was impossible. My new master did not visit, but surprisingly Martin checked in on me several times and told me the gossip of the castle, even being as kind as to sneak apples and some almonds from the stores. But his visits were rare and so I had to be content with my own thoughts as I plotted my escape from Vivar, hatched a plan to find Azarola and kill him and fulfil my quest for revenge. Each plan ended in death, imprisonment or, worse still, with me in Azarola's clutches.

Two months passed before I was able to get out of bed, and even then, I had to use two sticks to help me walk about, since my leg had not fully healed. I did not go far, just to sit in the church and stare at the beautiful stained-glass depictions of scenes from the bible. I braved the wintry world for some fresh air, and to see the faint sun in the sky, before the cold forced me back to the warmth of my bed.

I felt liberated when the boards were finally taken off my leg. I eased the weight on to it and was relieved when I felt no pain, just a little stiffness. I walked around the courtyard of the castle to get used to being on my feet again and some of the servants seemed pleased to see me. An old guard even congratulated me on killing the boar, which I was sure would irk Arias, but luckily, he was not within earshot. I did not see him or Rodrigo that day, or the day after, and a part of me hoped they had forgotten about me, but soon enough one of Rodrigo's men came to the infirmary when the sky outside was black as ink, the moon full and a bitter wind howled through the corridors, and ordered me to Rodrigo's chambers.

I hobbled without delay. He must have heard I was back on my feet and wanted me to come to him instead of him making the effort to visit his slave. I pulled a cloak around my frame a little tighter as I entered the keep, climbed the spiral staircase to the top floor and found his chambers deserted. An oil lamp burned on the desk and several candles gently illuminated the room from a pair of iron stands. It was larger than the other chambers in the keep; the bed was ornately carved with wolves' heads on the corners of the headboards, a heavy chest sat at its base, and a weapons rack with two swords and a short knife sat in the corner, along with a mannequin which held his gleaming mail and conical helm. The shutters to the windows were closed but a chill clung to the air. I took a seat at Rodrigo's desk to relieve my aching leg and waited.

On the desk was a silver jug of wine and several goblets beside a pile of parchment. Casting my eyes over the scribble I saw one was lists of men in the garrison of the castle, another list with the names of the squires, and a half-written letter. I thought nothing of them at first, but my interested was piqued when I noticed my name on the letter. Curious, I held it to the candle light to read the contents.

It was a report on my presence in Vivar, but who the intended recipient was unclear. It mentioned my hardships and the fact I had spent more time in the infirmary than being any use as a slave. I squinted in the scant light to try and decipher the last few lines, but I did not get chance to read the full page.

'An orphaned wretch who knows how to fight and, it seems, to read.'

I span to see Rodrigo stood in the doorway, glaring at me. He stepped in to the room with Arias behind him, a look of distain on his face.

'I was just looking,' I said without conviction, let go of the letter. It drifted off the edge of the table and settled on the floor. 'I do not know what any of it says.'

'Liar!' Arias growled. 'We have been watching you for more than a few moments. You have been reading things that do not concern you.'

'Did Auderico defy my orders?' Rodrigo said. 'Did he teach you how to read?'

'No.'

'I will gouge out his eyes and make a damned martyr of him for this.'

'He had no part in it. I already knew how to read!'

A frown appeared on their faces and they looked at each other. 'I knew there was something about you,' Rodrigo said. 'Ever since that day with Gotinus…bandits do not fight the way you do, and they do not teach each other how to read. Tell me who you are.'

'I am Santiago Iniguez de Gijon, lord.'

Rodrigo stepped forward and glared at me, spoke in a cold tone. 'Do you know what will happen to me if I defy Sancho's orders and kill you? Nothing. I will be reprimanded but nothing will come of it. I will still be a knight of the realm and lord of Vivar, and you will be rotting in a ditch. Now tell me who you are.'

'I am Santiago Iniguez…'

Arias marched forward and struck me across the face. The blow knocked me in to the table and I cried out as the pain flared in my ribs once more, and fresh blood trickled from my mouth. Pieces of parchment fell from the table top and fluttered around the room as Arias hauled me up and grabbed me by the throat. I gasped for air and beat my hands on his strong arm as he squeezed hard.

'Do not lie to your lord, wretch. Who are you?'

'Santiago Iniguez,' I gasped.

Arias roared as he threw me against the wall. The pain was unbearable, and tears welled in my eyes as I felt the agony in my ribs and leg. Arias drew his long sword in one swift movement, stared me down with the blade poised in his hand. I looked to Rodrigo with eyes pleading for mercy, but the young knight's expression was like stone. He nodded at Arias.

'This is your last chance,' Arias seethed. 'Your lord demands you tell him who you are.' He towered over me and I cowered on the floor in his shadow. When I hesitated, he drew back the sword, ready to strike. 'WHO ARE YOU?' he roared.

'I am Antonio Perez de Lugones!' I screamed. The sword stroke never came. 'I am the son of Pedro Valdez. I am not from Gijon; I am from Lugones near Oviedo. My father is dead, my brother is dead, and my mother and sisters are captive. Everything I once had is gone. This last year I have known nothing but misery and pain, and I cannot take any more of it. If you want to kill me then go ahead and do it. Just kill me!' I curled in to a ball and sobbed like a child, expected the blow to come and finish me off.

But none came. Just silence.

I lifted my head to see Arias stood there, a look of shock now on his pale face. He took a step towards me and leaned forward, as if to study me closer.

196

'You are Pedro's boy?' Rodrigo asked. He was wide eyed as he stepped towards me.

'Yes, I am,' I said cautiously. 'But I am no traitor. *He* was no traitor.'

'I know.'

It was my turn to look at the pair of them in disbelief. Arias crouched before me, studied every inch of my face. He laid the sword down.

'My God, you have his eyes,' he whispered. There was something discernibly different about both men's demeanour. Rodrigo offered me his hand. I hesitated, puzzled by the sudden change in behaviour, before letting him haul me to my feet. He helped me to his bed before he crossed to his table and poured a goblet of wine, drained it in one before he filled it again.

'So…you are not going to kill me?'

Rodrigo's eyes flashed to mine above the rim of his goblet, dark and full of emotion. He poured a second goblet, and then a third, before he handed one to Arias and, surprisingly, to me too.

The young knight sat on the chair and leaned forward. 'No, Antonio. What you have just told us changes everything. Tell us how you got here. Tell us everything.'

'How can I trust you?'

'Because I owe your father my life,' Arias said as he sat on the edge of the table.

'And we have more things in common that you think,' Rodrigo added.

There was nothing to lose.

Seeing no alternative, I told them everything.

Nine

'We fought beside your father at Graus, and he saved my life.'

Those were the first words Arias had uttered in a while. I had recounted my tale and he and Rodrigo sat there and took in every word, every detail. He drank another draught of his wine and filled the goblet. Rodrigo listened intently with a solid, unflinching demeanour. It was late now, and a servant had brought a platter of fruit and bread, though none of us had an appetite, and a fresh jug of wine. It was a strange but welcome luxury, given what I had been through.

I stared at him as he continued. 'I and a few of the men were unhorsed by missiles and were surrounded. A knight came at me with his spear levelled at my head, but before he could reach me Pedro lead his small band of knights to head them off and caught him in the neck. Your father was untouchable that day,' he said passionately. 'God graced him with a strong sword arm and courage beyond any of us. It was his destiny to kill King Ramiro. He did not deserve what happened to him next.'

'Why did he die? What was he really arrested for?'

'The king and his allies will argue treason and theft, but there is an underlying reason behind it. Jealousy.'

'I do not understand.'

'Azarola's jealousy,' Rodrigo spat.

'You know Azarola?'

'The whole kingdom knows who Azarola is,' Arias continued. 'I have the pleasure of being acquainted more than others.' I raised my eyebrows as he swirled the wine around his goblet. 'Azarola is my brother by marriage. He is married to my sister, Beatriz.'

My jaw dropped. 'And are you on...friendly terms?'

'*Friendly terms?*' Arias frowned and leaned forward. 'I loathe that piece of shit. He has the favour of the king after he saved his life at Atapuerca a decade ago and uses it to his advantage whenever he can. He has become nothing but a lapdog for Alfonso. I should have gutted that cretin a long time ago,' he growled through gritted teeth.

'What has he done to offend you?'

'He beats my sister and treats her like a possession!' he slammed a fist on the table, made me flinch. Rodrigo must have known for he did not react to the flash of anger. 'My father thought the match would be beneficial to the kingdom; a Castilian noblewoman joined together with a Leonese knight. "It will increase our prestige in court," he used to say. "The king will look kindly on those who buy in to his unification of all the Christian kingdoms of Hispania." There were other candidates, better suitors with honour and good land, but Azarola is a member of the Beni Gómez, one of the most powerful clans in Leon.

'Their leader is Pedro Ansúrez,' Rodrigo added, 'and he just so happens to be a childhood companion of Alfonso. Collectively they hold much of the land in central and southern Leon. They are prolific in the court of the king and in his ear, able to influence policy and remove their rivals from the court with a few poisonous words. It's not the first time Azarola has disposed of his enemies,' Rodrigo put in. I raised an eyebrow. 'My father was his first victim.'

'But your father plotted against the king,' I frowned.

'He did not such thing,' he snapped back. 'He was loyal to the Fernando, but the Beni Gómez have had grievance with the Flaínez for generations. Azarola used his influence to smash the power of the Flaínez around Leon once and for all. Like Arias said, all he and his supporters had to do was conjure a lie that threatened the king and Fernando did the rest. In return Azarola received all the confiscated territory and handed it out to members of his clan. If unchecked, there is no limit to what he can achieve. There is a reason Bernardo's father give him the moniker Azarola – it comes from the Vascon word for fox. It fits his persona perfectly; sly, cunning and elusive.'

I squeezed my hands in to fists as anger boiled within me, enraged that my father was not the first victim of Azarola's scheming ways.

I turned to Arias. 'You were punished because you offered refuge to Diego's men.'

Arias frowned. 'How did you know that?'

'Father Auderico.'

Arias rolled his eyes. 'Damned priest has a mouth on him. But yes, I did, and I was stripped of my land and title for it. Diego was a friend of mine and I was appalled when I discovered his fate, and I am forever grateful to Teresa for offering refuge for my wife and daughter, to find a purpose once more. Some of the men who served Diego now serve his son. Loyal knights to the end, unlike Azarola and the Beni Gómez. They are snakes, and Alfonso sees him as an asset. When Fernando dies and his sons take their own kingdoms, Azarola will be an enemy of mine.'

'So why was Azarola jealous of my father?'

'Arias was not the only man your father saved at Graus,' Rodrigo said. 'Azarola challenged Ramiro himself, and the Aragonese king bested him and threw him to the ground. But that is when your father dealt him the killing blow. He saved Azarola from death, and for that he paid for it with his life.

'When Pedro was chosen to collect the *parias* from Saraqusta Azarola conspired with members of al-Muqtadir's court. Personal items of the amir were planted within the *parias* tribute and ended up in the possession of your father, and Azarola was the one who led the king's men to arrest him.' The image of my father being dragged out of the keep at Lugones with the Moorish sword and helmet came in to my mind. 'Naturally Fernando and al-Muqtadir were infuriated and tensions rose between the two, but the men who once lavished Pedro with praise poured condemnation on him. So, your father and uncle died and Azarola raised his stock in the eyes of the king.'

My initial thoughts were proven right; my father had been caught in a conspiracy to sully his name and wipe away the glory that had once been bestowed upon him. I was sickened. I was not an angry boy, but I had to clench my fists to supress my temper.

'How do you know all this?'

'My sister sent me a letter detailing it all,' Arias said. 'He confessed it all to her one night, drunk and arrogant, before he...' Arias went quiet and a rage rose inside of him as he gripped his goblet tight. He took a deep breath as the anger dissipated. 'Like I said, he beats her. But she sent this letter to me in trust, to prove the kind of man he was. We shared it with Sancho, and he believes it too, but the king dismissed any talk of it and condemned your father even more. His mind is made up. Such is the poison Azarola has spat in to his ear.'

'Somebody needs to put a stop to Azarola's games,' I growled.

Rodrigo narrowed his eyes at me. 'In the aftermath of your father's death you plotted to kill him, did you not?'

'Yes. It was Inigo's original plan. We were to travel to Dueñas and burn the castle down. But ultimately it does not matter how it happens. I want revenge. My father should never have died.'

'We will help you,' Rodrigo said.

I was taken aback by the abrupt statement, and even Arias frowned at Rodrigo. 'You would be willing to kill Azarola, despite the dangers you have just claimed, with his standing in the court of the king?' I exclaimed.

'If it means I can avenge my father as you seek to avenge yours then yes, I will do what was necessary.'

'I want him to feel the same pain I have felt every day this past year,' I said through gritted teeth, felt tears brim in my eyes. 'He destroyed my world; I want to bring his crashing down.'

Arias set his goblet down and folded his arms. 'Have either of you even set eyes upon Dueñas? It is a formidable fortress, and the king would hang you both for murdering a lord in cold blood, especially one with as much influence and as many supporters as Azarola. It is an impossible task, suicide in fact. You would not even get close to him.'

'Then what do you suggest?' I snapped unexpectedly. 'Should we let him get away with his antics? He needs to be punished!'

'We wait and bide our time, conjure a plan,' Rodrigo put in.

'For how long?'

'Until Fernando dies, and we find a way we can do this properly.' I gave Rodrigo sceptical look. 'Sancho and Alfonso may be brothers, but they have no love for each other. They know what they will inherit when their father dies, and they already want more. Eventually there will be a war between Castile and Leon. And when war does come Azarola will be our enemy. You can face him on the battlefield, and you can kill him without any repercussions, no fear of reprimand.'

I gave a bitter laugh at the suggestion. 'I cannot fight! I can barely swing a sword.'

'So you will become my squire.' Arias said. The statement caught me off guard and I sat in silence. 'I will show you how to fight. Many of the other boys here are cretins. You are the son of a true knight. When you beat Gotinus you showed great technique and skill and, most importantly, determination. That cannot be taught.'

'But look at me. I do not have the physique for combat.'

Arias sniggered. 'Antonio, turning boys in to men is what I am known for. Give me a year and you will be better than your brother ever was. Pedro told me Inigo had the makings of a true knight, one who was destined for great things.'

'He was,' I nodded in agreement. 'He was fated for a good life and I have no doubt he would have been a hero, but evil consumed his heart. He deserved the death you gave him.'

My gaze flashed to Rodrigo. He looked at me with eyes unnerved by the comment. Rodrigo knew he had done his duty by the king and by God by slicing open my brother's throat. I did not look upon my master with scorn. Part of me wanted to thank him.

'Make your father proud,' Rodrigo said as he leaned forward. 'Inherit the same zeal and passion the men of your family fought with. Become who you were born to be and restore his honour. Together, we will kill Azarola.'

I nodded and made a silent vow to see it done.

Rodrigo smiled and patted me on the shoulder as he finished the last of his wine. 'Good lad. I hope I can make Pedro proud and avenge him as much as you. Finish your drink and get back to your bed. When you are fully healed the hard work begins.'

'Hard work?'

Rodrigo looked at Arias, who nodded back to him then smiled at me.

'We are going to turn you in to a knight.'

* * *

It was a relief to be a slave no longer. Rodrigo looked at me in a different light, talked to me in a softer tone with no hint of hostility. And he treated me as a guest in the final days of my recovery, saw I was well looked after and catered for. He even allowed Father Auderico to give me one of his favourite books to pass the time; titled "The Song of Hroudland", it told the death of a Frank who served a great king called Charlemagne, who tried to invade the *taifa* of Saraqusta. After years of war Charlemagne accepted Saraqusta's surrender and marched back over the Pyrenees to his homeland, but the Moors chased him and slaughtered his rear guard, led by his nephew Hroudland, who died heroically. Auderico said it inspired Rodrigo to become a better knight, and I would do well to learn from its meaning. I decided it was best to learn how to fight before I learned about the qualities of being a knight.

The change in Arias's attitude went some way to showing how much he respected my father. There was none of his scornful looks or comments, and though I still served as the cup bearer he did not work me as hard as he once did. And all the while he talked more about Azarola, told me all he knew about him and made my hate for him fester evermore inside me.

The ancient ancestral home of my nemesis was the castle of Dueñas, located near Palencia, an important city which had been the seat of a bishopric since the time of the Visigoths. He was the cousin to the Bishop Bernardo of Palencia and held influence over the city, which had slowly expanded to the court of King Fernando. His castle on the banks of the river Pisuerga had recently been rebuilt to incorporate a larger keep and the stout stone walls of the town could repulse a great army. Hardened knights and militia tracked down Moorish raiding parties who crossed the Duero looking for plunder. He also had a son named Pelayo, who was named after the old King Pelayo of Asturias who fought against the Moors, and though Arias was reluctant to admit it he described Pelayo as a fine young man, handsome and charismatic, who would look to emulate his father's achievements.

I realised how pathetic Inigo's idea to kill Azarola had been. How could three young men virgin to battle sneak in to the castle of one of the most powerful lords of Leon and look to kill him in his own surroundings? Part of me was glad our venture had ended on the Camino de Santiago, and my brother and cousin were dead. If I was still with them, I would not have found service with Rodrigo, a man I now considered a valuable ally and a just lord, who had the means to help me. For the first time in a long while I felt happy. God truly does work in mysterious ways.

The snows continued to fall heavy and the days were dark by the time I was fully recovered. I had settled in to a new room of my own within the keep where a brazier burned away, and the flames swayed in the draught when Constanza's slender frame appeared in the doorway.

'Good morning, Antonio Perez.'

'Your father told you then?'

'Yes.' She stepped towards me and spoke in a remorseful tone. 'I wanted to say I am sorry for your loss. I cannot imagine what you have been through. I pray for the souls of your father and brother, and for the safety of your mother and sisters, wherever they may be. God will keep them safe. You must miss them.'

'Thank you, my lady. You are most kind.' I took a deep breath to suppress the feelings of grief that threatened to pour forth once more.

'You have friends here now. Know you are no longer alone.'

'I have felt alone my whole life. I never felt as though I fit in with anyone in my family. My father and Inigo were so alike, I so different. Now the only two people who I trusted in my life are gone.'

'Your brother and cousin?'

Though they were my family and companions for much of our ordeal I did not trust them, especially after the bloodshed and misery they had caused.

'I speak of my old teacher, Father Santiago, was killed when Azarola's men sacked our castle. And my only friend, Jimena…I let her down. I do not know if she would ever forgive me, should we meet again.'

'You will find her, and if she needs to forgive you, she will. Hopefully that day will be sooner rather than later.' She gave a smile. 'Remember, you have friends in Vivar. Do not feel alone ever again.' I gave a smile and curt nod in reply. 'Goodbye Antonio.'

As she walked away, I found myself wondering what it would be like to marry a woman of Constanza's beauty and stock. She would yield good sons and daughters and carry out her duties with gusto. I had to avert my gaze away from her swaying hips to suppress the feelings of arousal that stirred in my loins.

The weeks went by and Arias had me train with the other squires. In that winter I became stronger and faster, honed my fighting ability day after day, duel after duel. I once loathed the idea of fighting, becoming a knight, but now I was motivated to tread the path of the warrior. Whether it was on the battle field or in a dark corridor in some castle, I would kill Azarola.

The last of the snows had melted away when Rodrigo and I prepared to depart Vivar.

'We are going to Burgos,' he declared. 'It is time we met with Sancho and talked about what has happened with you. If he takes pity on you, he may grant you a pardon from your slavery.'

'But Arias has taken me as his squire,' I frowned.

'I have told no one of your identity yet. In the eyes of the crown you are still a slave. Sancho may allow you to be Arias's squire, or he may send you elsewhere, to be a slave for someone else. I will try and persuade him to go down the path of the former, but there are no guarantees.'

'That's reassuring, lord,' I said with a grimace.

We left early in the morning when the sun was low and pale, rode through barren fields dotted with small villages still gripped by the short, cold days. It was no more than an hour when we joined the small trail of traffic and approached from the north, passed under the gateway of the sturdy stone wall that ringed the city.

Burgos was the principal settlement of Castile and formed a crossroads for trade and pilgrimage. The Camino de Santiago passed through the heart of the city, parallel to the river Arlanzón that ran to the south of the city walls and flowed west to join the Pisuerga. The wide streets were lined with hostels, taverns and brothels for pilgrims who travelled to and from Santiago de Compostela, and there seemed to be a church on every street, no matter how large or small. Market stalls flourished with goods coming from the Moorish south or the Christian north, whether they travelled from the Bay of Vizcaya by sea or by road through Francia. As we entered through the northern gate we passed through sizeable Mozarabic and Jewish quarters, and the streets were lined with Jewish and Frankish merchants with their fine wares.

The scallop shell of Santiago hung on pendants around the necks of pilgrims in simple cloaks or robes, while the citizens of Burgos conducted their business in smooth, vibrant silks from Isbiliya and Garnata, or fine woollen garments spun from Castilian wool. The stout stone walls and sturdy militia protected the city from attack. Traders bartered with customers for the best deal, fresh meat spat on spits and roasted in Moorish spices on the street vendor's stalls, and everywhere were banners bearing the golden castle of Castile on a blood red background, or badges with the crest sewn on to the tunics of the soldiers that manned the walls and patrolled the streets. Though the people of Castile were firmly part of a united kingdom with Leon, they liked to remind all who came to their city of their autonomous roots.

Our destination was the palace, which was situated close to the southern gate, overlooked by the castle. It was a fine limestone building in the Visigothic fashion, built by Fernando to be his base when he had become count of Castile, and now the palace was Sancho's, who prepared for the day he would be king of Castile by acting as governor. The guards, recognising Rodrigo, waved us through to the palace complex. We found ourselves in a large square with a grand hall before us, surrounded on the peripheries by smaller halls and buildings connected by galleries. Scribes, administrators and officials buzzed and weaved around the palace as petitioners began to filter through to the main hall. We dismounted and left our horses by the stables near the entrance before Rodrigo scanned the plaza and, without warning, marched towards three men who laughed and jested as they made their way towards the hall.

'Lord,' Rodrigo called.

Sancho turned and frowned at first but waved us over. Beside him was a man of slighter height and stature. He had a crop of bushy mahogany hair and large eyes under a great frown when he saw us, but the thing that struck me was the cleft lip that blighted his handsome face. The other man I did not know but took him for some official. He was tall and wore a white tunic trimmed in gold.

'Who are they?' I whispered.

'The ugly bastard is Garcia Ordóñez,' Rodrigo hissed as we drew closer. 'His father Ordoño once served as *alferez* to Fernando. Garcia resides in the castle of Pancorbo to the east, which was the gateway to Castile from Navarre and Francia. He's a powerful man, not to be crossed. The other man is Vermundo, the seneschal of the palace.'

'Welcome, Rodrigo.' Sancho called warmly. 'To what do I owe this pleasure?' He noticed me stood behind and narrowed his eyes. 'So, has this cretin finally come to do penance?'

'We need to speak in private, lord.' Rodrigo looked at Sancho, then to Garcia and then Vermundo.

'Anything you want to say will be said now,' the prince said, straightened his powerful frame. Rodrigo was taken aback by Sancho's abrupt nature but held his nerve.

'Did you know who he is?' he motioned to me. 'Who he *really* is?'

Sancho narrowed his eyes. 'If I recall he is Santiago Iniguez...'

'He is Antonio Perez, son of Pedro Valdez de Lugones.'

Sancho frowned at me, seemingly puzzled. 'He told you this?'

'Yes. He confessed the truth of it through the winter.'

Sancho shook his head. 'That claim is nonsense, Rodrigo. You should know better than listening to the lies of slaves. The sons of Pedro are dead, confirmed by the count of Oviedo himself.'

'The count is lying,' I stepped forward. 'Only one son of Pedro is dead, my brother Inigo, and Diego would not have seen his body.'

'Diego told the king Pedro's sons Inigo and Antonio were part of their father's conspiracy. They were chased and caught in a granary south of Oviedo, but it caught fire and they died in the flames. Personal items belonging to them were found on their bodies and presented to the king.'

'We did not have time to gather personal items. We barely evaded capture.'

'Were the bodies charred beyond recognition?' Rodrigo asked. Sancho hesitated then nodded. 'Seems a little convenient, does it not? It would be easy to find two boys who matched their description and put them in a fire. And after Azarola ransacked the castle it would not be difficult to take a few items and make them a little charred, to add meat to the bones of the lie.'

Sancho grimaced when he realised Rodrigo might be right.

'You can confirm who you are, can you?' Garcia Ordóñez said to me.

'Put me in front of the count and you will see a look of horror when he sees I am alive. Failing that, his sons and his daughter Jimena will confirm it too. She was my best friend before I left Lugones. I am who I say I am. I grew up in Lugones with my father, mother, brother and sisters. Bernardo Garces de Dueñas had every man of worth in my father's service killed, and my mother and sisters were taken captive, their fate unknown. As for Inigo,' I turned to Rodrigo, 'my lord killed him on the Camino de Santiago when I was captured. And my cousin Emiliano took the javelin to the chest.'

There was no hint of emotion on Sancho's face, just a frown as he took in my words. He paused for thought before he turned to Garcia Ordóñez.

'Go on without me. I have urgent business to attend.' Garcia nodded and headed in to the palace. Vermundo hesitated, looked at me with curiosity before he followed Garcia. Sancho turned to me. 'If your claims are true you are not safe. There are unwanted eyes and ears everywhere. Come.'

Sancho led us to the castle on the plateau of a small hill in the centre of the city, surrounded by another stout stone wall. It was made up of a small keep with guard houses and stables, workshops and armouries. There was little activity, only a few guards changing shifts and moaning about the chill the day brought. We were led in to the corridors of the keep where the sun's warmth failed to pierce the cool air, but Sancho and Rodrigo seemed unaffected by the cold unlike I.

Tapestries and Castilian banners lined the walls, with flickering torches providing scant light. We entered a small room with a window that allowed sunlight to stream through but contained little more than a table with several chairs around it, and two desks along the walls. A large vellum map was held down by small wooden castles, one in each corner, which showed Hispania, divided in to its many small regions and factions, some of which were faded beyond recognition. Sancho told us to sit, and I told him my story.

At some parts he seemed shocked and appalled; at others he did not show any hints of emotion. Throughout he listened intently, took in every word, every detail of my ordeals. I took my time and told him everything; I told him about Juande, the priest and where he could find the bodies of the pilgrims we had killed. When I was done, he sighed.

'I am truly sorry about your father. He fought well at Graus and it was an honour to know him. But you are still a criminal. The death of a priest is shocking enough, and at the hands of brigands whilst on pilgrimage is unthinkable. You should face trial for your actions, but I will leave it for my father to decide. Still, your account has proved...useful. You mentioned a Moor who was with Azarola the day he came to your father's castle. Do you remember much about him?' I nodded. 'Tell me everything you can recall.'

I explained what I knew, scant at best, but the mention of the Moor's scar on his cheek seemed enough. 'That sounds like al-Muqtadir's cousin. His name is Nasr al-Baytar. He was the general who led the forces of Saraqusta at Graus. I never liked the sour faced bastard. He is known to oppose cooperation between Christians and Muslims, even when his amir appealed for our help. I believe he may have been part of the reason your father was arrested.' I whispered the name to myself and vowed to find out more about this Moor. 'It would not be so hard to believe he was involved in the atrocities in this past year.'

'What atrocities?' I asked.

Rodrigo gave me a baffled look. 'The retaliation for the attack on Barbushtar.' I gave a vacant expression. 'How have you not heard of this?'

'I was you slave, remember? I did not hear much of the outside world.'

'There has been a great slaughter of Christians in the *taifas*,' Sancho said. 'Hundreds, perhaps thousands have died. In Saraqusta a church was burned to the ground whilst those inside took part in morning prayers. And the unrest spread south in to Tulaytula and Balansiya too. It is a shock this is the first you have heard of it! Some were murdered in the streets where they walked whilst others were crucified out on the roads. My father has sent envoys to demand al-Muqtadir explain his actions, but it seems little more than a prelude.'

'A prelude to what?' I asked.

'War.'

I never thought I would end up marching to war like my father once did, but if Rodrigo was called to fight and Arias intended for me to serve as his squire, I would be expected to join the army. I had scant knowledge of war and I loathed the idea of witnessing two armies clash as men hacked and stabbed at each other, screamed war cries and cried in pain. The thought brought back the terrible memories of our flight from Leon and the slaughter on the Camino de Santiago.

'I do not know what the future holds for you, Antonio Perez,' Sancho continued. 'Your father was a good man, a loyal man and one who should not have died. But my father does not see it that way. When he hears you are alive, he will summon you. Fortunately, he will have more important matters on his mind dealing with the Moors. For now, I release you from your slavery and will allow you to serve as Arias's squire. Go back to Vivar,' Sancho said to Rodrigo. 'Tell your men to prepare for war in the coming months. Choose your most trusted men and go to Leon. We should know soon enough what is going to unfold.'

We returned to the palace and prepared to leave, but before we could retrieve our mounts Rodrigo stopped and stared. I followed his

211

gaze to see Vermundo the seneschal talking to a hooded man on a horse. He handed him a letter. Both men returned our glares, and there was a tense standoff before the hooded figure spurred his horse towards the city gate. The tall man hurried back to the hall, keen to avoid us.

'What do you suppose that was about?' I asked.

'I do not know, but there are eyes and ears everywhere, willing to pass on whispers to the right people who will pay for the information. Something tells me your identity is no longer a secret.'

*   *   *

Rodrigo had granted permission for Gonzalo to forge me a blade. The smith happily agreed to make a sword, and the finished product was better than I thought. The cross guard was straight with a round pommel and black leather tang, and the steel was polished to a gleam so I could see my hazel eyes and the first stray whiskers of a beard in the reflection. It was simple in decoration but practical in its use, light and well balanced but strong and accurate. I always carried it with me as a symbol of pride and began to feel the part of a squire.

I also asked Gonzalo for another blade, one he raised his eyebrows at in surprise, but he nevertheless set to it. It was a dagger, no longer than my forearm from the pommel to the tip of the blade and was essentially a smaller version of my sword but with no cross guard. But what made it unique was the inscription I asked Gonzalo to etch in to the steel. It read, "I am Vengeance, born of hatred. I thirst for the blood of those who betrayed Pedro Valdez de Lugones". Its purpose was to end the lives of Azarola and al-Baytar, and I would always keep it with me, ready for the moment to strike them down. Nothing would stop me in my quest.

As well as my new weapons Arias gave me a padded tunic, strong leather boots and a simple bowl helm with a long nose guard and a leather cap to wear underneath. He presented them to me in the courtyard along with a bay colt with a long white patch on its nose and a blonde mane and tail. I ran my hand along the smooth coat and the horse snorted gently, sniffed at my sleeve and my hand when I offered it. He was not as big as Guerrero, Arias's chestnut stallion, nor was he as graceful as Rodrigo's white beauty, Babieca, but he was strong and well groomed, a fitting steed for any nobleman.

'He is a good horse,' Arias said, 'enduring and responsive, but has yet to be tested in battle. Perhaps you will tread that path together.'

'Does he have a name?'

'Asbat. It means "reliable" in the Moorish tongue.'

'He is a Moorish horse?'

'All horses in Hispania have Arabic blood. If they do not, they are not worth keeping. I took a Moorish noble captive a few years back, ransomed him for his mount. I have never found a suitable recipient for him – until now. Treat him well and he will be a willing servant.'

'Asbat,' I whispered. The name seemed fitting, and I hoped he would be a reliable and loyal friend for as long as we were together. It was strange to have so many gifts presented on me, but it only went to show how much Arias respected my father and wished to help me. I did not argue and humbly accepted them.

Rodrigo led us south with six of his knights and their squires from Vivar to Burgos, then set off on the long journey to Leon. We followed the main road, passed trade caravans as we went, and spent the night in the wilderness or within the walls of a lord who would welcome us. As spring replaced winter the frosts no longer hardened the ground and the morning sun cast a warm glow over us, and after four days we arrived in Leon, the city I had come to loathe. I had arrived first as an outlaw, then as a prisoner for my crimes. Now I arrived as a squire. God works in mysterious ways.

'I will find Sancho and find out the current situation,' Rodrigo said as we reached the main square of the city. The bells of the church tolled for the call to midday prayers. We had left our escort, horses and baggage in the barracks of the palace, but Rodrigo insisted we did not accompany him. 'I would advise you to keep yourselves scarce for a few hours. I will come and find you.'

'We will not go far, but do not keep us waiting too long,' Arias replied.

Rodrigo turned to me. 'You will have to prepare yourself. The subject of your father's treason has split opinion over what is fact and fiction. You will be called as a witness to give your account of what happened at Lugones.' He leaned in close and spoke quietly. 'It is imperative you mention every detail of Nasr al-Baytar. It may change the minds of a few of the lords of this realm, including the king. Can you do that?'

'I want justice for my father,' I said sternly. 'I will face the king and say what needs to be said, if I have to.'

He gave me a nod. 'Good. Now stay safe, both of you.'

As Rodrigo turned and marched towards the palace a troupe of around fifteen horsemen galloped hard in the same direction, shouted as they went. Most were knights and several seemed to be high ranking lords. All looked as though they had been hard on the road for days. Rodrigo's pace quickened at the sight of them and he followed as they dismounted and rushed straight in to the palace, left several onlookers bewildered at their haste.

'Come on,' Arias said, thinking nothing of it. 'Let's get a drink.'

We found a small tavern named the Apple Core where we dined on fresh bread, trout and blood sausage, and it served some of the best cider I had ever tasted, but Arias was reluctant to let me drink too much. It was barely passed midday and the tavern was quiet. Rodrigo's other knights had gone elsewhere in the city. Most of the usual revellers worked on the stalls or workshops around the city, but nevertheless we sat there in the corner and tried not to attract attention to ourselves.

We were part way through our meal and Arias was about to call for more wine when I noticed two men walk in to the tavern. I immediately stiffened.

'What is it?' Arias frowned.

'Two men have just walked in. I know them.' One was clean shaven with a long scar through his left eye, and the other was taller with a great black beard; distinguishable features that stuck in my mind. Both wore long brown cloaks over their black tunics.

'Friends of yours?'

'They are Azarola's men. I remember seeing them at Lugones.' The faces of most of the soldiers who sacked Lugones had been partially concealed by hoods or helms, but some had removed them when the slaughter was complete.

'The day your father was arrested?'

I simply nodded because one of them stared straight at me. He tapped his comrade on the arm and they both started towards us. Arias looked over his shoulder and cursed under his breath. I could see the glint of steel beneath their cloaks, and knew trouble was coming for us.

'Just stay quiet. Let me talk,' Arias whispered.

'Arias Benítez?' the bearded man said.

'Who's asking?' Arias said, not looking at the men. He cut another piece of blood sausage and popped it in his mouth.

'We have orders to escort you to the palace.'

'We are fine where we are.'

'You need to come with us,' the man stressed.

'On whose authority?'

'Prince Alfonso's.'

'The orders did not come from him though, did they?' Both men held their tongues. 'Tell my brother by law if he wishes to speak to me, he should get off his arse and meet me here. The food is good, and if he is lucky, I might buy him a cup of wine. Otherwise, tell him to go fuck himself.' Arias gave the men a wry smile before he went back to his wine.

'There are more of my men waiting outside,' said the scarred man. 'We will have no hesitation calling them in if you will not come quietly.'

'If you dare challenge me, you will need more men,' Arias growled as he stood and towered over the man, who tried to stand his ground, but doubt flickered on his face. 'I will not be talked down by a cretin like you.' The hustle and bustle in the tavern slowly died as the few revellers turned and stared at the scene.

'We are keen to avoid any blood, so if you would not mind stepping outside.' He stepped to the side to allow Arias and I to be escorted away. Arias seemed content to continue the argument, but I stopped him.

'Lord,' I called. He glared at me. 'Perhaps it is best if we go with them.' He did not want his pride to be damaged, nor did he wish to take advice from his squire, but he reluctantly gave in. He let out a heavy sigh before he stormed out of the tavern and I followed, tried to keep pace with him. Outside the air was cool and the sun bright, the city full of life. Stood before us were five armed men. We said nothing as the scarred man led the way, guided us through the streets as curious bystanders whispered to each other. Arias ignored them and walked with his head held high.

We were led to the palace, walked through familiar corridors until we reached an open plaza with colonnades around the edges. The interior was full of lush plants, trees bearing apples, oranges and lemons, and a small fountain with stone benches facing it. Beside one of these benches were two men in conversation, but their hushed words were distorted against the gentle drips of the fountain's water and chirp of nuthatches and warblers hidden in the trees. Our footsteps caught their attention and a young man turned to face us.

He looked to be in his mid-twenties, with a trimmed beard and black hair that fell in loose curls to his shoulders. His eyes were large and bright above a small pointed nose and thin pursed lips curled in to a shrewd smile when he saw us. His tunic was fashioned from fine silk, vibrant royal blue in colour and trimmed in gold, and was fitted to his slender frame by a black leather belt with a golden buckle. A large golden crucifix studded with rubies and sapphires hung around his neck, and two rings in the same fashion glinted on his fingers as he clasped his hands before him.

'Lord Arias Benítez. Welcome to Leon,' he said politely.

'Highness,' is all Arias said, without the respect the rank bestowed.

'Have you spoken with my brother yet?'

'I will speak with Sancho soon enough, highness.'

Alfonso, the second son to King Fernando and the one who would inherit Leon upon his father's death, seemed very different to his eldest brother. Sancho was tall, strong and imposing, yet Alfonso could not match him in stature, although he seemed well spoken and educated. 'I have a few questions for you and your…companion.' His gaze turned to me and studied every inch of my demeanour. 'Is this the boy?'

'He's a bit taller and fuller, but it is him, lord.'

Bernardo Garces de Dueñas, the man they called Azarola and my nemesis, stepped out from behind the prince.

I felt a pang of fear when I saw his face; the demonic vision that haunted my dreams every night was stood before me, mocked me with that smirk I had come to loathe. My fists tightened as anger boiled within me. I had Vengeance hung from on my belt, freshly forged and thirsty for blood, and it was all too tempting to draw it.

'You are meant to be dead, Antonio Perez,' Alfonso said.

'You sound disappointed,' I hit back.

'I do not like being lied to,' Alfonso frowned. 'Diego swore the bodies recovered were those of you and your brother. But it does not matter. You have arrived in Leon safe and well, so you can now stand trial.'

'On what charge?'

'Treason. The whole of the Perez family was declared enemies of the crown and are to be punished for it.'

'He was a fifteen-year-old boy!' Arias exclaimed. 'What involvement could he possibly have in his father's alleged crimes?'

'Inigo and Antonio stole the items that belonged to the amir of Saraqusta.'

217

A stunned silence hung in the air as I contemplated Alfonso's words.

'I did not go to Saraqusta, highness,' I eventually said. 'I was due to travel to Palencia to become a squire, but that was to be after my father returned. Inigo too stayed in Oviedo.'

'We have witnesses who place you in Saraqusta when the items were stolen. Do you have evidence to suggest otherwise?'

I knew my words would fall on deaf ears. There was no one left to testify for me; my father, Inigo and Father Santiago were dead along with everyone in my father's service, and my mother and sisters were captive and would not be allowed to give evidence, wherever they were.

'Your silence proves your guilt. I suspect the same will happen when you face trial.'

'I look forward to seeing him plead for his life like his father did,' Azarola smirked.

'Do not talk about my father, you bastard,' I snarled.

Azarola shook with mirth. 'Pedro was defiant to the last, even when the evidence against him was overwhelming. Though I do remember the way he begged for his life when we placed the noose around his neck, the way he blubbered and sobbed like a child.'

'Liar!' I cried. 'He did not weep. He stood tall and died with honour.'

My outburst amused Azarola even further.

'There was nothing honourable about your father. He was nothing but a scrap of shit on the underside of my boot, and his death was justified.' He turned to Alfonso. 'If there is nothing else, highness, I will take my leave.' Alfonso nodded and Azarola gave a smug smirk before he started towards the colonnade. But I was not done yet.

'How did it feel when my father saved your pathetic life?' I called to him. He stopped and turned with a puzzled look on his face. 'I'd wager your pride was dented, was it not? You wanted to kill King Ramiro yourself, but you were furious my father delivered the killing blow and took all the glory for himself. You could not stand the shame of having my father revered for such a prestigious achievement.' The puzzled expression descended to a frown. 'The truth is you are a jealous coward. My father was a proud warrior and won recognition for it, but you are nothing but a snake that spits poison in to the ears of those stupid enough to believe it.'

Anger and emotion fuelled my words. No one in their right mind would launch such a scathing attack, but I did not care. I felt a pang of satisfaction when Azarola's mouth twisted in fury and he began to march towards me, but Alfonso held out his hand. Being the obedient dog, Azarola halted and held his tongue.

'You will do well not to insult the men who may well preside over your trial,' Alfonso advised me. 'Azarola is a loyal man who offers sound advice. Do not chastise him for your father's crimes.' I was about to protest when he cut me off. 'I do not want to hear another word from you. Take them to the dungeons.'

'You will do no such thing.'

The voice was accompanied by dozens of footsteps from the colonnade. Prince Sancho strode tall, with Rodrigo behind him and a handful of his men. He seethed as he surveyed the scene, allowing his gaze to settle on his younger brother.

'What do you think you are doing?' he growled.

'This does not concern you, brother,' Alfonso said calmly.

'Oh, but it does. These men are here on my orders. Arias is one of Rodrigo's men. You have no right to arrest them.'

'This is one kingdom, and as such every man, woman and child are subject to the same laws. A guilty man is a guilty man.'

'Antonio Perez is no criminal, and neither was his father.'

Alfonso frowned. 'I assume you have proof of this?'

'I do.' Alfonso's eyes widened in surprize. 'If it comes to a trial the witness will come forth. Until then Arias and Antonio will be under my protection. They will spend no time in any dungeons.'

'Are you going to stop me?'

Alfonso's tone was not hostile, but Sancho did not like the challenge. Sancho was tall and strong, a proud warrior, where Alfonso was lithe and unimposing. But it did not stop the younger brother standing up to his sibling. There was no fear, only defiance. Sancho strode forward and towered over Alfonso and tension gripped the air. Men reached for the hilts of their swords.

'There will come a time when I will stop your pathetic defiance,' Sancho snarled. 'One day you will run your mouth and defy me, and you will rue the day when I answer with steel.'

'I look forward to the day, brother.'

A great booming voice dispelled the hostility.

At first the voice was distorted, loud and irate. The princes looked concerned and walked towards the colonnade to see the source. A tall, older man strode in to the sunlight surrounded by a priest and several officials.

'Where have you two been?' he barked. 'I have been looking for you both for an age.'

'Father,' Alfonso said with a slight bow. 'I and Sancho have been addressing an important matter which requires your attention.'

'Whatever menial issue you fools are quarrelling about this time can wait. We have urgent business that affects every one of us. I want every man of worth in this city in the hall in an hour. Every knight, every official, even the priests!'

My eyes widened as I caught my first glimpse of King Fernando of Leon-Castile. His hair was black streaked with grey, as was his beard, both of which were long but well-groomed and neat. He was tall and powerful, handsome and lavish. A gleaming golden circlet sat on his head, studded with diamonds, rubies and sapphires, and jewels adorned his fingers and the crucifix around his neck, made him look every inch the regal ruler he was rumoured to be. He had named himself Emperor of Hispania, which was a bold claim to make, but he backed that claim by subduing many of the Moorish *taifas* and even Christian kingdoms, and defeated them time and time again, exacted tribute as he went.

Under his command his armies had conquered Portugal down to Qulumriyyah and the Mondego river, annexed Navarre and subjugated Aragon from his brother. Isbiliya, Saraqusta, Batalyaws and Tulaytula all paid the *parias* to Leon-Castile for the promise of peace.

'What has happened?' Sancho asked.

'Al-Muqtadir has crossed a line. The amir of Saraqusta has not only killed Christians by the hundreds, he has now declared he has no intention in paying the *parias* any longer. The bastard grows too bold, and now I intend to answer with steel. We march to war!'

*   *   *

The hall was crammed with men. The sour scent of sweat from the close press was rife in my nostrils. There were dozens of lords and knights with their squires, officials and even priests from the various churches around Leon, or those who were attached to Fernando's travelling court. Though united there was a clear divide; the small contingents from Castile, Asturias and Galicia grouped together at to the left of the dais whilst the Leonese, greatly outnumbering the rest, were dispersed around the rest of the hall.

Situated at the front of the hall were Sancho and Alfonso, now accompanied by Fernando's third son, Garcia. He looked to be in his early twenties and was short and stocky with a neat beard and a full head of blonde hair cropped at the shoulders, whilst his small, darting eyes scanned the room. He would inherit Galicia, the western part of his father's kingdom and the largest part given Fernando's recent conquest of Qulumriyyah, complete with the *parias* from the *taifas* of Isbiliya and Batalyaws. Sancho and Alfonso had placed their younger brother between them, their earlier quarrel still fresh in their mind.

I stood with Arias and Rodrigo, along with Rodrigo's most trusted knights deep within the Castilian contingent, with a scant view of the rest of the hall. I scanned the faces of those gathered, searching for Azarola, but I could not pick out his visage in the close press of men.

After Fernando had demanded every man's presence in the hall Sancho had me and Arias ushered away to his private chambers, much to Alfonso's displeasure. Any trial, Sancho said, would wait until the conflict with Saraqusta was over. In the meantime, he said we were to accompany Rodrigo during the campaign. The king was to lead a great raid in to the Ebro valley, to burn the land and retaliate for the actions of al-Muqtadir before we marched on Saraqusta itself.

Men still streamed through the doors as King Fernando marched in to the hall and took his place on the dais where his throne sat. The hustle and frantic chatter subsided as the king prepared to address the congregation. He stood tall in a chainmail hauberk with the red and white surcoat of Leon-Castile over it, and his fine long sword hung from his hip. He looked around the room with a grim expression on his face, but I could tell anger brewed deep within him, waiting to be unleashed.

He waited until the hall was silent before his voice boomed.

'I thank you all for your presence, comrades, but I bring grim tidings that must be addressed without delay. As all of you will know, last year Christian forces took the city of Barbushtar from the amir of Saraqusta, the revered Ahmed al-Muqtadir. This conquest was ordered by the Pope, and though his actions were well met by the kingdom of Leon-Castile, we did not support the endeavour. It was the Catalans and Aragonese who leant their support to the Franks whilst we raised our flag above the walls of Qulumriyyah in the west. We were not involved in the great slaughter of Muslims when Barbushtar fell. If it was me, I would have spared them all, so long as they swore fealty to us, and those who know my reputation recognise this well enough. But it is us who have been punished for the actions of these invaders.

'Incensed by the massacre at Barbushtar, the Muslims of the *taifa* of Saraqusta have retaliated and slaughtered Christians in their droves. The unrest spread to the *taifas* of Tulaytula and Balansiya too, where they danced on the corpses of the slain. I wept when news of the atrocities reached me, and I vowed to make al-Muqtadir, a man I once considered an ally, answer for his crimes. A delegation was sent to Saraqusta to collect the *parias* and demand he answer for the slaughter, but not only did he refuse to pay this year's tribute, he set his men on the delegation and drove them from the city.'

A murmur of discontent echoed through the room and some men shouted their displeasure at the statement.

'I will not tolerate this insolence. Was it not my own son who marched to al-Muqtadir's aid and drove the Aragonese from his lands? Do we not offer the Moors protection when the Catalans and Aragonese sniff around their dwellings, looking for blood? The amir of Saraqusta bites the hand that protects him, so it I intend to make him pay. The kindness he abused has now manifested in to fury. And with the help of God we will make him kneel and acknowledge Fernando, Emperor of Hispania, as his true overlord once and for all. We march to Saraqusta, and to war!'

A great roar greeted the king's speech. The men of Leon-Castile were incensed by the news of the slaughter and they wanted revenge. King Fernando had given them the chance for that retribution.

The year was 1065, I was seventeen years old, and I marched to war.

Part Four

The Road to War

Leon, 1065 AD

Ten

We returned to Vivar, and Rodrigo gathered as many men as he could muster. The king had issued a charter that all men with a horse were called for service for the great raid in to the *taifas*. In the following weeks Rodrigo had raised twelve knights from his own household with their squires, and fourteen men drawn from the militia. These were men who plied their trade as merchants and craftsmen but owned a horse and could afford their own arms and armour. Royal knights of the king usually wore chainmail and carried large, round shields, or kite shaped influenced by the Franks, but the militia wore leather or scale armour and carried round shields and javelins as well as their spears, swords and hand axes. They were capable fighters and would expect their share of any plunder taken from Saraqusta which, given the wealth the Muslim *taifas* could amass, would be substantial.

Any spare moment I had was spent training with the other boys and honing my craft. Some squires were well trained and brave, others cautious and clumsy like Jorge, Rodrigo's squire. I faced off against him one day and he did not land a single blow, and I put him on his arse every time. Rodrigo looked on with a pained expression, but no less offered encouragement to his squire. By night, after we had finished our duties in the hall and around the castle, we sat in the squires' dorms and shared stories. I spoke of who I was without fear now, but some boys looked at me as if I was mad. One, a boy named Domingo, shamed my father and I felt like driving my sword through his belly, but Arias heard of the slander and clipped the boy on the cheek and chastised his master for training an insolent swine. He did not mention my father's name again.

It was mid spring before the army of Leon-Castile gathered at Burgos. We were some of the first to arrive, and everyday a new column of men approached the city, banners bright in the sun and fluttering in the breeze. Soon, there was close to two and a half thousand knights, squires and militia camped outside the city with servants and baggage. I had never seen so many men assembled for war, every man with their panoply and trusted steeds.

The army was preparing to march when Arias led me through the ranks of men. He called to some by name, embraced them as brothers and asked after family, exchanged japes and promised to outdo them in the war. When I was introduced, I was accepted without the usual cynical looks. We were all part of one army and there was no time for animosity within our ranks. There were men from both Leon and Castile, all flying the colours of the king, but all I could think of was Azarola and finding the opportunity to strike at his heart, no matter the consequences. All that mattered to me was revenge.

'So, is this your first taste of war, lad?'

A pair of Rodrigo's knights wandered over as I brushed Asbat's coat. They were brothers, Vascons, named Mancio and Aigeru, and had been Arias's men before his banishment from his castle at Frias. They were both powerful, tall and well built, sported clean shaven faces with moustaches upon their upper lips. They were experienced in war and had fought many battles, and their mail hauberks were well worn and patched with fresh links here and there where it had been pierced.

'It is, yes,' I replied.

'Shitting yourself yet?' Aigeru chuckled, his accent distinctly different.

'Lay off him,' Mancio retorted. 'He comes from good stock, this one.' He turned back to me. 'We fought at Graus, and we saw what your father did. He was a brave man. I raised a cup in his honour when I heard of his death.'

'Thank you, lord.'

'Does the same bravery flow through your veins?' Aigeru asked.

I hesitated. 'We will find out soon.'

'I will offer some advice, if I may?' Mancio asked. I nodded. 'Do not try and be a hero. You're only a young pup, inexperienced. I do not see you doing much fighting, for this will be more of a raid than a campaign of conquest. Raid, pillage and back home before you know it. But leave the hard work to the knights. Make sure you earn your belt before you try to play the part.'

I nodded to show I accepted the advice. When a squire was deemed worthy of ascending to knighthood, he would be given a belt from the king, or someone with authority. It would be worn with pride and granted a man the rank of a knight, along with all the benefits. A squire would train for around seven years before he was deemed ready. I was still years off before I would even be considered.

'Trying to scare him off already?' Rodrigo called from behind me. I turned as he wandered over.

'Just offering words of encouragement, lord,' Mancio said cheerfully.

'Do you not trust Arias to keep him on the right path?' Rodrigo chuckled. 'You will do well to listen to these men. They are veterans who know how to kill and how to say alive.'

'And you will do well not to piss your lord off, lest you suffer a worse fate as his enemies,' Aigeru offered with a wink.

'Careful,' Rodrigo cocked his head. 'Squires are not the only ones to suffer the wrath of Arias.'

Aigeru raised his hands in feigned apology.

'I feel sorry for the poor souls who will get on the wrong side of him when we fight,' I laughed. 'I vow to never make an enemy of him. And thank you for the encouragement, my lords.' Mancio and Aigeru bowed their heads then took their leave to prepare. 'And thank you, lord.'

'For what?' Rodrigo frowned.

'Believing me when no one else would.'

'Do not get soppy on me. I will have Arias clip you around the ear.'

'You already did, remember?' Rodrigo grimaced, but I gave a grin to show I took it in good faith. 'I will not falter, lord. Know that I pledge my service to you, until the day I die.'

He was taken aback by the unexpected statement. He placed a hand on my shoulder and shook me a little. 'So be it. As far as I am concerned you are now one of my own kin. I am sure you will serve me well.'

A small vigil was held in the church of Burgos, where the bishops of the kingdom blessed the king and his endeavours against the enemies of God, before Sancho held a feast for the leading men of the army and the nobility and clergy in the great hall. At dawn, the army began the long march to Saraqusta.

To war.

*   *   *

We left Burgos and travelled east to Logroño on the river Ebro, and the course of the river became our path in to the *taifa*. We first came to the region of La Rioja which was part of the kingdom of Navarre, but Fernando had reduced the land to a vassal state and so we travelled unhindered. From there we crossed in to the *taifa* itself with its lush valleys and irrigated fields abundant with grapes and dates, figs, pomegranates and olives. The army was split in to two columns; King Fernando, accompanied by Alfonso, led the royal knights and the men of Leon, whilst Sancho led the contingent from Castile. Our forces crossed the Ebro and devastated the land to the east while Fernando's men harassed the western banks. A small number of men were left to defend the baggage train as it followed the route of the river. The rest of our men galloped in all directions, stole, pillaged and burned as they went. The fury of Leon-Castile was unleashed.

Dozens were put to the sword, their homes burnt, and their possessions taken for our plunder. Arias revelled in the chance to spill blood. He had not fought in a battle since Graus, almost two years previous, and all that time spent idle in Vivar had made him angry and itching to kill. I remember how he laughed as he rode down farmers and shepherds, the way his eyes lit up like a wild beast on a hunt as blood arced through the air to stain the ground. I rode with the other squires a little distance to the rear of the knights, watched the horror unfold before us. When I walked amongst the corpses, I saw crosses around some of their necks, indicating Mozarabs fell as easy as the Moors. I raised the point with Arias after the second village lay in a smouldering ruin, but he simply shrugged.

'They may live in God's name, but they serve al-Muqtadir. We have no qualms about killing Aragonese and Navarrese, so why would we care about these people?'

'They have done nothing wrong. They are innocent,' I protested.

'So were the Christians slaughtered after Barbushtar.'

'And what about those slaughtered *in* Barbushtar?'

Arias glared at me. 'We follow the king's orders. If he says they must die they will die. Muslim or Christian, it matters not.'

Castles too fell to our fury. Some lords opened their gates in the hopes of appeasing us, but under Sancho's orders we showed them no mercy. The prince himself killed the naive lords and left the fortifications in ruins, and we feasted in the halls and afforded ourselves some luxury in a time mostly spent in the saddle and sleeping under the stars. Some of the more wary lords scorned us from their walls and showered missiles on us if we strayed too close, and they were the lucky ones for we were not to be drawn in to any sieges. We wanted to devastate the land, not fight a prolonged war.

The raiding and occupation of the outlying lands lasted in to the early summer, until we were ordered to march to Saraqusta itself. Our carts were already laden with loot and the men itched for a real battle over butchery, but they would not be fighting in the foreseeable future. We had penetrated deep in to the east of the *taifa*, as far as Lleida, but none of the amir's men would face us, and so we found a tributary of the Ebro and followed the *huertas* bursting with fruit trees and fields full of sorghum and rice before we joined the great river itself. The sun rose high and the warmth made sweat trickle down our backs and settle on our brows, so many of us rode without our armour. Only the knights rode in their full panoply, for their bodies were honed to survive in the most extreme of conditions and still be ready to fight at a moment's notice.

A white speck appeared to the south, and as we drew closer the speck manifested in to a great city on the southern bank of the Ebro which shone bright in the beating midday sun. Neighbourhoods had been erected outside of the city, full of curious and fearful people who glared at us as we rode in silence. King Fernando's men were already in the city and patrolled the streets, and we could see the gates to the city open with more of our men standing vigil. We crossed the old Roman bridge over the Ebro and entered the northern part of Saraqusta.

The city consisted of two parts: the inner city was built within the ruins of the old Roman walls of Caesaraugusta, and the new Moorish city. The outer limestone walls were strong and formidable and a great city had flourished within them, but the Roman walls were crumbled and for the most part the stone had been reused to build other structures within the city, yet at some points they still stood tall and proud as they once had hundreds of years ago. The remains of the Roman forum were now the site of a grand mosque surrounded by thriving markets and the theatre, with its marble facade stripped to reveal weather beaten stone.

It may have been a Moorish city, but its Roman foundations were still firmly in place.

As we marched through the streets the citizens of Saraqusta, be they Moor or Mozarab, willingly gave us the road. There was a distinct difference in their appearance; the Moorish elite were adorned in fine garments and headdresses of silk with intricate patterns, whereas the Mozarabs wore woollen tunics and trousers in the Arabic fashion and hid their crucifixes in public, though they were still permitted to attend church. Everywhere the sound of bartering came from the various stalls on street corners and wide-open plazas with larger markets selling spices, glassware, pottery, metal work, ivory and silk. Old men sat in the shade of gardens and discussed theology and science as the imams called out to the people of the city for prayers. As we rode, a strange beast appeared from one of the side streets. It resembled a horse but with gangly legs and an elongated neck, covered in shaggy hair with a hump on its back. It stared at me with big bulbous eyes and peeled its thick lips back before spitting at the hooves of Asbat, made me flinch and accidently tug at his reins. The horse showed his annoyance with a heavy snort.

Arias laughed. 'That is a camel. They come from Ifriqiya, far to the south. First time you have ever seen one?'

The beast was led around a corner and made a strange barking noise as it went. Though situated in the north of Hispania, surrounded by Christian kingdoms, Saraqusta was a different world.

We passed through the ruins of a Roman gatehouse and wound through the streets of the Moorish city, so narrow in parts we had to travel in single file to allow the traffic to flow freely. Side streets lead to cul-de-sacs secured by iron gates. We marched under the shadow of a Moorish gate and came to great open field where the bulk of the Leonese army was camped, but behind the rows of tents rose a great citadel. It was a square complex with walls even grander than the Roman walls would have been, with rounded towers on each corner and a wooden bridge which spanned a moat that surrounded the whole

233

citadel and led towards a large wooden gate. If the city was attacked it was a last bastion for the invaders to conquer before the city was subdued, but judging by the many work tables and artisans' tools around the gate, it was being converted in to a palace for the amir. Today the gate was open, which indicated he had no desire to fight.

Leonese soldiers held back crowds of people from the main road to the palace, who shouted and waved their arms in anger. A troupe of knights escorted a small group of Moorish men bound in chains, their fine clothes torn and soiled with dust and blood. One of them shouted in his own tongue and thrashed as a soldier dragged him by the scruff of his neck. It was not until the troupe was close enough and had passed us that I saw the wicked gash on his left cheek.

'That man,' I exclaimed. 'It's Nasr al-Baytar.'

Arias flashed his gaze to the man, and he guided his horse parallel to the group, tried to catch a glimpse of the man's face. He shouted at the men to halt, which they duly did, believing he was a lord.

Rodrigo had noticed the sudden halt and rode over to us. 'Arias, what are you doing?'

Arias held his hand up to his lord then waved me over.

'What is your name?' Arias asked as he dismounted. The man held his tongue.

'Arias, Antonio,' Rodrigo barked.

'You are Nasr al-Baytar,' I said through gritted teeth as I too jumped from the saddle. He frowned and still did not speak. It was enough for me to be sure.

'Let go of him,' Arias ordered the guard. Al-Baytar straightened and kept his gaze on me, unfazed by the interruption.

'You do not know who I am, but I know who you are,' I growled. 'You came to my home when my father was arrested. You were responsible for his death.'

'What of it?' al-Baytar replied, unflinching. He understood our tongue well.

'My name is Antonio Perez de Lugones.'

He sniggered as if amused.

'The son of Pedro the traitor. I heard you had died, but I am so glad you still live. Perhaps you might feel the same pain as your father did when he dangled like a piece of meat, begging for mercy.'

I drew my fist back and smashed him in the nose.

The months of intense training had given me strength I did not know I possessed. He collapsed to the dirt. Blood poured from his nose.

'That is for my father, you bastard!' I kicked him hard in the midriff, made him gasp for air.

It took Arias and another two knights to prise me away. A red mist had descended over me and I wanted nothing more than to send al-Baytar to his grave. My anger only increased when Azarola stepped out of the crowd of gathered soldiers and strode towards us.

'What is the meaning of this?' he said calmly. Though Arias wanted to retort he sensibly held his tongue. 'You allow squires to do the dirty work now?' Arias simply glared back. Azarola turned back to me. 'What do you think you are doing?'

'He deserves it.'

'He does, but you do not deserve to give the punishment. Step aside and let the men continue their work.' I stood my ground, felt my fingers twitch as they longed to grab Vengeance and plunge the blade in his neck. Azarola stepped forward and towered over me. His breath was pungent with the stench of some unfamiliar spice. 'Step aside, cretin, or I will have you whipped like the dog you are.'

Neither of us backed away. Azarola's snout flared and his bulbous lips bared snarling teeth. I had attracted too much of an audience, all eyes on us both now, and so I took several steps back. I kept my gaze fixed.

Rodrigo stepped forward and pulled me to one side. 'What makes you think you can assault prisoners like that?'

'He is the reason my father died,' I hissed.

'He is the reason many fathers have died, and mothers, sons and daughters. Do not think you are alone in that respect.'

'I thought you would understand.'

'I do, and I would have gladly let you enact your revenge if it were possible. But like Azarola said, you are a squire. The king himself wants to bring al-Baytar to justice, so do not think you can take matters in to your own hands.'

'I am sorry,' is all I could manage.

'Make sure it does not happen again. And make sure you keep him in check,' he said to Arias. The older knight gave a slight nod. 'Now go and get the horses. We have been assigned to the southern gate.'

I watched as al-Baytar resumed his thrashing as he was led in to the citadel. My gaze fell on Azarola, who gave a smug smirk before he followed the procession. I gripped Vengeance on my belt and knew the day would come when I would wipe the smirk from his face once and for all. In the meantime, al-Baytar would be tried and he would feel the wrath of Fernando and al-Muqtadir.

Or so we thought.

Because in the morning his cell was empty, and al-Baytar was gone.

*   *   *

'Someone let him out in the dead of night,' Rodrigo said, 'and the king wants the head of he who was responsible.'

'I would wager my entire wealth Azarola was involved,' Arias replied.

It was something that had crossed my mind as well. We were standing on the ramparts of Saraqusta's walls gazing south and east where the wide Ebro ran swift, snaked through the land to where to would empty in the Mediterranean. The sun was high and hot in the vibrant blue sky. Behind us the city was full of life under the watchful eye of our men, with an extra buzz as news of al-Baytar's escape filtered around. King Fernando was furious and blamed al-Muqtadir,

236

but the amir protested his innocence and claimed he had as much reason to keep his cousin behind bars.

'It cannot have been him. Azarola has an alibi.'

'What was he doing, sticking his head up Alfonso's arse?' The comment brought a rare snigger from Rodrigo. Arias grimaced as he continued. 'He has men that could have done the dirty work for him, and paying off some of al-Muqtadir's men would not be much of a problem for someone of his influence.'

'It does not matter. We cannot prove a thing.'

Arias sighed. 'Do we know where al-Baytar has gone?'

'No, but he has supporters in the south. Tulaytula or Balansiya, perhaps. And with this new development King Fernando has announced we will continue our campaign against both these *taifas*.'

Arias turned to Rodrigo and raised an eyebrow. 'He wants to raid both?'

Rodrigo nodded. 'When al-Muqtadir was grovelling, he claimed he tried to stop the killing of Christians, even though he wanted justice for Barbushtar. But al-Baytar, acting with men from both Balansiya and Tulaytula, was instrumental in drumming support and even killed innocent Christians with his own hands. Al-Muqtadir claims he was held hostage by his own court and was forced to bow to their demands, to make an enemy of Fernando.'

'And what do you think?'

Rodrigo shrugged. 'It does not matter. Al-Muqtadir has pledged his full support to Fernando and even claims he will increase his *parias* payment. As far as he is concerned Fernando may do whatever he pleases to al-Baytar when we capture him. I think he knows now there are consequences for betraying King Fernando's trust.'

'It only took razing half his kingdom to persuade him.'

'And to uphold his end of the new agreement,' Rodrigo continued, 'Fernando has claimed he will not interfere with al-Muqtadir's plans to recapture Barbushtar.'

'Fernando would allow that?' I exclaimed.

Rodrigo nodded. 'Fernando had no part in that war. It was the Pope who ordered the attack, and we have no business in Barbushtar, so why would he care? He has other matters to attend, and he has killed enough Christians in recent times. If the Pope wishes to keep Barbushtar in Christian hands let him and his puppy dog Franks fight for it when the Moors march to their walls.

'As for you,' Rodrigo frowned at me, 'Sancho has managed to smooth things out with the king. Azarola ran to Alfonso regarding your little assault on al-Baytar and petitioned the king to have you punished, but Sancho claimed you were provoked. Since the king thought al-Baytar deserved a beating he let it go; he even chortled at the idea of a squire striking him, much to Azarola's displeasure. He wants nothing more than to have you suffer like your father did. Stop attracting attention to yourself,' he pointed his finger at me. I felt my cheeks blush but held my tongue and gave a nod of acknowledgement.

We stood in silence, listened to an imam preach to a scant audience on a street corner. I looked at Rodrigo and noted how remarkable it was a man so young, in his early twenties, spoke with so much authority. Arias did not take too kindly to reprimand, yet he took Rodrigo's words without protest. People respected and listened to his opinions. From his time as Sancho's squire his skill in battle was supposedly parallel to the greatest knights in the kingdom, and he was educated and well versed in Latin and the Visigothic law which the men of Leon and Castile adhered to. Should he win enough renown in the eyes of the king he could gain new lands and be able to call more knights to his side, make himself a powerful lord of Castile. I felt content knowing I served such a man.

'What is our next move?' Arias asked.

'We are staying here for a while whilst we gather more men. The king has sent messengers to the Catalan counties, promising the riches of al-Andalus for any man who wishes to fight. Then we are going south.'

'Balansiya is further than we have ever been before.'

'If we want to drive the Moors from Hispania for good, We will have to go all the way to Jebel Tariq. There's still a long way to go yet, my friend, but it will start with Balansiya.'

Weeks went by and high summer arrived, when the midday sun was unbearable in the weight of armour. Though the hostilities had ceased with Saraqusta we were always ordered to keep our weapons with us, more for a show of strength rather than preparation for a conflict. Arias was sure to work me hard for the incident with al-Baytar; I groomed the horses more often, cleaned his arms and armour morning and night and ran enough errands during the day to make my legs ache when I was relieved of my duties. But he did allow me to wander the city once or twice and take in my surroundings.

I visited the markets near the great mosque and marvelled at the traders from various regions of Hispania, be they Christian or Muslim, but some came from Francia, even from Constantinople, Ifriqiya and the Holy Land far to the east. A cacophony of languages called out as the bartering filled the air. The whole area was lit with brilliant colours from trinkets and wares, headdresses and garments in yellows, oranges, blues and greens; gold and silver coins glinted as they exchanged hands.

I passed one of the stalls that sold jewellery when the merchant sprang forward, arms open in welcome.

'Greetings, friend of Saraqusta!' he beamed, coaxed me towards his wares. 'It is a fine day. God truly blesses us!'

'He does,' I said, taken aback by his enthusiasm.

'You are one of King Fernando's soldiers?' I nodded, to his delight. 'I thank you for making our city safe again. You get special discount.'

'I am not buying...'

'Look at the craftsmanship on this!' he picked up a small statue of a lion carved from ivory. 'A lion for a brave pup of Leon?' He grinned and bared a jaw of discoloured teeth.

'I could not possibly afford that.'

'Hmm, perhaps ivory is a luxury for your kind. I have smaller pieces, perhaps a pendent? I have a few of your Christian crosses from Constantinople, ivory or silver or even fine glass. Look at them.' He motioned to a row of necklaces on a small wooden frame as he moved on to entertain a wealthy looking Moor. I browsed the wares and found they were indeed delicate and well-crafted. One caught my eye over the rest, a silver chain with small glass beads of emerald green and vibrant amber. The green reminded me of Jimena's eyes, and so I decided to purchase it and send it to her, if I were to return to Castile. We haggled over the price and I parted with the little coin I possessed. I surely paid more than its true value, but it would be worth it if only for Jimena to know I still thought of her.

News came that King Fernando did not take too kindly to. Much to his displeasure the response from the Catalans was unfavourable and only a handful of men, barely fifty knights and their squires, answered his call. These men were Burgundians, and had been persuaded that abandoning Barbushtar to carry on their fight further south was prudent given news of al-Muqtadir's impending attack on the city. The assistance of the Catalans would have bolstered our numbers, but Fernando had to be content with fewer than three thousand men at his disposal. Instead of being disheartened, he put his faith in us and claimed three thousand men would be enough to conquer every *taifa* in Hispania. Buoyed by his words and with Saraqusta subdued, we marched.

We headed west and south through the mountains towards Qalat 'Ayuub, another important city in the *taifa*. A track ran through the mountains and though it made for a quicker journey, part of me was wary about the heights and precipices above us that would be suitable for an ambush. I imagined what would happen if al-Muqtadir went against his word and sent men to rain missiles on us, and I thought of how it would have been for the Frankish knight Hroudland who met his end in similar fashion in the Pyrenees. I doubted many of the knights of Leon would meet a glorious and revered death like Hroudland had;

there would be no songs for men impaled by javelins or felled by an arrow in the neck. But no one else seemed concerned by our surroundings; in fact, most sang songs or called japes to each other to pass the time, and so I let the troubling thoughts go.

Two petty *taifa* kingdoms of Sahlatu Bani Razin and Al-Sahla stood on the road to Balansiya, but they surrendered without a fight. And once we had passed them the raiding commenced. The wrath of King Fernando was unleashed against the land around Balansiya. We caused more devastation than we did to the lands of al-Muqtadir, slaughtered or enslaved villagers and drove the survivors to the safety of the castles that dotted the land. Mosques were stripped of their wealth and the loot from the campaign was piled high in to the carts until every man felt they would return to Leon a rich man. We feasted on goat and lamb laced with spices accompanied by the bounty of the many *huertas* we encountered; spinach and artichokes, rice and sorghum followed by sweet oranges. At night we drank pillaged wine and sang of our victories before we set out the morning after and engaged in the same bloodshed. For three weeks we savaged the land like a pack of rabid wolves, destroyed the economy of the *taifa*. Then we marched to the city itself.

King Fernando had desires to reduce Balansiya to another vassal state like Saraqusta, but the optimism brought on by our pillaging dwindled when we stared at the great walls before us. They were taller and thicker than those at Saraqusta or Leon, and the spears and helms of the defenders glinted in the sunlight as they stood defiant against us, dared us to throw ourselves at the walls and die trying to dislodge them. It was clear we would not be entering the city any time soon.

Instead, the king ordered us to make camp around the city, to cut off entry to each gate and fortify our position while he decided on our next move. We were situated next to the river Turia and so could draw fresh water, and there were abundant *huertas* around the city to keep us fed, tended by forage parties and the multitude of servants that had accompanied us. Skirmishers patrolled the edge of our new domain lest an attack came from the city, but we knew none would come. The men of Balansiya knew it would be folly to leave the safety of such a formidable defence.

We settled in for a siege.

Days went by, and life settled in to a tedious, repetitive routine. From dawn until dusk we collected water and firewood and maintained the tents and practised, always practised, for the time when we would fight. The extra work was hard, but I was used to it now. Some days I saw a young man named Braolio, who was Azarola's squire and came from the city of Zamora in southern Leon. He would stare at me and I would return the glares, and they intensified when he was with his master. Azarola would narrow his eyes at me before he smirked and carried on with his duties. He would not be smiling when I killed him. But getting close to him when he was surrounded by his own men would be impossible. I knew I had to bide my time.

The men of Balansiya showed no sign of coming forth from their walls and given the size of the city they would be well provisioned. We could not starve them out before the campaign season came to an end in the late autumn. Every day men with headdresses or helms patrolled the walls and jeered us, or else watched our camps, tried to gauge our actions. Many of our own men were thinking the same thing.

'How long can we remain like this?' growled Arias. 'We are not equipped for a siege. We should be on the way back to Leon.'

Some of the knights clashed in mock duels in an open area in the camp. Rodrigo was one of them and he cast aside opponent after opponent, undefeated in every contest. Blunted steel rang loud between the groans and cries of men, and iron and sweat glistened in the sunlight as knights kept themselves occupied. They were proud warriors who relished the chaos of battle, but in the heat of the sun, besieging an impregnable city, they grew idle all too quickly.

'Why do we not attack?' I asked.

'We would all end up dead, that's why,' Arias replied.

'Then why are we besieging them?'

'Why not go and ask the king that same fucking question, see if he will give you an answer?' He growled, before he sighed and composed himself. Rodrigo knocked another man flat on his arse, which was greeted by a chorus of cheers. 'Fernando wants a great victory. He foolishly thinks he will get one here.'

'He wins everywhere he goes.'

'He can defeat any man in the field, but against that?' he motioned to the walls of Balansiya. 'There is no victory.'

'What do you say, Arias?' Rodrigo called. 'Fancy an arse kicking, you old goat?'

Arias smirked. 'I look forward to smashing a few of your teeth out, boy.' He tied his hair in to a knot, retrieved his shield and picked a blunt steel from a rack. 'If I were you, Antonio, I would find something to keep yourself occupied. Something tells me we will be here for a long time, and for no real gain.'

Days turned to weeks, and each day was the same. But it would not remain so forever.

As the siege dragged on the problems began.

*   *   *

It started with flames in the night.

As the army slept and the sentries watched the walls of Balansiya, tents caught fire. The men inside screeched as they were roasted alive in the inferno. The darkness was illuminated with bright orange light and shadows danced as men frantically rushed here and there to collect water to douse the fire; petrified horses thrashed and the sickening stench of burning flesh caught the back of my throat and made me gag. As the fires raged, we heard cries of *"Allāhu akbar!"* call out in the night, and then there was silence.

'Fucking cowards!' the king roared after them. 'Come and face us like real men, you damned turds!'

But there was no answer. Just silence.

King Fernando doubled the number of sentries on duty, but the attack had the desired effect. The men were already restless and now their morale had taken a blow. Tensions rose and boiled over as arguments over petty things spiralled out of control. Fernando had several prominent trouble makers flogged in public, and one knight of Leon was stripped of his rank after he nearly killed a comrade in a heated dispute. The king would not allow discipline to dwindle.

Then the sickness began.

Tributaries of the river Turia were our sources of water and they served us well for the most part, until dysentery spread amongst the soldiers. Our bowels turned to water and our vomit was nothing but bile. The stench was unbearable, and we walked the camp with cloths over our noses. Some of the infected died and the disease spread further, ate away at us like a plague of locust to a crop. My own bowels burned with everything I ate or dared to drink. The strength in my limbs waivered, as it did with many, and in such a state the men of Balansiya would have an easy victory if they attacked. But still they stayed behind their walls.

Even the king was struck with the disease, confined to his tent, tended by priests. Those same priests wandered the camp and called blessings to the dying, told them their pain would dissipate when they reached Heaven. Sancho, assuming command in the king's absence, sent patrols up the tributaries, and they found the rotten carcasses of goats and sheep dumped on the banks of at least two of them from where we collected our drinking water. Their infected entrails had seeped in to the water we drank. The carcasses were cleared and burned, but it made little difference. The damage had already been done. The Moors had inflected another defeat upon us.

'If the king does nothing this army will die,' Arias said bitterly. We stood by the edge of the camp and gazed at the city walls. It was now late September and the sun was setting behind us, gave the sky a violet tinge as a cool breeze caressed our cheeks. The siege had dragged on week by week and dozens had succumbed to dysentery, with hundreds more recovering or still reeling from the effects.

'Do you think we can take the city?' I asked.

'No.'

'You could not be more correct.'

Rodrigo wandered towards us with a water skin in his hand. He offered it to us, and I hesitated as pain flared in my stomach again.

'Do not worry. It's fresh. Not all of the water sources are tainted.'

He took a swig himself to banish any hint of uncertainty. I took a draught before I passed it to Arias, who took it from me but simply stared at the walls of Balansiya.

'How would you take it?' he asked Rodrigo.

The young knight narrowed his bright eyes. 'A city like that cannot be taken by force without an army of at least ten thousand. Perhaps incite a revolt within the population? Balansiya is a city well stocked with provisions and internal water sources. They can last for months, perhaps a year. A besieging army cannot.' He gazed over our camp, sapped of morale and riddled with disease. 'The men of Balansiya have showed great cunning in poisoning our water and attacking us in the dead of night, and they are buoyed by such victories. We have been here too long. We should have raided the land, moved on to Tulaytula and returned to Leon rich men, but Fernando wants another great victory. The truth is we lost this war before it even started.'

'I imagine we would be going home soon?'

'The king needs his victory first.'

'Well he will not get one here.'

A silence ensued as we stared at the walls, broken only by a loud groan which erupted from my stomach. They both stared at me. 'I need to shit again. Excuse me.'

A painful cramp engulfed my innards as I waddled to an area of latrines and pits away from the camp. The stench was rancid, but having lived with it for weeks I had grown accustomed to it. As darkness closed in torches were lit to illuminate the camp. There were only a handful of men at the pits and so I found a spot away from the others before I dropped my breeches, squatted and closed my eyes, let my body do its business.

I breathed a sigh of relief when the pain dissipated, before I cleaned myself and pulled my breeches up. It was dark now, and the cool evening air was pleasant as I started back towards the camp. Silence ensued save for a few voices japing in the camp and my own boots that scraped on the dirt.

A shuffle to the left caught my attention.

I peered in to the darkness, scanned for any movement. All was silent again and the torches provided only scant light, not enough to pierce the gloom. I took a few wary steps forward, kept my eyes peeled. I heard it again, closer now, quicker than before.

'Hello?' I called. Silence greeted me. 'Who's there?'

A knife scraped from its scabbard.

The shadow moved swift from the black abyss, the knife reflecting the torchlight. The figure was hooded and moved with such speed I barely had time to react. As the knife was drawn back and thrust at me, I threw myself back, landed on the floor with a thud. My attacker was undeterred and launched himself at me again. I rolled out of the way as the knife blade sank in to the dirt next to me. I panted and tried to scramble away but my leg was taken from beneath me. I turned on my back as the figure loomed over me, and a fist caught me square on my cheek. Pain flared throughout my head and I sensed the figure raise the knife in both hands, ready to strike again, but I kicked out hard and caught him in the crotch. A bestial howl filled the night as my attacker doubled over, and it gave me the moment I needed to dart back to the camp.

'Help!' I cried as I ran, my assailant stumbled after me. 'Help me, please!'

My calls were answered, and as I entered the camp dozens of men appeared from their tents brandishing weapons. Arias and Rodrigo arrived, and I ran straight to them. A thud and a commotion sounded from behind me and the hooded figure was on the floor, apprehended by three soldiers. The assassin tried to wriggle free, but when one of the soldiers held a sword to their throat, they knew resistance was futile and the fight ebbed away. Their hood was pulled away to reveal the face of a Moor, mid-twenties perhaps, with olive skin and thick black hair and a beard that extended past his chest. A scar ran from his cheek through his upper lip, the pale flesh shining in the torchlight.

'Why was he chasing you?' Arias studied the man.

'I do not know,' I panted, caught my breath.

'He is one of Nasr al-Baytar's men.'

Sancho strode from the darkness with his brother Alfonso. The Moor stiffened at their presence. Alfonso looked at him with curiosity as Sancho glared, said something in the Moorish tongue in a harsh tone. A brief conversation ensued before the Moor nodded towards me.

'He says he was sent here to kill you,' Alfonso said as he turned.

All eyes turned to me.

'Why would he want to kill me?' I muttered.

No one could provide an answer. It was then I saw Azarola in the crowd. There was no smug expression on his face; only annoyance, fury almost, as if he was disappointed I was still alive.

'You,' I growled at him. 'If you wanted me dead why not do the deed yourself?'

He stepped out from the crowd. 'Watch your tongue or I will cut it out, you insolent shit,' he replied coldly.

'Not before I gut you first.'

'Antonio,' Rodrigo called in warning.

Azarola paced back and forth, addressed the congregation with a raised voice. 'Am I expected to endure the taunts and threats of a traitor's son? I would not allow such a cretin to live, but to give him a knife in the dark? That is beyond me. I look my enemies in the eye when I end their lives.'

'Enough,' Alfonso barked. 'This matter with you has dragged on too long. We will end this once and for all.' He looked at Sancho, who nodded in agreement. 'Antonio Perez, come with us. It is time to face the king's justice.'

Alfonso marched through the press of men towards the centre of the camp as two of the soldiers escorted the Moor in the same direction. I did not move, but soon found myself being shoved long by Sancho. Through the camp we wound until we arrived at the centre, at the tent of King Fernando. Two knights stood vigil by the entrance and stiffened when the princes approached.

'Is my father still awake?' Alfonso enquired.

'He is, your highness, but he is still tender from illness.'

Sancho and Alfonso entered the tent with the Moor, and I was left outside. The sky was black as pitch and the breeze had died down, so the air was warm and stale. The two knights stared at me as they kept vigil, even more so when my stomach groaned. I did my best to hide my discomfort and gazed at the starry sky, tried to pick out shapes from the constellations.

It felt like an eternity had passed before the brothers exited the tent.

'My father wants to see you,' Sancho said.

'What is to become of him?' I asked, motioning to the Moor. He thrashed and cursed as he was dragged away.

'He will be executed. He told us all we needed to know, so now he is expendable. Go in. My father will not be kept waiting.'

I took a deep breath and passed through the open tent flap.

We knew the illness had afflicted the king more than most, but the scent of incense did little to mask the stench of shit that cloyed the air. A few candles had been lit to offer scant light and most of the interior was shrouded in shadow, but an elaborate helm and sword were laid on a table top next to a circlet studded with precious rubies and sapphires, glinted in the light like stars in the night. In the centre of the table with a map of Hispania held down with weights. A figure rose from a chair behind it.

'So, you are the son of Pedro Valdez,' a raspy voice said. I held my tongue, not wanting to incur the wrath of the king by contradicting his judgment. My silence annoyed him. 'Speak, boy. I did not bring you in to my tent just to gawp at me.'

'Yes. I am Antonio Perez, son of Pedro Valdez de Lugones…highness.'

King Fernando moved in to the light. His complexion was pale and his cheeks and eyes gaunt, and the red tunic he wore was loose on his slender frame. He had not been seen for some time during the outbreak of dysentery, and now it was plain to see why. The illness had taken its toll.

'Everyone seems surprised to see you alive,' he said.

'I consider myself lucky to be alive, highness.'

'So, tell me why I should not have you executed right here in my tent?'

I swallowed hard. 'On what charge?'

'That is the question. You have been quite the trouble maker I am led to believe. Men whisper you were involved in the theft of personal items of al-Muqtadir, amongst other things, which we will come to later. I have heard many conflicting views, two from my own sons at least. What am I to believe on this matter? There are those who call for your execution like your father, yet you stand before me now and I have my doubts as to whether that would be the correct course to follow.'

I could not stop my brow rising in surprise but held my tongue.

King Fernando planted his arms on the table and glared. 'I will ask you plainly. Were you at Saraqusta with your father?'

'No, your highness. I was in Lugones.'

He stared at me a moment, before he nodded to himself. 'I can believe that. Al-Muqtadir confirmed himself he has never set eyes upon you or your brother. What is more, he claims your father was innocent of the crimes he was tried for.'

My jaw tightened and my fists clenched with anger. My inkling had been correct all along; my father was innocent of treason. But now I knew he died for nothing.

'I understand this must be difficult for you to hear,' Fernando said, sensing a change in my demeanour.

'He was set up. He was innocent,' I growled.

'That is why I want Nasr al-Baytar and his supporters – alive. He has shed too much blood in recent years, and I intend to make him answer for it. He is one in a long line of Moors who wish to disrupt amicable relations between Christian and Muslim, and help deliver al-Andalus back in to the hands of a Moorish Caliphate. But he is guilty of more than slaughtering people and treason against his own cousin. It was he who planted the items in the treasures gifted to your father by al-Muqtadir.'

'You should look closer to home as well, your highness.'

'Bernardo Garces,' he said slowly. I nodded, which was met by a long sigh, as if it was a reluctant subject for the king. 'What evidence do you have to support his involvement?'

'He arrested my father at Lugones.'

'I ordered him to.'

'He was the one liaising with al-Baytar at Lugones. They looked like they were working together.'

'Al-Baytar was there on orders from al-Muqtadir to recover his property. Azarola was there to assist, so it is natural they worked together.'

'He was jealous!' I said more passionately. 'Azarola was angry because he had the chance to kill Ramiro at Graus, but my father saved his life and killed your brother himself. Azarola was envious of the prosperity my father received after the battle and fabricated this entire ploy with al-Baytar because he is a pathetic weasel who cares only for himself. You should arrest and execute *him*!'

I surprised myself at my rant to the king. I expected some sort of reprimand, a threat of violence or imprisonment. But the king just stared at me, his grey eyes bright in the low light. He reached for a goblet on the table and drank a draught of wine.

'Do you know Azarola saved my own life, once?' he said softly as he placed the goblet down. I nodded. 'It was during the battle of Atapuerca when we fought my brother, Garcia, who was king of Navarre. I was in the thick of the fighting and my horse was struck by a javelin. I was trapped beneath the beast, helpless, defenceless. Azarola stood over me and fought off every man who dared come our way before I was dragged from underneath my horse. I hailed him as a hero, and he has had my gratitude ever since. Now tell me,' he leaned forward, 'why would I so easily cast aside the life of the man I owe my own to? If someone were to accuse Azarola of treason they had better bring me some damned good evidence. Only then would I entertain the idea.'

'But my father...'

The king held a hand up for me to stop before he rubbed his tired eyes. 'My judgement is passed. I am tired and will waste no more time on it. But now you will tell me of your crimes on the Camino de Santiago. Tell me of your sins.'

I told him everything, from the death of the priest to Rodrigo's capture of us, and everything that went before and after. He listened intently, and allowed it all to sink in before he spoke.

'Do you think you will go to Hell, Antonio Perez?'

'Yes, your highness.' I had no doubt of it.

'Do you think I will?'

'Of course not, your highness,' I frowned. 'You are a king. When your time comes your place by the Lord is assured.'

'Is it?' he spat. 'You have killed a handful of men, a priest among them, yet I have slaughtered thousands. I killed one brother, and allowed my son to kill the other, so I could call myself king with no rival. Why would a king be exempt from joining the devil in his domain for his crimes? No Antonio, you are wrong. I *will* go to Hell. But I will beg for God's forgiveness until my dying breath, in the hope he will see me repent. Like me, when you return home you will do penance for your sins. Then I will decide if you have been punished enough.'

'What about Azarola?'

'You will give him no more thought. It is my judgement that he had nothing to do with what you speak of, and when al-Baytar is captured and reprimanded you will be content your father is avenged. I will hear no more of it. Do I make myself perfectly clear?'

'Yes, your highness,' I replied meekly.

'Good. Now go and start packing your lord's things. Tomorrow I will order the retreat from Balansiya. We are going home.'

'Home?' I exclaimed.

The king nodded. 'We should have raided these lands and left with all the loot we could. That would have been enough vengeance for the slaughter brought on by al-Baytar's bloodlust. But I thought we could subdue Balansiya and Tulaytula in a single swift campaign. How wrong I was. So yes, tomorrow we will return to Leon. Now go, leave an old man in peace.'

Come dawn the news of the impending retreat filtered around the camp. Our gear and loot were loaded back on to the carts and mules. The last of the bodies of those who had died from illness were given burial in the land around the city, presided over by the priests who prayed for their souls. Mid-morning came and we began the long march.

It was a glorious day as the sun beat down overhead and the sea breeze gave bursts of cool against the heat. The mood was sullen, as if we had suffered a defeat, but many men were glad to be returning to Leon. Then a buzz filled the air. We were barely a few miles from the city with the river Turia on our left, let the river guide our way, when riders from the rear guard rushed to the king. Soon the news they carried reverberated throughout the whole army.

The gates of Balansiya had been thrown open.

And the Moors within came for us.

Eleven

A council of war was hastily called, with all the leading lords in attendance. The rest of us waited with bated breath. Some were nervous at the prospect of battle, whilst others licked their lips in anticipation of the impending bloodshed. I found myself in the camp of the former. I was untested in battle, apprehensive about taking the plunge and entering the carnage. No amount of training could prepare me. I gripped my sword hilt tight so stop the trembling in my limbs.

'I can see you are shitting yourself,' Arias chuckled as he took a long draught of wine from a skin. He offered it to me, but I declined.

'I have been shitting myself for weeks. I do not want to die today.'

'If we are to fight, you will be nothing more than a spectator. It is the knights who must do the fighting. Keep up with your training and one day you might experience it, Antonio.' He looked in to the distance, relived some past conflict. 'War is a glorious thing. The way the ground shakes as hundreds of horses gallop across the plain; the way the whites of your enemies' eyes light up at the sight of the spear point coming for him; the way men scream and bones crunch and blood sprays as the charge hits home.' He turned and grinned at me. 'I have missed it.'

'Are men truly supposed to love battle?'

'A man who does not love battle is as good as dead at a time like this. These men who will ride with me have embraced the way of the sword and are willing to die by it. The warrior culture is embedded in our society; it is our world, our life. It has been ever since the Visigoths conquered this land from the Romans, and it will still be here when we conquer the land from the Moors. So, my advice to you is to accept it, just as your father did.'

My father had said things in a similar ilk. His father had been a knight, and so had his for many generations. We were descended from a noble Visigothic family who had settled in Asturias hundreds of years ago, after arriving from lands far to the north and east where vast forests cover the land and rain soaks the fields for most of the year. It was my father's wish for me and Inigo to carry on that legacy, but he had not held much hope for me. Now would be the time to prove him wrong.

The council dispersed and the leaders addressed the men. Prince Sancho spoke to the Castilian contingent, in a booming voice so all could hear.

'There are five thousand Moors coming our way.' A murmur of excitement and discontent rumbled through the men. 'They have hid behind their walls, ground us down and sapped our morale, and now they think they can finish us off. But we're going to show them the Kingdom of Leon-Castile has more fight in it than they could ever have imagined.'

'We are going to fight them, lord?' Arias called.

'No. We are going to slaughter them!' He drew his sword and thrust it skywards in a salute, which was greeted with a great roar of approval that erupted from the gathered men, buoyed by the prince's words.

On our retreat from Balansiya we travelled a dirt road north and west, followed the river Turia as it snaked through the land. The banks were heavily wooded and the land to the north was also pocketed with thick forest. The outriders had reached a long loop in the river that bent south and west before it resumed its course north, with a shallow ford which would allow us to cross. Here, it was decided, was where we would make our stand.

Part of the baggage train was sacrificed to provide bait for the oncoming Moors. Around five hundred men were chosen to be the anvil, and the rest of us were to be the hammer that would flank the Moors and drive them in to the river. Some of the wagons were moved close to the ford and several of the wheels hacked off, to make it look as though they had broken down as we tried to cross. Two hundred men were left to guard them, most of them citizen militia who would use their spears on foot and defend the wagons from the approaching enemy. Another two hundred men were stationed across the ford with the rest of the wagons, posed as the rest of the guards for the baggage train and ready to assist when needed. The handful of camp followers and wagon drivers who could use bows and crossbows were positioned in the woods flanking the ford. The rest of us were to hide in the forests to the north and wait for the time to strike, where we would fall upon the rear of the Moorish lines and slaughter them.

'Are you ready, Antonio?' Rodrigo asked as we made for the woodland.

'Will I ever be ready?'

'No, but if there is ever a time it is now.'

'What am I to do in the battle, lord?'

'Stay with the other squires. The knights will charge and try and break them. If we are unsuccessful, we will retreat, and I need you to be ready with another spear. Do not look for me or Arias; just give it to any knight who needs it. If you must fight make sure you are not alone; I cannot guarantee you will live to see the day through, and it is best to die beside your own men.'

'You know how to reassure me, lord.'

'Welcome to war,' he said with a wink. 'God bless you, and I will see you when the day is done.' Rodrigo kicked the flanks of Babieca and joined Arias and the rest of the knights as I guided Asbat towards

255

the rear of the concealed men, kept the spare spear close to me. Horses were settled in the cool shade of the canopy, and the general chatter died down as each man said their prayers to God and partook in pre battle rituals and superstitions. Then we waited.

Less than an hour passed before the Moorish outriders arrived.

A troupe fifty strong galloped in a loose group along the dirt track on swift horses, in hasty pursuit of a group of our scouts chosen to watch the enemy. The Moors stopped when they saw the overturned wagons. Their scale armour shone in the midday sun, and their green tunics and white headdresses were vibrant. Our men were told to act casual and go about the tasks at a leisurely pace, to not draw attention to the trap, but when the Moors arrived, they were to descend in to chaos, feign panic at the approaching enemy. They played their part well, rushed around and tried to make hasty the repairs to the wagons as a portion formed a shallow battle line. But the Moors did not attack. They were there to watch, to intimidate and to keep us in check.

Soon the bulk of the Moorish army arrived.

They marched in a great column that snaked down the dirt road, their footsteps like the rumble of faraway thunder growing louder with an approaching storm. There were spearmen and axe men in leather or scale armour, with small crescent shields covered in hide or leather, and archers with short bows marched under green banners with a black serpent and phrases written in white Moorish script. Two columns of horsemen flanked them and rode strong, swift horses, and were equipped in the same fashion as the infantry, save for a few dozen at the head of the army with coats of mail. And at the helm of these men was the leader of the army, the amir of Balansiya, Abd al-Malik ben Abd al-Aziz al-Mansur.

He sat resplendent on his horse, wearing a coat of chain mail that covered his face and head with only his eyes exposed, and a pointed helm with a long plum of horse hair sat on top. An emerald green cloak of silk hung from his shoulders, another from his horse hemmed with white Moorish script, and a curved sword scabbard hung by his side, trimmed with gold and studded with emeralds and garnets. He led his horse ahead of his army and stared at our men by the overturned wagons, by now formed in to a semi-circular shield wall bristling with spears. Everything was quiet as both armies stared each other down. Asbat snorted gently and I stroked his neck to calm him as my own heart pounded against my chest, waiting for the inevitable.

Al-Malik drew his fine sword and held it to the sky as he called out a mighty battle cry in his own tongue. His men followed his lead and filled the air with the same cry that echoed across the land, beat weapons on shields, tried to dishearten our men. Then they advanced.

The Moorish infantry moved forward at a steady pace, kept a close formation as the cavalry took position on the flanks. Our own men packed tight together but stood firm, and the men across the ford spurred their horses through the water to protect their flanks. We already knew they would lose a fight if it came to it. Their task was to merely hold the Moors in place before we could strike at their heart.

As the Moors closed in the arrows and quarrels from the hidden archers and crossbowmen flew from the trees and sent the Moorish lines in to disarray. Our men jeered them as the enemy stumbled forward over dead bodies, shields raised high. The Moors quickened their pace at the expense of their cohesion. Next came the exchange of javelins; the Moorish missiles bounced off the shields of our men, whilst our own found their target here and there and added more bodies to the dirt. A great roar sounded as the fractured line of Moors charged, followed by the clatter of wood and metal as battle was joined. The quarrels and javelins continued to fly, and the blood flowed and stained the earth.

I heard a whistle somewhere in the forest, followed by the thud of horses' hooves as the long lines of our cavalry trotted forth from the trees. Rank upon rank of knights took their positions, grouped in to squadrons of forty men, and did last minute check of equipment. I was with the squires in the rear ranks, ready to rearm the knights with fresh spears if they turned back for a second charge and lend our support if those initial charges failed to break the enemy. I prayed to God that would not be the case.

King Fernando rode forth from our ranks. His magnificent helm sat upon his head; his white cloak was immaculate, and his polished mail glinted in the sunlight. We were all surprised yet buoyed by his presence, for many believed he would be too ill to take part in the battle, but Fernando needed a victory before we returned to Leon and would not allow his sons to take his glory away.

'Let us drive these heathens from this land!' he cried in a voice feeble for the great king. It was enough to catch the attention of the Moors who, upon seeing a long line of knights to their rear, frantically tried to reform their ranks. 'For God, and the kingdom of Leon-Castile!'

The war cry erupted throughout our lines. Two and a half thousand men roared like lions and clashed their weapons upon their shields, fired up for a fight after months of frustration. On the king's signal the knights advanced.

The front rank of our cavalry burst forward. The horses of a thousand knights set off at a canter, and before them rode a loose line of skirmishers, mounted on the swiftest of horses who carried a handful of javelins that would disrupt the enemy as they tried to organise themselves. The long line broke in to three groups and they slowed their pace as they neared the Moorish lines, and those lines bent in to crescents that slowly manifested in to circles. The skirmishers galloped around these circles and, once they neared the enemy, launched a javelin, and repeated the action until all their missiles were discharged. Only a handful of Moorish missiles hit their mark against the ever-moving targets. The constant barrage kept the enemy in check and created holes in their formation, ready for what was to come.

The skirmishers, having done their duty, galloped back towards our lines and through gaps made by the squadrons of knights as they trotted forward. Those gaps closed and the pace quickened to a gallop. Hooves beat against the earth and rumbled like thunder, caused a thin haze of dirt to kick up as they went. The knights rode side by side, so close their legs almost touched, to present a wall of horseflesh and steel tipped spears. A wave of death surged towards for the Moors. Al-Malik rode behind his lines and shouted encouragement, but the Moorish line was bent and fractured from wavering courage.

The knights crashed in to the Moors in an explosion of noise.

Lances were shattered on shields and helms, pierced flesh and bone. Horses were skewered on spears, and men were thrown from the saddle or flung in to the air from the impact of the charge. Blood flowed as if fountains had sprung forth from the earth, drenched everything from weapons and armour to flesh and cloth in a sickly crimson tide. Dust kicked up and hung over the battle in a haze, obscured vision and cast a shade across the fight. It was difficult to see what was happening and I could not imagine what it must have been like to be close to the enemy, hacking and slashing at anything that moved.

The charge devastated the Moorish lines, but they held firm. A series of horns rang out and the knights turned their horses around to regroup. With their backs exposed they were easy targets for the Moorish archers who picked off several with their short bows and sent the brave men to the dirt. Rodrigo led his men back to the lines, and Arias brought up the rear. His spear had been cast aside and his sword was thick with crimson that dripped and stained the dirt. I gripped his spare spear in my hand and prepared to hand it over, ready for when the knights rallied and launched another assault.

That is when I saw the steel flash in the sunlight.

At first, I thought another knight had rallied to his side, but Guerrero's rear leg buckle, and with a piercing screech the horse went down. Arias was thrown from the saddle and crashed to the ground, powerless to avoid Guerrero from toppling on to him. It was only when I saw the nearest knight to Arias did I realise what had happened. That knight was Azarola.

The bastard had hacked at Guerrero's leg and drove the beast down, and now Arias was isolated between us and the Moors. And now a handful of the Moors saw him defenceless and rushed from their scattered lines to finish him off. Azarola looked behind to see if his attack had the desired affect and spurred his horse harder to join the reforming ranks of knights.

A great void opened in my stomach. I wanted to spur Asbat forward and come to my lord's aid, but my muscles were frozen. Fear had gripped me. Fear of charging in to the fray, of bloodying my sword and the risk of grievous injury or death. The long months of training could not prepare me for the terror that struck my heart from gazing on so much destruction wrought on the human body. But my father's voice came in to my mind, stern and authoritative as ever.

Do not let Azarola win, his voice said. *Be brave. Make me proud.*

A tear trickled down my cheek as I remembered him and thought of what he would have done to protect his kin, his comrades and his kingdom. He had inspired victory at Graus with his actions. Arias was helpless. He needed me. I had a duty to protect my lord.

Be brave.

I tightened the grip on the spear in my hand and roared my father's name in a battle cry as my heels kicked Asbat's flanks. The horse reared and darted forward, and before I knew it, I had wound through the retreating knights and galloped towards the advancing Moors.

I paid no attention to the calls that ordered me back to the lines. My only thought was to save Arias, the man who had taken me beneath his wing. My mouth became dry, yet my brow and upper lip were saturated. I gripped the reigns tight and guided Asbat headlong at the enemy, close enough now to see there were five of them only a stone's throw from Arias, all on foot, two of them with spears and the rest with the short axes favoured by the Moors. Others had already reached wounded knights and finished them off with a cut to the throat and a spear through the neck of injured horses, and I knew I could not allow that to happen to Arias. They expected easy pickings, but they realised all too late I came for them.

I thrust at the first Moor, struggled to keep Asbat steady. The aim was true, and the impact launched him in to the air. I let go of the spear as my enemy thudded in to the ground, gasped for air as the life drained from him. I paid him no heed as I drew my sword, slowed my pace and attacked my next opponent, but he was prepared and he ducked my first strike, sidestepped the second and swung his axe which I parried. Asbat circled and kicked one of the Moors in the face with a sickening crunch as I continued my attack. The height advantage offered by my horse proved fruitful as a strike from high caught him in the neck.

The two remaining Moors lunged with their spears and Asbat reared in panic. I tried to keep my balance but could not stop myself tumbling from the saddle. Pain engulfed my right side as I thudded on the ground. Fear gripped me when I saw my sword had been thrown from my grasp, and I desperately lunged after it, only to be blocked by one of the Moors. I scrambled to my feet, gritted my teeth and fought through the pain and held my small round shield up to block a spear aimed at my torso. I sprang forward and shoved him with my shield to put some distance between us before I deflected another strike from his comrade. They both levelled their spears and tried to flank me, but I backed away, gave myself time to conjure a plan of action. But I was bereft of ideas.

'Antonio!'

I spun to where Arias lay, still trapped beneath Guerrero. He threw his own sword my way. It landed at my feet and I hastily picked it up. The feel of the smooth leather tang in my grasp brought a surge of renewed confidence and I faced my two attackers down, watched them above the rim of my shield and studied their posture. They were cautious now, intimidated, and I used it to my advantage. I sprang forward, kept my shield high as a spear prodded the wooden planks before I dropped to one knee and stabbed forward. I felt the tip pierce flesh and grind on bone, which was followed by a howl of pain. I stabbed again and again, and soon my opponent fell to floor, his belly and thigh stained with blood. I went to stamp on his face, but the second Moor was too quick for me and his spear battered the side of my head. A great light blinded me, and the warmth of the sun beat on my face as my helmet was knocked clean off by the blow. With my vision no longer stifled the world brightened, and the colours became more vivid and the details enhanced. Thick blood was everywhere, dripped from weapons, splattered on flesh and garments and congealed in pools in the dirt.

I tried to drive my opponent away with my sword in great arcs, but each time the Moor stabbed at my face with his spear. A sharp pain along my temple made me wince and grit my teeth, and the trickle of blood betrayed the gash where the spear had caught me. For the next few moments I dodged darting spear thrusts, edged backwards. I did not see the body of the Moor behind me until it was too late. I tripped and fell over the corpse, rolled on to my back and tried to scramble away. But the Moor was quick and shouted in his own tongue as he loomed over me, lifted the spear, ready to strike. I muttered a silent prayer to God, begged him to allow me in to Heaven, certain my time had come.

A great mass darted passed, and the glint of steel as a sword took the Moor in the back. He shrieked and collapsed as Rodrigo reined in Babieca and stared at me.

'You all right?' he called as more squadrons of knights charged passed us towards the reformed lines of the Moors, fresh spears poised for the charge. A mass of squires followed them, looked to add weight to the charge and put the enemy to flight. The knights and squires of Vivar caught up to their leader and awaited his orders. I could not speak but managed a relieved laugh then nodded, took a moment to saviour being alive. 'Good. Now get up and get back in the fight.' He turned Babieca and shouted to his men. 'With me, men of Vivar!'

As the battle raged on, I crawled over to where Arias lay beneath Guerrero. He was still but managed to open his eyes when I knelt beside him.

'Lord, are you okay?'

'Never felt better,' he croaked. Blood covered his mouth, and when he coughed fresh crimson coated the dried patches. 'Couple of broken ribs...a shattered leg I imagine. A flagon of wine would not go amiss.'

'I will get help to move your horse.' Guerrero was a large horse and would take several men to lift him enough to slide Arias out. I looked around for help, but Arias waved me away.

'You will get back on your horse and help win this battle, boy,' he barked. 'Leave me and go. I will still be alive when you get back.'

I hesitated, but the glare he gave me persuaded me to carry out his wishes. I retrieved my sword and helm, mounted Asbat and said a prayer to God to keep me safe.

I kicked Asbat's flanks and entered the fray.

*   *   *

It felt like a dream as I galloped in to the field of death.

I looked at the bodies strewn on the floor, their faces contorted in grotesque expressions, frozen in pain and suffering. Limbs lay hacked off like animals to the slaughter, bits of bone and jellied meat amongst the blood, corpses slumped in heaps where they lay without dignity. If those men who sing songs and write accounts of battles saw this side of it, would they sing of the screams and butchery? The blood and the shit from voided bowels, the bestial noises men make as they desperately hack at each other? Of course not. Those tales are meant to tell of victory and inspire men to fight. If men virgin to battle knew of this side of war, they would stay safe behind their walls. I was in no haste to join the corpses, and so focused on the battle that raged ahead.

The knights had hit the Moorish lines in a second charge and penetrated deep in to the main body of men. Many Moors lay dead but there were still a great host who fought on, and the Moorish cavalry had joined the fight. The battle descended in to a desperate slog. Knights had discarded their shattered spears and hacked and slashed with swords and axes. I followed Rodrigo as he led his men towards the flanks to attack the Moorish cavalry there, to encircle the enemy. I slashed left and right, kept momentum and tried to maintain balance, sensed my blade scrape off metal and bite in to flesh.

A Moor on a grey steed came at me, sword raised in his hand, and my arm jarred as the blades kissed. We hacked and parried as our horses wheeled, whinnied and thrashed, then my opponent's horse shied away from a corpse on the ground as he thrust with his sword, knocked him off balance. I hacked down with my sword and felt the blade cut through leather, flesh and bone as his hand was severed from his arm. The Moor looked dumbstruck as he stared as his stump, as the blood spurted forth, but before he could scream, I drew back and slashed. His throat exploded in a fountain of crimson and a bestial gargle came forth from his mouth. I recoiled as the blood splashed in my eye, face and the front of my armour, made me gag as the sickly scent filled my nostrils. Asbat flinched and thrashed, but soon retained his composure.

A monster of a man in a gleaming scale coat screamed in his native tongue and lunged at Gotinus with a spear. The block headed squire kept his mount active, tried to swat away the attack, but his assailant was skilled, and a precise strike caught him in the right shoulder, pierced the hardened leather and drew blood. Gotinus cried out, could not prevent another strike clip the side of his helm and knock him off balance. But before the Moor could finish him off, he roared in pain as Mancio's sword took him in the back of the neck, slumped to the ground in a heap. Mancio gave the squire a nod of reassurance before he spurred his horse off the follow Rodrigo.

The lord of Vivar was untouchable. His sword was slick with thick crimson blood, rose and fell with ferocity as all before him succumbed to his might. Babieca's shimmering snow coat was blighted by streaks of pink, but the steed was unfazed. I sat upon Asbat and stared in awe, enthralled by the ease of the killing. He had led his knights in to the midst of the elite Moorish cavalry, and more lords and knights had followed his lead to outflank the enemy, cause a rout and win the day. Rodrigo caught a strike aimed at his head in mid-air from the right, pushed the enemy's blade away then slashed with such vigour his foe's head was almost cloven from his shoulders. His head had already turned to the left and the tip of the blade pierced the shoulder of another Moor, who looked to best Aigeru, then a hack from high finished off a dismounted opponent. He was engrossed by the battle joy men feel when the blood of a foe runs slick upon your arm. Yet Rodrigo was but one man, and many Moors remained. I plucked up my courage and looked to enter the fray once more.

Then I saw him.

At first, he looked like any other Moor who fought for his life, wore fine scale armour with a yellow cloak sullied by blood and grime upon his shoulders. Most had mail hoods or helms that obscured their faces, but he was confident for he wore nothing on his head but a yellow headdress. The wicked gash on his left cheek was all too familiar. My heart thumped against my chest and anger boiled within me, and then came the anticipation at the prospect of finally gaining revenge for the death of my father.

'Nasr al-Baytar!' I screamed.

He turned in his saddle and stared at me. I removed my helm and allowed him to see my bare face. Though covered in blood he recognised me, and a savage grin curled upon his face. He stood before me, defiant, ripe for the taking. I replaced my helm and knew what I had to do.

I kicked Asbat's flanks once more, levelled my sword and bellowed my father's name as I charged towards him. He grinned and accepted my challenge, spurred his own horse forward. Fear gripped me as the gap closed quicker than I had anticipated. I let out an almighty roar as I raised my sword and al-Baytar lifted his own, a long sword with a single curved edge favoured by the Moors. We swung and our blades collided, beginning our sword song.

The force of the impact jarred my arm and pain burned all the way to my shoulder, but I gritted my teeth and turned Asbat around. Al-Baytar was quicker and slashed at my left side, scraped paint off my shield. I had to let go of the reins to move my shield around freely, to deflect sword stroke after sword stroke that beat relentless on the wood. It was difficult to defend and keep my balance in the saddle, and being the better rider al-Baytar took advantage of my inexperience and moved his horse around the back of me, tried to slash at my back. I shifted my legs to the right and deflected with my sword, but the sudden movement left me unbalanced.

Al-Baytar's blade slashed at my torso and a sharp pain engulfed my ribs. My jerkin had failed to stop the cut and the gash seeped crimson, though it was not deep enough to cause too much damage. But whilst I was distracted al-Baytar lashed out with a boot, and the force knocked me from the saddle. The impact made me grunt and cough, Asbat whinnied and galloped away, and before I could react al-Baytar slashed once more. I rolled to the side, saw my shield had been thrown from my grasp and so raised my sword to block his attacks. The swords embraced time and time again as he drove me back, the savagery of his attacks unrelenting, the expression on his visage bestial.

He raised his arm to strike from high, and I seized that moment to lunge forward with my own sword. My aim was true, and the tip pierced his thigh and scraped against the bone. As he recoiled from the pain I draw back and hacked at his shin. The leather greave took the edge off the blow, but the sharp edge cut in to the meat of his leg, and a howl erupted from his mouth. I tried to attack again but this time his sword clashed with mine, jarred my arm, and through gritted teeth al-Baytar intensified his own attacks. The pain in his leg had whipped a rage within him. My muscles burned and each attack sapped my strength more and more until I had nothing more to give. I slumped to one knee, my vision blurred as exhaustion took hold and both my hands gripped along the tang of my sword, prepared for the blow that would finish me off.

But that blow never came.

Through the sound of carnage around us, horns blared in the distance. Al-Baytar's expression descended in to panic as he frantically looked around. He gave one last glare of contempt before he reined his horse in and galloped away as fast as the beast's legs would go. The Moors were in full retreat, with the men of Leon-Castile in pursuit.

Those on foot were ridden down without mercy, hacked in the back by swords or skewered like boars with spears, but those lucky enough to have horses made good their escape back to the city. Al-Malik himself was one of the furthest away, content with saving his own skin rather than dying with his men.

I leapt to my feet and staggered after al-Baytar.

'Come back you coward!' I roared. 'I am not done with you yet! I swear by God I will kill you one day. My face will be the last thing you ever see in this life!' The anger released a torrent of emotion, and I did not fight the tears as they cascaded down my cheeks. My sword dropped from my hand and I removed the helm from my head, threw it on to the dirt, crouched down and breathed heavily. Several moments passed as the emotion slowly ebbed away. I had survived the battle, and I had come face to face with one of the men I loathed, but I was not strong enough to kill him. My father's face flashed in my mind; his expression locked in the same visage of disapproval I was acquainted to.

I felt like a failure.

When I looked up again the sky burned with a deep orange glow as the sun began to set in west, as if the fires of a great forge had burst in to life. There were bodies as far as the eye could see; Christian and Muslim embraced in death's grip, blood and entrails and scattered limbs littered the ground. It was a scene from Hell, one that sent a chill down my spine. The mood was solemn as the men of Leon-Castile gathered the bodies of their fallen comrades and those of the enemy. Graves were already being dug for our men as the priests gave last rites to the dying, while the Moors were thrown on to great pyres ready to be burned, their arms, armour and valuables stacked high to be divided as spoils of war. Surgeons tended to the savage wounds of screaming victims and carrion birds circled high and pecked at the dead, attracted by the gagging stench, and returned too quickly when chased away by the soldiers.

I looked at the wound on my torso. Blood still trickled gently down my tunic. I winced at the pain emitted with the deftest touch. I knew I would need cleaned before it became infected, but the ache in my limbs prevented me from moving. The relative tranquillity after the carnage of the battle was well received, and I took a moment to savour it.

A shadow moved across me and I looked to see Rodrigo. He wiped his sword clean of blood with a scrap of cloth taken from a corpse, and his mail was splattered with sickly pink stains. A relieved smile adorned his face.

'It is good to see you alive, Antonio.' He sheathed his sword and offered me his hand. I accepted it and got to my feet. My legs were shaky from the exhaustion, but I took a moment to get my balance. 'You are wounded,' he said, motioned to the gash on my torso.

'My first true war wound,' I replied, tried to pass it off as nothing. 'No doubt it will not be the last. Nasr al-Baytar inflicted it upon me.'

'He was here?' Rodrigo asked. I nodded. 'What became of him?'

'I wounded him, but he managed to escape. I could not finish him off.' I hung my head, still ashamed and feeling a failure.

'Do not be disheartened. He is a great warrior, and that you stand before me now proves you were not just lucky. He knows now who you are and what you are capable of. He will not rest easy knowing you are out there. Something tells me he will fear the day he crosses paths with you again. You will be a better warrior when that day comes. And you will kill him.'

'I hope so.' I let my mind wander and tried to conjure an image of my knife plunging in to al-Baytar's neck, before I snapped back in to reality. 'Where is Arias? Does he live?'

Rodrigo nodded. 'He is alive and well, because of you. What you did was incredibly reckless, but today I saw a squire show more courage than many of the knights in this army. Your bravery has been noted, Antonio Perez. I will see you are rewarded for it when we return to Vivar.' He offered a smile and I was buoyed by his words. He sighed and shook his head. 'Damned Moors and their bows. They must have known that Arias fought like a daemon and sought to shoot him in the back rather than face him like a man.'

'It was not a Moor that brought Arias down. It was Azarola.'

Rodrigo raised an eyebrow. 'What do you mean?'

'I saw him hack at one of Guerrero's legs, which caused him to fall. He turned only to see his plan had worked; he had no intention of helping him, which is why I rode out. I could not give Azarola the satisfaction of another victory over me.'

'That is a serious accusation,' he replied cautiously.

'Why does nobody ever believe me?' I cried out in frustration. 'Azarola hides behind his reputation and his good fortune with the king. He is untouchable and he knows it, which means he can do whatever he likes and get away with it. My father's death, the attempt on Arias life; all his handy work, yet he faces no repercussions.'

'And exactly what do you plan on doing about it?'

No words came out of my mouth, because there was no plan. Just a desperate idea. 'I do not know, yet.'

'You were reckless today and it paid off. Now you must bide your time. There will be opportunity enough in the future.'

'What do you mean?'

'The king was wounded in the battle,' he grimaced. 'He took a spear in the side as he led the second charge.' He motioned to where the king's tent had been erected in the middle of the battlefield, surrounded by knights and militia who tried to catch a glimpse of Fernando. 'The priests and physicians are doing their best to patch him up, but the wound is deep and is sure to fester. We fear he will not last the year. The king does not have long to live.'

'And so, the kingdom will be divided?'

'Yes. Azarola will be our enemy. So now we bide our time.' I nodded to show my understanding. 'Go to your lord. He's been asking after you.'

He patted me on the shoulder and walked away. His words provided comfort in my pessimistic frame of mind. To fight in a battle was one thing, but to survive when combat does not come naturally, and given my reluctance to learn to fight, was a feat I believed was beyond me. A wave of optimism for the future surged over me and gave my limbs renewed vigour. But while my own future felt secure, that of the kingdom of Leon-Castile was shrouded in obscurity.

We had won the battle but, the king was dying.

Twelve

Why are some men so obsessed with war?

The stories passed on in books and the tales men bring from battle tell of heroic deeds, triumphant duels and feats of unrivalled courage. The truth is there is nothing glorious about killing men. Those stories omit the part where your body aches from combat; the way blood sticks to your skin and sword, and after a thousand washes to stench of death still lingers; the way your enemies' screams wake you in the dead of night and the deathly visages haunt your mind. Their deaths of the men I killed were not dignified. Men still boast of such feats, but not I.

The ride back to Vivar was long and the mood despondent.

Each man was concerned for the king and the slow pace to Saraqusta was meant to ease his discomfort, but his condition deteriorated with every passing day. By day he travelled in a litter surrounded by his sons, priests and physicians to tend his every need, with periodic stops to change dressings and offer blessings. By night the howling wind of the waning autumn did little to hide the moans and wails coming from the king's tent. As we travelled further north many believed the king would slip away, but he clung to life, stubborn as he was.

Arias's injuries did not slow him, but he did take to cursing more often. Despite his broken leg and ribs, he insisted on riding. I offered him Asbat and rode a mule instead. Guerrero was mercifully killed due to the injuries suffered in the battle. Arias wept for his horse as a man would weep for a brother, because Guerrero had been with his lord since Arias had become a knight.

'We have been through many battles together,' he said solemnly. 'He was the very best of horses, strong and obedient. My father gave him to me when I became a knight, and he was with me through everything.'

'I am sure you will find another horse, lord, just as loyal and strong.'

'True companions are not so easily replaced.'

Nothing came of Azarola's treachery, as I expected, because all attention was the king's health. No one believed the words that came from the mouth of a simple squire. I had to endure his glares, but where he once looked with contempt, he now looked with caution or frustration, as if my defiance had dealt a blow to his confidence. I returned those looks and conjured different ways of killing him in my head, hoped one day just a single plot would bear fruition.

The king stayed in Saraqusta for some time and al-Muqtadir's physicians did their best to aid in his recovery. His sons and sworn knights stayed by his side whilst the rest of us returned home with the loot we had gained, our services no longer required. As we travelled further north and west biting winds howled from the mountains and a lashing rain soaked our cloaks and dampened our spirits. Elation filled us when the castle of Vivar appeared on the horizon in the early morning, a blanket of fog hanging above it. It was late autumn when we arrived, and the relief on everyone's face when we returned was evident. It was uncommon for armies to be in the field beyond the autumn when the conditions for fighting became unsavoury, and with the lack of news coming from the south Teresa feared the worst. She embraced Rodrigo and beamed with pride at his exploits and the heap of loot he returned with. Dometza cradled Arias and tended to his every need when she saw his injuries, and grieved with him for Guerrero. Father Auderico too beamed at our return and praised God for keeping us safe, and even Gonzalo the smith was happy his handiwork had kept us alive. Yet no one was happier to see me more than Constanza.

When we locked eyes, she gave a relieved smile and embraced me tight.

'It is so good to see you again, Antonio,' she beamed. Her chestnut hair smelt of lavender and was pinned high to reveal her slender neck. She had matured in the year since I departed on campaign. Her eyes were brighter, her cheeks more defined and a woman's body hid underneath her dress.

'It is good to see you as well, my lady.'

'When we did not hear news, we feared the worst. I had visions of you not returning.'

'I found I am a harder to kill these days, my lady.'

'I have missed you,' she said, taking an unexpectedly sincere tone. 'It has been a terribly long year. I did not realise how much I would miss male company around the castle.' Her cheeks blushed. 'There are only so many of Father Auderico's japes and stories I can take. I am sure you have some tales to tell, so what say you tell me all about them later?'

Before I could answer Arias hobbled over and embraced his daughter.

'My dear daughter, how you have grown!'

'It is good to see you alive and well, father,' she replied with a smile.

'That is only down to the actions of this one.' He slapped me hard on the back, made me lurch forward. Both father and daughter shared a laugh. 'I have exciting news for you. Through the boredom and carnage of this past year, I have found you a husband.'

273

She was taken aback but smiled, nonetheless. 'You honour me father. It is such delightful news. May I ask who he is?'

'Garcia Ordóñez de Pancorbo.'

I was as surprised as Constanza. Despite the cleft lip that blighted his visage Garcia was a young knight with a growing reputation, and was fast becoming one of the most powerful men in Castile. His father had once served as *alferez* for Fernando, and there was a consensus Garcia would also hold that office when he matured. Arias had done well to arrange a marriage to such a high-profile figure. Yet Constanza did not look enthusiastic, forced a hollow smile, which Arias did not seem to notice.

'How wonderful! I look forward to the union, and I hope he will make me happy.'

'He better, or else I will cut off his manhood,' Arias said with a grin before he hobbled towards the keep. Constanza's smile descended to a slight grimace.

'You are not pleased, my lady?'

'No…I mean, yes, of course I am. Just a little…unexpected, is all.' Her smile returned as she brushed the conversation aside. 'Would you still care to join me after the feast? I would like to hear of your experiences of the campaign.'

I accepted her invitation, which was greeted with a genuine smile, before she left me to go about my duties.

Rodrigo declared there would be a feast to celebrate our victory and mourn the dead. A messenger had been sent ahead of our arrival and servants were already busy in the kitchens as they prepared food and raided the winter stores. The great hall had been decorated with new drapes, fresh rushes were strewn across the floor and benches set out for a large host. Come nightfall the hall was packed tight with men as a savage storm brewed outside, and the food and wine were never ending. Musicians entertained us with jovial tunes on their ouds and lyres, and light hearted banter echoed through the hall as the revellers enjoyed the festivities.

Rodrigo placed me at the end of his table, a high honour for a squire, and I joined in conversation with some of the men I had fought side by side with; the Vascon knights Mancio and Aigeru, and another two Castilian knights named Osmundo and Suero. We traded our accounts of the war and shared blood red wine and salted pork from the stores. The wine was sweet and quickly became a favourite of mine, and sipping from a solid silver goblet made me feel more like a lord than a squire. They were impressed a squire had saved his lord from death and offered a toast to my achievement. The feeling of being praised was a foreign to me, yet appreciated, and I wonder if my father felt the same when men congratulated him on killing Ramiro of Aragon.

As darkness closed in Rodrigo picked out several individuals who had fought valiantly for special commendation and presented them with valuable items looted from the south. Rodrigo had brought back two carts laden with treasure, from bags of coins, Moorish weapons and armour to bolts of cloth and silk, and even an ivory Mozarabic reliquary. This he dedicated to God and offered it to Father Auderico for the chapel, which he was most pleased about.

When the presentations were done, he asked me to stand.

'Our hot-headed castellan would not be here if it was not for this lad, Antonio Perez.' The statement drew laughter as Arias raised his cup. 'At first, we took him for a cretin and a murderer, and worthy of nothing but misery. Now, I consider him a dear friend. It was he, and only he, who risked his life to save Arias when he was defenceless, surrounded by enemies.' He proceeded to spin the tale of what happened, spared no detail in my heroic defence, yet omitted Azarola's treachery. 'This man is a worthy successor to his father's legacy. Pedro Valdez, the hero of Graus, would be proud of his son Antonio, a hero of Balansiya.'

Rodrigo held his goblet towards me and bowed his head, which was met by a rapturous salute from the men gathered in the hall. I was not used to such praise and gave only a slight bow in thanks before I sat and secluded myself from the limelight.

'So where is your reward, lad?' Mancio asked as I sat. 'Saving Arias's life like you did, you would imagine he'd give you a big bag of gold or something?'

'I do not want anything from him. He's already given me enough.'

The chance of revenge was worth more than any riches in the world.

The few women at the feast retired as the wine continued to flow, and as the night dragged on the guests stumbled out of the hall in to the raging storm outside to their lodgings in the castle and village. Eventually I pushed myself from the table, bid goodnight to Rodrigo and Arias and staggered out of the hall. But rather than retire to my own bed, I made my way to Constanza's chambers.

The corridors funnelled bitter air throughout the keep that nipped at my fingers and made the torches along the walls flicker. It was eerily quiet as the midnight hour approached; the only sounds the sporadic shuffle of my boots and the rain that lashed outside. The wine had been potent and my head span as drunkenness took hold of me. An unwelcome belch almost made me vomit, but I managed to keep it down.

I arrived at Constanza's chamber and knocked thrice upon the door, heard a voice inside and entered.

The room was modest in size and furnishing, bright from the trio of candle stands that held a plethora of candles on each, which flickered and danced from the draft. A small bed with furs beneath a blood red silk bedspread, neat and smooth, dominated one wall, above which hung a wooden crucifix gilded with gold. The shutter of a small window on the opposite wall rattled as the wind howled outside, beneath which was a table and two chairs, whilst a chest sat by the remaining wall. Constanza stood in the centre of the room with her hands clasped before her. She wore a simple gown of green silk trimmed in silver, her hair was pinned high and a silver necklace hung around her neck. She looked radiant and I gave a gasp, which made her smile.

'Hello Antonio.'

'Evening, my lady,' I said with another belch.

Her face dropped. 'Are you drunk?'

'I think so…never really been like this before. Father never let me drink wine. Said it was a man's drink.'

'My father is the same, says it is unladylike to be drunk. But…my father is not here now.' She gave a wink then walked to the table which held a large jug and two goblets, filled one of the goblets and, surprisingly, downed the contents in one. She grimaced and I thought she would vomit, but she composed herself and filled her goblet again, then the other and held it out to me.

'Please, sit.'

We sat and talked for what seemed like an eternity, though it was mainly me that answered her questions. She asked about the campaign and what I saw, heard and did, and I told her everything from the markets of Saraqusta, the siege of Balansiya and the battle. She listened intently and a tear welled in her eye when I described how her father had been forced to the ground and trapped under his horse, only for a smile to appear when I describe my heroics. She then insisted I describe Lugones, my childhood and my family too. She wished to know everything about me, but I duly talked, held back tears when I recalled the happier moments in my life and those who I had left behind.

When the wine ran dry and the hour was late, I decided to take my leave.

'I think it is time for me to go, my lady,' I said, then stood and started for the door. 'Your father would flog me if I slept in.'

'You do not have to go,' she blurted out as she rose and held an arm out to stop me. 'You could…stay.'

'What do you mean?' I frowned.

'Is it not obvious, Antonio?' I greeted the question with a vacant expression. She held her tongue and her bright eyes were fixated on me. After a hesitation, she stepped forward and kissed me. She allowed her lips to linger, but I broke away and stepped back a few paces as I panicked.

'We cannot do that! Your father…'

'I do not give a damn what my father says,' she said in a passionate tone, her stern eyes locked on to me.

'But you are betrothed to Garcia Ordóñez. I simply cannot.'

'I do not care about Garcia, or any other man. I want you.'

She kissed me again, more intense than before. I had never kissed a girl and did not know what to do, but when she wrapped her arms around my neck, I instinctively followed her lead, grabbed her waist and pulled her tight. The wine that pumped through our veins heightened the intensity of our embrace, and before I knew it, she had dragged me to the bed and shoved me on to my back. She climbed on top and hesitated, stared at me, panted profusely. Her emerald eyes were vibrant and compelling, her complexion flawless like a work of art. She gave a nervous giggle, something I mimicked as any tension began to subside, before she planted a softer kiss on my lips and changed the pace of the encounter to slow and sensual.

In that moment nothing else mattered but me and her; I spared no thought for Azarola or al-Baytar, my father or Inigo, all the events that led to my embrace with my lord's cherished daughter. Constanza undid my breaches and loosened the tunic from my body, and I helped lift the dress from her slender frame. Her nipples were hard against the cool air that hung in the chamber. She let out a subdued moan as she eased herself on to me, and I closed my eyes and lay back as she writhed in ecstasy on top of me.

And that night I became a man.

*   *   *

It was barely dawn as I stumbled through the keep, half dressed, back to my chamber.

I had stirred to find myself naked in Constanza's bed, her bare body draped across mine. The fear of being discovered made me wiggle from beneath her, grab my clothes and quietly exit her chamber. My heart thumped against my chest, so loud I thought it would wake the entire castle as I pulled my clothes on and stalked the corridors. Every shadow had me spooked and I was relieved when I returned to my room, eased the door closed and collapsed on the bed. Sleep did not come as the potential consequences gnawed away at me. Would Constanza tell her father? And if she did, would he geld me like he had promised? As cold sunlight crept through the shutters I rose and donned a fresh outfit, full of dread for the day ahead.

The day was torture, made harder by the lack of sleep and thumping head from too much wine. I did not see Arias, and Constanza did not make an appearance all day, perhaps kept indoors by the light blanket of snow and the chill wind that descended over Vivar. Was she ashamed of what had happened? Did she regret laying with me? Anxiety took hold and I flinched more than not, jumped at every face I saw and expected to face Arias's wrath at any moment.

It was later that evening when I was summoned to Arias's chamber.

I knocked on the door and eased it open. Arias was sat at his table as he brooded over a document in his hand. I noted his sword was propped against the wall next to him. I moved gingerly in to the room and closed the door behind me, which caught his attention.

'Ah, there you are Antonio.'

'Good evening, lord. How is the leg?'

'Much better now I have a steady supply of wine to ease the ache.' He smirked and held up a silver goblet of wine. To my relief he seemed in good spirits. 'And Auderico said it has healed well, so I should be back to fighting in no time.' My eyes widened, much to his amusement. 'Do not worry, Antonio. We are not going to war for a while yet, though Castile does not lack a choice of enemy. Who would you prefer; the Moors, Leon or Navarre?'

'If truth be told, just a single Moor and Leonese will satisfy my bloodlust.'

A dark frown appeared on his face. 'I could not agree more. Perhaps we will get that opportunity sometime soon. God, I hate him. Azarola and I have had a troubled relationship ever since my sister was carted off to become his wife. Our hate for each other was subdued, tolerable, but ever since you came along it has intensified. Azarola tried to eradicate your father's bloodline, but I am here to preserve the remaining font. The only way this feud will end is when one of us is dead.'

'This is my fight, lord. I cannot ask you to die for me.'

'As your lord I am expected to protect those under my command, and if it is God's will I die then so be it. But enough of that. There is another reason I asked you here.' He poured more wine for himself before he offered me a seat and a similar goblet. I sat cautiously, unsure of his motive.

'I never thanked you properly for saving my life. It was reckless, but a brave thing to do and I am in your debt. Such feats deserve just reward.' He crossed over to a chest in the corner of the room with delicate steps, opened it, and pulled out a heavy object that jingled when he carried it over to me. 'This coat of mail belonged to a mercenary who fought for the Moors at Balansiya. I will have Gonzalo repair and clean it, so it is good as new.' Several of the links were broken at the midriff where a spear had punctured it. 'The metal appears to be from Tulaytula, and Tulaytula is famed for the quality of its steelwork. Unfortunately, it does not stop a spear tip from a knight charging at full speed.'

Arias did not lie when he said it was fine work. It glimmered in the light offered by the flames and felt heavy in my arms. I stared as a child would look when he gazed on a shiny jewel for the very first time.

'You honour me, lord, but this gift is beyond someone of my ilk.'

'Bullshit. You are seventeen years old now, Antonio, no longer a child. One day you will become a knight, and a knight needs proper tools of war. He needs other things as well, such as land and a lord to serve. But he also needs a woman in his life, to bear him children and continue his legacy.' He sat forward and stared in to my eyes. 'After much thought, it is no longer my wish for Garcia Ordóñez to wed my daughter. Instead, I want you to be her husband.'

My jaw dropped. It was the last thing I expected him to say.

'But he is one of the most powerful men in Castile!'

'Garcia will find another woman worthy of him.'

'I am a squire. I have nothing to offer your daughter. I am not worthy.'

'Bollocks to that. I will speak with Sancho and he will give his blessing to the proposal, because he has no choice in the matter. It is my decision. But I will request one condition to the marriage; you will bow to the king's wishes and do penance for your crimes. He has not forgotten about what you did on the Camino de Santiago. I would not want my daughter married to a man who has not repented for his sins.' That did not surprise me. Sancho seemed like he held a grudge for a grievance, and by doing penance I would cleanse my soul of sin. I would be reborn as a different person, marry to a highborn lady and continue the path of knighthood.

A new start.

'And what has Constanza had to say of it?' I asked cautiously.

'She has already spoken to me about your…time spent together last night.' My jaw hung loose, and no words come forth, but he laughed at my discomfort and held a hand towards me. 'I am not angry with you. I was surprised, of course. If that had happened before I knew who you were, I would have gelded you and fed it to the pigs. But I have become fond of you, and so has my daughter. There are hints of your father in you, yet you are an altogether different creature. You have a grasp of learning and education not many take to, and your skill in combat is improving every day. It is Rodrigo's belief you will become a fine knight one day. Who better to wed my daughter to?'

I should have been elated. Relief was something I felt because Arias would not hurt me for laying with his daughter, and I should have been ecstatic I would be wed to a woman of Constanza's stock;

highborn, beautiful, and a true lady. But there was only ever one girl I loved.

Deep in my heart I wished it was Jimena who I would wed.

My childhood friend would always have a special place as the girl who accepted me for who I was. She made me laugh and smile and forget about all the times I was made to feel worthless. But when she helped me in my hour of need, I had let her down, failed to be the friend I promised I would be, which was something I was adamant she would never forgive me for. There was never any hope for me and her.

Jimena was a part of my past. Constanza would be my future.

'I am honoured, lord. I promise to treat her with respect and honour.'

'I know you will, because if you do not, I will do more than cut your manhood off.' I gave a nervous laugh, and though he produced a beaming grin I knew he was serious. 'In the morning you can take that mail coat to Gonzalo. Then we can plan for the union in the spring.'

He offered me his hand and I accepted it, winced as he squeezed hard, before he grabbed me in a headlock and rubbed the top of my head with his knuckles. The pain was unbearable, and I had to wiggle out of his vice like grip. He grinned even more as I grimaced.

'I am looking forward to having you as my son by law.'

My relationship with Constanza flourished in a relatively short time. She told me she had been smitten with me since I came to the castle, despite me being a slave, and she used to stare at me from the castle windows as I was worked to the bone. But I had gone to war for the best part of the year and left her to brood over her feelings and live every day with a sense of dread that I would not return. And when we did return, she told her father of her feelings for me, and Arias had brooded long and hard but felt it was the right choice.

Life was good in those final weeks of the year. Frost hardened the ground as the hellish Castilian winter set in, and a mist constantly hung over the plains. When I was not doing my duties, I would spend hours with my betrothed. We quickly fell in love with everything about each other, and would dine with Rodrigo, Arias and Dometza and laugh and jape, exchange stories and discuss the world we had seen and longed to see. Life was so very different to what it had been in Lugones, where perfection was demanded of me and joyful times were few and far between. But on the day before we heralded a new year in to Vivar, a messenger came from Leon with grave news.

King Fernando was dead.

*   *   *

The snow-covered city of Leon was in mourning.

We arrived late in the evening after a long, cold ride and found a tavern to spend the night. It was a cosy place named the Scallop Shell, homage to the pilgrim heritage of the city, with a roaring fire to warm us as we ate our supper of salted boar, fresh bread and nuts. The tavern's owner told us the king's fever had come and gone since the battle at Balansiya, and the cold weather that hovered over the land sapped his strength and led to his demise. The mood was sullen, and we were tired from the journey, so me and Constanza retired to a room, Arias and Dometza shared another and Rodrigo to one of his own. Father Auderico lodged in a hostel set aside for monks and pilgrims travelling the Camino de Santiago. The next day we donned our finest clothes, pulled thick cloaks over our shoulders and went to pay our last respects to the king.

The Basilica de San Isidoro was a new building within the old Roman city, the previous church having been destroyed when Leon was sacked by Almanzor less than a hundred years before. The façade gleamed even in the low winter sun whilst the other churches we passed looked dated and weather beaten, with the odd stone missing and statues with faded faces. It gained its name when Fernando had the remains of San Isidoro transferred from Isbiliya to Leon and dedicated the building and all the relics within to the saint. The amir of Isbiliya willingly returned them as part of the *parias* tribute and a sign of peace

283

between the Moors and Christians, but Fernando claimed the repatriation of one of Hispania's most revered saints was seen as a victory over the Muslims in the quest to take back Hispania. Queen Sancha considered it the most holy site in the city and had chosen it as the mausoleum for herself and her husband. Now her king resided with the saint.

Our boots crunched on the fresh layer of snow from the night before and entered through the southern threshold of the basilica. The air was bitterly cold, and our breaths appeared before our faces in the scant light that filtered through the stained-glass windows to our right. I put an arm around Constanza and rubbed her shoulder to generate a little warmth, and she gave a delicate smile. Curls of her hair showed from beneath her black headdress, and her eyes shone against the drab colour of her garments. Our footsteps echoed against the low chants of clergymen. Other mourners moved like shadows, interrupted by the spectre-like priests in their white vestments, stood like statues with their hands clasped in prayer.

The funeral had taken place some days previous, but the king's body was laid near the altar so those travelling from afar could pay their respects before he was interred in the crypt beneath the basilica. Fernando was laid beneath the altar on a bier draped with a great shroud which bore the arms of Leon-Castile, scattered with ashes and ringed by candles that gave him an ethereal glow. A monk's robe adorned his body, his once powerful frame was now thin, his flesh pale and his cheeks gaunt, and his thin hair had been tonsured. He was a shadow of the king who conquered lands from the Moors, instilled fear in to their hearts and pride in our own. No gold shone upon him, no crown or precious jewels. The king had given up his royal rule in the final moments of his life, wished to be judged by God for his sins as a simple man. It was a humble, anticlimactic end for such a revered man.

Sancho mulled around the altar, his gazed fixed on his father. He gave a curt nod as we prostrated ourselves in front of Fernando and offered our prayers. I gave a silent offering in my head, asking God to guide Fernando's soul to heaven before I walked over to Rodrigo and Arias, who offered their condolences to the man who would be their new king.

Sancho echoed the tale of the innkeeper, stated the king never recovered from the wounds he suffered at Balansiya. His fever waxed and waned with every passing day, and though he managed to ride through the gates of Leon as a hero it was barely a week later when the strength left his body and he was left bed bound. It pained him to breathe some days. He insisted on taking prayers, no matter how many times he stumbled or fell making the short journey to the chapel, but his body finally gave in. In his final days he set aside his crown and royal possessions, donned the robes of a monk and let the Lord take him. He died the day after Christ Mass, and in the following days loyal lords braved the cold to pay their respects and weep for their king.

As the lords conversed, I noticed a small group of men and women enter the basilica and process down the centre of the nave. My stomach knotted when I saw who led them. His head was held high but there was a sombre expression on his face, a change to the smug smirk that seemed permanently in place.

'Antonio?' Constanza laid a hand on my arm. They saw I stared at Azarola as he went to the bier where the king lay. He knelt and clasped his hands together in silent prayer.

'If he says anything to you do not rise to his words,' I heard Dometza whisper to Arias. My lord breathed deep as I sensed anger bubble within, but even he knew better than to cause a scene when we mourned the king. When Azarola was finished he stood and walked back down the centre of the nave and waited for the rest of his group, oblivious to our presence.

Arias's boots thudded on the stone floor as he strode forward and paid no attention to Rodrigo, who hissed warnings after him.

'Bernardo,' he called. He stopped a few paces away so his brother by law was in earshot. I stood behind my lord and glowered at my nemesis.

'Ah, Arias,' he said with a smirk. 'It is good to see you back in health.'

'Beatriz?' Arias's sister was noticeably absent.

'I am afraid she was feeling a little…delicate. She could not make the trip.' Arias's face twist with rage and Azarola smirked again, knowing full well any mention of Beatriz would irk him.

'Is everything alright, father?'

A young man came and stood at the side of Azarola and this, I guessed, was Pelayo. He was everything Arias had said he was; tall and handsome, and he carried himself in a confident manner, perhaps two years my senior. His hair was short and the colour of wheat in the sun, his beard neat and his eyes bright. Though he did not possess the same snout or bulbous lips as his father, his hard face was one I instantly disliked.

'Everything is fine, my son. I was just catching up with your uncle.'

'Hello uncle,' Pelayo bowed his head. At least he showed respect, unlike his father. He frowned at me. 'Who is this?'

Azarola sniggered. 'Antonio Perez, son of Pedro Valdez de Lugones. The traitor's son, and one your uncle seems to have taken a liking to.'

'I was not aware our family had relations with the spawn of traitors,' Pelayo said as he inclined his head. I clenched my fists to suppress my growing anger.

'If I were you, I would spend some time acquainting yourself with Antonio, because soon he is to be a member of our family,' Arias said. Azarola raised an eyebrow. 'Antonio and Constanza will be married in the spring.'

Azarola's eyes widened in shock and for a moment he was speechless, before he frowned and snarled like a beast. 'You're a disgrace, fraternising with traitorous cretins such as he. The king should never have allowed him to live. He never would have approved this union.'

'*My* king has blessed the union,' Arias bit back. 'I do not give a care as to what *your* king will have to say about it.'

'His father deserved his death, and you will deserve everything coming for you.'

Arias started towards him, but Rodrigo held him back. Arias's body trembled with rage and his complexion deepened to crimson. The commotion attracted the attention of others within the basilica and a priest wandered over to try and diffuse the situation, whispered in Rodrigo's ear. The young knight said something back and eased his hold on Arias, whose temper slowly dissipated. He still glared at Azarola, and if he had carried a weapon, he would have drawn it and spilled blood right there.

Without another word Azarola and Pelayo exited in to the cold outside, which allowed us a moment to gather ourselves. But I was not content. I ignored the calls behind me and marched out of the basilica, scanned the square as a light snow drifted down from the dark clouds and strode over to where they walked away. My business was not yet done.

'Bernardo.'

The older man stopped and turned, sighed as if annoyed by my presence. He waved to his companions to go on without him. Pelayo hesitated, then soon turned and walked away, but not before giving me a sharp look. I had only met the boy, but the feeling of hate was already mutual.

We stood only a spear length apart, and I realised it was the first time I had been alone with him. I was determined to get answers.

'At Balansiya I met with the king. He told me my father died because of a conspiracy. I know you were involved. What did he ever do to you?'

'He got in my way,' he shrugged. 'What do men of worth want in this life? Wealth? Good health? A gorgeous woman to hump every night and bear children to carry on his name? All those things are desirable, yes, but there is one thing men truly covet. Power.' He poured emphasis on the word as if it was the only thing that mattered. 'Let me give you some advice, boy. If you want power, you had better learn to spill blood to reach the top and grasp it. No one will give you power; you take it for yourself. Your father trod on my toes and took the glory I was owed away from me. I could not accept that grievance, so I destroyed him.'

'You took the coward's route. A true man would have challenged him face to face.'

'When you have a chance to strike a man in the back you should take it. Their armour is weaker, the flesh softer and the blow more likely to end him.'

'Perhaps the same thing will happen to you one day.'

It was my turn to snigger as he frowned in confusion.

'I have something to show you.' From underneath my cloak I drew Vengeance from the sheath and held it before me. I cared not that weapons were forbidden in the basilica; I always carried my small blade on me. A flicker of uncertainty appeared on Azarola's face as his eyes scanned the sharp edge of the blade and the words inscribed in the metal. 'I had this made for you. I named it Vengeance, because its only purpose is to seek out those who were responsible for my father's death. Would you like to know what it reads? It says, "I am Vengeance, born of hatred. I thirst for the blood of those who betrayed Pedro Valdez de Lugones".

I sheathed the weapon then stepped forward and squared up to him, so close I could see the fresh stubble on his face, smell his sour breath. 'One day I will plunge this blade in to *your* back, and I will smile as you draw your last breath. My face will be the last thing you ever see, haunting your visions in the afterlife for all eternity, just as you have haunted mine these past two years.'

Fear flickered on his face. My words had the desired effect.

'What makes you think you can kill one of the most powerful lords in Leon?' he snarled. 'Dueñas is a fortress, impregnable even if you had ten thousand men at your back. The Beni Gómez, my brethren, look after one another. They will not tolerate threats to one of their own, no matter how hollow. Many have tried to end me, and all have failed. What makes you think you can achieve what no other man can?'

'Because I have justice on my side, and justice always finds a way of prevailing in the face of adversity. I will not stop until you are dead. So, sleep tight, Azarola, because your days are numbered.'

I walked away, content my warning had the desired effect, before I stopped and turned to him again. 'Oh, and one more thing. Give my regards to Nasr al-Baytar. Let him know death comes for him as well, and next time I will not let him get away.'

Azarola snarled as I turned and walked away. My companions waited by the entrance to the basilica. Arias and Rodrigo glared at Azarola, and a tense standoff ensued

'Are you all right?' Constanza asked.

'Of course, I am. Nothing like getting acquainted with my new family,' I said with a grin. The comment made Arias smile as we prepared to return to Vivar.

*   *   *

Before we left Leon, I sought out Fernando, Jimena's brother.

I had heard he had accompanied his father and brother and stayed in the city for a while, but Jimena was still at Oviedo. As his father was a count he stayed in the royal palace, and it was only through Rodrigo's relationship with Sancho did I get the opportunity to talk. I met him in one of the gardens where the foliage was blanketed in snow, as a grey sky hung overhead.

'Thank you for meeting me. I do not know how I can repay you.'

'An apology for my sister's treatment would be a start,' he growled. Fernando clearly still felt bitter, and justly so, for the treatment of Jimena by my brother.

'I cannot apologise enough. If I had the power to stop Inigo I would have. You know I would never want to see harm come to her. We were desperate.'

A tear welled in my eye, and Fernando's demeanour softened.

'How is she?'

'It took her a while to recover after you left, but she is well. She has matured in to a fine young woman. I remember the tears of joy she wept when she found out you were alive. Know that she misses you.'

A lump formed in my throat. It was all I wanted to hear. Though he did not say as much, Fernando's words went so far to quell the fear that Jimena blamed me for what happened to her. I held my tongue and pulled out a parchment and a rag. Fernando frowned as I held it out to him. He plucked it from my grasp.

'It is a letter for Jimena. Please do not read it. It is for her eyes only.' Fernando's frown moved from my eyes to the rag. It contained the necklace I had purchased in Saraqusta. 'And that is a gift for her. A small token to show her she is ever in my thoughts.'

Fernando placed both objects in a satchel slung around his left shoulder.

'If she wishes to send anything back, for any reason, tell her to send it to Vivar. It is not far from Burgos.'

'I will tell her so, but do not expect a response anytime soon, if at all. I am sure the contents of your letter will be hard for her to digest.'

Fernando gave a curt nod then left.

In the letter I had told Jimena everything that had happened since the day Inigo attacked her; the execution of my father, the horrors on the Camino de Santiago, my time spent under Rodrigo and the campaigns against Saraqusta and Balansiya. And I told her of my impending marriage to Constanza. My heart longed for the girl I had fallen in love with from a young age, and it always would, but I would never have her. Jimena was my past and Constanza was my future, the woman who would bear my children.

We left Leon and braved the cold winds as we travelled east along the Camino de Santiago. The road was for the most part deserted, and the hostels had plenty of room to accommodate us. We passed the spot where we had massacred the priest and pilgrims from Roma and Pisa, and I stopped and looked around at the terrain, tried to remember who had died where. The blood had long been washed away and the bodies of the pilgrims may still have been in the monastery, nothing but charred skeletons, undignified in death. I once had designs to return and lay their remains to rest, perhaps restore the monastery and help form a new thriving community. But that idea was wild and a long way from fruition, if it would ever happen. My gaze fell one last time to the west, took in the rolling hills and mountains of Leon, before I gently touched the flanks of Asbat and re-joined our small group.

I bid farewell to Leon and Oviedo, to Jimena and my childhood home.

And I prepared to become a citizen of Castile.

We arrived in Burgos on an eve where the sky was awash with vibrant orange and deep purple rays. Sancho, king of Castile now in all but name, had declared that if I was to be accepted in to his realm I was to honour his father's wish and do penance to make my peace with God. In his eyes I was still a sinner and I had to answer for my crimes.

We rose early at dawn, so the church was quiet and gloomy. The rising sun's rays had barely pierced the windows to the east, so we were in darkness save for a few candles that provided scant light. Stout columns ran down either side of the aisle and supported the vaulted roof, and the aisle led to a stone altar draped with a tapestry of the birth of Christ. Our footsteps echoed and the chill nipped at my cheeks, made me shiver in the plain white robe I had donned. Father Auderico, my only companion, wore the white vestments of a priest and it was a wonder he did not shiver as profusely as I did with the cold. Perhaps his layer of blubber kept the worst of the chill away.

Father Auderico offered to hear my confession, and I was happy it was he I would speak to. He had made me feel most welcome on my arrival in Vivar and we had struck a friendship. I did not expect him to understand what I had done, and there was a chance his attitude towards me would change, but it was a chance I was willing to take.

Father Auderico stood at the altar and I knelt before him. The stone floor numbed my legs and chilled me to the bone, but I did not complain. I was here for an important reason and I would see it through.

The priest spoke in a stern voice, a contrast to his usual pleasant tone.

'Do you wish to confess your crimes in the eyes of the Lord and cleanse your soul of sin?' his voice echoed around the hollow nave.

'I do, Father.' I pulled a small crucifix from around my neck and clasped it tight.

'Then speak, and let God judge you.'

'I wish to confess murder and being an accessory in murder. I am guilty of extorting wealth from innocent people and using the name of the Lord to do so.'

'Confess.'

I swallowed hard. There was no denying I had lied about what had happened in the past two years. The falsehoods I told had felt like armour that protected me from the stark truth, the severity of the crimes. But here I would be judged by God, and I was naked.

'There was a guard in Leon,' I started meekly. 'He chased me through the streets after I and my companions tried to save our fathers from execution. He had every right to seize me and throw me in a prison, but I killed him in an alley and left his body for the dogs. I killed pilgrims, too.' I hesitated and looked at Auderico, who gave a nod for me to continue. 'These men accompanied a priest who was on pilgrimage from Roma on the Camino de Santiago. We had joined with a hermit and tried to take wealth from pilgrims by claiming to have the bone of a saint and offered miracles in exchange for coin. It was a shameless act, but we did not care. The priest saw through our debacle and tried to stop us.' Tears brimmed in my eyes. 'There was blood. Too much blood. The priest was killed along with many of the pilgrims, and a pair of knights. Some died by my own hand. I did not wish for a fight, but I was too weak to stop the bloodshed.

'More murder I committed when we went on campaign with the king...'

'Murder in war is not a sin,' Auderico interjected. 'You were given your command by the king, and a king's actions are sanctioned by God. You will not be judged for these.'

Was I supposed to feel comforted by those words? They did not have the desired effect. I wept like a child. I lowered my head to the cold stone floor in supplication before God and begged his forgiveness.

'I am sorry. I am so, so sorry. I did not want to do any of those things, but I had to. I just wanted to save my father. He was innocent. He should not have died. None of this should have happened.'

'No, it should not have.' I turned my head to see Sancho stood in the nave with Rodrigo and Arias. The first rays of dawn illuminated the church behind them. They strode towards me as Sancho continued. 'Will God forgive him, Father?'

'I believe the Lord will accept he is sorry. Some of his crimes were out of his hands, other were avoidable. But his soul will be pure again.'

'Good. Then let us dunk him in some water and finish it.'

I thought Sancho jested at first, but soon I was led outside and made to stand in a barrel of icy water. My body shook profusely as Father Auderico laid a hand on the top of my head and submerged me several times. The shock of the cold made me gasp when I came up for air. There was nothing but darkness followed by the dark grey sky above. Sancho, Rodrigo and Arias watched in silence as Auderico muttered prayers. It was necessary, Sancho said, to wash away the sin so both body and soul were cleansed. When Auderico was done Sancho and Arias hauled me out of barrel and led me back in to the church, where I was placed in front of a brazier to warm my frozen body.

'So, is that it, then?' Arias asked.

Sancho looked at me before he nodded.

'Yes. He has paid enough for his crimes.' He slapped me on the back, hard enough to almost push me in to the brazier. 'You did well, lad. I am sure your father would have been proud of you.'

'Standing in a barrel is not too difficult, lord,' I replied, still shivering.

'Not just that. There's courage inside of you I'd wager you did not know was there, and a strength and determination to survive. These qualities have kept you alive. You are no longer a boy, Antonio. You're a man, a warrior in the making. Rodrigo and Arias will guide you, and one day we may make a knight of you, give you land and titles.' He stepped forward so the light of the brazier illuminated his strong jaw, piercing eyes and stern brow. 'Are you ready to be renewed in the eyes of God and your king?'

'Yes, lord.'

'Rise, Antonio Perez.' Sancho held out a hand. 'Rise as a citizen of Castile.'

I took his hand and rose, no longer the cautious, frail boy from Lugones, but now brave, matured and toughened.

I was reborn.

Thirteen

We did not return to Vivar, for Burgos was alive with a jubilant buzz due to the impending coronation of Sancho. Everyday new lords arrived in the city from the furthest reaches of the new kingdom, as far north as the Bay of Vizcaya, east from the border with Navarre and south to the Duero. Arias busied himself with greeting old acquaintances and traded war stories over a cup of wine, and I shadowed him, listened to the tales and the banter and was ever present to tend to my lord, who still felt the effects of his wounds suffered in the recent war.

We found suitable lodgings in a tavern until the coronation was over. We were not expecting to stay in the city long, for in the days after my penance the preparations were well underway. Hunters brought fresh kills through the streets each day, new drapes and banners bearing the golden castle on a red background hung from every street corner, and every tavern and hostel was crammed with any man of worth in the kingdom. With the wealthiest of the kingdom gathered in one place the traders braved the winter chill to flog their wares and maximise profits. Within days the city was hastily prepared for the coronation. Sancho wanted to waste no time in placing a crown upon his head.

On the day of the coronation we donned our finest garments, save for me who was provided with a uniform to be would be worn by all servants at the feasts. As a squire I was nominated to provide service for the guests. Only when I became a knight would I be one of the privileged guests who would gorge on fine food and drink my fill of wine. The uniform consisted of red tunic and white hoes, with a red cloak trimmed in white fastened by a clasp in the shape of a castle, topped off with a small red woollen cap. Arias could not help but chortle at my appearance, and even Constanza stifled a snigger.

'Do not worry, I have had the same punishment before,' Arias grinned. 'I will make sure I drink your share of wine.'

'I will make sure I do not pour any on your head,' I retorted, much to his amusement.

I did not attend the coronation, for I was busy preparing for the feast in the grand hall of the palace. It was held in the church of Santa Maria attached to the palace and was presided over by the bishop of Oca, as Burgos did not have a bishop in those times. There, Sancho II of Castile was crowned with a golden circlet fashioned like his father's own crown, and presented with the sword that had been passed down from Fernando's maternal grandfather, Sancho Garcia of Castile, intended to be a symbol of those who ruled over Castile. The ceremony lasted longer than many believed it should and indeed would have liked, and Arias had to be nudged awake by Rodrigo as the bishop of Oca droned on for what seemed like hours about Sancho's divine right to rule, through endless sermons and hymns. Then the congregation rejoiced; Castile was once more an independent kingdom.

Guests filtered in to the hall and took their places at the long trestle tables. The hall had been scented with garlands of fresh mint and jasmine, torches brightened the room and braziers burned to provide heat against the winter chill as Castilian banners and richly coloured tapestries adorned the walls. A dais had been set up at the back of the hall with a table and chairs, and a grand throne for Sancho, with four long tables with benches for the guests running from the dais to the door. Silver goblets and platters covered the tables, gold for those on the dais. There was even a small wooden stage to the side of the dais for musicians, who were setting up as Vermundo, the seneschal of the palace, clapped his hands and called for quiet.

'Lords and ladies of Castile, I present to you your new king: Sancho of Castile, the second of his name, firstborn son of Fernando and Sancha of Leon and ruler of this land by God's decree. Long may he reign over us.'

Sancho strode in to the hall with the pale winter sun at his back. He wore a blood red silk tunic and white trousers, and draped over his broad shoulders was a cloak in the same fashion bearing the golden castle of Castile, trimmed in white wolf fur. Gold and precious gems adorned his belt buckle, the rings on his fingers, the chain around his neck and the circlet upon his head. He looked every part a king, a strong king that would lead his people to glory. He processed down the centre of the hall with his head held high as guests prostrated with a bow of the head. Yet the king looked very much alone, because Sancho was without a wife and childless, and so behind him came his most trusted knights and advisors. Among them was Rodrigo, who walked by the side of Garcia Ordóñez.

The procession took their places at the tables, and when Sancho stood before his subjects there came a great cry of 'Long live the king!' as each man and woman held their drinks aloft in salute.

An awkward silence ensued. Sancho looked around the hall, searched for something.

'Is your new king destined to be thirsty at his own coronation?' he barked. 'This is meant to be a celebration. Where is my damned wine?'

The congregation let out a bark of laughter as a red-faced servant hurried to the dais and handed Sancho a golden goblet encrusted with red stones. The king took the goblet and drained it in one, an action greeted by a loud cheer. The seneschal of the hall clapped his hands and the musicians began a tune on their flutes, drums and ouds, signalled the beginning of the feast.

It was hard to keep up with the demands of so many lords and ladies. A layer of perspiration coated my brow from the constant rush back and forth to the kitchens and amongst the close press of people, on top of filling goblets and clearing platters of half eaten food. My stomach growled in protest at the sight of so much boar and venison, fresh trout from the Arlanzón and rabbit stew served with a plethora of breads, cheese and fruits. I snuck a few scraps when nobody was looking, which went only so far to satiate my appetite.

The wine flowed and things soon became rowdy. Two men started to scrap from either side of a table, and I had to duck to avoid an ill aimed cup of cider that clattered off the wall before both men were ejected from the hall. And when I spilt some wine on one lady's dress she stood and slapped me hard on the cheek, which was met with boisterous laughter, then cursed as she exited the hall. I slunk to the side of the hall whilst my embarrassment subsided.

A pair of arms wrapped around my waist and squeezed gently.

'I do not like the look of you in a uniform,' Constanza whispered in my ear. 'I think you should take me somewhere quiet and show me what's underneath this horrid thing.'

'You know I would love to, my dear,' I protested, wriggled free to face her, 'but I cannot. My absence will not go unnoticed.'

She frowned and pouted. 'You are no fun.' Her eyes seemed heavy and she swayed as she stood, a sign she had already had plenty of wine.

'It would not be fun to think what your father would do to me if we did.' I looked over to see Arias. He stared at me with a disapproving look on his face. Constanza was ill amused and rolled her eyes. 'Later. You will not be disappointed, my lady. I promise'

Her frown changed to a slight smile. 'I never am.' She gave me a kiss on the cheek and returned to her place with Arias as I returned to pouring more wine.

The low sun had long set, the braziers blazed, and the feast was in full swing when Sancho rose from his seat and addressed his guests. Several servants still carried platters and dishes to the tables as Sancho spoke, filled goblets as they went. It was then I noticed two servants who carried a great boar towards the dais. There was nothing untoward about their behaviour, but what drew my attention was most of the servants were squires like myself, or else young men employed in the palace, yet these two seemed older. I studied them as they went, their heads bowed towards the floor as if trying not to attract attention.

I saw the scar on one of their faces. A tight knot formed in my innards.

I had seen it before. At first it came from a distorted memory and I could not figure out where, but a second look at his companion left me with no doubt. That second man should have had a great black beard, except he was now clean shaven, but his features became all too familiar.

Sancho had descended from the dais and addressed his audience with some speech about his father, but I could not pay attention. I was oblivious to everyone else in the room save these two men and what they were doing. What they intended to do.

I stalked them from the side of the hall, kept pace as they went. I reached the end of the table ahead of the two men and waited, ignored several lords as they held their goblets out to be filled. They reached the end of the aisle and turned towards me, then knelt and placed the boar on the floor. I would have expected them to rise and return to the kitchens, but they stayed knelt and seemed to be fidgeting. I watched and waited, unsure of their intentions as the hall was oblivious to their actions.

My eyes widened when I saw the faint glint of steel.

'Assassins!' I screamed.

I sprinted forward as the two men drew short swords from beneath the carcass and turned to Sancho. The king looked confused at first, shocked when he saw the steel coming for him. He backed away as they started towards him, hate in their eyes, intent on plunging the blades in to the newly crowned king.

A figure leapt from the side to tackle the taller assassin to the floor as I threw myself at the scarred man as he was about to lunge. The world span and pain shot through my shoulder as we crashed to the floor. I found myself on top on him, but as he regained his wits, he tried to shove me off and threw a fist. Pain flared in my nose and a steady stream of blood trickled to my mouth, and he used that moment to reach for the sword. My response was quicker than he anticipated, answered with my own thump to his temple before I grabbed his head and smashed it off the stone floor. The blows dazed him, enough to deter him from the blade. Guards rushed over and apprehended the assassins, pinned them to the floor even as they thrashed and tried to wriggle free. I rose and stepped out of the way, wiped a smear of crimson from my nose on to the back of my hand. I looked to the other assassin and saw Rodrigo had stopped him and proceeded to make a bloody pulp of his face. The young knight seemed unfazed as he stood and backed away as spear armed guards pointed their blades to the attackers' necks. More armed men had formed a barrier before the king, but now Sancho eased those men out of the way to study the attackers. They sensed their moment had passed. The flails stopped and they lay there, breathed deep, furious and fearful at their failure.

'How is it that you, and only you, knew they were going to attack?' Sancho asked me, still in shock.

'I know who they are, your grace.'

'Tell me.'

I studied their faces, and knew they were Azarola's men. The man with the scar was all too familiar. They had been there when my father was arrested, and they had escorted me and Arias to Alfonso when we had arrived in Leon before Fernando announced the campaign against Saraqusta. My gaze shifted to Arias, and the expression on his stern face told me he too knew who they were.

'Tell me!' Sancho barked as he grew impatient at my silence.

'They are from Navarre,' I said.

Murmurs of shock rippled throughout the hall as Arias glared at me. I risked a glance at the assassins, who stared back with confusion.

'You are sure of this?'

'Yes, your grace. When I first came to Vivar as a slave, Rodrigo took me on an expedition to track down a party of Navarrese who were believed to be raiding deep in to our territory, but he left me in the wilderness and declared I was to make my way back to Vivar with nothing but my wits and the clothes on my back.' I kept my focus on Rodrigo as I spoke, his face embedded with a tense expression. He knew who they were, and knew I played a dangerous game with the lies I spun. 'These men were part of that raiding party, cut off from their comrades, and when they found me, they tried to take me back to Navarre. I had no intention of becoming a slave to another king and managed to escape back to Vivar. But there is no doubt they are those same men.'

The grumbles of discontent grew louder at my words. Sancho paced before the men, who averted their gaze, so they did not meet his piercing glare. 'So, the king of Navarre wishes to give me a knife in the back at my own coronation. Such actions need to be met with retribution. Rodrigo, take them away. Do with them what you will.' As Rodrigo nodded and removed them from the hall Sancho laid a hand on his arm and stopped him. 'Make them suffer.'

Rodrigo hesitated then bowed his head. He signalled to several men who hauled the prisoners away. They struggled and flailed upon hearing the king's words. Sancho gave me a curt nod of thanks before he picked his goblet from the floor. A servant hurried over and filled it to the brim with blood red wine. Sancho ascended the dais once again, took a sip from his goblet before turning to the congregation.

'This transgression will not spoil a good occasion. Feast – your king commands it!'

A mighty roar erupted from the guests as the festivities continued. I returned to where I was serving, but Arias marched over and cut me off.

He pulled me to one side, out of earshot, and whispered in an intense tone.

'What the hell was that? Why did you not say they were Leonese?'

'It would have given Sancho an excuse to start a war with Leon.'

'Well you have given him an excuse to invade Navarre. One need only look at Sancho in the wrong way and he will treat it as an offense. We have not long returned from Balansiya and the kingdom lost good men there. Sancho would have given Alfonso a warning and nothing more, for the sake of their mother. He sees Navarre as a viable target for conquest. This will lead to war and many more men will die because of you. The blood will be on your hands.'

'I will not apologise if that is what you are asking of me. This is personal.'

My cold tone made Arias hold his tongue. It was not often I would stand up to him and the defiance caught him off guard.

'Antonio.' I turned as Aigeru approached. 'Rodrigo would like a word with you. Alone.'

I took one more look at Arias before I nodded and followed the Vascon knight. I heard Arias curse under his breath then walk back to his place at the table, but I paid him no more heed.

If I could not get to Azarola then I would seek vengeance on those in his employ.

*   *   *

I was escorted to the castle, battled against the biting wind that had descended upon the city, and found the prisoners in a small, windowless cell in the bowels of the fortress. The stench of death and decay filled my nostrils and a brazier burned gently in the centre of the room, but did little to deter the chill from the air. The prisoners knelt at either side of the brazier, their faces beaten and bloody, and they shivered from the cold. I stepped in to the room and they stared at me with scorn as

302

Rodrigo paced, hummed a tune with his sword rested upon his shoulder. When he saw me, he stopped and grinned.

'Antonio. Thank you for coming.'

'What can I do for you, lord?'

'You said these men are from Navarre, but we both know that is not true. You lied about their identity.' I swallowed and he took it as a sign he was right. 'They are from Leon, and you have indeed seen them before, have you not?'

'Yes, lord. I do not know their names, but they are Azarola's men. They were there the day my father was arrested.'

Rodrigo's grin curled a little more in the faint light.

'Thank you for confirming it. My memory was a little hazy. This day grows more interesting by the minute.' He spat at the feet of the prisoners. 'Leonese dogs. What sort of man sends cretins like you to slit a king's throat at his own coronation? The men of the Beni Gómez clan are cowards.' The prisoners said nothing as the scarred man continued to stare at me, baring his teeth in fury. 'This is not the first time they have offended you. They deserve to be punished. So, tell me, Antonio, what would you do with them?'

It was too easy to say I would slit their throats and throw their bodies in to the Arlanzón. The thought initially sickened me, but given whom they were and what they had attempted to do I had designs to take Rodrigo's blade from his hand and do it myself. I found myself itching to end their miserable lives, but I decided I had seen enough death in recent times.

'I would let them go.' Rodrigo raised an eyebrow. Even the prisoners seemed surprised. 'I would let them go, allow them return to Leon in shame and deliver a message to the dog they call a king. Not everything has to end in blood.'

'A message...I like that idea. Very well, we shall send them back to Leon, as you say. But some offenses demand blood.' He grinned as he looked at the prisoners, and the grin had an unnerving effect on all of us. It signalled impending torment.

303

Rodrigo called in Mancio and Aigeru, Suero and Guter, who held the prisoners down on their knees. As he sheathed his sword and drew a long knife from his belt the scarred man begged for his life, pleaded they be allowed to return to Leon unhindered like I suggested. His words made Rodrigo think twice about his actions as he stood and thought a moment, then sheathed his knife.

'This one talks too much,' Rodrigo muttered. 'Fetch me some tongs.'

Guter found a pair of tongs from the blacksmith's hut in the castle and plunged them in to the brazier. The black iron soon glowed a bright orange as the whites of the offending prisoner's eyes cut through the gloom, focused on the instrument. Rodrigo donned a pair of thick gloves before he lifted the tongs from the coals and admired the hot glow that emitted.

'Hold him down.'

Mancio held the scarred man's head and his mouth was forced open as Rodrigo grabbed his flapping tongue with the tongs. I wanted to look away but found myself transfixed by his desperate flailing. A searing hiss entwined with cries of anguish, and then came the sickening snap as Rodrigo yanked with all his strength and ripped the scarred man's tongue clean from his maw. Bestial howls of agony echoed through the narrow corridors. Though I winced at his misery I felt no pity. Did he feel pity as my father hung from the gallows in Leon? I did not care. I wanted him to suffer.

Rodrigo tossed the tongue on to the brazier. His victim flailed and howled and sobbed on the cold floor. Blood gushed from his mouth and the sickly scent of the burning tongue made me gag, but I kept my composure as Rodrigo turned his cold glare at the other prisoner. Fear was embedded there now. He did not know whether to plead for his life or hold his tongue in the hope he would keep it.

Rodrigo sensed the fear and crouched before him.

'Do not worry, friend. You will need your tongue, because you will be the one to deliver our message to King Alfonso.' The man sighed as

Rodrigo laid down the tongs. 'But you will need your companion, for he will guide you back to Leon.'

'I...I can guide myself.'

'How will you do that without your eyes?'

The prisoner did not understand at first. As the scrape of Rodrigo's knife loosening in the sheath cut through the silence, panic gripped him. His eyes widened and he tried to plead his case, but it was futile. Rodrigo placed the tip of the knife in the brazier and allowed the metal to glow once again, before he retrieved it and forced the blade in to the eyes of his captive. Blood spurted and flowed thick and time and again the agonising scream filled the room. Those screams made me wince.

By the time Rodrigo was done the eyes were nothing but mangled, bloody messes, singed from the heat of the blade, smouldered in the low light. The horror was something more akin to the depictions of demons on the tapestries and vellum pages composed by monks. Both prisoners knelt and whimpered and sobbed like children, and though I did not smile I felt a strange satisfaction at their fate.

Rodrigo knelt before the blinded man, his tone now malicious.

'I have two messages for you to deliver. I do not believe Alfonso would be stupid enough to send you to kill his brother, which means your master must be the one who gave the order. But you will tell Alfonso that if such a transgression occurs again, the armies of Castile will march to the gates of Leon and burn the city to the ground. And as for Azarola, tell him Rodrigo Díaz de Vivar has not forgotten what he did to his father. It is not only the blade of Antonio Perez he should fear. His days are numbered.'

Rodrigo stood and addressed his men.

'Strip them naked and beat them bloody. Then give them simple robes, lash them together, and guide them to the Camino de Santiago. Perhaps some pilgrims will take pity on them and help them to Leon. Otherwise it is a long and lonely road.'

He motioned for me to follow him out of the cell as his men kicked and stomped on the maimed men. The cries of anguish intensified. The

305

sound sent a shiver down my spine, or perhaps it was the winter chill in the air.

'Do you think I was wrong to do that?' he asked as we walked.

'They tried to kill our king. To me they do not deserve life.'

'Could you do what I just did?'

I hesitated. I used to think I could never hurt another soul, but now there was no limit to what I could do. 'I have done things I did not think I was ever capable of, lord. I would not discount it.'

'Good. We will keep the identity of those men our secret and hope our message reaches Azarola's ears. His time will come. I have a feeling war is coming much sooner than any of us could have anticipated. The three brothers of Fernando have pledged to be civil whilst their mother still lives and resides in Leon. But when she dies? Well, let us hope there are some years left in her yet, for the sake of the Leonese.' He gave a wink as he draped an arm on my shoulder and led me upstairs. 'Come. I need some wine and a good woman.'

We returned to the palace where the celebrations continued with raucous laughter, rowdy banter and light hearted music. Sancho spoke with several men at the dais, but when he saw us enter, he held up a hand. The noise gradually died down so there was little more than the shuffle of feet and the occasional cough from somewhere in the room. The silence had an unsettling effect on me, even more so with all eyes on me and Rodrigo.

'Antonio Perez. Come here,' Sancho's great voice boomed.

After hesitation I marched over to the king. He towered over me, yet swayed slightly, and the raw eyes and sour stench of wine on his breath signalled he was drunk. He clicked his fingers and a servant rushed over with a platter with several silver goblets and a fresh jug of wine.

'I was wrong about you. When you first came to me, I took you for nothing but a murderer and a sinner. You saved my life and I owe you my thanks. There is honour in you. I saw that same honour in your father.' He picked up a goblet from the tray, filled it and handed it to me before he repeated for his own goblet. Some of the wine sloshed on to my hand but I did not complain; kings were not meant to hand wine to mere squires like me.

'I, King Sancho of Castile give my thanks to this boy, Antonio Perez. He has shown courage beyond what is expected of him. He is the hero of my coronation, just as his father was the hero of Graus. Pedro Valdez de Lugones was a loyal man and did not deserve the death he was dealt. So as one of my first acts as king I will do something my father should have done a long time ago. I abolish all blame afforded to Pedro Valdez and his brother, Velasco Valdez, for their alleged part in the theft from the *parias* tribute from al-Muqtadir. They were set up by jealous schemers and their names will be besmirched no longer. They were good men, honourable men, and should have died the death of heroes, not that of common thieves.'

I could not believe what Sancho had said at first. He did not have to say what he had because he was king of Castile and my father was Asturian, now part of Leon. But Sancho had always held my father in high regard like Fernando had once done, and even when Fernando had slandered my father for his alleged treason Sancho had refused to believe the lies and petitioned his release in vain. A tear welled in my eye at the words, but I forced myself to remain strong.

Sancho saw the emotion in my eyes and nodded towards the guests.

'Go and enjoy the rest of the feast with your woman. You have earned it.'

'Thank you, lord,' is all I managed as I made my way back to Constanza and Arias. Guests offered curt nods and slight smiles as I passed, and I offered my own nod of thanks in reply. Constanza placed a delicate kiss on my cheek and even Arias inclined his head a little, but it was plain to see he was still seething from our earlier encounter.

'Before we continue,' Sancho announced, 'there is one more matter I wish to address. Every king needs a champion. My father had noble men who served him well as *alferez* and there are many in this room who would serve with the same duty and honour. But in recent times there is only one man I trust above the rest. Rodrigo Díaz de Vivar, step forward.' Murmurs of shock echoed through the congregation as Rodrigo cautiously advanced toward the king. Sancho towered over his subject and placed a strong hand on Rodrigo's shoulder. 'You, too, saved my life today. I need someone who will protect my kingdom and be my champion. I have known you for many years now, ever since you came to Burgos as a squire, and I have watched you grow in to one of the finest soldiers I have ever seen. You have served me well, yet I call on you to serve me longer still. I want you to be my *alferez*.'

Rodrigo usually carried himself with confidence, yet even he seemed taken aback by the statement. He hesitated, struggled to find the words, then fell to one knee and bowed his head in supplication.

'Thank you, your grace. I will not let you down.'

'I know you will not. Rise.' Rodrigo did as he was instructed as Sancho turned to the guests. 'I hereby declare this man, Rodrigo Díaz de Vivar, is now the *alferez* of Castile. He will bear my banner and lead our knights in to battle. He is the sword that strikes at the hearts of our enemies and the shield that protects the realm. His voice carries the authority of the king in my absence. There is no greater warrior than he in my kingdom.' Sancho grabbed Rodrigo's arm and thrust it in to the air. 'Hail, your *alferez*!'

A great roar of approval erupted around the room and each man and woman raised their cups in salute. Soon the name of Rodrigo Díaz reverberated in a great chorus as the young knight beamed before them. Only Garcia Ordóñez, the man widely expected to be named by Sancho, refused to celebrate. His face was twisted in to a bitter visage, his cleft lip made him look hideous, and his glare bored through Rodrigo's soul. It was the look of pure hate. Rodrigo may have gained a powerful position in the kingdom, but from the way Garcia looked at him he had made a great enemy.

'Castile will need her champion to fight well in the coming months,' Sancho continued. His voice carried intensity, perhaps due to the wine and the anger at the assassination attempt. 'If the king of

Navarre thinks he can give me a knife in the back then I will respond with a sword thrust through his damned gullet. My father reduced Navarre to mere vassals, yet should have ended them when he had the opportunity. He had too much respect for his homeland when they showed him none. Now they have grown in power again and become too bold in their actions. We will bring fire to their walls and put their people to the sword. We will rape their women and carry their treasure back as the spoils of war. When we are done the Kingdom of Navarre will be no more. And we will not stop there.

'My father was the most powerful Christian king this land has ever seen, and as his eldest son I should have inherited his legacy. But he wounded my pride when he allowed my brothers to inherit land which is not rightfully theirs. I will not allow it to endure. When Navarre is gone, we will conquer Aragon and the Catalan counties, and after that Alfonso and Garcia will feel my wrath. And then, when all the Christian lands north of the Duero are united under the banner of Castile, we will turn our attention south. For too long the Moors have occupied the land our forefathers settled for themselves. Every *taifa* will bow to us and we will expel the Moors from our homeland. Castile will be triumphant. We will be the masters of Hispania!'

There was no doubt the roar that echoed from the hall would have been heard throughout the city. Sancho had declared his intentions and the lords of Castile had unanimously hailed their support. A host of blood thirsty warriors was unleashed. They had lived in the shadow of Leon for too long; under Sancho, they wanted to become the lords of Hispania, no matter the challenge.

'Are you happy now?' Arias snapped at me. I held my tongue. 'You have just unleashed a beast and condemned us all to war.'

'It does not matter what I did, lord. Sancho wanted his war, irrespective of the enemy, and now he has it. You cannot blame me for something that was inevitable.'

Arias refused to speak to me for the rest of the feast, but I would not apologise to him. I wanted Azarola to feel fear and know we would one day come for him. I and Rodrigo were making plans.

One day, we would have our vengeance.

*　　*　　*

We returned to Vivar, to normality. The threat of conflict hung in the air and so I took to the practise yard with the squires daily. We donned armour and climbed ladders twenty times a day, and lifted heavy bales of hay to improve our fitness, under the watchful eye of our lords. Rodrigo would take us to the outlaying fields and teach us drills and manoeuvres upon our mounts. We danced in duels, steel clashed with steel above the grunts and cries. The light snows that covered the land deterred us not.

During a spar with Esidero I paused for a moment, sucked cold air in to my lungs and allowed the ache in my limbs to alleviate. Sweat dripped from my hair and stung my eyes as it trickled down my forehead. The blunted steel in my right hand felt like a part of my arm rather than a hindrance it used to be.

I looked behind me, expected to see my father glaring down with the same look of scorn, the same jaw twisted in fury at my futile attempts at combat. But he was not there. Instead, Rodrigo looked upon the yard, scanned over his wards as if we were all his own children. His face was emotionless, and when our eyes met, he gave little more than a curt nod. It was a simple gesture, but one that instilled confidence. I returned the nod and turned back to Esidero, coaxed him with taunts about his blemish pocked face. Enraged, he flew forward and tried to hack at my midriff, but I twisted and tripped him with the flat of my blade, sent him tumbling in to the sloshy mud.

The thrill of combat felt strange. Not two years before I had stood in the yard at Lugones and wished with every passing minute the ordeal would end once and for all. But now I welcomed it. I welcomed the burning in the muscles, the clang as steel blades kissed and the pride at seeing an enemy on his knees before me. Those who had offended me would beg my forgiveness, and I would smile.

My father and brother were dead, my mother and sisters lost to me. I had made friends and I had made enemies, and I knew our paths would cross in the years to come. The old Antonio, the one coveted by Father Santiago for being a bright pupil, was gone. The new Antonio had an agenda and a burning desire to see it through, no matter the consequences.

The seed of vengeance had been sown. A feud had been enacted that would not stop until one side was gone and the other left to claim the spoils of victory. But I had justice on my side, and fear had been struck in to the hearts of my enemies. I was a warrior, a young man on the path of knighthood, instilled with courage and confidence that I would achieve my goals.

And I would not stop until Azarola and Nasr al-Baytar were dead.

Author's Note

This book has been five years in the making. It can be a lonely task to write, and so I wish to thank several people who have helped the novel grow over the years.

Firstly, I would like to thank Laura and James of Writer's Block North East for providing the opportunity to develop my career as a writer, and believing this project was good enough to support. The fellow writers who I sat with on the course proved to be inspiration in their own distinct ways, and I thank them too. To the proof readers and beta readers, your comments and input were invaluable, and helped me spot glaring mistakes where my own eyes were blissfully unaware. And a final thank you to all of the writers and readers across social media over the years; your advice, banded together, has moulded me in to the writer am I today.

If you would like to know more about the context of this novel, please visit my website at www.stuartrudge.wordpress.com. I plan on adding articles relating to each book I publish, and do not think a few pages here can do justice to the history of both Rodrigo Diaz de Vivar and the period.

Printed in Great Britain
by Amazon

45091564R10185